MW00529366

FAILED STATE

A PROSECUTION FORCE THRILLER

LOGAN RYLES

Severn River Publishing
SevernRiverBooks.com

ISBN: 978-1-64875-476-0 (Paperback)

ALSO BY LOGAN RYLES

The Prosecution Force Series

Brink of War

First Strike

Election Day

Failed State

Firestorm

The Reed Montgomery Series

Overwatch

Hunt to Kill

Total War

Smoke and Mirrors

Survivor

Death Cycle

Sundown

To find out more about Logan Ryles and his books, visit

severnriverbooks.com/authors/logan-ryles

For Gary, the voice of Reed Montgomery.
Go bird teams!

1

Russian Foreign Intelligence Service (SVR)
Moscow, Russia

"Are you sure about this?" SVR agent Ivan Sidorov kept his voice low as the knot of FSB agents closed around him. The room was small and dark. The four men quiet and cold. They were young, also. Ivan couldn't help but notice. As decades had swept him farther up the ladder of Russian intelligence, he marveled at how young the men who filed in beneath him appeared.

Just kids, really. Too young to die.

But that was their decision.

"We know what you did, old man," the lead officer sneered.

Ivan peered deep into his eyes. "Do you know what *he* did?"

The officer's gaze flickered for just a moment, then his face became stone hard. "*Get in.*"

Cold steel pressed against Ivan's rib cage—the muzzle of an FSB-issued Grach handgun. Forcing him deeper into the small room as the men closed around him, weapons drawn. They shoved Ivan into the machinery room built into the basement of SVR headquarters—a soundproof space Ivan himself had often used for interrogations—then one of them reached for the door.

"My condolences," Ivan said.

"To whom?" the officer said. "Yourself?"

"To your wives."

The door slammed shut, and Ivan sprung. He took the man in front first, grabbing his outstretched gun and wrenching the weapon to one side. The man by the door had his back turned, and the two on either side of the officer opened fire. Ivan clamped his hand down on the officer's trigger finger and sent a 9mm slug spitting into the chest of the man to the left, even as he felt an identical bullet sting his flesh somewhere beneath his shoulder. With one man down, the trigger finger of the officer snapped, and Ivan wrenched the handgun free.

The cramped room was rank with gun smoke as he pivoted the Grach straight into the gut of the broken-fingered officer and drove four slugs into his stomach. Then the last two were on him. Ivan drove a right elbow into the face of the first, knocking him back before shooting him in his throat. But he couldn't get to the fourth man in time. The last FSB agent's shoulders were driven against the door he had just closed. His Grach rose toward Ivan's chest, barely a meter away.

He fired. Ivan fired. Simultaneous blasts echoed off the steel walls, and another slug tore into Ivan's chest, the bullet aimed for center mass. Just as the FSB had trained the young man to shoot.

Ivan staggered back, but the agent went down—one round tearing right between his eyes. Just as the KGB had trained Ivan to shoot.

Ivan slouched against the wall and probed his chest to find the wounds. Two of them, the first scraping his rib cage beneath his shoulder, ripping and tearing skin and cartilage but doing no real harm. The second was more serious. The bullet struck just beneath his collarbone, ripping straight through his body and exiting the other side. A full metal jacket round—something Ivan opposed for use by Russian security forces, but now he was grateful. A hollow point would have expanded on impact, likely tearing through an artery and ensuring his demise before he even hit the ground.

As it was, he still bled. A lot. Ivan clamped one hand over the entry wound and moved for the door, keeping his breaths slow and steady to minimize the efforts of a strained heart. Shoving a body aside with one foot, he dragged the door open far enough to squeeze through, still holding the dead officer's gun. He locked the door behind him, then moved immediately to the left, down a subterranean hallway of the SVR's headquarters. There was almost no one down here, which was why the FSB had taken him here to die. But that emptiness also gave Ivan precious time to escape.

He had spent most of the last decade as one of the senior agents inside this building. Now it was no longer safe. The entire city was no longer safe.

Russia was no longer safe.

Ivan felt blood sliding down his back as he stumbled to a utility closet and pulled the door open. It was filled with cleaning chemicals, mops, brooms. And a first aid kit. He grabbed it off the wall and snapped it open, sliding onto his knees and working quickly. Still breathing smoothly. This wasn't the first time he'd been shot. It likely wouldn't be the last.

The wound gel lay at the bottom of the case in a foil wrapper. He tore it open with his teeth and quickly swabbed handfuls across his chest and back, reaching over his shoulder and gritting his teeth to fight back the pain. It was a battlefield compound, designed to quickly stem blood flow. It worked, a little slower than he would have liked, but in time to keep him from bleeding out.

Ivan leaned against the wall, panting and scrubbing blood off his hand. Then he dropped the magazine on the Grach and checked the load.

Eleven rounds remained. Not enough to get him out of the building by force. But Ivan knew another way.

He abandoned the first aid kit and returned to his feet. Down the hall, a stairway provided access to the hot water pipes that ran within the building. It was a cramped, narrow crawl space, but it eventually connected to the city sewers, and from there provided a path beneath the streets of Moscow. In decades gone by, the KGB had used that path on occasion to meet with undercover operators working deep inside Western embassies.

Now it would be Ivan's highway of escape.

He found the ladder, found the crawl space, and gritted his teeth as his heart thumped and his head pounded. His chest was on fire with pain, his hands damp with sweat. By the time he reached the sewers, his mouth was dry and he felt dizzy on his feet.

But he didn't stop. He proceeded straight along the network of sewer lines, moving toward the edge of the city. There was another utility closet built beneath a manhole cover where Ivan had long ago stashed cash, another handgun, fake passports, medical supplies, and the keys to a Soviet-era Lada parked in a garage half a mile away.

Because in the business of Russian intelligence, what had happened today was always a possibility. He'd spent most of his career with one eye on a route of escape, half his animal brain calculating his own preservation should the ground vanish beneath him.

He never planned for it to happen. Never actually believed his country would burn him. But it wasn't just a lowly farm boy from outside Voronezh that Moscow planned to kill. Unless he was outside Russia by nightfall, thousands—maybe millions—more would die.

Ivan Sidorov was on the clock.

2

Fayette County, West Virginia
Three Months Later

Someplace deep in his soul, Wolfgang knew he was a coward for bringing Collins's body back to West Virginia. He could have easily buried his baby sister on the small plot of land he owned in rural upstate New York—alongside the only woman Wolfgang had ever loved.

That grave was only half a mile through the trees from the house Wolfgang called home. It would be an easy trek to lay flowers on Collins's headstone, just as he laid them on Megan's headstone every Sunday.

But if he was honest, Wolfgang knew he didn't want to see Collins's headstone every Sunday. Even after a decade, it was hard enough to accept his own responsibility for Megan's death. Collins was a bridge too far. Bringing her back to their childhood home in the mountains of rural West Virginia was a convenient excuse to hide her fate from his own miserable existence.

Early February brought snow flurries to the air as the hearse backed into the little church graveyard nestled on the hillside. The grave crew huddled around their backhoe, drinking hot coffee from a thermos and rubbing their hands together, eager to cover Collins's casket and go someplace warm.

Wolfgang stood next to the grave as the funeral home crew placed the casket on suspension straps. There were no pallbearers. No friends of the recently deceased Collins Ward to stand around her as she was finally laid to rest after a multi-decade battle with a crippling case of cystic fibrosis.

Just Wolfgang and the Protestant minister of the church who had graciously allowed him to purchase a plot. It wasn't their childhood church. Richard Ward Senior didn't believe in churches.

It was just some hillside in West Virginia, under a roiled gray sky. Alone in the cold.

"Would you like me to say a few words?" the minister offered.

Wolfgang detected genuine sympathy in his voice, but it rang hollow in the reality of the situation. He simply shook his head. The minister retreated with the funeral home crew, leaving Wolfgang alone next to his dead sister.

He might have cried, but there were no tears left. His right thigh throbbed over the prosthetic leg mounted beneath it, now icy cold in the open elements. Every part of him felt numb, not just by the cold, but by the emotional erosion of the past decade.

The loss of Charlie Team. Then Megan. Then those long, brutal nights in southeast Asia. The bloodshed in Dubai. The years of throat-cutting as *The Wolf*, piling up dollars and medical diplomas in a frantic effort to save Collins.

And it all came to this.

Wolfgang recognized the familiar pop of gravel beneath heavy tires and looked up to see a black SUV roll through the gate of the graveyard. It was muddy with a fogged windshield, the bare-bones look of a rental vehicle. Steam rose from the hood as snowflakes melted against hot metal, then the engine stopped, and doors swung open.

A tall man with broad shoulders stepped out. Dark-haired, wearing sunglasses despite the clouds overhead. He helped a blond woman from the back seat. She carried a small child on her hip, both of them bundled up like Eskimos for the twenty-degree West Virginian weather.

They were all from the Deep South. This wasn't the winter they were used to.

Doors on the other side of the SUV swung open, and another tall man got out—taller than the first, and heavier. Also bundled up, but not as aggressively. He was from the mountains of Tennessee. He'd seen snow before.

The woman who accompanied him was Asian, wearing only a long-sleeved shirt and a light jacket. Because she'd spent most of her life without the luxury of climate control.

The group ascended the hill, the Asian woman cradling a large bouquet of colorful wildflowers. The men looking somber.

Reed reached Wolfgang first, wrapping him in a big hug without comment. Wolfgang accepted, feeling the iron in Reed's grip as the big man pulled him close and held a beat longer than was necessary.

There were tears in Banks's eyes as she put an arm around his neck and kissed his cheek.

"I'm so sorry," she whispered.

Wolfgang just nodded. There was nothing more to say. He accepted the flowers from Sinju and an awkward handshake from Turk. Then they all circled the grave and stood silently over the casket.

Deep in the clutches of a West Virginian winter. Under a roiled gray sky.

The diner in Wolfgang's hometown hadn't changed since his childhood. Enough years had passed so that nobody recognized either him or the group of cold and hungry friends who joined him at a table in the corner, but Wolfgang recognized several of the faces around him. Tired and haggard, cold and worn by the rough life of an Appalachian coal town now robbed of its chief industry by the slow march of time.

He knew this place. He felt it in his bones. He hadn't sat in this diner since he was fifteen and had just watched his drunken father cartwheel to his death off the New River Gorge Bridge.

Now he wondered why he had come back.

"You headed back to New York?" Reed asked.

Wolfgang grunted, cradling black coffee but not drinking it.

"You should join us in the Bahamas," Turk said, his mouth full of eggs and bacon. "Me and Sinju are headed down for a long cruise. The weather is warm. Be good for that stump of yours."

Turk prodded the prosthetic with the toe of his boot.

"I've got some things to do," Wolfgang said. "Another time, maybe."

The conversation died, consumed by the clink of battered steel utensils against scratched dinner plates. Reed's young son fussed, and Banks wiped grape jelly off his face. Sinju cooed and helped calm the child, her cheeks glowing as she tickled him.

Wolfgang turned back to Reed and Turk, lowering his voice.

"Any news?"

Reed gulped coffee, glanced sideways at Turk. The big Tennessean seemed just as hesitant to answer.

"I've had a rough enough week." Wolfgang spoke through gritted teeth. "Don't piss me off."

Reed set the coffee cup down. "Still no word. It seems we've been ghosted."

Wolfgang wasn't sure if he believed Reed. He'd known the ex-Marine for a few years now and had come to trust him with his life. But Reed liked to play things close to his chest, and it was no secret that he and Turk were willing to sideline Wolfgang. Not just because of his missing leg and grief-stricken life.

Because he wasn't like them. They were fighters. Warriors in the most primitive sense of the word. Wolfgang was an outsider to their world of bloodshed and gunfire, but he was still related to it. The three of them had been tied at the hip since the origination of the Prosecution Force—the off-the-books black ops team invisibly linked to the CIA and under the direct command of the White House.

Reed and Turk were the blunt instruments. Wolfgang was the ghost behind the scenes, pulling strings and watching their backs.

But ever since their failure three months previously to capture Stepan Belsky, an exiled Russian oligarch believed to be behind President Trousdale's attempted assassination, the Prosecution Force had been left in the dark.

No communication from Washington. No communication from Langley.

No communication at all.

It pissed Wolfgang off, and he knew Reed and Turk were equally pissed. Some good men had died while chasing Belsky. Somebody had to pay for that bloodshed.

"They can't just bench us," Wolfgang said. "We've still got work to do."

"They say Belsky is dead," Turk said. "They say he went down with the ship."

"But you never *found him* on that ship. And even if he is dead, we all know there were people behind him."

Nobody answered. Wolfgang lowered his voice. "Get Trousdale on the phone. We've given her three months. The trail is growing cold."

"I've tried," Reed said. "They're isolating her."

"Who is?"

"The White House. They say she's in recovery."

"So she's turned chicken?"

"I doubt it," Reed said. "My gut says something else is at play here. Somebody else wants us sidelined."

"Stratton?" Wolfgang named Trousdale's vice president, a man who had fallen under suspicion during their investigation into the identity of her would-be killer. Jordan Stratton stood to benefit from his boss's death, it was true. But he also had a reasonable explanation for the circumstantial evidence they brought against him.

"Maybe," Reed said. "Or somebody else in the administration. Somebody near the top."

"What are you gonna do about it?" Wolfgang pressed, an edge slipping into his voice.

Reed remained calm, digging a credit card out of his pocket and handing it to the waitress. He took his time answering.

"I'm going to look after my family, Wolf. I'm going to buy a house, and maybe a truck. I'm going to live my life."

"Are you freakin' kidding me?" Wolfgang's voice rose into a low growl, attracting the attention of both women and the old couple dining next to them. Wolfgang didn't care. "You've gone soft."

His voice turned sharp with venom. Reed stiffened, shoving his plate aside and leaning forward.

"Is that what you think? You think I don't see those Coast Guardsmen every night, blown to hell by some faceless coward? Don't hear that gunshot and watch *my president* hit the hardwood?"

Wolfgang glanced around the diner, suddenly aware that all eyes were on them. He didn't answer, and Reed relaxed a little. He signed the check and pocketed his credit card, then pushed his chair back.

"I'm a soldier, Wolfgang. I kick doors down and I ventilate bad guys. But when I'm out of people to shoot...I go home. And so should you."

3

Washington, DC

White House staff had cranked the heat up, but President Maggie Trousdale still felt cold. Not just chilled on her skin, but frigid in her bones. Her body ached beneath multiple layers of presidential sweatshirts. When she looked at her hands, they were chalk pale. Her Louisiana tan had faded, and she'd lost weight. A lot of it.

The assassin's bullet that tore through her liver the previous November had failed to take her life but had still taken a toll, and that toll wasn't strictly physical. The nightmares were regular. The shooting pains almost constant.

And the basket of pill bottles the White House physician prescribed were enough to keep her head buzzing and her stomach in knots. She hadn't even been able to deliver her own inauguration speech. Jordan Stratton, her running mate and vice president, had delivered one in her place.

Seated halfway down the length of the polished mahogany conference table situated in the Cabinet Room, Maggie blinked through a mental fog and surveyed the people around her. Stratton, directly to her left. Victor O'Brien, Director of the CIA, sitting across from her. Her chief of staff, Jill

Easterling, situated next to the director, her petite fingers working a pen as she took rapid notes.

And to Maggie's right, barely inches away, James O'Dell. Rising with her from the governor's office in Baton Rouge, O'Dell was her longtime bodyguard turned Secret Service liaison turned...

Maggie wasn't sure. O'Dell hadn't left her side since she'd been shot. His face was the first she saw when recovering consciousness. His fingers the first she felt wrapped tightly around her own. Those kind, dark eyes...

"Madam President?"

Stratton's deep voice jolted her from the brain fog. Maggie slurped water, her torso aching with the movement, and sat up. She wasn't sure what question she had missed. She didn't care. She'd called this meeting for only one purpose—the only thing she had cared about since returning to the White House.

Finding the man responsible for her attempted assassination.

"Where are we with Belsky, Mr. Director?"

She addressed the question to O'Brien. The owlish chief of the Central Intelligence Agency blinked behind round glasses, his bald head shining under fluorescent lights, and looked to Stratton. Maggie snapped her fingers.

"Look at me. I'm your boss."

O'Brien flushed just a little. Maggie didn't so much as blink. During the pain-filled weeks that followed the bullet tearing through her gut, Stratton had assumed many of the responsibilities of the commander in chief, essentially running the country in her absence. Her staff had become used to reporting to him.

She couldn't blame him. But it was time to take the reins back.

"As stated previously, ma'am, we believe Belsky went down with his yacht." O'Brien's voice was as measured and controlled as ever, a man who kept his emotions on a leash so tight Maggie had never seen him crack a smile. He was a long-time spook and a man she found difficult to trust—not like she had an option.

"So why can't you find a body?" Maggie pressed.

"We're working on that, ma'am."

Maggie gritted her teeth. The hunt for the exiled Russian oligarch

Stepan Belsky had commenced the moment the Prosecution Force had identified Belsky's yacht, *Everstar*, as the delivery vehicle for Fedor Volkov, the Russian sniper who shot Maggie. *Everstar* exploded and went down in the Straits of Florida, carrying most of its crew and—presumably—Stepan Belsky with it.

But Maggie didn't buy it. She still wanted a body. *Needed* a body. She had Volkov, and that was something. But there was a greater conspiracy here. People behind people, like dominos in a line. She wanted them all, and Belsky was the next domino.

"Until you lay his cold, dripping carcass on this table, he's not dead," Maggie snapped.

Nobody spoke. Stratton and Easterling looked away.

O'Brien blinked his owl eyes. "That may be difficult, Madam President. *Everstar* went down in over five thousand feet of water. At that depth, it's very likely that the wreck disintegrated. The Navy is still deploying deep-sea drones to locate it. They've found bits of wreckage, but the bodies could have been swept away by undersea currents or buried in the sand. Even if they survived, marine life would consume—"

"Are you telling me you've got nothing?" Maggie demanded. She felt the blood leave her skull, and she braced herself against the table.

O'Dell put a gentle hand on her arm. During the weeks since leaving the hospital, she'd become used to his touch. He often assisted her in and out of chairs, and she usually needed it. But she didn't need it now.

She jerked her arm away and remained fixated on O'Brien. The director kept his cool.

"I'm telling you that Belsky is dead, ma'am. And we may never be able to prove it."

The room fell silent. Maggie felt suddenly at a loss for words. She wanted to dog cuss the director. Drag him down a notch or two and threaten his job if he didn't produce results.

But she simply didn't have the energy. She drank water instead, stalling for time. Her body still felt chilled, and the strain in her mind was translating directly into increased torso pain from her still regenerating liver. The doctors expected her body to make a full recovery, but the road was long and hard.

The stress of her preoccupation with Belsky wasn't helping.

"Ma'am, if I may." Stratton spoke softly, his large fingers interlaced over the mahogany. Dressed in an impeccable black suit with a red power tie and an American flag pin, and with his slicked, jet-black hair, Stratton looked the picture of a political superstar.

Not like Maggie.

"The investigation into your attempted assassination will continue, but at present, you should consider other priorities."

"What does that mean?" There was more edge in Maggie's voice than she intended, but maybe that was okay. Stratton needed to remember who was boss.

"Your administrative agenda, for a start," Stratton said, keeping cool. "It's been twenty-three days since your inauguration, and you still haven't made a public appearance. We've communicated no legislative priorities to Congress. There's a certain amount of political momentum that comes with a landslide victory such as ours. We need to capitalize on it before it melts away."

"*Ours?*" Maggie demanded.

Stratton kept his chin up, his voice calm. "We were both on the ticket, Madam President. That's all I meant."

"The vice president is right, ma'am." Jill Easterling spoke for the first time, her voice a little squeaky in the large room. Known as *The Cannonball* around Washington, Jill had quickly developed a reputation as a political force of nature. Maggie selected her to be White House Chief of Staff for a reason—Jill's instincts were outstanding, and her ability to keep the sludge moving unrivaled.

"I've assembled a proposal for a legislative agenda," Jill continued. "It's focused primarily on political reform and domestic energy production. Things we campaigned on, messages your base resonates with. There's still time to make an impact in your first hundred days, but we need to move quickly."

"I'm already working the Senate," Stratton jumped in. "I've got connections on both sides of the aisle who are committed to making meaningful strides this session. If we hand them a reasonable proposal, gridlock shouldn't be a problem. My old colleagues in the House assure me they are equally committed to playing ball. Nobody wants to be the guy standing in the way of a wounded president who won by a landslide. This is a golden opportunity—"

"Get out," Maggie hissed.

The room fell deathly quiet. Nobody moved. O'Dell reached for Maggie's arm again. She pulled it away.

"*Out*," she snapped. "Both of you! Now."

The room remained still a half beat longer, then Stratton and Easterling rose, each taking their time. Stratton buttoned his jacket, and Easterling collected her notes. O'Brien moved to stand also.

"Not you," Maggie said.

The doors closed behind the ejected cabinet members. Maggie finished her water and mopped sweat off her forehead with a napkin. She didn't care that she looked like she hadn't yet showered or that there wasn't a hint of makeup on her face. The ripping pain in her gut and the cocktail of medications erased any concern about her appearance.

"Mr. Director, I don't *care* about legislative agenda. I don't care about my first hundred days or capitalizing on political capital. Somebody *shot me*. Do you understand? Somebody *shot* the President of the United States."

Maggie's voice turned hoarse as it grew in volume. Her fingers knotted into a fist, and she leaned across the table.

"I wasn't elected to pass token laws and make fancy speeches. I was elected to lead this country through the storm, and I can't do that if I don't even know who's shooting at us!"

Maggie tasted sweat as it ran off her lip. The director didn't blink.

"Now, you're going to *find* Stepan Belsky. Alive or dead, I want his ass on this table. Do you understand?"

O'Brien didn't move. He let the moment linger.

"Lean on your people," Maggie said. "Cash in some favors. Make deals with the devil. I don't freaking care. I want you to run this asshole to the ground, whatever it takes. Am I clear?"

"Ma'am, I would advise caution—"

"Save it, Victor! You're not paid to advise. You're paid to figure things out. So do your job. Find the people who shot me. And don't come back until you're dragging them in by their hair."

4

Caracas, Venezuela

From the wide picture window built into his executive office inside Palacio de Miraflores, President Cesar Moreno could see right into the heart of Venezuela's business district. Proud skyscrapers of gleaming stone, glass, and metal shone in the late afternoon sun. Most of them dated back to the eighties and nineties, built during the boom years of the Venezuelan oil economy.

Built by Chávez and his Bolivarian Revolution. An energized era of promise and limitless wealth, literally pouring out of the ground as fast as Venezuelan pumps could swing. Millions of barrels of it, feeding a greedy American economy while the dollars rolled in by the truckload.

Moreno remembered it well. He'd stood alongside Chávez as the *Comandante* ushered Venezuela into a new age of socialist paradise. Flush with oil dollars, Chávez spent money like water, investing into housing, parks, subsidized food programs, education. Anything and everything his people wanted—he nationalized the oil industry and ran that cash cow day and night, three hundred and sixty-five days a year.

And right into the ground.

Moreno's stomach tightened as he stood with his hands clasped behind his back, the warmth of the afternoon sun washing across his face and easing some of the tension in his neck. Some, but not all. The stress Moreno felt in his stomach was a natural outgrowth of the hellscape he now viewed. One or two kilometers away, those towers appeared tall and proud, but a closer inspection revealed another story.

The shine was only surface level. Many of the skyscrapers were empty, their offices and executive suites long abandoned, their lights flickering on and off with the irregular blackouts that rippled through the city. Employees had now dispersed, trading tall stacks of hyper-inflated Bolivars for paltry returns of merchandise.

The *Comandante* was gone. And so was his socialist paradise.

A soft knock rang on the door behind Moreno, but he didn't turn from the window. The ache in his skull intensified a beat as thoughts of the voice on the phone returned to his mind.

An angel or a devil, Moreno wasn't sure. But a savior, either way. Wasn't that enough?

"Señor Presidente?" The soft voice of Moreno's secretary echoed across the polished wood floor, a little timid. Or maybe just tired. "Señor Belsky is here for you."

Moreno swallowed. He couldn't help it. He stared at the proud skyline and felt, just for a moment, that voice in the back of his head. That soft warning, like the distant flash of a red police light.

But he ignored it. Because the President of Venezuela couldn't afford to be squeamish.

"Show him in," Moreno said.

He turned from the window and approached the tea bar resting against the wall. Many Venezuelans, like most South Americans, enjoyed fine coffee, maybe from Colombia. But Moreno hated coffee, and he hated Colombians. Elegant tea suited him like the fine tailored suits he wore and the gentle cologne he imported from France.

In a world so savage, a man must find his refuge.

Heavy footfalls thumped against the polished wood as Moreno stirred honey into the tea. He didn't have to look up to know who had entered. He could smell the man. All grease and sweat and fat—a total slob.

"Got any vodka?" The Russian spoke in English. He didn't know Spanish, and Moreno pretended not to know Russian.

"I have tea," Moreno said, turning slowly and sipping from a china cup. "And water."

Stepan Belsky stood just inside the door, dressed like he smelled in lint-coated slacks and a white dress shirt unbuttoned to halfway over his gut. No undershirt. A sweaty tangle of gray and black chest hair billowing out like a storm cloud.

Suddenly, Moreno lost his taste for the tea. He turned for his desk, and Belsky helped himself to the tea bar, pouring it black into a cup and shooting it like liquor.

"Nice and strong!" The Russian gargled. "Not half bad."

Moreno settled behind the desk. Belsky refilled the cup and sat across from him, slouched in the high-backed mahogany chair, his stomach rolled out across his thighs. It was all Moreno could do not to wrinkle his nose.

Belsky was easily one of the world's richest one hundred men, but it seemed there were some things money couldn't buy.

"What is the update?" Moreno cut straight to the point, eager to get the Russian and his odor out of the office as expediently as possible.

"Two of my ships will make dock this afternoon," Belsky said. "Drilling equipment, mostly. And some pipe. We'll lay lines out of the oil fields."

"Won't that waste time?" Moreno questioned.

Belsky snorted. "It will *save* time, Señor Presidente. Once you have pipes, you will suck black gold like ten-dollar hooker, yes?"

Moreno said nothing. Belsky laughed.

"Excuse me. Like ten-million bolívar hooker."

Belsky raised his teacup. Moreno remained expressionless. The red light in the back of his mind flashed a little brighter, a little more vibrant. He thought he heard alarm bells, but he shut them off.

He'd made his decision. Not like it was a decision at all. When a man's back is against the wall, what choice does he have? Moreno knew the feeling of a wall pressed against his shoulder blades like he knew the gaunt faces of his hungry citizens.

His constant companions.

"Speaking of hooker," Belsky continued. "The accommodations you provided are very comfortable, but I must confess, somewhat lonely. Perhaps there are…how do you say…*señoritas* who could visit? I will pay their rent for a year!"

Another raucous laugh, spluttering tea across the desk. The red lights were gone now, replaced by a dull burn in Moreno's knotted stomach.

But he didn't show it. He wouldn't give this slob the satisfaction.

"I'll see what I can do," Moreno said simply.

Belsky nodded, swirling the tea. Then his grin faded, and the warmth in his face seemed to fade with it.

"I hear you're having trouble at the Colombian border."

Moreno tensed. He hadn't expected the question, even though the Colombian border had been on his mind all week, keeping him awake at night. He decided to play it cool.

"No trouble."

"I hear otherwise. I hear ten thousand Venezuelans fled the country last week."

"Our border posts report no such departure." Moreno kept his voice cool.

Belsky snorted a derisive laugh. "I imagine they don't. But Russian satellites tell different story. And you know the thing about satellites? They do not lie."

Belsky's gaze turned hard. He finished the tea and stood, then walked casually behind Moreno's desk as though he owned the place, pocketing his hands and looking out through the picture window.

"Our benefactor is concerned about domestic security. He would like you to close your borders."

The comment was dropped with all the grace of potatoes spilling out of a sack. Just dumped in Moreno's lap without any pretext or warning.

"Excuse me?" Moreno pivoted in his chair.

"This is no time for instability in Venezuela," Belsky said, his back turned, his shirt streaked with sweat. "We'll need people to work the oil fields. People to rebuild Venezuela's economy. Close your borders, and order people back to their homes."

Moreno stood, the warmth in his gut now building into something closer to outrage.

"Señor Belsky, you are not here to advise me on matters of governance. You are here—"

"To put your country back together," Belsky snapped, wheeling on Moreno. "Because you ran it into the ground!"

Moreno didn't move. Belsky's eyes bulged, and his face flushed red. He took a step closer, bringing his bulging, sweaty gut to within inches of Moreno's flawless Armani suit.

"Do not mistake my advice as coming for free. You are not the only man here with his back against the wall. When our benefactor makes a request, it is not option. You play ball, or you leave ball field. Is this clear?"

Moreno didn't blink. Belsky stared him down, his matted hair clinging to his scalp like a muddy rug.

"Close the border," Belsky said, stepping around the desk and moving toward the door. "And have vodka and women sent to my room. Plenty of each."

The brass doorknob clicked. Moreno breathed slowly, forcing his heart rate to calm even as his knuckles tightened into a fist.

But he didn't move. Because Belsky was right.

The footsteps paused. Moreno looked over his shoulder to see Belsky smirking at him.

"Relax, Señor Presidente. Our benefactor is a kingmaker. The wealth of Chávez will return."

5

Upstate New York

The house sat by itself on a low hill surrounded by tall hardwoods. Wolfgang's Mercedes purred past the automated gates and wound along an asphalt driveway, snow and ice crunching beneath the tires. More of the same was piled high to either side of his path, heaped amid the trees in drifts as tall as Wolfgang, frozen solid amid a precipitous New York winter.

Wolfgang had the drive cleared regularly, but with more snow in the forecast, he'd probably be stuck at home for a few days. He was okay with that. It wasn't like he had any place to be.

After rolling into the attached garage, Wolfgang cut off the engine and sat in the rapidly cooling cabin for a moment. Despite the heated seats, his body felt stiff. His mind numb. He thought about the mound of rocky soil piled over Collins's casket, and all he felt was failure. He pictured the custom laboratory built almost directly beneath him in the home's basement and thought about the thousands of hours he'd spent there.

The thousands of hours more he had invested into advanced medical education. The extracurricular reading. The obsession.

And in the end...it meant nothing.

Wolfgang pushed the door open and stepped out, his stump of a leg aching. With practice it wasn't difficult to drive with the fake leg. He could climb stairs, take long walks amid the trees, and even jog. Modern prosthetics were a working miracle, but despite his ability to remain active, Wolfgang felt very little desire to do so. For his entire adult life, he'd remained in flawless shape, with a rippling six-pack and the stamina of a racehorse.

Now he was fifteen pounds overweight, a little out of breath after climbing out of the basement, and uninspired to hit the gym. Why did it matter? Collins was gone. Reed had benched him. His health seemed very unimportant.

Wolfgang slid his key into the door lock, already contemplating a freezer dinner and a hot shower, and then he froze.

The door was unlocked. Both the deadbolt and the knob. Momentary confusion was joined by instantaneous self-doubt—had he forgotten to lock up?

Wolfgang drew his phone from his pocket and held the glowing screen across the face of the deadbolt. Tiny, almost imperceivable scratches marred the brass face. Wolfgang's spine tingled, and he pocketed the phone before reaching beneath his coat.

The Glock 29 strapped to his hip housed ten rounds of hollow-point 10mm rounds—a soul-stopping load, capable of inflicting instantly terminal damage. Wolfgang knew, because Wolfgang had seen it happen.

He held the gun close to his chest and eased the door open, waiting for the familiar chirp of the alarm system.

The house remained silent. Still. But not empty. Wolfgang felt it in his gut.

Slipping through the door, he cleared the mudroom with a quick sweep of the Glock, finger near the trigger, a flick away from unleashing hell.

The laundry room passed under quick inspection. Then a short hall, and the kitchen. There was a knife lying on the counter, smeared with mayonnaise. Bread crumbs on the floor, and half of a sliced tomato.

Wolfgang's heart began to thump. He kept his back near the wall, easing to the next corner. Turning toward the living room.

Then he heard the first sound—a gentle slurp. A soft sigh.

Wolfgang's finger dropped over the trigger, depressing the safety blade and stopping only a couple pounds short of firing.

Then he rounded the corner, Glock first.

Only one person occupied the shadowy living room, seated in Wolfgang's easy chair with his back turned. A shirtless man with a head full of tangled black and gray hair, and bulging biceps that reached to the sides of the chair and stuck out like bear legs. He cradled one of Wolfgang's glasses, half-full of something clear, sitting perfectly relaxed. Unmoved by the deliberate smack of Wolfgang's shoe against hardwood.

"Don't move!" Wolfgang growled.

The man did move. He took a long sip from the glass, remaining seated, his free hand resting unthreateningly in his lap. He swallowed and let out a long sigh. Then he set the glass down.

"Hello, Amerikos."

Wolfgang rounded the chair, still leading with the Glock, still depressing the trigger to within a flinch of firing.

The burly man occupying his living room didn't so much as blink as the gaping mouth of the handgun covered his face. He only smiled dryly, exposing dirty and crooked teeth housed inside a mouth large enough to consume a turkey leg like a chicken wing.

"*Ivan*," Wolfgang snapped. "What the hell are you doing here?"

Wolfgang didn't bother to conceal the anger in his tone. Half of him wanted to shoot the intruder right then and there—empty the Glock into Ivan's chest. God knew it would take a few rounds to bring down the beefy Russian.

But he didn't fire. Not only because he knew the man, but because he had additional questions. Questions like how Ivan had circumvented his extensive electronic security. Or how Ivan had even found the house in the first place.

The location of Wolfgang's home was a carefully guarded secret. He'd told no one. Not even Reed.

"It is good to see you, my friend." Ivan spoke in weary English, but he didn't stand. He knew better.

Wolfgang eased off the trigger—more because he was nervous about an accidental discharge than because he had in any way relaxed. He kept the gun up.

"*What* are you doing here?" Wolfgang repeated. "How did you find me?"

Ivan snorted. "Were you hiding?"

Wolfgang was, but he didn't take the bait.

"I keep track of my friends, Amerikos. Especially the ones I like."

Another flash of the crooked teeth. Wolfgang looked quickly over his shoulder, sweeping the kitchen again, then looked down the hallway toward his bedroom.

"Relax," Ivan said. "I am alone. Nobody knows I am here."

"How can I be sure?" Wolfgang said.

"Because if they did, I would already be dead. And so would you."

Wolfgang said nothing. He dropped his gaze across the Russian and noticed what he hadn't before. Gaunt circles beneath Ivan's eyes. Skin that hugged his ribs, and arms that, while muscular, were not so taut as they had been the last time Wolfgang had seen him, barely three months prior.

And worst of all, a nasty scar just beneath Ivan's right collarbone. A mass of white skin, gnarled together and twisted with the distinct marks of a makeshift stitching job. A bullet wound, Wolfgang thought. A relatively fresh one.

Wolfgang lowered the gun, just a little. He kept it pointed between Ivan's legs.

"What are you doing here?"

Ivan's face fell, the grin melting away. He suddenly looked very tired. Very battered.

And very resigned.

"I need your help, Amerikos."

6

"Stay there." Wolfgang backed away from Ivan, keeping the gun on him as he retreated to the digital thermostat mounted on the wall. It was freezing —barely fifty degrees in the house, and Ivan was shirtless.

Freaking Russians.

Wolfgang switched the heat on, then pivoted around the room to a spare chair, sitting with his back to the wall and the handgun resting on his knee. Still pointing at Ivan.

"You better have an excellent explanation for this," Wolfgang said.

Ivan's face twisted into a frown. "Is this how old friends greet each other? When you email me last November, and I meet you in Minsk, I offer good drinks and warm embrace."

"That wasn't in your *house*. It wasn't breaking and entering. And it seems you've already helped yourself to my drinks."

"Water is no drink, my friend. Your liquor cabinet is heartbreakingly empty."

"That's because I don't have one. Enough small talk. What do you want?"

Ivan relaxed into his chair. His shoulders loosened, and his eyes closed, but he didn't answer.

"Why aren't you in Russia?" Wolfgang probed.

Ivan's eyes opened, now rimmed with red. He drained the water glass.

"I am no longer welcome in Russia," he said simply.

"Why?" Wolfgang didn't indulge in any sympathy. He kept one hand wrapped around the gun.

"When you come to meet me in Minsk...you have questions about Russian sniper."

"Fedor Volkov," Wolfgang said. "*The Ghost of Grozny*, you called him."

"*Da.*"

"What about him?"

"I told you he never worked for Russian government. That he disappeared."

"Right..."

"This is not quite true."

The tingle returned to Wolfgang's spine, racing this time. He sat up.

"What are you telling me?"

"You are familiar with oligarchy, yes?"

"Super-rich Russian jackasses," Wolfgang said.

That brought a dull smile to Ivan's lips, but it didn't last. "Yes. Wealthy business owners who capitalized on the fall of Soviet Union."

"What about them?"

"Have you heard of man named Stepan Belsky?"

Wolfgang's blood ran cold. "Who?"

He kept his voice calm, but Ivan saw right through it. The grin returned, drier than before.

"So you know."

"Let's say I don't. Who is he?"

"Belsky is Russian oligarch. Very powerful one. At one time, not long ago, the most powerful, maybe. He made his money off oil and natural gas. Very big industries in Russia, as you know. Billions of dollars."

"And?"

"And he became a threat to Moscow."

"You mean to President Nikitin."

Ivan shrugged. "One and the same, these days. As President Nikitin rose to power, Belsky paved the way. But at some point, Nikitin fears Belsky is too powerful. So he work in secret with other oligarchs, and Belsky is banished. Or so we think."

Wolfgang's eyes narrowed. "What does that mean?"

"Belsky was kicked out of Russia. His domestic holdings divided amongst Nikitin's supporters. He live aboard a yacht and wander the world, living off his foreign businesses."

"What does any of this have to do with Fedor Volkov?"

"He is man who shot your president, no?"

Wolfgang didn't answer. They both knew it was true.

"I told you Volkov never worked for Moscow. In one way, this is true. He never worked directly for the government. But...he did work for the oligarchy."

"In what capacity?"

"Men of power like the oligarchs have problems, sometimes. Politicians, government officials, even religious leaders, perhaps. People who stand in the way of their business interests. Volkov solved these problems."

"So he was an on-call killer."

"You may say so."

"You're telling me Belsky hired Volkov to assassinate Trousdale?"

"Your government already believes he did. This is why they track him to Straits of Florida and blow up his yacht."

"We didn't blow up his yacht." Wolfgang let the words slip before he could stop himself. Ivan smirked.

"No. You did not. Belsky did."

"Why?"

"To cover his trail. The boat sink in very deep water, no? Difficult to find the body."

"So he was never on the yacht?"

"He was on the yacht. But shortly before your Coast Guard get there, he left it."

"That's not possible. No aircraft or other vessels were sighted in the region."

Ivan nodded slowly. "Not above the waves, anyway."

Wolfgang's mind spun. And then it stopped. He leaned forward, the muzzle of the Glock dipping, that tingle in his spine turning icy cold.

"What are you telling me?"

"After we meet in Minsk, I return to Moscow to conduct my own investigation. What you say about Volkov was deeply concerning. So I start to dig, and I find connections between Belsky and the Kremlin."

"Are you telling me..."

Ivan's voice dropped. "What I am about to tell you, you must not tell anyone. Not until we have a plan. I need to know this."

"Or what?"

"Or I will have to kill you."

There was no bravado in Ivan's tone. No humor. Just blunt truth.

"This is serious, isn't it?" Wolfgang pressed.

"Deathly so."

Wolfgang didn't move. He stared into the Russian's eyes and wondered who he was really looking at. He'd known Ivan a long time, dating back to his first mission as an espionage operative in Paris, nearly ten years prior. That first meeting wasn't a friendly one, and neither was the second, in Moscow several months later.

But by the time he and Ivan collided for a third time in Sydney, Wolfgang and the battered Russian had developed something of an understanding. Maybe not a friendship. Certainly not an alliance. But a mutual respect. Ivan had delivered when Wolfgang needed it most, and when lives were on the line, Ivan put humanity above politics. That made him somebody Wolfgang was inclined to trust, but Wolfgang had learned the hard way not to fully trust anyone, ever.

And yet he knew he was at an impasse. He would either agree to Ivan's terms, or the Russian would leave, and there would be nothing Wolfgang could do to stop him short of gunning him down.

Wolfgang breathed deep. Then he nodded once. "Okay. I promise."

"The Kremlin conspired to kill your president," Ivan said bluntly.

"And by Kremlin, you mean..."

"Makar Nikitin."

"You can't just say that. That's an earth-shattering statement. You need proof."

"I was finding proof. Then I was discovered."

"And shot." Wolfgang jutted his chin toward the wound in Ivan's chest.

"Yes. I escaped Moscow and hid in Russia. It took weeks to escape. I had to travel south into Ukraine. Use a military transport to sneak into the West. All the while trying to recover. Once I was in Poland, things become easier. I have fake Latvian passport that bought me passage into Canada. Then I come here."

"Why?"

"Because what I know could trigger world war, and I must stop this. I need somebody who I can trust. Somebody who thinks with level head."

"And that's me?" Wolfgang snorted a laugh.

"No. But you are best I could find."

"So what do you know?" Wolfgang pressed. "All of it."

"I know that Nikitin was in communication with Belsky while your people were chasing him. I know that Nikitin deployed Russian attack submarine to recover Belsky from Straits of Florida. And I know Belsky is now in Caracas."

"Venezuela?"

"*Da.*"

"Why?"

"This I do not know. I have spent many hours trying to think…no obvious answer has come to me. But he is not simply hiding. Nikitin sent him there for a purpose."

Wolfgang leaned back, picking one fingernail against the finger grooves milled into the Glock's slide. He should have been rattled by what Ivan said. Alarmed, certainly. Maybe even panicked.

But he wasn't. A decade of grueling work as an espionage operative, then an assassin, and now a member of a black ops team that didn't exist had taught him to expect the unexpected and not to overreact to any of it.

He still had questions, though.

"Why would Nikitin want to kill Trousdale? That's an insane move."

"Nikitin is insane man. I have followed his career since he was in KGB, and I tell you, the man is obsessed."

"With what?"

"What else? Power. Not merely prestige, but total dominance. He is a Soviet without a Union. A man drunk on the promise of his own glory. Much has changed since the Cold War ended. His predecessor's failures in

Ukraine have shown Nikitin just how weak Russia has become. Our economy is broken. Our military outdated and under-equipped. In fact, were it not for nuclear threat, Russia would be no super power at all."

"Killing Trousdale doesn't change any of that," Wolfgang said. "All it does is risk Russia's total annihilation. We've got nukes too, you know."

"Yes. Which is why I believe there is bigger plan. Somehow, Trousdale stood in the way."

"Nikitin couldn't seriously think he could get away with gunning her down."

"Hasn't he?" Ivan said, tilting his head. "She survived, yes. But until I tell you this, your government has not suspected Moscow."

It was true. Wolfgang knew Washington and Langley had hit a dead end tracking down the origins of the president's assassination attempt. If they hadn't, the Prosecution Force would have been deployed by now.

"Okay," Wolfgang said. "You've told me. So what do you want?"

Ivan settled into the chair. He looked old again. "Do you love your country, Wolfgang?"

Wolfgang didn't answer immediately. He wasn't sure what to say. Not because of how he felt about America, but because of how he felt about love. He wasn't sure what the word meant.

But this wasn't the time for a philosophical definition of patriotism. Wolfgang merely nodded.

"I love Russia like I love myself," Ivan said. "It is home. It is blood. It is...life."

Ivan's eyes watered, and his hand trembled. He swallowed. "For many years my people have suffered. The gears of war, be they hot or cold, grind on forever. Always there are madmen who will escalate. Men who will push and push. And one day...it will be too much. The rockets will fire. The earth will stand still. And then everything is over."

Ivan sat forward. Rested his elbows on his knees and stared Wolfgang right in the eye.

"I never before ask for help from an Amerikos. But the Russia I love is under control of a madman. We must stop him."

7

Number One Observatory Circle
Vice President's Residence
Washington, DC

The old mansion lay quiet. Vice President Jordan Stratton had sent his wife, Carolyn, and their twin daughters back to Chicago to visit with her parents under the guise of a winter getaway.

In truth, he simply wanted his family out of the house long enough for him to think. Crowded days packed with presidential duties kept him hunted and harried, running from one meeting and appearance to the next, doing his best to hold together a faltering nation with a wounded president.

It wasn't the job he signed up for, and yet, in a weird way, it was exactly the job he signed up for. As Maggie's VP, Stratton hoped to be an involved member of her legislative agenda. He wanted to be an active vice president, spearheading initiatives and leading diplomacy on the White House's behalf.

But his true purpose—the purpose the vice presidency was originally created for—held a higher calling. In the absence of an able-bodied president capable of leading the nation through war and peace, the Twenty-Fifth Amendment kicked in, and the VP stepped up.

Stratton believed in the Constitution. He was proud to serve. But the events that dragged him into this position in the first place were far from ordinary, and the knowledge he withheld from Maggie concerning the identity of her would-be assassins haunted him daily.

Not because he really knew who those faceless enemies were, but because he suspected, and the possibility of that reality was worse than hell on earth.

Stratton poured three fingers of Buffalo Trace into a glass, then slumped into a desk chair in his executive study on the second floor of the mansion. The house was quiet, all the staff having completed their nightly functions and now departed for the evening. On occasion Stratton could hear the click of a dog collar as a pacing Secret Service agent and his K-9 partner circled outside his window, but otherwise all was still.

It was just him, the bourbon...and that unopened envelope resting on his desk.

Stratton tipped the glass back and enjoyed the liquor's burn as he fixated on the envelope. It was small—only about three inches square—and bulged in the middle from the one item it contained. Stratton knew what that item was. Even though the envelope was unmarked, it didn't take a rocket scientist to feel through the paper and identify the contents.

It was a thumb drive. A small storage device containing files that were too sensitive to be transmitted via email—even the highly encrypted government email of the vice president.

Stratton reached into his lap drawer and withdrew three items—a punch cutter, a yellow flame lighter, and a hand-rolled Cuban cigar. He worked quietly with the tools, focusing as he removed a plug of tobacco from the end of the cigar, then wet it with his lips. He took his time lighting it, holding the tip a half inch above the top of the flame and toasting the tobacco slowly, preventing any risk of charred smoke on that first draw.

Cigars were as much a part of Stratton's elite heritage as fine suits, dirty money, and political corruption. But of all the trappings that his last name thrust upon him long before adulthood, cigars were the item that he most genuinely enjoyed. Maybe for the heritage, or perhaps for the ritual. Certainly for the flavor.

Alcohol could numb his mind, but tobacco truly calmed him.

Stratton took a slow virgin draw, relishing the perfectly smooth flavor of Cuban excellence. Nobody could do it like Cuba, embargoes be damned.

He relaxed in the chair and closed his eyes, rolling the cigar between tired fingers and traveling back in his mind. Three months prior, sitting in another office chair, in another office.

The Oval Office.

The room had been dark. The White House still. But one man stood in front of him. Tall and dark, dressed in black clothes. Stratton never learned his name—he had cleared Secret Service security with an ID that was later determined to be fake—but he remembered the man walked with a slight hitch, as though one leg were stiff or injured.

After a brief and hostile meeting, the man was on his way to the door when Stratton asked a final question.

"You said Belsky is in bed with Cunningham Enterprises?"

The man looked over his shoulder. "Does that surprise you?"

Stratton hadn't answered. The man had left, leaving him in desolate silence, with a lead weight in his gut the size of a dump truck.

Because no, he wasn't surprised. He had suspected for years that the Stratton family's close friend, Harold Cunningham, was in bed with shady foreign interests. Sitting atop the monumental energy conglomerate, Cunningham Enterprises, Harold had long made his views about the merits of international partnerships clear. He saw no moral barrier in partnering with any nation, regardless of human rights atrocities or political disagreements, in order to keep the money flowing. He never had.

But now Harold was suspected of partnering with Lenkov International, an energy firm owned and operated by the man suspected of pursuing the attempted assassination of the president: Stepan Belsky. A connection like that, landing so close to the family of the man who would assume office if Maggie Trousdale died, was more than suspicious. It was politically terrifying.

Stratton ripped the envelope open. The thumb drive was marked with a case number written on a white label in black Sharpie. He pressed the drive into his personal computer and input a password on demand, holding the Cuban between his teeth.

The screen blinked, and then the files displayed in a field of tiny square icons. Dozens of them.

Stratton's stomach fell. He knew before he input the password what he would find, but he still hoped he would find nothing. A single document, maybe. A letter from the agency, explaining their failure to dig anything up.

But PPI—Premier Private Investigations—never failed to dig something up. Stratton had used the firm many times during his years as a businessman, then a senator. Staffed almost exclusively by former FBI agents, many of whom had been ejected from the Bureau for ethical violations, PPI didn't have a website and they didn't advertise. They operated exclusively by word of mouth, leaning on the trust of the American elite they served, and running a menu of investigatory services that rode the line between bending the law and breaking it.

If you had to ask how much they cost, you couldn't afford them. If you inquired too deeply about their process, they dropped you like a hot rock.

But if you wrote the checks and accepted the results, they came in spades. Because PPI could find dirt in a snowstorm. The truth in a barroom full of drunk liars. A person's deepest, darkest secrets no matter where they were hidden.

And they could do it without being caught.

PPI was the first call Stratton made after learning about a possible connection between Cunningham and Belsky. His request was simple: *Get me everything.*

By the look of this drive, PPI had done exactly that. They had found everything and then some.

Stratton rolled the Cuban to the side of his mouth and clicked a pen open. He sipped more bourbon.

And then he went to work.

8

Birmingham, Alabama

The little rental home in the hills of Birmingham's Mountain Brook neighborhood had served as Reed's home longer than any address since he was forced to torch and abandon his cabin in the mountains of north Georgia, two years prior. It wasn't a large place. Two bedrooms and a thousand square feet littered with baby toys and parenting paraphernalia, with a fridge full of baby sauce and beers—not to be consumed by the same individual.

Reed never intended to call it a permanent home, and after over a year of paying inflated rents and stumbling around cramped rooms, he was ready to move along. The CIA paycheck for his assistance in investigating Trousdale's attempted assassination had been slimmer than the last two. No overseas trips, no significant risk to life and limb—at least in the eyes of the CIA. But despite the shortchange, Reed had squirreled away the better part of two hundred grand in a simple savings account, and even after paying his taxes, he felt confident there would be enough left to purchase a nice piece of property someplace outside of town.

A few acres with a project home. A barn where he could fully restore his father's 1969 Chevrolet Camaro, now showing the signs of age and abuse. A tree where he could hang a tire swing for Davy. A room where Banks could hang her guitar and write music.

A family home. A place to put down some roots and finally feel like he belonged somewhere.

"What about this place?"

Reed sat across the living room from Banks, scrolling through listings on his phone. She was fixated on social media, checking up on friends from her past life and grunting positively or negatively depending on the listing he sent. The house was a wreck, and an empty pizza box still lay on the coffee table.

But at least Davy was asleep. That brought some temporary calm to the storm.

"It's kinda far out," Banks said, flicking through pictures of the three-bedroom ranch on four acres of rolling St. Clair County.

"Well, yeah. We're not gonna find something in our budget near the city. Besides, don't you want some space?"

A neutral grunt. No emotion.

Reed returned to the listings and continued to scroll, narrowing his search to bring the zone closer to Birmingham. Prices shot up immediately, and his stomach tightened in frustration. He didn't want a mortgage. He didn't want the payment. With a fully owned home he could find a way to cover their monthly expenses, even outside another invitation to work for the White House.

"Carla got a deal," Banks said suddenly.

"Who?"

"We used to sing together sometimes. She's more pop than I am. She just got a record deal."

"That's great," Reed said, selecting another listing. A new house, closer to the city. Much smaller yard. About fifty grand over budget. But a fifty-thousand-dollar mortgage wasn't the worst thing, right?

"What about that one?"

Banks flicked her thumb across the screen, inspecting the home quietly for a long moment. Then she looked up.

"Do you really...want to live here?"

Reed tipped his beer bottle back, draining and dropping it next to two of its twins on the table next to him.

"What do you mean?"

"I just mean…there's nothing really happening here. We could live anyplace, right? Maybe a bigger city."

"We can't afford a bigger city. I thought you liked Birmingham?"

Banks shrugged. "It's okay."

She returned to her phone, and Reed dug his fingernail into the beer bottle's label as renewed frustration burned in his chest. It had been like this ever since returning from West Virginia. Banks had felt…off. Disengaged. Attentive to Davy, but little else. When he'd tried to initiate the night before, she claimed to have a headache.

It wasn't like her. She'd always been warm and engaged. Even clingy.

"I thought you'd be excited about a home," Reed said. A little irritation crept into his voice, and he didn't try to hide it.

Banks only nodded, still fixated on her phone.

"Can you put that down, please?"

She looked up. "Put what down?"

"The phone. I feel like I'm talking to an android."

She clicked the phone off and set it down, her face just as blank as before. "What do you want to talk about?"

Reed didn't answer immediately. He fingered the bottle and cocked his head. "What's going on? What's with this attitude?"

Banks's chin lifted indignantly. "This *attitude*?"

"I'm trying to have a conversation here. We're looking at houses. Why do I feel like I'm pulling teeth?"

Banks didn't answer. Reed abandoned the bottle and rested his arms on his knees, leaning forward.

"What's with you? You seem completely checked out. Did I say something? Did Turk say something?"

Banks shook her head but didn't answer.

"Well?" Reed pushed.

"You just tell me what you want to do, and that's what we'll do," Banks said.

"Excuse me?"

"You heard me, Reed. Tell me where we're gonna live and when to pack."

"That's not what's happening here."

"Really? You sure?"

Reed drew a breath, then hesitated. He looked to the phone. "Is this about Carla? The music deal?"

No answer.

"Look. I'm not a mind reader. If you've got something to say, you better say it."

"Maybe I'm feeling a little closed in, okay?" Banks snapped. "Maybe you're talking a house in the woods and another baby on the way and that's just not...that's not what I thought life would be."

"What do you mean, another baby? Are you pregnant?"

"No, I'm not pregnant. That's not the point. You're not even listening."

"I'm listening, I just have no idea what you're saying. Why don't you try again?"

Banks ran a hand over her face, grunting irritably. "See, there it is. That right there. That tone. It's like you're in charge, and you tell me what to do, and that's what we do."

"I'm lost, Banks."

"Like this house!" Banks said, throwing a hand up. "Like this city. Like our entire lives. Ever since we got back to the States, it's never been what we want. We've never even talked about what we want. You just decided what we need, and that's what happens. Like, why do we even live here?"

"I'm literally trying to find us a bigger place as we speak," Reed said.

"Not the house, Reed, the *city*. There's a whole world out there. I'm twenty-eight. My old friends are signing record deals and moving into nice apartments. They're traveling the world and going on tour. What am I doing? Picking up baby toys and cleaning bathrooms, waiting around while you traipse around the world getting shot at, not knowing if you'll come home. Then you do come home, and boom, we're moving out of the city. Like, what the hell, Reed?"

Banks began to sob, now curled up on the couch. Someplace deep in his gut the confusion Reed had felt minutes prior morphed into something hotter. Something more frustrated.

"Are you shitting me right now?" He spoke through clenched teeth, working to keep his voice down.

"What?" she said.

"I have given you *everything* you've ever wanted. I said you should have that life. You should be a singer. But *you* wanted to be together. You wanted to get married. So we did, and we came back here, and I'm doing my *damnedest* to make it everything you want. You don't have to work, you don't have to worry, you—"

"Do you hear yourself right now?" Banks cut him off. "Do you realize how sexist you're being? How condescending?"

Reed swept his arm across the table, knocking the beer bottles off. Banks sat up with a jolt, her eyes widening.

"You wanna know what I hear?" Reed said. "I hear a whole lot of ungrateful whining. That's what I hear. I've been from Iran to North Korea doing what I had to do to take care of this family. Getting shot at. Risking my life. Doing whatever it takes. And you've got the nerve to come at me grumbling about record deals?"

Banks just stared, eyes wide and full of tears. In the spare room, Davy awoke, probably startled by the falling beer bottles. Now crying loud enough to wake the dead. Reed ignored him, teeth still clenched, the molten heat in his stomach growing.

He looked at Banks, but he didn't see her. He saw the ball of fire as Belsky's yacht detonated, blasting half a dozen US Coast Guardsmen into hamburger meat in a millisecond.

Just the latest in a long slew of trauma and failure.

"What's happening to you?" Banks whispered. "Reed...we aren't like this."

Reed's phone buzzed from the table next to him. He ignored it, still glaring. His mind felt numb and sort of shut off. He saw his wife crying and knew that should trigger a caring, heartfelt response from him. But he couldn't feel anything.

"You gonna deal with him?" he snapped, jabbing his chin toward the back room. Banks blinked hard, her faced contorted into something between disbelief and pain. Then she got up and rushed down the hall.

Reed sat in the sudden stillness, still feeling numb, and yet somehow stunned by it. The phone next to him buzzed again, and he snatched it up. He didn't recognize the number, but he recognized the prefix—upstate New York.

He stood up and walked to the TV cabinet resting against the wall, then lifted the decorative bowl of fake flowers that sat there. Banks didn't like him to smoke around Davy. He'd promised to only smoke in his car, when he was alone. But he still kept a pack in the flower bowl, alongside a lighter.

On the back patio, he lit up before redialing the New York number. The line connected in only two rings.

"Wolf?" Reed spoke as he exhaled a cloud of glorious nicotine. The drug was already taking the edge off. Already calming his disoriented mind.

But still leaving his hand trembling with restrained emotion.

"Is this a bad time?" Wolfgang's voice was all business.

"I've got five. What's up?"

"I've got a situation. We need to meet."

"What kind of situation?"

"The prosecutable kind."

Reed froze, the smoke halfway to his lips. He took his time answering, drawing a long pull and breathing out.

"Turk?" Reed said at last.

"Yes. ASAP."

"Where?"

"Remember that time we had dinner by the water? You had a sore throat."

Reed remembered. He'd never forget.

"Tomorrow at noon," Reed said.

"Copy. And Reed?"

"Yeah?"

"Don't call anyone. Especially Saint."

A dull chill ran up Reed's spine. He hung up, staring at the phone as the cigarette smoldered between his fingers.

Especially Saint.

It was Trousdale's Secret Service call sign, a nod to her Louisiana heritage. What could Wolfgang have possibly stumbled into that he'd need to hide from the White House?

Nothing good.

Reed pocketed the phone and finished the cigarette, then smoked one more. By the time he ground it out on the patio with the heel of one shoe, his blood pressure had started to calm, but his mind still felt blank. It was like he stood outside himself, knowing what he should be thinking. What he should be feeling.

But he just felt numb.

A cabinet door slammed behind him, and Reed looked over his shoulder into the kitchen to see Banks scooping baby food into a bag. A suitcase sat upright behind her, and Davy was buckled into his detachable car seat, a sippy cup of apple juice clutched in one hand.

Reed tore the door open and crossed into the living room. "What are you doing?"

Banks ignored him, shouldering the bag and grabbing the suitcase with one arm while she reached for Davy with the other.

"Banks. What the hell are you doing?"

"I can't do this, Reed. I don't know what's happened to you. You're not the man I married."

Reed cut her off on her way to the hall, placing a hand on one shoulder and pulling her back.

"Wait. You can't just walk out. This *is* about the record deal, isn't it?"

"You wanna know what it's about?" Banks turned on him. "Here's what it's about, Reed. It's about me sitting up late nights wondering if my son is going to have a father. Wondering if you're gonna get shot up or imprisoned in some shithole country on the other side of the globe. It's about the fact that I married you, but you're married to the fight, and I'm done playing second fiddle."

She hefted Davy and turned back for the door. Reed pulled her back again.

"You think I *want* to do this stuff? You think I want to be shot at? I'm done, Banks. I did what I had to do to get us free. You want to live someplace else? Fine. Name the place. Throw a dart in the map. I'm right here!"

"Are you?" Banks challenged.

Reed's shoulders dropped. He saw the wall behind her eyes and finally felt something. Confusion. And pain.

"Of course. I'm right here."

"Then who were you on the phone with?"

Banks lifted her chin, shoulders square. Those gorgeous blue eyes he fell in love with blazing.

He opened his mouth. And then he shut it.

"That's what I thought," Banks said. "Good luck, Reed. Good luck being shot at. I won't ride that train anymore."

She pushed through the front door, grabbing her Volkswagen keys on the way out. Reed stood dumbly in the hall, staring at the door as the SUV rumbled to life and its tires chirped against the concrete.

He stepped out onto the front porch just in time to see Banks disappear around the corner, taillights fading into the night. Taking his son with her.

Leaving him struggling to feel at all.

9

Chattanooga, Tennessee

Reed booked a midmorning flight out of Birmingham, and Turk picked him up at the airport in his race-red Jeep Gladiator. Originally from Knoxville, Turk now lived in Nashville with Sinju and made the short trip down to Chattanooga his favorite way: behind the wheel of a cramped, loud, rough-riding vehicle.

Once a Marine, always a Marine.

Reed tossed his overnight bag into the back seat and clambered in, banging his shins against the doorframe and biting back a curse. He hadn't said anything to Turk about Banks. Hadn't called her or even tried to untangle the spaghetti of mixed emotions he felt picturing those taillights vanishing into the dark. He simply called his old battle buddy and told him where to be and when, and Turk rolled out—as faithful as the sunrise.

Reed lit up a cigarette from the airport convenience store as Turk navigated toward downtown Chattanooga. They rode in silence, the easy comfort of long-time familiarity bridging any need for small talk. Reed couldn't help but notice the abandoned hair bands in the cup holder and the exhausted lipstick tube rolling on the floorboard.

Sinju was adjusting well to the abundance of Western culture. It was good to see some of Turk's rough edges worn down a little by the presence of a female touch, but Reed didn't want to think about a female touch just then. He didn't want to think about anything.

The Jeep rolled to a stop in a parking lot facing the slow churn of the Tennessee River a hundred yards down the hill. Bright sunlight spilled over the anchored mass of *Southern Belle*, an antebellum-style river boat now loading passengers for a lunch cruise. Next to the *Belle*, a metal pier shot out over the black water, American flags lined up at the end over small brass plaques.

Reed knew the spot well. It was the site of his second encounter with the man he'd only known as *The Wolf*—an elite assassin tasked with bringing Reed into early and permanent retirement during his days as a contract killer.

Wolfgang had managed to wrap a choke wire around Reed's throat that night, almost strangling him to death. Hence the reference to Reed's sore throat.

Always a sense of humor.

Reed glanced to the left of the river boat to where a small restaurant clung to the bank, with a boardwalk and a deck overhanging the water. Standing just outside the restaurant, wearing his customary black peacoat to block out the winter chill, Wolfgang raised a hand in a two-finger wave.

Reed dumped the cigarette butt out of the Jeep and slammed the door, feeling the heft of the SIG P226 riding beneath his left arm in a shoulder holster—a provision Turk had brought with him from Nashville. Despite the years of friendship and growing trust that had distanced him from his last meeting with Wolfgang alongside this river, Reed couldn't help but indulge in a cautious glance around the parking lot.

Bad memories triggered predictable instincts.

They found Wolfgang waiting at a secluded table on the deck. Plastic sheets covered the windows, blocking out the wind, and propane space heaters kept the space comfortable enough to relax in but not warm enough to justify removing their coats.

Smart Wolf.

Two glasses of bourbon on the rocks waited for the two men. Wolfgang sipped water, looking gray and hard, much as Reed had seen him four days prior in West Virginia. Turk ordered a round of appetizers and breadsticks, and Reed contemplated a steak. He hadn't eaten anything since the pizza he and Banks shared the night prior. The emotional tutorial of the evening had burned a lot of calories but left him with no appetite.

Part of him wondered where she had driven to or how long she would be away. It wouldn't be hard to track her. They used a joint bank account, and he could see the location of her phone using a tracking app they shared, but he hadn't bothered to check.

Right now, he just needed to cool off.

"Good flight?" Wolfgang asked.

Reed only grunted and gulped bourbon. The server took their orders, and Reed requested the steak anyway. Maybe a good cut of meat would bring his appetite back. As soon as the woman left, Wolfgang leaned over the table.

"I found Belsky."

Reed stiffened, the bourbon glass halfway to his lips. "Where?"

"Caracas."

Reed set the glass down. Glanced sideways at Turk.

"How—"

Wolfgang held up a hand. "Just wait. There's more."

The server came with a basket of breadsticks. Wolfgang gave her time to leave.

"Do you remember my contact from Moscow? The guy I flew to Minsk to visit."

"Right..."

"He was at my house last night."

"What?"

"Things went sideways for him in Russia. Apparently, the questions I asked in Minsk triggered some concerns of his own. He was investigating and got busted. He barely got out alive."

"Investigating *what*?"

"Who hired Belsky to kill Trousdale."

"And?"

Wolfgang's voice dropped to a whisper. "He thinks Nikitin."

Reed's blood ran cold. The restaurant around him dulled out of existence as his mind spun, racing instantly to a picture of the ultimate worst-case scenario.

Then ratcheting quickly back to reality.

"Where's the proof?"

"He doesn't *have* proof," Wolfgang said, irritated. "Did you miss the part where he barely got out alive?"

Reed wiped his mouth. Finished the bourbon in one gulp and set the glass down. He held Wolfgang's gaze but didn't say anything.

"You don't believe me?" Wolfgang snorted.

"I didn't say that."

"But you don't."

"I don't know this guy. You've been particularly obscure about your sources, Wolf. And I've never pressed you. But this is something else. You realize that, right? Do you hear what you're saying?"

Reed's unintentional use of Banks's same question from the previous evening jolted his mind. He buried the thought and focused on Wolfgang.

"I wouldn't have called you if I didn't think it was legit." Wolfgang spoke through gritted teeth.

"So who is your source?" Reed asked.

A long pause. Wolfgang looked to Turk, but the big Tennessean offered no support. He picked his teeth with a toothpick and waited.

Wolfgang's shoulders slumped.

"He's from before, back when I worked in espionage. His name is Ivan Sidorov. He was KGB, then SVR. We collided on a couple of European ops before working together on a counter-terrorism mission in Sydney. I wouldn't call him a good guy, but he's proven himself reliable. He's a solid source."

"KGB?" Reed questioned.

"*Ex*-KGB."

"No such thing," Turk drawled. Reed had to agree.

"Why would he lie about this?" Wolfgang said, cheeks flushing. "If what he said is true—"

"We're staring down the barrel of a world war," Reed said.

"*Exactly*. Why would he lie about that?"

"Plenty of reasons, I'm sure. What's his explanation for coming to you?"

"He's anti-Nikitin. He's trying to forestall a war."

"Of course he would say that," Turk muttered.

Wolfgang stiffened, shoulders rolling back. Reed held up a hand.

"Cool it, Wolf. These are fair questions."

The server came with the entrées. Prime rib for Turk. A ribeye for Reed, with all the trimmings. Wolfgang stuck to a chicken Caesar salad, ignoring it while Reed and Turk dug in.

"Why didn't you call O'Brien?" Reed said.

Wolfgang folded his arms. "I thought we should talk first."

"Why?"

"Have you seen Trousdale lately?"

Reed shook his head. "Nope."

"Exactly. Nobody has. She's been squirreled out of sight for months."

"Your point?"

"Only that we don't know what her current mental or physical condition may be. We don't know who's actually calling the shots right now. Could be Stratton."

Reed paused, a forkful of potatoes halfway to his mouth. Pictures of the vice president flashed across his mind. Tall and austere, the polished figure of a born politician. A Republican from Illinois with direct ties to Cunningham Enterprises, a corporation wrapped deep under the sheets with Lenkov International.

Belsky's company.

Wolfgang himself had confronted Stratton about the connection the previous November. Stratton had reasonable and compelling explanations for his innocence. Reed wanted to believe him, but a worm of doubt still ate away at his mind. Wolfgang's suspicion of the VP could be well founded.

Reed set the fork down. Wiped his hands.

"Why does Ivan think Belsky is in Caracas?"

"He says he found Russian naval command ordering a stealth attack submarine to the Straits of Florida at the time of Belsky's yacht sinking. He believes the sub fished Belsky out of the water and carted him to South America."

"Why?"

"He doesn't know. But he doesn't think Belsky is simply camping out.

There's some kind of a connection here. Belsky, Lenkov, Moscow...an attempted assassination."

"What do you mean?"

"Think about it. Let's say Ivan is right. Let's say Nikitin used Belsky as a middleman to knock off Trousdale. What does that mean?"

Reed sucked his teeth. Glanced at Turk. The question was rhetorical, but it demanded a direct answer anyway.

"He's making plays," Reed finished.

"Aggressive plays. Bigger plays than his predecessor ever dreamed of. He's either crazy, or there's a lot more coming."

Turk finished his prime rib while Reed stared at his half-empty plate and calculated. It was difficult to believe Wolfgang, but not because the stoic killer had ever proven himself to be dishonest.

Everybody's emotions were ragged. In addition to the slain Coast Guardsmen on Belsky's yacht, Reed and Turk had watched their own president topple under an assassin's bullet, right in the heartland of America. Wolfgang, while perhaps less emotionally invested in either Trousdale or the events off the Florida coast, had just lost his baby sister. Nobody knew about Reed's marital issues, but he wasn't so irrational as to ignore their impact.

Emotional stress eroded good judgment. It clouded clear thinking.

And that made Reed think of Trousdale. Because Wolfgang was right—the nation had neither heard from nor seen their president since Christmas, and nobody had more right to be emotionally supercharged than the actual victim of that bullet.

The thought of a mentally compromised president was only slightly less concerning than the prospect of a corrupt vice president pulling her strings.

"We can't sleep on this," Turk said, mopping gravy with a dinner roll.

"I agree," Reed said. "But we can't keep it from the White House, either. We don't have the resources to act on our own, and if we sideline them, they sideline us."

"But what if Stratton's involved?" Wolfgang pressed.

"Then I'll cut his throat on the White House lawn. But the only way to know will be to get close."

"They're gonna send us after Belsky," Turk said, suppressing a burp. He didn't appear stressed by the prospect, but Reed could see the focus in his eyes. Turk was already zeroed in on the mission at hand.

"I'm counting on it," Reed said. "If Stratton is dirty, Belsky might know."

"Or Stratton might set us up," Wolfgang retorted.

"I'll take my instincts over his," Reed said. "I've been dodging bullets for a long time. Let's get O'Dell on the phone and tell him we want a meeting with Maggie directly. That way we can gauge her condition."

"What do we tell him?" Wolfgang said.

"Only what he needs to know. If anything Ivan claims is true, we're talking about a major risk of real global conflict. The kind that leaves a few million biting the dust. We'll hold our cards until we know who to trust."

Turk grunted his agreement, picking his teeth again. "Where is he, by the way?"

"Who?" Wolfgang said.

"Ivan."

"At my house. Laying low. He snuck in on a fake passport. The Russians are looking for him...or so he claims."

Wolfgang finished the sentence with a slight shrug.

"You better get back up there," Reed said. "Put him someplace safe and out of sight. The CIA may need him."

Wolfgang nodded. Reed thumbed two hundred-dollar bills on the table to cover the check.

"I'll call O'Dell. Once we get a meeting arranged, we'll update you."

Wolfgang shook his head. "No. I'm not riding the bench this time. I want to be there to see Trousdale."

Reed didn't answer right away. He held Wolfgang's gaze and noted the strain in his eyes. The gaunt circles riding beneath them. The disheveled hair, uncharacteristic of the killer.

Reed knew that look well—he'd seen it in the mirror more often than he cared to admit. The look of a man nearing rock bottom, looking for something to sink his teeth into. Like a hungry wolverine.

Emotional stress, eroding them all.

"Deal with the Russian," Reed said simply. "And stay close to the phone."

10

The White House

The private dining room of the presidential residence flickered with candlelight. Maggie was as much use in a kitchen as she was behind the controls of a fighter jet, but the perks of being POTUS included a world-class kitchen crew who prided themselves in catering to the palate of the president.

That meant Cajun food. *Really good* Cajun food.

The table was laden with steaming dishes of crawfish étouffée, red beans and sausage, gumbo slimy with chopped okra, and plenty of white rice to ladle it all over. All the best fixings of Maggie's homeland—swampy southern Louisiana.

O'Dell sat next to her at the little table, dressed in a simple black suit with no tie, his shirt open at the collar. He smiled politely as Maggie ladled étouffée onto his plate, ducking his head but not commenting. She smoothed the dress over her thighs, ignoring the shooting pain that raced through her torso like a bolt of lightning.

She'd come off the pain meds in the past week. The White House physician was happy to keep writing prescriptions, but Maggie was concerned about the long-term risk of opioids. She didn't feel like herself on them.

And at the same time, she was growing to like them too much.

"Wine?" she asked.

"Please."

O'Dell's New Orleans drawl carried just the hint of formality—an undertone she'd been unable to shake since she woke in a Chicago hospital room with his fingers clamped around hers. She wasn't sure what she felt in that moment—the moment when their eyes locked, and she experienced hope for the first time since toppling under the freight-train blow of a sniper's bullet.

She only knew she wanted to explore it. And she hoped he did, too.

Maggie poured a generous measure of Sauvignon Blanc for them both, then broke French bread into a wad to mop through the gumbo in her bowl. The dishes were all the finest White House china—an obvious choice, she thought, when she first invited O'Dell to dinner. Now she regretted the dinnerware. The stiffness in his posture couldn't be helped by the landslide of ornate trappings surrounding them.

"I don't think you've ever told me about your daughter," Maggie prompted.

A smile lifted O'Dell's cheeks. He hesitated, the wineglass held midair.

"Holly? She lives with her mother. In Austin."

"Do you get to see her very often?"

"No, ma'am—"

O'Dell broke off, and their eyes met. He flushed just a little and shifted.

"No. Not often."

Maggie winced, feeling suddenly very awkward and somehow embarrassed. O'Dell looked away, and she felt the blood rush to her cheeks.

Maybe this had been a mistake. She'd known O'Dell for years, tracing all the way back to her initiation as governor of Louisiana. He served as her bodyguard at the time and quickly became her constant shadow, sticking to her like the rice on her spoon.

Security slowly grew into companionship, professional concern manifesting into unquestioning loyalty. She trusted O'Dell like she trusted almost nobody. When she awoke in Chicago, limp on a hospital bed, clinging to life by the skin of her teeth, O'Dell was there. And he didn't leave.

There was something in his eyes, something more intimate than platonic loyalty.

Or at least she had thought so. But as his faultless loyalty and constant concern failed to develop into the new year, she began to question the roadblock.

Tonight's quiet dinner was meant to stir the fire. Probe the darkness and see what lay unspoken between them.

It wasn't working.

Maggie smoothed her hands across her dress again, a little red number that struck a balance between elegant and sexy. As much of a balance as a woman half shot to death could strike, anyway.

"James...can we talk?"

She looked up. His wide, dark eyes were fixed on her. The wineglass in his hand, rotating slowly. He only nodded.

"I'm...well. I'm not very good at this."

She laughed nervously. O'Dell's face remained expressionless. Her stomach tightened.

"What I wanted to say...I mean. What I've been wanting to say..."

The words caught in her throat. She stopped, unsure where to go. His eyes remained fixed on hers, a little wider now. Completely unreadable and leaving her questioning everything she had ever felt.

"Yes?" O'Dell's voice was soft, the wineglass now frozen in his fingers.

"Well." She looked down at her hands.

Find your guts, dammit.

"These last few weeks...I mean, really, these last few years. They've meant a lot to me. You've meant a lot to me. And..."

She looked up. "I wanted you to know—"

The sharp shrill of a cell phone cut her off mid-sentence. O'Dell flinched, and his face flushed just a little. He dug into his suit jacket and produced the offending device, glancing once across the screen, his thumb hovering in indecision. His shoulders tensed, then slumped.

"I'm sorry. I should take this."

Maggie waved a dismissive hand. "Sure, dude. Whatever you need."

O'Dell rose to his feet, answering as he moved to the door. Maggie felt the blood rush to her face as she scooped up the glass and gulped wine.

Sure, dude? What were they, high schoolers making out in a pickup truck? Why the hell had she said that?

The Sauvignon washed down her throat but failed to carry away the sting of her own embarrassment. She cursed herself silently and wished she'd never planned this stupid dinner.

What *was* this? This wasn't her. She never lost her nerve like this.

The doorknob rattled, and she stiffened, looking over one shoulder a little too quickly. O'Dell stepped back in, the phone held in one hand, his head up and his shoulders back.

His business stance. That familiar bulk of a muscled chest and chiseled jaw that made her feel safe in a world full of flying bullets. And made her feel…other things.

Maggie blinked. The wine was getting to her.

"Everything okay?"

"That was Montgomery, ma'am."

This time O'Dell didn't seem to notice his application of formality. The word stung, but Maggie didn't show it.

"Yes?"

"He needs to meet. They've found Belsky."

11

Caracas, Venezuela

The Brazilians called them *favelas*, but the Spanish word for makeshift slum houses was *barrio*—a shantytown, built of scavenged sheet metal, blocks, repurposed wood, and whatever else the starving masses of Venezuela could get their hands on.

Caracas was full of them. Rising over the rolling hills that dipped into a wide mountain valley near the coast and spilling around the broad highways built by Chávez during the golden years of Venezuelan wealth. As abandoned factories succumbed to dismantlement by the homeless, the barrios grew. They spread deep into the countryside, where the impoverished residents of inland Venezuela would kill for a home as fancy and dry as a barrio.

Such was the nature of Venezuela's national heartbreak, and it was this inescapable reality that brought Luis Rivas to build his national headquarters in the heart of the barrios. Not just because Venezuela's destitution was a reality that Rivas's political rival, Cesar Moreno, refused to acknowledge, but also because there was an unspoken understanding in Caracas that Rivas was a dead man walking if he ventured too far outside the confines of his own territory.

Moreno wanted Rivas in the ground, and hordes of *colectivos*—paramilitary gangs founded by Hugo Chávez and now loyal to Moreno—would be only too happy to arrange a convenient accident on Moreno's behalf.

Rivas wasn't safe in the wealthy, pro-Moreno neighborhoods that surrounded Miraflores. But deep in the barrios, where he was lost among the people he longed to protect, Rivas had friends. Hundreds of thousands of them. Starving and desolate men and women who longed for the vibrant and happy Venezuela their grandparents so enjoyed—a country that was second only to the United States in all the New World. A wealthy, powerful, influential nation.

A nation Rivas was born to lead.

Twice now, he had campaigned against Moreno in national elections for President of the Bolivarian Republic. Twice he had been soundly defeated.

There was no doubt in Rivas's mind that both elections were stolen. He wasn't the only one who thought so, either. Since 2019, the United States had joined in his protest of Moreno, recognizing Rivas as Venezuela's true president and sanctioning the Moreno regime into oblivion.

Perhaps the Americans were pure in their intentions, but their approach to managing the human crisis in Venezuela was both ham-handed and absolutist. Rivas was no closer to Miraflores now than he was five years prior, and the American sanctions had brought his entire homeland to its knees.

Food was scarce. Oil production had fallen from 3.5 million barrels per day in the late nineties to barely 310,000 a day at present—not enough to supply Venezuela's domestic demand. The national currency, the Venezuelan bolívar, was worth less than the paper it was printed on. Literally.

Bureaucracy and centralized regulation had choked the life out of Venezuela's industry, rendering over eighty percent of her once proud factories as empty hulks. The highways, the office buildings, and the supermarket shelves were all empty. Life expectancy was in the toilet.

All while Rivas stood over an untapped oil reserve greater than any nation on planet Earth.

Standing on the balcony of his headquarters, looking down a long and grungy street clogged with trash and the occasional starving dog, it was difficult for Rivas not to embrace the rage. Not only toward Moreno, but also toward the world. The dozens of developed Western countries that turned their backs on Venezuela without more than token support for the revolution he was fighting to ignite.

If there was one thing Rivas knew about Venezuela's future, it could be captured in only a few words: they were on their own.

"Luis. We're ready."

Rivas glanced over his shoulder to see one of his political advisors standing in the shadows well inside the door, unwilling to step outside for fear of a sniper. Unlike Moreno, Rivas didn't boast a big cabinet or any sort of large staff. His unrecognized presidential headquarters was nestled inside a three-story, pre-Moreno building, held together by duct tape and goodwill. Inside the dusty upstairs room, he relied on kerosene lamps for light as the unreliable Venezuelan power grid blinked on and off at random —a problem Moreno blamed on the United States.

Maybe Moreno was right.

Rivas ducked inside and joined a small crowd of his lieutenants around a low table. Spread across it was a map of Caracas, marked in detail with a red pen. Little *X*'s highlighted the locations of Moreno's presidential palace, his key government buildings, and garrisons of the National Guard—Venezuela's national police, weaponized into regime enforcers by Moreno.

For what Rivas had planned, the locations of all these little points were as critical as a brain surgeon's understanding of a patient's anatomy. Knowing where the National Guard was stationed, how quickly they could respond, and where the weak points in their grasp on the city lay were all crucial elements in breaking that grip.

But knowledge alone was insufficient. Rivas had been around long enough to understand that. Everyone in Venezuela knew how bad things had become. Even if the majority blamed those realities on Moreno, blame alone wasn't strong enough to displace the corrupt leader.

Rivas needed outrage. He needed gasoline for the fire.

"If we disperse our protests to the east of the palace, Moreno's soldiers will be spread too thin to suppress them all." One of Rivas's advisors spoke quietly, tracing the map with a pen to mark his suggested locations. "They will resort to containment and circle in to protect the palace. That will draw attention away from the station."

He circled another spot on the map to the south and west of Miraflores. Situated in the foothills, above the city. Difficult to reach, chosen for its geographic position above downtown.

Not a military station. A television station. *The* television station, in fact, controlled by Moreno and regularly projecting *cadenas* across the city—mandatory governmental broadcasts that automatically interrupted all prior programming.

They were an incessant nuisance, ignored by Rivas's supporters, many of whom didn't even own televisions. But they were watched religiously by the middle class and wealthier residents of the city, many of whom supported Moreno. And that made the *cadenas* the key to Rivas's whole gamble.

"It's good," Rivas said. "We'll take the station a few hours after the protests begin. Light some fires someplace on the outskirts and throw some tires on them. The smoke will alarm people. Get more eyes on the television."

A grunt of agreement rang around the table, but nobody said anything. Rivas could feel the tension in the air. Uncertainty that built into fear, palpable enough to cut with a knife. He'd expected his people to become nervous the closer they came to executing their plan, but he couldn't afford cold feet. This was an all-or-nothing play. The stuff revolutions were made of.

"Amigos." Rivas placed both hands on the table, looking each man and woman in the eye and holding their gaze before passing to the next. Only five people in total, counting himself. No more than a conspiracy, but even wildfires could be ignited with a single match. "This is our moment. What we've waited for. You cannot grow timid on me now."

No immediate answer. Everyone looked away.

"What if Juan doesn't come through?" one woman whispered. It was the question Rivas knew they were all thinking. A reasonable fear, all things considered. Rivas's secret informant, Juan Blanco, was the key to this entire operation, and he was a man Rivas knew almost nothing about. He didn't know where Juan lived, whether he had a family, or if Juan Blanco was even his real name.

He only knew that Juan worked deep inside Moreno's government and that Juan knew things. Things that could serve as the gasoline Rivas so desperately needed to burn away Moreno's support.

"Juan will come through," Rivas said, projecting more confidence than he felt. "Don't doubt him. He's putting his life on the line for his country. For his people. We can do as much."

Soft, hesitant nods. No great votes of confidence.

Rivas straightened. "I love our country, amigos. It is *our* country. Our Venezuela. We will take it back—for our children. For our children's children. *Sí?*"

Another round of hesitant nods. Rivas broke into a wide smile that he didn't feel.

"*Viva Venezuela!*"

The cheer was returned with a little less heart but a few weak smiles. Rivas patted backs and squeezed shoulders as his cabinet resumed preparations, debating avenues of approach and the best locations for the core of the protests.

All key ingredients for what was to come.

Rivas reached into his pocket for a cigarette—a frequent indulgence that calmed his nerves. He'd barely lifted it to his lips before he heard the door explode open on the ground level and a commotion ensue. Everyone panicked. One of the men nearest Rivas ran directly for a side table, reaching into a drawer for a pistol. Rivas held up a hand, moving himself to the stairwell. Voices called for him to stop as he hauled the door open, and the commotion below broke onto the stairs.

But Rivas didn't hear the pounding boots of *colectivos* coming to assassinate him. He heard a woman's desperate cries, repeating his name as she clawed her way up the stairs, tripping and being hauled back by his personal bodyguard, a former soldier of the Venezuelan army.

"Señor! Señor, please! I must speak to Rivas!"

Rivas pushed down the stairs, finding the woman in the sparse living room below. He waved a calming hand toward his bodyguard, lowering himself into a crouch next to the fallen woman. "It's okay, Mateo. I will speak with her."

Mateo backed off reluctantly, the AK-47 he wore like a personal accessory riding from a sling.

Rivas sat next to the woman, offering a calming smile. She was skinny and battered, with lines in her face and tears streaming down her cheeks. One of those cheeks was swollen and bleeding a little where she had collided with a wall. Rivas wiped her forehead with one thumb and called for a damp rag.

"Calm yourself, señora. You are safe here. Take a breath."

She gasped as he wiped the blood off her face, then offered her water. She shook her head and began to cry again.

"What is it?" Rivas asked. "What happened?"

"My husband," she sobbed. "He was taken by the police. They dragged him out of our home this morning. They wouldn't tell me why. They took him to El Helicoide."

A dull chill ran down Rivas's spine, and he could tell by the icy silence that filled the room that everyone around him felt the same. El Helicoide was a large, oblong building situated in the heart of Caracas, looking something like a spaceship with multiple layers of glass-encased floors. The ostensible headquarters of the Bolivarian National Intelligence Service, Moreno's secret police.

But everyone knew El Helicoide's darker purpose—that of political prison, a last stop for any and all enemies of the Moreno regime. A gulag for Venezuela. A veritable hell on earth.

"Take a breath, señora," Rivas said again, still speaking softly. "Who is your husband? Maybe I can help."

The woman swallowed hard, still fighting back tears. But when she spoke, her voice was strong.

"Juan Blanco. My husband's name is Juan Blanco."

12

Washington Dulles International Airport
Dulles, Virginia

Reed tried Banks before boarding the plane to DC, but the call went straight to voicemail. He checked her location and found that Banks had disabled location services from her end, blocking him from viewing her place on the digital map.

For the first time since leaving Birmingham, he felt real uncertainty. Not quite fear, and not regret. His gut was still tense with irritated frustration that bordered on anger. But he started to wonder if he had screwed up. If somehow, during the mix of flying accusations and irate challenges, he'd missed the forest for the trees.

He didn't know, and he still didn't have the energy to figure it out, so he buried the questions instead and boarded a 737 straight to DC. Turk rode quietly beside him, relaxed in the cramped economy seat, but Reed could tell his best friend's mind was grinding with racing thoughts, the same as his own.

Wolfgang's claims bordered on the insane, but if even half of them were true...

A jet-black Chevrolet Tahoe waited for them outside the arrivals terminal at Dulles. The rear hatch opened as they approached, and they both deposited their overnight bags before climbing into the back seat.

Only one person sat up front—tall and broad, with bulky shoulders and dark skin. Darker glasses shielded his eyes, but Reed knew he was watching them via the rearview mirror.

James O'Dell.

Reed grunted once and ducked his head. O'Dell chewed gum and shifted into drive, rumbling into traffic without a word. They navigated amid clogged metro streets toward the heart of DC. Reed watched the cityscape pass, noting the towering spire of the Washington Monument gleaming in early morning sunshine.

Everything looked as it always looked. Alive, preoccupied. Nearly a million people invested up to their necks in the busywork of their own lives, heedless of any storm brewing in the distance.

Reed used to resent that, but since Davy was born, he somehow appreciated it. The ignorance of the masses was a childlike innocence, in his eyes. The ability to enjoy life without an intimate knowledge of the horrors erupting just out of sight in places unknown was perhaps the greatest American privilege. It was what he joined the Marine Corps to protect and now found himself still protecting in a much darker capacity.

It was also, in his mind, the most fragile part of an already fragile society. The spit wad holding up a house of cards.

O'Dell pulled through the main entrance of the White House and flashed an ID at the guard. Moments later, the SUV rolled behind the building and pulled into a low garage sheltered by trees and shrubbery. Half a dozen men in black suits stood by, at least two of whom openly brandished FN P90 submachine guns.

O'Dell cut the engine and looked into the mirror with a dull smirk. Reed raised both eyebrows.

"Seriously?"

"Drop your pants, Montgomery."

Reed and Turk submitted without further objection, handing over sidearms and stripping down to their birthday suits in the chill of East

Coast winter. O'Dell stood back and chewed gum, barely concealing his satisfaction as Reed and Turk were poked and prodded far beyond the necessity of presidential security.

This was O'Dell's world. His own little kingdom, and he was taking full advantage. Despite Reed's sacrifice and service to the Trousdale administration, there was bad blood between him and O'Dell, and it clearly hadn't been washed away yet.

As Reed re-buckled his belt and pulled his jacket on, he shot O'Dell a look. "Satisfied?"

O'Dell shrugged and led them out of the garage. Two of the Secret Service guys followed, walking just out of sight over Reed's shoulder. He ignored them, stopping at a subdued side entrance near a back corner of the old mansion.

O'Dell put his hand on the knob, then stopped. He turned around, removing his glasses and tucking them into his suit jacket without comment. For a long time he just stared them down, still chewing the gum. Then he spoke quietly in his syrupy Cajun drawl.

"The president is still recovering. She doesn't have energy for bullshit."

Reed didn't answer. O'Dell leaned forward, just an inch.

"You stress her out, I'll kick your ass."

"You fantasize about that, don't you?" Reed said.

O'Dell's lips lifted in a snarl. He spat the gum into a nearby flowerbed, then pulled the door open.

Reed had been here before, the first time he ever visited the White House. It was a service entrance, leading into the basement of the old building where staff quarters, janitorial closets, and scuffed hallways ran like the legs of a spiderweb deep into the dirt. O'Dell led the way, navigating with ease as he brought them into the West Wing, still underground, then took the stairs up one level.

The two agents hung close behind as they ascended into the operations center of the Free World, passing offices packed tight together over a field of blue carpet. O'Dell stopped at the entrance to a conference room, looking once more back to Reed. Steel in his eyes.

"Why didn't you want Stratton present?" he asked, his voice barely above a whisper.

Reed motioned to the door. "Why don't you find out?"
Another hardened glare from O'Dell. Then he pushed the door open.

13

The West Wing
The White House

The room was large but occupied by only three people: Chairman of the Joint Chiefs, General John David Yellin; Director of the Central Intelligence Agency, Victor O'Brien; and President of the United States, Margaret Trousdale.

Maggie looked like absolute hell. She sat at the end of the table, pale-faced and slumped in a chair, her hair held back in a ponytail, a royal blue sweatshirt emblazoned with the presidential seal clinging to her shoulders. She'd never been a very heavy woman, but she'd lost weight since Reed had last seen her, lying in a hospital bed with tubes and wires running out of her like some kind of science experiment.

He couldn't help but stop cold in the entrance of the room, noting her thin lips and the yellow tinge of her skin. He'd seen her without makeup before, but never like this.

She looked like she was dying.

"Hello, Reed," Maggie said. Her voice was confident but didn't project very well. Reed glanced sideways at O'Dell. The president's bodyguard was no longer watching him, his dark eyes fixed on Maggie instead. Reed saw deep pain in those eyes.

Pain and...

"Have a seat." Maggie's words broke off his trail of thought. She motioned to twin chairs a few seats down from the head of the table, directly across from O'Brien and Yellin. Reed knew them both by name and didn't bother to offer a greeting. They didn't bother either.

He sat next to Turk and cracked open a bottle of water, taking the temperature of the room. Yellin was tense, his bulldog shoulders bulging beneath Army Class A's. O'Brien looked as he always looked—stone-faced and impassive, housed within a plain black suit. His owl eyes inspected Reed behind round glasses, but he didn't so much as twitch as their gazes locked.

"We found Belsky," Reed said simply. No point in beating around the bush.

"So you claim." O'Brien was the first to speak, and it caught Reed off guard. The spook had never been one to lead a conversation before.

"Butthurt?" Reed asked. "I wouldn't be. You could fill a library with the things the CIA doesn't know."

O'Brien didn't blink, the insult washing off his back like water droplets off a duck. Somehow it irritated Reed. Not because he actually cared about offending anyone, but because he resented not being the most unreadable man in the room.

"Why don't you start from the beginning?" Maggie suggested. A steaming cup of something dark sat next to her. She raised it for a slow sip, her hand trembling just a little. O'Dell had taken position behind her, and Reed momentarily considered having him ejected from the room prior to diving into Wolfgang's report.

No point, really. Something told him O'Dell had wormed his way about as deep inside the administration as a person could get. Even deeper than the vice president or Maggie's chief of staff, apparently.

"Our associate was recently contacted by a source of his. Somebody deep inside Moscow."

"And by *associate*, you mean Wolfgang Pierce?" Again O'Brien took the lead.

"I mean our associate."

"Where is he?"

"Not here."

O'Brien's lip twitched, just a little. Maggie held up a hand.

"*Enough*. I don't have time for this. Reed, get to the point."

Reed decided to give a little ground, just to make things easier. "Wolfgang has a contact inside Moscow, like I mentioned. A high-ranking SVR official. Somebody Wolfgang trusts. He was the man responsible for providing us with the Fedor Volkov lead. Wolfgang met with him in Minsk while Turk and I were working in Chicago."

Reed glanced around the table to make sure everybody was following. Yellin still hadn't spoken. Maggie was cupping her mug, fixated on him.

"Following the assassination attempt," Reed continued, "Wolfgang's contact ran an independent investigation into Belsky's activities. Apparently, he had some concerns of his own. One thing led to another, and he was busted by Russian authorities, fled the country, and wound up rendezvousing with Wolfgang."

"Here?" O'Brien demanded.

The man misses nothing.

"Somewhere," Reed said.

"Why?" O'Brien pressed.

Reed stopped, taking his time formulating his next statement. It was the core of this entire meeting. The moment when he decided how many of Ivan's radical theories to share—and how many to hold back.

"Wolfgang's contact claims that Belsky is still alive. He escaped the yacht explosion in the Straits and is currently hiding in Venezuela."

"That's not possible," Yellin said, his voice a dull growl. "We've deployed naval deep-sea scans to the wreck site. The largest piece of that boat could fit on this table. The Coast Guard swept the seas for days—there were no survivors."

"Wolfgang's contact claims that Belsky was removed from the yacht prior to the blast," Reed said carefully.

"In Miami?"

"No. At sea."

Yellin squinted, but Reed could tell he was putting it together.

"There were no surface vessels in the region," Yellin said slowly.

"Exactly. No surface vessels."

"What are you saying?" Maggie's voice gained a little strength. "Cut to the chase, already."

"Wolfgang's contact believes that Belsky was fished out of the water by a Russian attack submarine before being transferred to Caracas."

Dead silence. This time even O'Brien blinked. Reed tapped one finger on the tabletop, waiting for the reality of what he claimed to sink in.

Yellin was first to speak. "Are you saying *Russia*—"

Maggie cut him off, holding up a hand. A little color had risen to her cheeks, and her body tensed.

"Where's the proof?"

It was a great question, and it reflected a presence of mind on Maggie's part that reassured Reed, if only a little. She was thinking rationally.

"We don't have any," he said. "The contact claims he was assembling proof when he was busted. He barely escaped Moscow with his life."

"*Who* is he?" O'Brien said, his voice charged with a hint of angst.

"Does it matter?" Reed said.

O'Brien finally broke. He snorted, teeth flashing. "*Of course* it matters. For all we know, this is an elaborate Russian sting operation—"

"A sting operation incriminating their own government?" Turk took that one, his Tennessee drawl rising in incredulity. "Come on, now."

"So maybe it's a Chinese sting," O'Brien snapped. "We've got a lot of enemies, Mr. Turkman. Any one of them would dearly love to send us tripping down a wild goose chase—"

"Mr. Director, please." Maggie cut him off. The room went silent. She sipped from her mug, then wiped a trail of sweat from her forehead. She turned back to Reed.

"You're a lot of things, Reed, but an idiot isn't one of them. I need details."

Reed gave them, recounting Wolfgang's story, beginning in Minsk and working up through Ivan's unexpected visit. He kept Ivan's identity a secret, and he skirted any direct mentions of Makar Nikitin.

He wasn't sure why. It was just something in his gut. By the time he finished, Maggie's mug had stopped steaming, and he held the president's full attention.

"Where is he now?" Maggie said.

"Who?"

"*The contact.*"

"Wolfgang has him."

"Here?" Maggie said. "In the States?"

Reed hesitated. Then he nodded. "Yes."

Maggie's fingers worked around the handle of the mug. O'Dell reached for a carafe sitting on a table nearby, but she waved him off.

"If Russia facilitated Belsky's escape...," Yellin began.

"That can only mean one of two things," Maggie said. "Either they need him alive, so they fished him out of a sticky situation..."

"Or they sponsored the assassination from the start," Turk said.

O'Brien's face flushed. He laid both hands on the table with dull, fleshy smacks. "This is *absurd.* Madam President, you can't seriously treat this fantastical, unverified nonsense as actionable intelligence. If Mr. Montgomery refuses to disclose his source's identity and location, why should we entertain—"

"Because it might be *true,*" Reed snapped. "Use your head, dammit. It doesn't matter who my contact is. It doesn't even matter if he's lying. It only matters if some of what he's saying is true. If there's even a possibility of a Moscow connection, we have to assume the worst is yet to come."

"You're out of your depth," O'Brien snarled. "You have no *idea* how deeply complex the intelligence world is. Misdirection and bad information roll in by the truckload. We verify, reverify, and verify again before we believe *anything,* let alone take action on questionable information that could lead—"

"To a *war,*" Yellin snapped.

Nobody spoke. Reed looked from O'Brien to Maggie, and his shoulders sagged. He knew there was only one possible outcome of this conversation. A part of him relished it, remembering the brave Coast Guardsmen Belsky's detonating yacht had slaughtered.

But another part of him was tired. Because he knew that no matter how bad things appeared...they were guaranteed to get worse.

"The director is right," Reed said. "You need verification, Madam President. And there's only one place to get it."

"Caracas," Maggie said.

"If Belsky is alive, we need him to stay that way," Reed said. "You need a chance to interrogate him. Get ahead of this thing, whatever it is."

"Why would he be in Caracas?" O'Brien demanded.

"A great question," Reed said. "And more reason to find him."

Maggie traced the top lip of her mug. She took her time responding.

"If there's even a chance this is true, we need Belsky on ice yesterday. There's no time to waste."

"It could also be a trap," O'Brien broke in.

"Good thing your ass will be safe at home," Reed said, not even attempting to hide the disgust in his voice. O'Brien bristled, but he didn't clap back. He turned to Maggie.

"Madam President, I'm imploring you. It would be incredibly ill advised to take potentially catastrophic action based on the incomplete and unreliable reports of an unknown and untrusted source. The Agency has worked around the clock since your attempted assassination to identify the actors behind Volkov, and—"

"And has gotten *nowhere*!" Maggie's voice cracked, and she sat upright, blood rushing to her cheeks. O'Dell closed in, concern creasing his face. She pushed his arm back and extended a finger toward O'Brien.

"You've had three months, Mr. Director, and your hands are as empty now as they were while I was bleeding to death in Chicago. This is the first lead of any sort that we've had since uncovering Volkov in the first place, which apparently was also the work of this nameless contact."

"*Exactly*," O'Brien said. "You must see the correlation there. We're taking all our information from the same unproven source—"

"Did you find Volkov?" Maggie said.

"Ma'am?"

"Did you recover Volkov's body from the yacht wreck?"

O'Brien stiffened. "Yes, ma'am."

"And it was, in fact, Stepan Belsky's yacht?"

Another protracted moment, followed by a nod.

"Then it seems, Mr. Director, that Wolfgang's source is not so unproven after all."

Maggie turned directly to Reed, not giving O'Brien further opportunity to object.

"Will you go to Venezuela?"

Reed knew the question was coming. He wouldn't have flown to Washington at all unless he was prepared to carry the mission into Caracas. But he also wasn't in the habit of volunteering for things on anything less than his own terms.

"Only if I'm allowed to operate freely under my own stipulations," he said flatly.

"Done." Maggie didn't hesitate. She turned back to O'Brien. "Mr. Director, please facilitate the Prosecution Force's deployment into Caracas. Give them whatever they need, stay in contact, and report back to me as the situation develops. Reed, I want Belsky's ass secured and dragged back to the States, whatever it takes."

"Understood," Reed said.

O'Brien's lips pressed into a tight line. "I feel obligated to advise everyone present that kidnapping a foreign national from within the borders of a hostile country is extremely illegal. If even a sniff of our involvement leaked to Russia, or even our allies—"

"That's why we have a Prosecution Force, isn't it?" Maggie said. "Full deniability. They get caught, you hang them out to dry. They get the job done, you freaking write the check. Okay?"

Her voice rose until it cracked, her hands shaking against the tabletop. Nobody moved.

"I was *shot*, Mr. Director. You want to talk about 'extremely illegal,' save it for the lawyers. I want this done. Right now."

Reed exchanged a glance with Turk. He saw a reflection of his own concern in the bigger man's eyes.

O'Brien ducked his head. "Yes, ma'am."

The four of them stood. Maggie held up a finger.

"Reed, a moment."

Turk's eyes narrowed, but he filed out of the room behind Yellin and the director. O'Dell stayed behind. Reed noted the way he hung close behind Maggie. Like a protective dog.

"Why did you request Stratton to be excluded from this meeting?"

Reed pocketed his hands. He held Maggie's gaze a long while, weighing his options. He could see her frayed mind in the way her lips pinched together and her knuckles turned white around the mug. In her tense shoulders and pale face.

Muddy Maggie Trousdale was alive and kicking. But a long, long way from a hundred percent.

"Assume the contact is right," Reed said. "Assume Russia had a hand in your attempted assassination."

She didn't answer.

"They must feel pretty good about your replacement," Reed said simply. Maggie flinched.

"Watch your back, Madam President. I'll drag this Russian scum in by his hair."

14

Victor O'Brien could feel the veins in his neck pulsating as he left the West Wing. It wasn't his terse exchange with Montgomery or even how the president had shot him down that riled him. O'Brien had worked in the upper echelons of the American intelligence world long enough to be familiar with politicians and how to manage them.

No, his problem was much more foundational and much less personal. O'Brien was entering his thirty-first year of service within the CIA, beginning as an analyst and climbing over the bodies, straight into the director's chair. He'd served under seven presidents and a slew of congressional oversight committees. He'd scraped intel off the grimy streets of four continents and actually worked the field on five separate occasions.

O'Brien knew the CIA better than he knew himself, and in all those years, during all that chaos, he'd *never* been put in the position of facilitating a black ops team that neither reported to nor answered to the CIA.

It wasn't just an ego thing. The Prosecution Force was dangerous in its very inception. Reed Montgomery was effective, granted, but he was also reckless, brash, and had somehow wormed his way right to the heart of the Trousdale administration.

The very *idea* that an operator of any sort would even speak to the president, let alone sit in the West Wing and direct the winds of American foreign policy, was beyond preposterous. It was unheard of. Pure insanity. There was a reason why decades of espionage protocol called for the president to make requests, while the many layers of anonymous and invisible agency assets who made magic happen operated independently. *Without* direct White House contact.

It wasn't just about plausible deniability for Trousdale. It was about operational integrity for the Agency. A politician, even a savvy one, didn't know the first *thing* about intelligence work. It was unthinkable for the president to be this closely involved, let alone for Montgomery to be using the CIA like his own personal concierge service.

But the situation was now well out of O'Brien's hands. His best bet would be to manage the fallout while he searched for a way to sideline the Prosecution Force, or else bring them under his direct control.

Sliding into the back seat of his waiting armored Cadillac, O'Brien directed the driver to return him to Langley before he dialed the first number on a long list of favorites. Not his wife. Not a trusted family friend or advisor. O'Brien had none of the above. The first name on his list was Dr. Sarah Aimes, Deputy Director of the CIA, and his right-hand woman.

"Yes, sir?" Aimes answered with predictable expediency and professionalism.

"Contact SAC. We need a flight out of Andrews, for Caracas. Two passengers, undercover. No agency links."

A keyboard rattled in the background. Sarah was taking notes. He waited for her to finish, knowing that no part of the request was particularly unusual for her. Even while diplomatic relations with Venezuela and the Moreno regime were icy at best, the CIA maintained a field office in Venezuela. Not in the embassy—Moreno had ordered a full expulsion of all American embassy personnel in 2019, and the building now lay boarded up and empty. But the CIA station, now reduced to a handful of field officers and a station chief, remained in a covert office, off-site.

Just because the country had gone to hell in a handbasket didn't mean the Agency was uninterested in it. SAC jets flew in and out of Venezuela semi-regularly.

"Who are we flying?" Aimes asked.

O'Brien gritted his teeth. "Montgomery."

Aimes was quiet. O'Brien collected himself and ran her through a surface-level highlight of the mission. His cell phone was fully encrypted, but he still preferred to reserve critical details for in-person discussion.

"Have our people on the ground reported any Russian activity in the region?" Aimes asked.

"Negative."

Aimes was quiet again. O'Brien knew she was thinking what he was thinking. That this was insane.

"Make contact with the station chief," O'Brien said. "I want an escort waiting for Montgomery and his team the moment they touch down. Wherever they go, I want our people on them like white on rice. If Montgomery picks his nose, I want to know how wet the booger was."

"Understood, sir. Anything else?"

O'Brien hesitated. Ninety-nine percent of him thought Montgomery's wild Belsky story was pure fantasy. But that one percent...

"Reach out to our station in Moscow. Have them poke around for reports of missing SVR agents, particularly high-ranking ones. Any ripples in the water since the president was shot."

"Will do, sir."

O'Brien hung up and worked his jaw, watching through bulletproof glass as Washington slid by. He didn't allow himself to embrace the rage he felt. He didn't give himself a moment to panic, or fume.

He only calculated. Because calculation had led him this far, and he'd be damned if he let everything he built be hijacked by an upstart from Louisiana.

15

Caracas, Venezuela

Kirsten Corbyn was a bloody good spy.

Not her words, of course. She was confident, but not so brash as to self-label the quality of her work. It was her field instructor back in London who made the declaration, a startling departure from his usual stinginess with any form of praise. The fact that he followed up the compliment with a five-minute monologue on her operational deficiencies didn't dampen the warmth that moment of praise had brought her. It was the first time in nearly six years that Corbyn had felt, deep in her gut, that she belonged somewhere. And it was a feeling she had craved ever since her American-built Royal Air Force Chinook helicopter went down in smoke and flames over northwestern Iraq, taking her dreams of a career in British military aviation with it.

Her pelvis shattered on impact, along with one knee and both ankles. The doctors said she would never walk again, let alone fly. They were right about the second part—the RAF discharged her with honors, a medical pension, and an award of the King's Commendation for Valuable Service. A very nice "screw you," in Corbyn's mind.

She didn't want medals or pensions. She wanted to fly. But even after two years of brutal recovery put her back on her feet, and even won her third place in a Scottish ultramarathon, the RAF wasn't interested. They'd moved on, found other pilots. And anyway, the war in the Middle East was finally drawing down.

The King needed fewer service members, not more. And certainly none with metal brackets in their hips.

That was when Corbyn found the Secret Intelligence Service, colloquially known as MI6. She wasn't recruited via a shadowy meeting in the smoky back corner of a London football pub. It was nothing so romantic—or easy—as that. She hit upon the idea of being a spy after sifting through mountains of application requirements for every manner of military and governmental service she could think of.

The SIS was the only one she could find that promised the chance at fieldwork without automatically disqualifying her for her injuries. And Corbyn longed for fieldwork. She'd fallen in love with it as a pilot and knew she could never be happy riding a desk or working a computer, no matter how well it paid.

She wanted to *go* places. She thirsted not only for the adrenaline but for the strangeness of it all. Waking up in a new locale surrounded by people who spoke another language. Pushing her mind and body to overcome new challenges and embrace new skills, all while serving the country she dearly loved.

No, MI6 wasn't her first choice. But after applying—and twice being rejected—Corbyn became obsessed. She kept applying, ringing phones off their hooks and bending the ear of anybody from the inside who would listen to her, until at long last she was offered a shot.

Not a job. Not even the consideration of a job. Just a chance at a chance.

And she blew it out of the water.

Four years of training, education, and hard work later, and she had finally landed her first independent field assignment—Caracas.

The United Kingdom didn't really have an interest in Caracas, or Venezuela, for that matter. The rising concern of the day was Moscow and how much farther into Eastern Europe Nikitin might press after his predecessor invaded Ukraine. But the SIS had learned over long decades of hard lessons that no corner of the globe was unrelated to the UK's interests.

Terrorism, corrupt global trade, and the prospect of sprawling Chinese and Russian conquest was a threat almost everywhere. It was worth keeping your eyes open.

So Corbyn was sent, alone, to Caracas. Her mission? To be on standby. To keep her ear to the ground. To leverage the rich complexion her Sicilian father had blessed her with, combined with her own mastery of the Spanish language, into mining any information that may be of use to London.

It was a backwater assignment, and Corbyn knew it. All the SIS gave her was a shabby apartment, a shabbier SUV, and a select assortment of technical gadgets that were all decidedly less than lethal. But Corbyn wasn't discouraged. Caracas could be a path back to the Middle East. And the Middle East could easily be a path to the Far East, or even the holy grail of intelligence operations: Moscow.

She was content to bide her time. So long as her feet were in the field, she was ready, able, and eager to impress.

So when the dossier concerning a number of dilapidated container ships transporting unidentified cargo out of West Africa, across the South Atlantic, and into a rural Venezuelan harbor dropped into her secure email inbox, Corbyn was only too eager to jump on it.

The SIS wasn't initially concerned with what the ships contained. Lots of shady, unmarked cargo traversed the shipping lanes between Africa and South America on the daily. What piqued their interest was the fact that three of these container ships were registered to Lenkov International, an energy company associated with some Russian guy named Belsky. The Americans had recently made inquiries to both MI6 and the Mossad concerning information on Belsky. They wouldn't say why, but what concerned the CIA concerned the SIS, and anyway, it wasn't like there was a hell of a lot going on in Caracas. Why not have a look?

Corbyn was only too happy to have a look. British satellites had tracked the most recent container ship to a Venezuelan port about five hundred klicks east of Caracas, some place called Pedernales. It would take a few hours to navigate her battered Toyota Land Cruiser down pothole-infested Venezuelan highways to the port.

Good thing gas was cheap in Venezuela. Thanks to government subsidies, a thousand liters of fuel cost less than a bottle of water. If you could find it, that is.

She tossed her backpack into the back seat, loaded with nondescript personal items, a change of clothes, and nothing more suspicious than a pair of binoculars and a Nikon camera with a lengthy lens. She was a bird watcher, traveling from Argentina.

Not a threat to the local regime. Certainly not an international spy. Just an attractive, thirty-four-year-old woman with dark hair and a quick smile, bumping through rural Venezuela in search of rare, winged creatures.

And, just maybe, a few Russian container ships.

16

Washington, DC

Reed and Turk caught a taxi from the White House to a Marriott hotel across town. Understandably, Maggie didn't want them hanging around as another chaotic day in the West Wing got underway.

And also, Stratton would arrive soon. Reed figured the president wanted to dispense knowledge of the evolving situation in Venezuela on her own terms, if at all. He was fine with that. Now that he had informed Maggie of his suspicions concerning her VP, Reed considered himself finished with the issue. He had other problems to worry about, anyway. Problems like how to find Belsky in a city of four million people.

At the Marriott, Reed stripped down and showered, changing into fresh clothes before digging out his phone to call Banks. He didn't know if she would answer, and part of him hoped she wouldn't. There was no possible way he could explain what he was about to do without dumping truckloads of gasoline on the marital fire they were already engulfed in. Just the thought of dealing with her outraged protests made him want to punch the wall.

But there was another thought, too. Another possibility. She might not care at all. She might simply say, "Okay," and then hang up. Because she was done.

And the thought of that was finally enough to break through the head fog he'd been fighting for weeks. It was enough to drive him to call her.

The phone went straight to voicemail, not even ringing. Banks's chipper voice invited him to leave a message, but he didn't know what to say, so he simply hung up. Maybe her phone was dead, but more likely she had placed it in airplane mode. When he checked their tracking app, her location was still turned off, and that sent a fresh flush of heat to his face.

Reed turned his own location off, then retreated from the window, digging two one-ounce bottles of cheap whiskey from the mini fridge before collapsing into a corner chair. The whiskey was weak, leaving him wishing it was Jack Daniel's poured over ice, with the rest of the bottle close at hand. His go-to arrangement.

Turk sat on the bed at the other side of the room, staring at his phone, but Reed could easily see that the screen was black. He pinched his eyebrows together, a wash of guilt passing over him as he realized he had barely checked in with his friend since meeting him in Chattanooga. More preoccupation with his own life.

"You good, bro?"

Turk glanced up. "Huh?"

"You've been...abnormally quiet. Barely said a word on the drive or the flight."

Turk scratched his cheek. "Yeah, man. All good."

"How's Sinju?"

Turk nodded a little too quickly. "Good. Real good."

Reed waited him out, draining the second bottle.

"What happened?" he asked.

Turk looked back at his phone, tapping it against his knee. Then he made his own pilgrimage to the mini fridge, selecting vodka in place of whiskey. Three bottles.

Something was up.

"You ever just...feel like...like, wow. It's big. Like it's more than you can manage."

"With Banks?"

"Yeah."

You have no idea.

"Sure. Why?"

"Well...lately it's just been kinda like that. Like, I don't know, man. I guess...well. I feel like a bitch for saying it. But I don't know if I'm up for it."

Reed frowned, digging a cigarette from his pocket, and lit up. The Marriott would complain, but the CIA had booked the hotel. Their problem.

He took two drags and wondered what sort of relationship advice he was qualified to give. He didn't want to share the gory details of his fight with Turk, or with anyone, for that matter. He was still trying to process it, and somewhere in his gut he knew he was culpable for the situation. He didn't want to be told that by a third party.

At the same time, it felt dishonest to comment on Turk's fledgling relationship without admitting his own failures. He had the vague feeling that there was something Turk wasn't telling him. Something that would lead to a much lengthier, more complex conversation that Reed simply didn't have the energy for. He knew he was a bad friend for doing it, but he still took the first exit he could think of that wouldn't result in more questions.

"Do you love her?" Reed asked simply.

"Like crazy." Turk didn't hesitate.

"Then don't worry about it. You'll be fine."

Turk nodded slowly, then drained another bottle, leaving Reed to wonder if his own advice was worth the oxygen it consumed.

The day wore on, and Banks didn't call back. Reed called in the midafternoon when he knew Davy would be down for a nap. Again the call went straight to voicemail, and this time he left a brief message, whispered quietly enough to keep Turk from hearing.

"Call me. We need to talk. I don't want us to be this way."

As he finished the message, a sharp knock rang against the hotel door. It was O'Brien, and he wasn't alone.

Reed ended the call and admitted the director into the hotel suite.

O'Brien wrinkled his nose at the stench of cigarette smoke, then swept his gaze across a small pile of empty liquor bottles.

The disgust was palpable. Reed didn't care. Of the four men standing in this room, two of them weren't likely to be dodging bullets over the next week.

"Surprised to see you," Reed said. And he was. A cabinet meeting was one thing. For the director himself to descend from the top of his glass tower and make an appearance in a mid-grade hotel room said something.

Reed just wasn't sure what.

O'Brien flicked a thumb toward his associate.

"Dr. Matthew Perez, Venezuelan intelligence expert."

Reed offered the newcomer a nod. "Care for a drink, Doctor? The Agency is buying."

Perez shook his head. O'Brien walked to the suite's dining table but didn't sit down. He placed an oversized tablet on the table and tapped on the screen, calling up a map of Caracas. Reed recognized it from his own reconnaissance over the afternoon.

"Ever been to Venezuela?" O'Brien said, his voice laden with protracted condescension.

"As a matter of fact, I have. Just so happens I was married there."

O'Brien's owl eyes twitched toward Reed, betraying genuine surprise. Reed twisted open another whiskey and shot it.

"Care to lay off on that?" O'Brien growled. "This is serious."

"I wouldn't be drinking if it weren't." Reed flicked the bottle into a trash can. "What've you got?"

O'Brien stepped back, and Perez stepped in. The doctor was small, with a pale complexion but dark hair and eyes that betrayed his South American heritage. He may well be from Venezuela, Reed thought. Second generation, maybe.

But intimately familiar with the country.

"Caracas is a large city, about four million people. But significant portions of the business and commercial districts are now vacant. Are you familiar at all with Venezuela's history?"

"Hit us with the Cliffs Notes," Turk said, settling into a chair across from the tablet.

"Thirty years ago, it was one of the richest, most powerful nations in the western hemisphere, second only to the United States. The Bolivarian Revolution placed Hugo Chávez in control of a socialist economy built almost entirely atop a booming oil industry. Venezuela has more proven reserves of crude oil than any nation on earth—and it isn't close. Chávez drilled like a maniac and used the proceeds to fund a tsunami of social welfare programs. Subsidized everything—housing, food, transportation, schools, parks, jobs, and, of course, gasoline. They fell short of absolute communism, but not by much. Chávez nationalized the oil industry, and the party hit overdrive."

"Until...," Turk drawled.

"Until oil prices plummeted in the nineties, and national revenue could no longer keep pace with national spending. From there it was a slow spiral of escalating debts and frantic stopgap efforts. Bureaucratic corruption and incompetence took hold, leading to further inefficiencies. By the time oil prices rose again, it was too late. Human rights abuses led to international sanctions, and Chávez died in 2013, leaving a wrecked empire to his right-hand man, Cesar Moreno."

"How bad are things now?" Reed asked.

"Much worse. Moreno is even less of an economist than Chávez. He's printed the bolívar into literal worthlessness. Hyperinflation, unemployment, and empty shelves are now the national currency. Venezuela imports almost everything except gasoline, and they're somehow short on that also."

"Despite sitting atop all those reserves."

"Correct."

Reed studied the map. Sucked his teeth.

"What's the point?"

"The point is," O'Brien said, stepping in again. "Venezuela is a complex *mess*, and the last thing the president or anyone else needs is a diplomatic disaster."

"And you think I'm about to make one."

"I'll be perfectly blunt, Mr. Montgomery. I don't like you. I don't like your team. I don't like how you bend rules and operate so far outside traditional oversight. If it were up to me, you'd be back in Alabama watching NASCAR. Permanently."

"But you aren't the boss," Reed said.

"No," O'Brien said. "I'm not."

"So spare me the sniveling. What's the plan?"

O'Brien flicked his finger across the screen, then spun it around. Photographs of Reed and Turk had been matched with fake identities, printed across the face of Canadian passports. Excellent fakes, Reed had to admit.

"We'll use an agency aircraft registered to a shell corporation," O'Brien said. "You'll clear customs as international businessmen, then rendezvous with an agency asset who will have a hotel waiting for you."

"And then?" Reed asked.

"And then you *wait*," O'Brien said. "Until called for."

Reed nodded slowly, surveying the passport photo. It was taken from his DOD file, he was sure of it. Almost a decade old. He barely recognized himself.

"You're sidelining us," he said.

O'Brien smirked. "I may not be *the boss*, Mr. Montgomery. But this is still my show. You'll park your ass in that hotel unless and until called for. But don't worry." O'Brien cast a condescending glance toward the pile of empty liquor bottles. "We'll cover the tab."

O'Brien turned for the door, leaving Perez to recover the tablet. As they marched toward the door, Reed couldn't resist a final barb.

"You know the trouble with people like you, O'Brien? You've never been shot at."

O'Brien stopped. Pushed the glasses up his nose and looked back.

"And the trouble with people like *you*, Mr. Montgomery, is that being shot at is all you're good for."

17

The Kremlin
Moscow, Russia

Midnight had passed and early morning hours taken hold of the old Russian building, but President Makar Nikitin wasn't even a little tired. Despite traditional government operations that began at sunup and concluded sometime just before dinner, Nikitin preferred to rise around ten a.m. after as little as four hours of sleep and enjoy a leisurely start to his day that included a large breakfast and an intense workout before donning his suit and heading for the office.

His prime working hours lay between dinner and five a.m., while most of the nation lay fast asleep. The Kremlin was quiet then, enabling him and the army of aides he dragged along with him to be more productive and less distracted. But that wasn't Nikitin's primary motivation for the unusual practice. Nikitin worked the early hours of the morning because those were the hours when his enemies, on the far side of the world, were awake and moving.

Nikitin kept American news media playing on three separate television sets in his executive office, and while regular SVR updates informed him of crucial military and governmental intelligence mined out of Washington, the televisions provided another, even more crucial service: that of an arm cuff, reading the pulse of the American people.

And the American people were scared. Not only because their president had been shot, but because she had also gone missing. More than sixty days had elapsed since her last appearance, and all the White House press secretary would say about the matter was the same canned, meaningless line: *The president is experiencing a full recovery and is eager to get back to work.*

Except that couldn't possibly be true. Because, if it were, Margaret Trousdale would have made an appearance by now. The White House was hiding something, and the thought turned Nikitin on like watching a twenty-year-old stripper.

Yes, he wanted Trousdale dead. He could barely contain his rage when she somehow survived. But could it be possible...that this was *better*?

A wounded duck in the Oval Office, and a hamstrung vice president, operating on restricted authority. Washington was hog-tied and limping, and like any other hungry wolf, Nikitin was eager to pounce.

The phone rang, and Nikitin ripped his attention away from another monologue on CNN.

"*Da?*"

"We're ready for you, Mr. President."

Nikitin adjusted his suit jacket as he stepped into the adjoining conference room. Like most rooms in the Kremlin, his office was opulent in the extreme, with an abundance of ornate trim, expensive furnishings, and plenty of gold accents. But the conference room was something else altogether. More like the American president's Situation Room, this space was designated for operations, and that made it strictly functional.

Utilitarian tables and chairs. Soundproof walls. And a lot of screens.

Only three men occupied the room—the three members of his cabinet that Nikitin most trusted. The inner circle of the inner circle.

The only three who knew about Belsky.

Nikitin closed the door and nodded once to Igor Solisky, his Minister of Foreign Affairs. That was Solisky's title, anyway. His actual occupation was a lot more precise.

"Belsky's ships are in port," Solisky said. "It'll take time to off-load. The Venezuelans are struggling to find adequate trucks."

Nikitin took a seat, concealing his disgust with the practiced ease of a man whose rise to power included a lot of concealed emotions. But he felt it, nonetheless.

Damn Venezuelans.

"Is Moreno sufficiently motivated?"

"Belsky says he's become a little...squeamish." Alexey Falkov was the next to speak. A deputy prime minister, but one who seldom spoke to his supposed boss, the prime minister. Falkov reported directly to Nikitin, Russia's de facto leader.

"What does that mean?" Nikitin questioned.

Falkov shrugged. "Probably nothing. Belsky says he is concerned about Russian intrusion. He wants to protect the integrity of his government."

"His government lost all integrity the day Venezuelans began using bolívars as toilet paper. Tell Belsky to shut him up."

Falkov nodded. Nikitin turned to the last man at the table.

Unlike the first two, Anton Golubev was no official member of the Russian government, although he'd served under a half dozen meaningless titles. He wasn't a politician at all, or even an oligarch.

Golubev was something darker and far more menacing. The fly on the wall. The one who had always been there, right from the very inception of Russian politics. The man every president feared, every prime minister kept at arm's length.

The man with resources. The man who knew where the bodies were buried and had buried many of them himself. The fixer. The ghost of the Kremlin.

Unlike his predecessors, Nikitin didn't fear Golubev, because he understood the man. Golubev was an animal with a voracious appetite that could only be satisfied by one thing: power.

Nikitin understood that, because Nikitin was also an animal. So long as Golubev could play second fiddle, they would go far together.

"Security?" Nikitin asked.

"Fifty men," Golubev answered. "All mercenaries, completely untraceable. We hid them in one of Belsky's ships."

Nikitin nodded his satisfaction, but the nervousness from Falkov and Solisky was palpable. It was as though the temperature in the room had jumped fifteen degrees.

"This is…a big risk," Falkov said carefully. "If Russian forces—"

"Didn't you hear me?" Golubev cut him off. "These are not Russian forces. These are mercenaries. Who knows who they work for?"

Perfect stillness, but the tension remained. Nikitin gritted his teeth.

"Lost your stones?" he growled. Both men looked away.

"Tell Belsky to get to work," Nikitin said. "That will be all."

Falkov and Solisky both rose. Golubev remained seated. He knew his boss had more to say. As soon as the politicians had left the room, Nikitin turned to him.

"What about the other thing?"

Golubev grunted, remaining relaxed in his seat. The swollen white scars on his face from conflicts unknown were sheltered by a dense beard, but they paled when he was focused. It was a bizarre tic Nikitin had learned years ago.

He felt he understood Golubev better than most. One animal to another.

"It seems likely Sidorov escaped the country," Golubev said carefully.

Nikitin clenched a pen in one hand, slowly clicking it open. Then closed. Thinking about the missing SVR agent.

Nikitin had never heard the name Ivan Sidorov prior to six weeks ago, when Golubev first informed him of a potential intelligence breach. Apparently, Sidorov had been spying on the private communications of the Kremlin, a deeply treasonous act.

And now he was gone. In the wind. With what information?

"You have people tracking him?" Nikitin asked.

"I have people trying," Golubev said. "He is a difficult man to trace. Apparently, he was well prepared for a sudden escape."

Smart man. Another animal.

"Keep looking," Nikitin said. "Do whatever you have to do. And when you find him…"

Nikitin trailed off, but Golubev didn't need to be told. He nodded once.

One animal to another. Thirsty for blood.

18

Joint Base Andrews
Maryland

The SAC jet assigned by the CIA to transport Reed and Turk to Caracas was as generic as any of the CIA jets Reed had flown on in the past year, but not nearly as nice. In place of a Gulfstream, O'Brien had issued them a Learjet 60, at least ten years old, well maintained but much less comfortable. Reed watched the Air Force crews fueling the aircraft while the pilots sipped from water bottles nearby, probably postulating on the cause of their unscheduled trip into South America.

Painted on the fuselage of the plane, just above the windows, was a long blue line with the letters "EET" painted above it, like a logo. Reed had no idea what the letters stood for. "Elite Executive Transport," maybe? It didn't matter. It was a fake name for a fake business operated by an agency with zero actual investment in the transport of business executives.

And that was just what Reed needed.

Turk poked his head out of the open side door of the jet and shot Reed a thumbs-up, confirming the presence of the gear they had requested—tablet computers loaded with intel on Venezuela to digest during the flight, international credit cards without spending limits, and generic luggage that would hold up to inspection by nosy Venezuelan customs officers.

But no firearms. O'Brien promised that those would be issued at their hotel by whatever local agency asset was waiting for them. Reed didn't believe him, so he and Turk had smuggled their sidearms on board, wrapped in plastic bags beneath a bed of ice and sandwiches in a camping cooler. Just in case.

Reed cupped his hand over a cigarette and lit up. It might be his last for a while, or at least his last before landing, and he badly needed the nicotine to take the edge off the anxiety he felt. Not just about the mission, but about his marriage.

"Mr. Montgomery?" A door creaked behind him, and Reed looked back to the guard post rising out of the tarmac fifty feet away. A young lieutenant leaned out, his face pinched into a frown.

Probably ready to tear Reed a new one for smoking so near the refueling process.

"I'll put it out," Reed muttered.

"There's somebody asking for you," the lieutenant said. "A Mr. Pierce?"

"On the phone?"

"No, sir. At the gate. Should we let him in?"

Reed dropped the smoke, stamping it out. Momentary confusion was replaced almost immediately by concern, and he nodded. The lieutenant returned to his office, and Reed looked down the long concrete drive that ran perpendicular to the airstrip, leading toward the base's main gate.

He didn't have to wait long. An Air Force utility truck rolled up to the guard shack five minutes later, headlights blasting through the icy night as it stopped. Wolfgang got out of the passenger seat, toting a duffel bag. He exchanged a farewell with the driver, then approached Reed, limping ever so slightly on his prosthetic leg.

"What are you doing here?" Reed said, not giving him time for a greeting. "Where's Ivan?"

Wolfgang stopped a few feet short of him, the bag riding his shoulder. He looked tired.

And angry.

"He's gone," Wolfgang said simply.

"What do you mean, he's gone?"

"I got back to the house and he wasn't there. No note. Nothing out of place. It was like he never existed."

Reed's mind spun, and he instinctively glanced around the tarmac, wary of eavesdroppers. There was nobody, and the distant howl of an Air Force jet prepping for takeoff drowned out their voices, anyway. He stepped closer.

"CIA?" he asked.

Wolfgang shook his head. "I don't know how he found me, but it isn't a publicized address. The property is registered under a pseudonym. The address on my driver's license and vehicle registration is a fake street in Albany."

"What, then?"

"I don't know. I think he just split. Maybe he didn't feel safe there."

"Can you contact him?"

"I wouldn't have the first idea how. The man is a ghost."

Reed rolled another cigarette between his fingers, still calculating. He knew what would happen if O'Brien learned Ivan had disappeared. The mission would be scrubbed, ASAP. Wolfgang's fragile credibility would be sabotaged. Trousdale would be convinced to pursue other avenues of investigation.

And the moment Reed considered that possibility, he realized how eager he was to get on that plane. To be back in action, with the adrenaline pumping.

He needed it. Not just because he'd spent the last decade being shot at, but because it was something he could take control of. Something he understood.

"Don't tell anyone," Reed said. "Go back home and stay by the phone. We'll call if—"

"I'm going with you."

"What?"

"I'm already packed. I'm not riding the bench this time."

Reed shook his head. "Sorry, no. We don't know what we're walking into, and—"

"If you mention my leg, I'm going to throat punch you."

Reed stopped. He was about to mention the leg, and not without reason. Wolfgang looked stiff just exiting the truck. Out of shape, too.

"It's not personal," Reed said.

"Sure it is. It's personal for you, isn't it? Or do you really expect me to believe that you do this just for the paychecks?"

Reed said nothing.

Wolfgang adjusted the bag on his shoulder. "I need it too, Reed. I need something. I can't sit in that house another night by myself."

Reed couldn't argue with that. He looked over his shoulder to the jet. It was almost ready for takeoff.

"They arranged fake passports for us. We don't have one for you."

"Already covered," Wolfgang said, smacking the bag. "Brad Juniper. Detroit. Your personal assistant."

A dry grin crept across Reed's face, and he nodded again. "All right. But don't let me catch you lagging."

Wolfgang started for the jet, calling over his shoulder. "I'm already taking point. Get on my level."

19

Caracas, Venezuela

The CIA's Learjet made a refueling stop at Patrick Space Force Base, just south of Cape Canaveral, before turning for South America. Reed slept two hours of the seven-hour flight, spending the rest scrolling through an iPad laden with articles and dossiers about Venezuelan politics.

Perez wasn't kidding—the nation was a wreck, on the verge of total economic collapse. The State Department labeled Venezuela a *failed state*. Incapable of self-governance. Long past the point of self-recovery.

A snowball of collapsing social systems, gaining speed by the minute.

Not a bad place to hide, really. With diplomatic relations between Caracas and Washington almost nonexistent, and the CIA's presence within Venezuela's borders strictly unofficial, Belsky was safer there than perhaps anywhere else in the western hemisphere. Plus, if he really *had* been plucked out of the Straits of Florida by a Russian submarine, it was an easy trip south to a secluded Venezuelan port.

And yet...

Reed couldn't help but wonder *why*. Wouldn't it be just as easy of a trip to Africa? Or right back to Russia? Belsky was a multibillionaire, and

Venezuela was far from a resort. Why would a filthy-rich businessman with no connections in Caracas deliberately choose to be dropped there?

It made Reed question Wolfgang's intel. Or rather, Ivan's intel. The fact that Ivan had vanished certainly didn't assuage those doubts.

The seat belt sign flashed on a few minutes past four a.m., and Reed lifted his foot across the aisle to give Turk a kick. The big Tennessean was snoring like a lawn mower, but he jolted upright and reached for his belt with a grouchy yawn.

Wolfgang sat at the other end of the plane, gazing out the window with his hands in his pockets, much as he had the entire flight. Reed hadn't seen him touch a book, an electronic device, or even walk to the aircraft's built-in lavatory once.

It only served to reinforce his uneasiness.

"It's dark," Turk said suddenly.

Reed looked out the window. The Learjet was beginning its final approach, and he knew they were landing at some private airfield on the outskirts of Caracas. The city should be fully visible, just ahead of the right-hand wing.

But he saw only a small cluster of dim lights. Barely enough to mark a midsized town.

"Four million people, right?"

"Give or take," Turk said. "Metro."

So Caracas was roughly the size of urban Chicago. But it didn't look even ten percent as bright.

The plane touched down with a gentle shriek of rubber on asphalt, followed by a series of bumps and jolts. Apparently, the tarmac wasn't very smooth. They taxied directly to a dark hangar, and Reed couldn't see any people or lights through the window. He double-checked the SIG P226, now affixed to his hip, and shot a glance to Turk and Wolfgang.

Both men were up, bags in hand, waiting by the door before the engines even wound down. In an uncertain environment, it paid to be on your feet early.

The engines finally cut off, but the pilots didn't exit the cockpit. Reed guessed they would be back in the air as soon as the doors were closed.

Turk worked the latch, and the stairway lowered automatically. A blast of warm air washed through the cabin, a welcome change from the hostile chill of the East Coast. Turk led the way into the hangar, and the stairway hissed up behind them as their boots hit the ground.

The cavernous space was quiet save for the tick of the cooling airplane. There was no one around. No customs, no security.

Nobody.

A tap rang against glass, and Reed looked over his shoulder to see one of the pilots pointing. The guy nodded confidently, and Reed shouldered his duffel bag with an irritated grunt.

"We *are* in Venezuela, right?" Turk muttered.

Reed didn't answer, but the thought had already crossed his mind. If this was O'Brien's idea of a joke, he wouldn't enjoy the comeback.

They reached the hangar's entrance and stared out into a black night. Reed's hand slid beneath his jacket, finding the familiar grip of the SIG as his eyes began to adjust. The grind of the jet's engines shook the tarmac, and Reed's body tensed.

By the time he saw the SUV, it was almost on top of him. Streaking across the busted concrete from his left, the headlights were off, and the vehicle was jet black, blending almost completely into the dark of night. It ground to a halt directly in front of them—a Chevrolet Tahoe, eight or ten years old and showing it. Then the driver's door popped open, and a small head poked over the windshield.

"Montgomery, party of two?" the guy called in a heavy Bostonian accent.

"Party of three," Reed corrected. "Who are you?"

"Your ride. Hop in."

Reed hesitated. He wasn't sure what he expected upon landing. This entire mission had been strung together on a shoelace, all at the last minute. Somehow, this didn't feel right.

"Hey, buddy," the small head chirped. "I'm leaving, okay? You coming or not?"

Wolfgang moved first. He opened the back door, throwing this bag in ahead of him, then climbed in after it. Turk spoke without moving his lips.

"I'll sit behind him."

Reed grunted an acknowledgment and took shotgun. The little head disappeared inside, and the driver's door slammed.

As Reed took his place in the front seat, his nostrils were assaulted with the sour stench of...something. Foreign food of some kind; he couldn't place it. But the odor of stale, unfinished meals was distinct in any language. The seat creaked and sagged, and he almost elbowed over a travel mug of coffee as he jammed the duffel between his legs.

The guy seated next to him was proportionate to his tiny head. Five foot two, tops. Slender, with beady eyes and slicked-back hair that looked as though it were styled in a wind tunnel. He was dressed in a worn Metallica T-shirt that completely failed to conceal the Glock 19 strapped to his hip. The Tahoe's driver's seat was racked all the way up to give his feet access to the pedals, but he drove with the authority of a tank commander, whipping the SUV around as the jet taxied toward the airstrip.

"Welcome to Caracas!" the guy said. "I'm Stewie."

"Stewie?" Reed raised both eyebrows.

"Yeah, man. Like *Family Guy*. You watch *Family Guy*, right? Best show!"

Stewie retrieved the oversized travel mug and guzzled coffee, barely slowing the Tahoe as he blazed toward a guardhouse and a gate. Reed noticed two men dressed in olive drab uniforms positioned just outside the guardhouse, AK-47s slung over their chests. He stiffened, and his hand dropped to the SIG.

Stewie let his foot off the gas and lifted a two-finger salute as the gate swung upward. One of the guards returned the salute, and the big engine roared.

"Customs?" Reed asked.

Stewie laughed. "Amazing what a hundred bucks will buy, ain't it? That's nearly two years' salary for these schmucks. Crazy, right?"

Reed's hand relaxed a little as Stewie piloted them along a narrow highway, the path ahead now illuminated by dim headlights. Potholes littered the roadbed like fallen LEGOs, and Stewie made no attempt to dodge them, brain-rattling all four of them as they crashed along at fifty miles per hour.

"So where you guys from?" Stewie asked. "Wait, don't tell me. I heard a little something Southern in your voice. South Carolina? Or Georgia, maybe? You're not Falcons fans, are you?"

He slurped coffee and broke into a raucous laugh.

"Man, how about that Super Bowl? Talk about a *choke*! Nobody does it like Brady, am I right? Nobody!"

"*Who* are you?" Reed repeated through gritted teeth.

"I told you, bro. I'm Stewie."

"*Who* do you work for?"

"Who do you think? Same as you, I'd imagine." Stewie made air quotes with both hands, completely releasing the wheel. "The *Company*. Or is it *The Firm* this week? Wow, man. That's a great movie. You've seen it, right? Tom Cruise? Hey, nobody does it like Tom Cruise, am I right? What a freakin' legend."

Reed shot a glance over one shoulder. Turk sat behind Stewie, his long legs given room only by Stewie's abnormal driving position. The murderous look in Turk's gaze confirmed that Reed wasn't the only one ready to kick this shrimp out a window.

"You guys sit tight, now," Stewie said. "Gonna get a little bumpy."

Right, like I have any teeth left.

Stewie punched the gas, and the Tahoe surged forward. It was still dark outside, but the buildings that flashed by didn't look like organized dwellings. They looked more like a field of shacks, clinging to the hillsides in rough stacks, metal roofs affixed to block walls with little dirt tracks running between them.

"Favelas?" Reed asked.

"Barrios," Stewie said. "The Spanish version. But yeah, all kind of the same thing. We gotta pass through them to avoid a couple checkpoints. But don't worry, I do it all the time."

The Tahoe rumbled on, and the dark and shabby homes blended together. Reed didn't see any faces, and there weren't many lights. Occasional streetlamps cast weak pools of orange over mucky ditches, and loose trash blew across the pavement.

At last they topped a rise and the Tahoe nosed down, and then Reed saw the city. Or what could be seen of it, anyway. Spilling down between mountain ridges, a cluster of towers illuminated by spotty yellow lights rose toward the sky in a knot, surrounded by rolling black hills. It was the core of downtown, Reed was sure of it. But it looked half-alive, like a vacation city during the off-season.

"Why is it so dark?"

Stewie had been humming and slurping coffee, like a happy office drone on his way to work.

"Short on power!" he chimed. "Hell, they're short on everything. Food, clean water, even toilet paper. They shut a lot of the towers down at night to conserve electricity. Which is fine. I mean they're vacant, anyway."

Reed noted a few passing cars as they wound through dense city streets. They were all junkers from the eighties and nineties, held together it seemed by a hope and a prayer. Buses rumbled by on occasion, looking just as dilapidated. A few dozen motorcycles joined the mix as they neared the business district and the clock ground nearer to five a.m.

Nobody gave them a second look, but it was difficult for Reed to relax. Long, bloody experience had taught him the hard way to expect trouble around every corner.

At last Stewie pulled the Tahoe in front of a fifteen-story hotel, built of concrete with narrow windows and an orbiting glass door. Reed saw the outline of a familiar hotel brand on the grimy concrete, but the sign had been ripped away. Now nothing but white letters on smeared glass marked the nature of the establishment: *Hotel de Caracas*.

"Hey, it's not the Four Seasons, but it'll get the job done, am I right?" Stewie cut the motor and piled out. "We got you a suite on the top floor. Great view! I hear the breakfast is pretty good, also. Lots of eggs."

"Couldn't you get a room closer to ground level?" Reed asked, slamming the door behind him.

Stewie laughed. "Are you crazy? That's where all the noise is. You wanna be up top."

Not if I have to jump out a window.

Stewie led the way, bypassing reception and moving straight to the elevator. It was slow and made a lot of noise, Stewie standing near the door and whistling quietly. His Glock now rode beneath the shelter of a leather jacket, but Reed noted that he kept his right hand free and near the grip, using his left hand to open their hotel room door.

It smelled musty, but when Reed flicked the light on, he was surprised to find it reasonably clean. Two beds were joined by a breakfast table, a coffee station, and a bathroom with a walk-in shower. It all looked very nineties, but everything was in good repair.

"Sorry about the bed situation," Stewie said. "We were expecting only two guys. Guess a couple of you are gonna have to snuggle up, am I right?" He laughed and punched Wolfgang in the arm. Wolfgang shot him a glare that would break glass.

"Welp!" Stewie said, unperturbed. "I guess we'll be in touch. You guys make yourselves comfortable."

He turned for the door, and as if on cue, the lights flickered off. Reed reached for his gun as the room and the hallway outside went completely black. Through the smudged window he could see the city outside. It had gone dark also. Completely.

The gun cleared his holster, and he started for the door.

Then the lights blinked, clicked off again, and then returned.

Stewie stood by the door, a sarcastic smirk on his face.

"Welcome to Venezuela."

20

Puerto Pedernales, Venezuela
320 miles east of Caracas

Corbyn found the port six kilometers after leaving her Land Cruiser hidden in the jungle, just off the road. She navigated on foot, by compass, leaning on her RAF survival training to maintain her bearing through dense jungle.

There was a road, of course. Leveraging local maps and satellite imagery captured by MI6, she could have driven right into the port and saved herself some sweat and brush-cut arms. But what would be the point of that? Security at the port entrance would have turned her away, copied her license plate, and informed their superiors. Within an hour she might have a tail, and from then on she'd have to worry about constant surveillance by the Bolivarian National Intelligence Service.

No, better to slip in quietly from the dark. It was nearing five a.m., so she didn't have a lot of that darkness remaining. But as she crested a hill and dropped to her stomach, she smelled diesel fumes in the air, mixed with the grind of heavy engines and the clang of heavier machinery.

She crossed the next few meters on her stomach, worming along, her hair held back in a ponytail as sweat crept down her face. It was warm in

Venezuela. This close to the equator, it never cooled off unless you traveled deep into the mountains. The previous summer had been hell on earth.

But Corbyn didn't mind. The sweat and grime were all part of the adventure for her. And besides—the warmth was good for her busted pelvis. It had healed, sure. But cold would bring those bone scars to life in all manner of aches and pains.

Corbyn wriggled out of her backpack, slowing her crawl to a creep as she reached the edge of the vegetation. She could see lights now. They twinkled in the shallow valley beneath her, barely two hundred yards away. Work lamps on tall posts, shining down across a concrete dock.

Even before Corbyn reached for her binoculars, she made out the shadowy bulks of not one, not two, but *three* container ships. They were small—feeder-class ships, maybe six hundred feet long, each with built-in cranes to self-load and unload. Designed to transport cargo out of small ports like this into bigger ports, where the containers would then be loaded onto much larger ships for transcontinental travel.

Except these ships *had* conducted transcontinental travel. MI6 had already confirmed it. Two had set sail from Nigeria, and the third from Angola. Long trips for ships of this size.

Corbyn dug the binocular case out of the backpack and quietly unzipped it. Nestled inside was a brand-new pair of Pulsar Multispectral Fusion binoculars—a three-thousand-dollar toy, equipped with night vision, infrared, and a built-in video camera. All compliments of the British taxpayer.

Activating the device, Corbyn used her backpack as an armrest and brought the lenses to her eyes. It took a moment to calibrate the NV function and focus the zoom, but then everything snapped into perfect clarity. Better than standing close—just as bright as broad daylight. Nothing could hide from the sweeping eye of the Pulsar.

Corbyn measured her breaths to steady her view and hit the record button. A little light flashed to indicate recording had commenced, and she started with the nearest ship, working from the superstructure over the field of containers, pausing each time she reached a Venezuelan longshoreman.

She couldn't make out the name of the vessel, but she didn't need to.

MI6 already knew the names of all three vessels, along with their ports of departure and approximately what time they had arrived in Venezuela. What the satellite couldn't determine was what was hidden inside those crates, or why these vessels had made the trip.

It was probably nothing. Black market smuggling of any number of luxury commodities for a poverty-stricken nation. Small arms for the Venezuelan army, maybe. Coming from West Africa, it could be literally anything.

MI6 just wanted to make sure it wasn't something that could threaten Western security. Corbyn was more than happy to confirm.

She spent the next fifteen minutes recording a detailed sweep of the harbor, hovering over each ship and passing face, zooming in to note container numbers and following rail lines as they carried the containers out of sight, deeper into the jungle.

None were being opened. Nothing she recorded seemed particularly important. Even so, analysts in London would pore over the video, picking it apart and returning to her with a punch list of items they wanted better shots of. She'd probably have to return in a day or two, repeating the grueling hike through the jungle just to snap pictures of the same things.

Corbyn didn't mind. She was just glad to be in the field.

Sweeping left, she completed one final pass of the dock before tapping the record button, terminating the video. To her east, the sky was beginning to brighten, heralding a new day. Third-shift workers were removing their hard hats and gloves, shuffling off while fresh faces arrived.

Business as usual, by all indicators.

Then her eye caught something else. A vague glint, deep in the jungle beyond the third ship. Almost a thousand yards away, sheltered by overhanging trees.

Corbyn raised the binoculars again and zoomed in on the spot. In the growing light of early morning, everything appeared a little washed-out in the night vision. She adjusted her focus on the trees, sifting through the shadows in search of the glint.

She saw it again—a blink of light, lasting only a moment. A door closing? A curtain flicking open, for just a second?

Corbyn didn't know. She held her breath as she balanced on her elbows, leaning forward. Focusing. She thought she saw a vague outline. Rising out of the shadows, nestled in a finger of water offset from the rest of the port. Perfectly black, reaching twenty or so meters out of the water...was that a...

No way.

Corbyn smacked the record button and adjusted her angle. Fine-tuning the focus, she hovered over the spot, straining her eyes to pierce the darkness.

It was.

21

The White House

Stratton climbed into the back seat of his private limousine before six a.m., en route to the White House as a bright winter day broke over the nation's capital. With a fresh dusting of snow still white over the National Mall and not a cloud in the sky, it promised to be a gorgeous day, but the vice president barely noticed. His mind was lost in a maze of the documents held on that thumb drive.

And what they meant.

Stratton's starched white dress shirt crinkled as he settled into the leather seat. He sipped coffee from a travel mug, his body aching with sleeplessness, eyelids drooping. Despite the exhaustion, he knew he wouldn't be able to sleep even if he tried.

Premier Private Investigations had delivered, just as he knew they would. They dug up everything. But raw data this complex wasn't simple to draw conclusions from. He'd need another few days of mining through spreadsheets and transaction records before he could hope to find the smoking gun he was looking for.

And even then, he might find nothing. It was really a shot in the dark.

People like the ones Stratton was hunting hadn't climbed so high by leaving footprints to mark their trail. They were experts at covering their tracks.

But at least he knew how they thought—because like it or not, he was one of them.

The phone built into the console next to him rang, and Stratton lifted it automatically, like a robot.

"Yes?"

"Good morning, Mr. Vice President. This is Shelly, from the president's office. President Trousdale would like for you to meet with her privately in the Oval Office prior to the cabinet meeting this morning."

Stratton checked his watch. He would arrive at the West Wing barely ten minutes before the cabinet meeting was scheduled to begin. There wouldn't be time for much of a pre-meeting.

"Absolutely," he said. "I'm five minutes out."

He hung up and reached into his suit pocket for a bottle of eyedrops, taking care not to spill any on his pressed shirt as he held open one eyelid at a time. It wasn't enough to wash all the signs of sleeplessness away, but if he was going to submit himself to the private inspection of the president, he should look his best.

Maybe she'd be doped up and wouldn't notice even if he were wearing reindeer antlers.

The limo stopped at the entrance of the West Wing, and Stratton exchanged pleasantries with various members of the cabinet as he made his way toward the Oval. The president's operational headquarters was alive and kicking, even this early in the morning. It was Monday, and there was a long week of politicking ahead.

An aide let him in through the massive swinging entrance of the Oval Office. The seat of presidential power was decorated tastefully for the season, with an ornate rug stretched beneath plush couches and gentle accents arranged across bookshelves and end tables.

Not Maggie's touches. In Stratton's experience, the president had the decorative taste of a fifteen-year-old boy. But in the White House, these things took care of themselves.

Stratton stopped in front of the desk. The chair was turned to face away from him, but he could see the dirty-blond top of Maggie's head barely visible over the top. And for once, O'Dell was nowhere to be seen.

"Good morning, ma'am," Stratton said.

Maggie didn't turn. She remained facing the window, overlooking the South Lawn. Stratton stood with his hands clasped behind his back, a minute dragging closer to two before he uncomfortably cleared his throat.

"Would you get me a coffee?" Maggie's voice was soft but strong. "Fix yourself something, also."

Stratton turned for the side table laden with a carafe on a silver tray. "Cream and sugar?"

"No. Drop a shot of Jack in there, though. It's in the drawer."

Stratton paused, the carafe in midair. He glanced over his shoulder. Maggie was still looking away.

"I can't imagine that's good for your liver, ma'am."

Maggie laughed. "Life isn't good for my liver, Jordan."

Stratton fixed the coffee, held the Jack, and delivered Maggie's cup on a saucer to her desk. She turned slowly, revealing her face for the first time.

She didn't look good. A lot better than six weeks ago, certainly. But it was almost as though Maggie's recovery had hit a plateau. She was bone skinny, and despite a careful application of makeup, her skin still yellowed under the imperfect efforts of a recovering liver.

"Have a seat."

She lifted the cup, and Stratton noticed a tremor shoot across the surface of the drink. A gentle sip was followed by a quick return of the cup to the saucer.

"I see you held the Jack."

Stratton said nothing.

"Is that what you do, Jordan? Look out for me?"

Maggie flashed him a sudden, piercing gaze as Stratton took his seat, balancing his saucer in one hand.

"Of course, ma'am."

Maggie didn't blink. She simply rubbed the cup with one thumb, and Stratton felt a vague uneasiness enter his stomach. He didn't want to check his watch, but it must be nearly time for the cabinet meeting. What was she doing?

"How's your family?" Maggie asked.

"My family?" Stratton was taken off guard. Not only because it was an odd question, but because, truth be told, he'd barely thought of Carolyn or the twins since shipping them off to Chicago. His plate had been overloaded.

"Enjoying Washington?" Maggie asked.

"I sent them back to Illinois," Stratton said. "I thought they could see the family for a few weeks while I'm pulling some overtime."

"Ah, yes. Your overtime."

Maggie said it as though it were the next point on an agenda. Stratton just smiled.

"Not complaining, ma'am. Happy to serve however I'm able."

Maggie sipped more coffee, staring into the darkened depths. Her next question hit him like a brick in the face.

"Who do you think shot me?"

Stratton tilted his head. "Ma'am?"

"Who do you think really did it?"

"Fedor Volkov..." Stratton said it as though it were obvious—because it was. The Prosecution Force had proven it. Volkov was dead.

"Yes. But who hired him?" She didn't look away now. Didn't so much as blink.

"I really don't know, but I'm checking in with the FBI daily. I'm happy to forward you a memo, if you like."

Still no break in eye contact. No blink.

"Would you tell me, Jordan? If you knew?"

Ice crept into Stratton's stomach. A strange foreboding.

"Tell you what, ma'am?"

"*Who shot me.*"

Stratton set his cup down. Now it was his turn to hold his tongue, simply staring.

Did she know? Had Maggie somehow learned of his investigations with PPI? Did she know about the possible Cunningham connection?

If so, it would understandably lead her to suspect him. But that would be insane. It had to be the pills talking. Or maybe the Jack—had she been drinking?

"Do you question my loyalty, Madam President?"

Maggie didn't answer. She held his gaze as the coffee cooled, and Stratton didn't blink. Maggie waited a full minute for him to break, then she abruptly set the saucer down.

"We're late, Stratton."

She punched a button on her desk. "O'Dell? Can you assist me, please?"

The door popped open almost immediately, and O'Dell marched in. He helped the president to her feet and held her arm as they moved to the door.

They marched right past Stratton as if he weren't even there, leaving a wash of mistrust in their wake.

22

George Bush Center for Intelligence
Langley, Virginia

CIA headquarters was just beginning to come alive, but for Deputy Director Dr. Sarah Aimes, the workday began five hours earlier—out of bed in time for a ninety-minute calisthenics workout before a balanced breakfast enjoyed from a bottle, a hot shower, and then off to the office.

It wasn't a special day, it was just another day. Twelve plus hours of sifting through mountains of digital paperwork, managing half a dozen different teams, and fighting to stay one step ahead of America's enemies. An endless grind with no glory, no glamor, and not much in the way of a paycheck.

But it was what Aimes wanted when she chose a career in intelligence. She liked knowing things other people didn't. She liked neck-stomping terrorists even better. And since the arrival of Muddy Maggie Trousdale and the death of former president William Brandt, her job had accelerated quickly to redline. What once was a tornado quickly became a Cat 5 hurricane. Langley was consumed by constant chaos—a deluge of activity.

Air Force One. Then Pyongyang. Then an assassination attempt, right in the heart of Chicago.

And now Venezuela. The hits just kept coming.

Aimes poured herself another cup of steaming green tea and wished it were coffee. She wasn't a health nut; she just wanted to live longer. She began the workout routine eighteen months prior, followed by healthier eating. Coffee was one of the last dominos to fall. Most days she felt inclined to resurrect the habit.

The phone on Aimes's desk buzzed, and she startled, dripping honey across her hand instead of into her cup. She cursed and reached for a rag as the buzz repeated.

"Frazier, I told you to hold calls." Aimes contained the bulk of her irritation when she finally found the answer button, still scrubbing honey from the hem of her suit jacket. Why couldn't cane sugar be healthy?

"I know, ma'am. I'm sorry. I thought you'd want to know—it's Deputy Director Arnold."

Aimes stopped with the scrubbing, turning to the phone.

"SIS?"

"Yes, ma'am."

She sighed. "Okay. Give me thirty seconds, then put him through."

She gave up on the honey and dropped a plastic spoon into her tea, stirring what little had landed in the cup until it dissolved.

To hell with this.

She hit the buzzer. "Frazier?"

"Yes, ma'am?"

"Get me a Diet Coke, please."

Frazier's voice morphed with a contained chuckle. "Yes, ma'am."

Aimes enjoyed two fizzy sips before taking the call. The smooth flavor rolling down her throat erased the strain in her mind like freaking Ajax. A very miracle drink.

"Sarah, darling. How are you?"

SIS Deputy Director John Arnold's voice was as bubbly and active as the Coke, and despite how much she liked the man, it pissed Aimes off.

"It's Monday, Jack. All hell is breaking loose. How are things in the old country?"

Aimes had no direct relation to England. She knew for a fact that her family had been citizens of the New World since before the Civil War, which was as far as she cared to investigate. But she always used the phrase whenever speaking to Arnold, and he always got a kick out of it.

"Jolly good, old girl. Chelsea put a wallop on Tottenham last night. Truth be told, I was a bit hung over this morning. Almost missed my train."

"How does the missus feel about that late-night partying?"

"Between mistresses, as it happens. Had to part ways with dear Jingle Bells. You know, a laughing woman is a delight when you're drunk, but it really stifles the mood in bed, if you know what I mean."

Aimes didn't, and she didn't care to ask. As obnoxious as he could be, her London contact never called just to waste her time.

"What's up?" she asked.

"Got a memo you chaps had an interest in a certain Russian attack boat...let me see...the *Kron-shike*. No, that can't be right. *Kron-shad*? *Kron-shaft*? My lord, sounds like a bloody venereal disease, doesn't it?"

"*Kronshtadt*," Aimes said, sitting up. "You found her?"

Arnold laughed. "Don't act so keen, darling. I may be tempted to name a price."

"Jack, this is serious."

"Oh, well. Chill out, now. Yes, we found her. We think we have, anyway. One of our assets obtained images of what we think is the *Kronshtadt* at anchor...in Venezuela."

Aimes's heart skipped. She swiveled to her computer and tabbed back to the file from yesterday—the top-secret mission brief sent directly by O'Brien, with only a small handful of ranking officers as recipients. The one about Venezuela, and the unconfirmed reports of Stepan Belsky's escape...

Via Russian submarine.

There was no way to be sure if the reports were accurate, of course. But the first thing Aimes did after receiving the memo was to have a look at Russia's stealth submarine fleet. That didn't take long, because Russia didn't have much in the way of stealth anything. Really only one vessel caught her eye.

The *Kronshtadt*.

"Are you sure?" Aimes asked.

"Pretty damn sure, yes. I can send you the pictures. Old girl got close. Really risked her neck."

"Where?"

"Venezuela."

"Right, but where in Venezuela?"

Long pause. "Some port east of Caracas. We were looking into something unrelated. A shipping matter. I'll send you the details. But say, darling. Tit for tat. What's your interest in the Russki?"

Aimes leaned back in her chair, sipping Diet Coke and wondering how much she could share. Wondering how much she wanted to share. She trusted Arnold as much as anybody in intelligence trusts anyone. But that never meant she divulged information without cause.

"Classified, I'm afraid. Let's just say we're interested in all connections between Venezuela and Russia, at the moment."

"Well, then. I'd better forward you our file on these container ships. No relation, probably. Just a spot of busywork they've got us doing, but you might take interest."

"I appreciate it, Jack."

"My pleasure. And say, Aimes. Next time you're in London, you should really give me a call. I don't laugh in bed."

Aimes indulged in a rare grin. "I'll take that under advisement. Catch you later, Jack."

"Cheers."

Aimes hung up, and the smile melted. She remained fixated on the screen, rubbing one lip. Thinking about *Kronshtadt*.

Barely a minute passed before Arnold's encrypted email arrived, as promised. Documents pertaining to suspect Russian feeder ships crossing the Atlantic were shelved as she dug straight into the photos of the shadowy Russian attack boat.

The vessel was distant and a little grainy. But the silhouette was clear.

She reached for the phone.

23

Palacio de Miraflores
Caracas, Venezuela

Far beneath the ballrooms and opulent dining halls of Venezuela's presidential palace, the basement of the old building was built of solid block, dim save for flickering fluorescent lights. Not quite dank, but certainly musty, the sprawling space was subdivided into multiple rooms and used chiefly for storage, security operations, and, in a quiet back corner, sheltered by steel doors and armed guards, as a detainment facility.

There were only three chambers, and they almost never saw use. At the hands of his national intelligence service, national police, or sometimes the *colectivos* themselves, Moreno imprisoned most of his political enemies at El Helicoide, where the grisly work of interrogation and reeducation could proceed unobserved.

But not Juan Blanco. Following the arrest and detainment of Blanco, Moreno gave orders for him to be transferred from El Helicoide directly to Miraflores, locked in a chamber at the back of the basement, handcuffed and chained to the wall.

In the dark.

Right where Moreno could interrogate his former presidential aide personally.

When news of Blanco's betrayal first reached Moreno, his first comment had been "*Who?*" He had many presidential aides, most of whom he knew by face only. Blanco worked in his press department, helping to draft the regular speeches Moreno used as *cadenas*—addresses to the nation delivered on national television. He'd met the man maybe twice, and neither interaction was sufficiently interesting for him to place a face with the name his secret police handed him.

But what that name was accused of—siphoning critical intelligence straight from the heart of Miraflores and passing it to the rebel leader, Luis Rivas—was concerning enough for Moreno to want to meet the man in person.

And not just meet. Moreno felt a deep personal outrage at the thought of one of his own aides selling him out. Like a knife sliding into his back, it connected with his most primal defensive instincts. He wanted to squeeze this man, and keep squeezing until Blanco disclosed every little thing he'd told Rivas.

That squeezing had lasted the better part of an hour, now, and Moreno was growing tired. He unwound the athletic tape from his fists, breathing hard as two FAES members—a detachment of his national police reserved especially for such occasions as this—stretched Blanco's bound hands over his head and onto a hook screwed into the block wall. Blanco's head rolled over his chest, and blood streamed from every orifice on his head. Swollen cheeks were matched to busted lips and puffy eyes, red welts rippling down his neck and across his bare chest.

Moreno had put a beatdown on him—forty minutes of relentless hits, carefully calibrated to inflict maximum punishment while stopping just short of triggering unconsciousness. Moreno knew the technique well. He'd trained in various forms of boxing for most of the past twenty years, using the hobby to keep himself in shape and feeling manly even as old age set in.

It had been a long time since he'd pounded flesh the way he regularly pounded a heavy bag, and even though he'd never admit it to anyone, he didn't care for it. The reek of blood in the enclosed space was overpowering. Blanco's steady moans made him want to puke.

"Hold him," Moreno snarled before chugging water from a bottle. One of the soldiers stood next to Blanco, ratcheting the prisoner's head back as Moreno approached.

If Blanco could see at all, it was only by a slit between his swollen eyelids. Moreno didn't care. He brought the water bottle, pressing his sore fingers against either side of Blanco's mouth to force his jaw open prior to squirting a stream right into his throat.

Blanco choked and gargled, swallowing as much as he could. Moreno stepped back and drank another long pull, then handed off the bottle. Blanco's face rocked toward him, still manipulated by the fistful of hair the soldier clenched.

"You're a tough nut to crack, Juan. I'll give you that. I should have put you in my security detail, no? But then I guess you would have simply shot me."

Blanco's breaths came in dry rasps. Moreno reached down, beneath his belt buckle, and wrapped his throbbing knuckles right around Blanco's crotch, squeezing slowly.

Blanco choked and attempted to pull his hips away. A dull cry escaped his throat, and Moreno jerked, turning the cry to a shriek.

"Now, amigo. You will *tell me* what you told Rivas!"

Blanco's head slumped as the soldier released his hair. Blood ran from his mouth, and his body continued to tremor. The soldier cuffed him across the face.

"*Contéstale al presidente!*"

More streaming blood and racking coughs. Moreno waved the soldier back. He closed in until his face was only inches from Blanco's, conscious of the fact that both soldiers were carefully watching him. The stench of body fluids and misery sent Moreno's stomach flipping, reminding him of those early days long ago when he served in the Venezuelan army.

He hated blood, dirt, and sweat then, and he hated those things even more now. But with so much on the line between Moreno and Belsky—between Caracas and *the benefactor*—he couldn't afford to remain hands-off on this one.

What Blanco might know could bring the whole regime crashing down.

"Listen to me, Blanco," Moreno said. "I am not your enemy. I am your president."

Blanco didn't answer. Blood dripped from his lip onto Moreno's shoe, and Moreno placed his hand beneath Blanco's chin, lifting it until Blanco's swollen eyes made contact with his own.

"Everyone makes mistakes," Moreno said. "These things happen, *sí*? But we must fix them. This is your opportunity to fix things, before anyone is hurt. Do you understand me?"

"I...know nothing," Blanco rasped.

"You lie!" Moreno's voice cracked, and he squeezed Blanco's jaw. Crimson saliva ran over Moreno's fingers, and his stomach convulsed.

"Tell me now," Moreno said. "Tell me what you told Rivas, and I will make your death quick and painless. But—" Moreno lowered his voice to a whisper, bringing his lips close to Blanco's ear. "If you lie to me, I will bring your wife to this place. I will give her to my soldiers. They will do it in the next room, so you can hear everything. Every scream. Every plea. Every desperate call of your name."

Blanco began to shake. Moreno pulled his face away and wrenched his jaw around.

"*Tell me.*"

Blanco's lips parted. Bloodshot eyes blazed behind the swollen lids. His body shook.

Then he blasted a mouthful of spit and blood straight into Moreno's face.

Moreno stumbled back, clawing the goop out of his eyes. Both soldiers rushed in, slamming Blanco against the wall and raining blows across his stomach as he swung from the hook like a side of beef.

Helpless. Too weak to scream.

Moreno ripped a towel off a nearby chair and scrubbed his face and hands clean. He clenched his jaw to hold back the vomit and plowed through the door, back into the hallway. No matter how hard he scrubbed, he couldn't remove the metallic taste of another man's blood. It saturated his mouth like the oily smoke of a dark cigar.

Stopping at the end of the hallway, Moreno flung the towel down and snapped his fingers at the guard stationed there. The man hurried to offer him a fresh bottle of water, and Moreno guzzled.

Still, the flavor refused to die.

"Are you okay, Señor Presidente?"

Moreno lowered the bottle, suddenly conscious of the two other FAES members standing nearby. Watching him.

"Lieutenant!" He snapped his fingers again. The man stood to attention. "Find Blanco's wife. Find his children. Find his friends. Bring them all to El Helicoide."

"*Sí*, señor."

Moreno flung the bottle down and marched up the stairway even as a broken cry escaped Blanco's busted lips.

The FAES were unleashed now. Blanco should have talked while he had the chance.

The screams faded as Moreno reached the polished marble of the first floor. He ran the back of one hand across his brow, turning for the stairway to his presidential suite, already planning a long shower.

And then he ran almost headlong into Belsky.

The fat Russian was just rounding the corner, that overgrowth of chest hair billowing out of his shirt like an erupting volcano. He smelled, as before, but at least he was wearing a new shirt. He radiated with the semi-relaxed condescension of a man recently pleasured, and Moreno thought of the two Venezuelan whores he'd ordered to be delivered to Belsky's suite.

God save them.

Belsky swept a lazy gaze over Moreno, stopping over his disheveled shirt.

"Problems, Señor Presidente?"

Belsky spoke in English, his overbearing Russian accent deliberately butchering his ham-handed attempt at Spanish formality.

Moreno straightened his back, casually adjusting his shirt as though it weren't wrinkled and sweaty.

"Of course not, amigo. I was just working out."

Belsky's gaze drifted down to Moreno's shoe, where a wide pool of crimson was starting to dry. He grinned.

"Ah, yes. *Working out*. Hopefully with some excellent company at hand, no?"

A dry, disgusting laugh. Moreno gritted his teeth.

"If you will excuse me, señor."

Belsky held up a hand. "Just one thing. I thought you'd like to know—the cargo arrived on schedule. We are unloading as we speak."

The uneasiness Moreno had felt the last time he spoke to Belsky returned. This time all he could do was bottle it up, mixing nausea with nausea, and longing all the more for that shower.

"With any luck, we'll be drilling within the month," Belsky continued. "A cause for celebration, I think?"

Moreno forced a smile. "Of course, amigo. Meet me in the courtyard. I'll have my people open something vintage."

Belsky grinned, his discolored teeth gummy with thick saliva. "Excellent! And while you're at it, have them change the sheets in my room. Things got a little...violent."

24

As the door slammed shut behind Moreno, the guard hurried to collect the bloody towel and fallen water bottle off the floor. The two FAES soldiers were already marching down the hall, an anticipatory aggression in their step.

Eager to carry out Moreno's new orders.

Looking over his shoulder, the guard could hear the muted cries of Blanco as electric sparks cracked from the prison cell. The collage of gruesome sounds sent a shiver down his spine, and he reached for the phone. Punching out a memorized number, he waited as the phone rang.

Once. Twice.

At four times, he'd hang up. Somebody could barrel down the stairs or up the hall at any moment.

"*Sí?*"

He didn't recognize the voice on the other end, but he spoke quickly.

"I have a message for Rivas. They've got Blanco at Miraflores. Moreno just gave orders for his wife and family to be arrested. Get them to safety."

"Has he talked?" The voice turned anxious with the next question.

The guard looked back down the hall. Back toward the sounds of agony.

"I don't know."

The man by the phone snapped his fingers, then held up an open palm for the room to be silent. He clutched the handset close to his ear and breathed an anxious question into the mic.

"Has he talked?"

Long pause. Then he lowered the phone, hanging up with a dull click. He looked across the room.

Luis Rivas stood with both hands on the map table, his shirt collar open, a sheen of sweat glimmering across his forehead. A question on his face.

"Moreno is coming for her," the man said, tilting his head toward the adjacent kitchen. "And the family."

Rivas didn't hesitate. He rattled off a short command to two of his lieutenants, and they both departed immediately, out through the kitchen where they would collect Blanco's wife. From there they would visit the barrios, rounding up as many of Blanco's family members as possible before heading inland, into the jungles. Rivas wouldn't know where. He wouldn't want to know where. Just so long as they were safely beyond Moreno's reach.

Turning from the table, he ran both hands through his hair, wringing out sweat, and looked through the window. It was a new day in Caracas, with a clear sky and a bright sunrise. What little commerce remained in the city would come alive shortly.

Another grinding day beneath the Moreno regime.

"Has Blanco talked?" Rivas asked.

"I don't know," the man said.

Rivas chewed his cheek, tasting blood but not caring. A few years ago, he might have been angry with himself for being more concerned about whether Blanco had spilled than whether Blanco was alive.

But Rivas was now far beyond that point. The viselike grip of perpetual violence, hunger, homelessness, and economic devastation that he witnessed daily far outweighed the plight of a single man, no matter how desperate it may be. Rivas couldn't afford to fixate on that tragedy. He was too pragmatic.

"Luis." One of his lieutenants approached, her salt-and-pepper hair held back in a sweaty ponytail, her face just as exhausted and strained as his own. "What are you going to do?"

Rivas's head spun. What *was* he going to do? The operation Blanco was a part of had been underway for nearly two months. Not a long time, considering the gravity of the results they were hoping to achieve, but when an opportunity like this came knocking, you didn't overthink it. You had to *act*.

Now that opportunity was slipping away.

"Without the tapes, we have nothing," Rivas said. "We cannot proceed."

"Wait." The man behind him stood from a chair. "Surely you are not saying we should stand down?"

"What choice do we have?" Rivas spun, shouting but not meaning to. He pointed to the map. "Without the tapes, it's just another riot!"

"No." The woman shook her head. "Not just another riot. It's a riot with a *cause*. Make Blanco the cause! Call Moreno's bluff."

"It's not a bluff," the man said. "If Blanco breaks, Moreno will have enough to arrest you, Luis. Are you hearing me? He'll send the secret police. He'll have you in El Helicoide by nightfall!"

Rivas looked back out the window, toward downtown. Toward El Helicoide. He knew his lieutenant was right. The only thing standing between Moreno and his lust for arresting Rivas was the questionable strength of a man Rivas didn't even know.

Had Blanco already broken?

"Take the wind out of his sails," the woman said, pointing to the map. "Use his *wife*. Start a protest. Ask the media: Where is Juan Blanco? Moreno cannot answer without incriminating himself, and he cannot arrest you without admitting to Blanco's torture. Put his back against the wall, Luis!"

Rivas looked back to the map and thought about the carefully orchestrated protests and the thousands of angry Venezuelans ready to put their own health, liberty, and even their very lives on the line to make those protests happen.

He couldn't ask them to do that simply to save his own skin. But if he was arrested, what would be left of the resistance?

Not much.

"Luis." The man stepped around the table and put one confident hand on his arm. "We stand behind you. The people stand behind you. Don't let Moreno draw first blood. Hit him while he least expects it. *Tonight*."

Rivas looked to the woman. "Tonight?"

She nodded. "Tonight, Señor Presidente."

He looked back to the map. And then he nodded.

"Tonight. Call the media."

25

George Bush Center for Intelligence
Langley, Virginia

"How old is this?" O'Brien demanded, his hands spread wide over his desk as he peered down at the images displayed on a large iPad. Aimes stood across from him, a stylus in one hand as she flicked through each picture.

"Only hours. British intelligence captured them this morning."

"From the ground?"

Aimes nodded. "My contact indicated as much."

She stopped over the shadowy outline of the submarine. Even in the inky darkness, the shape was distinct. O'Brien chewed his lip, his computer-like brain spinning into overdrive.

Not so much about what he was looking at, but about what he should do with it.

"How sure are we that the boat is Russian?"

"It's impossible to be certain. I had an analyst run several silhouette checks. Most of the key identifiers aren't visible, but..."

"But?" O'Brien tilted his head up.

"We think it's *Kronshtadt*, and so do the British."

O'Brien settled in his chair, steepling his fingers and still studying the photograph. Then he looked up.

"Contact Montgomery. Have him look into it."

"The Prosecution Force?" Aimes frowned. "I thought you wanted them on the bench."

"I do. And this is a wild goose chase, three hundred miles outside Caracas. Far enough to keep them busy and out of trouble."

"So you don't think it's Russian?"

O'Brien shrugged, pivoting to his computer. Already moving on to the next task of an overwhelming day.

"Maybe it is, maybe it isn't. Doesn't really matter either way. So long as that jackass is occupied, he's off my back. Get it done."

26

Caracas, Venezuela

"Okie dokie, hotshots, time to roll!"

Stewie barreled into the hotel room barely four hours after he'd left, a half-eaten burrito in one hand, not bothering to knock. Reed was out of his chair, the SIG rising to eye level before he realized who it was.

Stewie held up an open palm. "Chill, brother. I ain't Tom Brady!"

Reed shot Turk a sideways look. Wolfgang was in the bathroom, taking a shower. The water cut off abruptly at Stewie's noisy intrusion. Reed could picture Wolfgang springing toward the door, leading with the gaping mouth of his 10mm.

Reed holstered the SIG. "You should knock."

Stewie took a massive bite of the burrito, talking through a mouthful of eggs and what smelled like roasted pork.

"I heard from the big cheeses. They got something for you to look into, down on the coast. Something the Brits found."

"What?" Reed said.

Stewie wiped his mouth with the back of one hand. "Some Russian sub? Station chief will have a full report ready when we outfit you. You guys can drive stick, right?"

Stewie drove the battered Tahoe, still scarfing the burrito, while Reed, Turk, and Wolfgang rode in irritated silence. Despite the sour stench of trash rolling around on the floorboard, coupled with Stewie's generally disgusting approach to consumption, Reed's stomach growled. The burrito smelled good. He hadn't eaten a full meal since the prime rib in Chattanooga.

Stewie navigated away from the hotel, weaving amid more narrow streets and taking only slightly more care to dodge potholes by the aid of broad daylight. Now that Reed could see the city, it was impossible to ignore the depression of the place. None of the architecture looked any younger than thirty years, with rusted roofs and sagging awnings overhanging battered homes.

Tangles of electrical lines ran down tight and winding streets, with trash piled in gutters and aged cars parked alongside busted sidewalks. It looked exactly like the bad side of any average American city—a place that used to be the "it" part of town but had since been relegated to poorer demographics by the slow grind of time.

Only, this wasn't just a side of Caracas. Even as Stewie topped hills and wound along low ridges offering panoramic views of the cityscape, it all looked the same.

"That's Miraflores, over there," Stewie said suddenly, pointing as he crumpled up the burrito wrapper.

Reed squinted into the morning sun, barely making out the glint of flagpoles rising out of a three-story structure, a few miles distant.

"What's that?"

"Presidential palace," Stewie said. "Best crib in the city. And look! There's Moreno's chopper."

He pointed again. Reed watched the glimmer of a small helicopter—a Eurocopter of some sort, he thought—gliding out of the clouds and descending in an elegant curve toward Miraflores.

"Must be beach day," Stewie quipped with a disgusted shake of his head.

"We were briefed on Moreno," Reed said. "I gather he's the problem around here."

He gestured in the general direction of the slums. The battered shacks were starting to fade now as they passed into what appeared to be more of a business district, but the potholed streets and busted sidewalks continued.

Stewie pried a bit of his breakfast from his back teeth with one finger. He shrugged.

"That depends on who you ask. We don't like him—officially. But you'd be surprised how many Venezuelans support him. *Chavistas*, they call them. People who liked Chávez, and now they like Moreno. Generally, the very rich or the very poor, which is weird. I guess the poor people still believe Moreno can resurrect Chávez's gravy trains, and the rich know better. But they're in on it."

"In on what?" Wolfgang asked.

Stewie replicated Reed's vague gesture toward the city. "Look around. This feel like a socialist paradise to you? Moreno is corrupt as hell. So was Chávez, but at least Chávez wrote a lot of checks. Now the money is gone. US sanctions, plus falling oil prices...a death blow to a place like this."

Reed looked out the window at a passing row of office buildings. One featured a red-and-white sign, with glowing letters reading *banco*—a bank. A couple hundred people were lined up on the sidewalk outside, filing slowly ahead, hands in their pockets, faded and threadbare clothes hanging over their backs.

They all looked skinny and tired, but not in a hurry. Maybe they had no place better to be.

He turned away and remembered the little houses he was looking at outside of Birmingham. They felt so peaceful and opulent compared to the devastation around him. Momentary frustration flashed in his chest as the memory brought with it thoughts of his fight with Banks. She still hadn't called, and he was finished listening to her voicemail.

Why can't she just be happy?

Stewie finally pulled the Tahoe off the street on the edge of downtown, just outside a ten-story building that looked mostly abandoned. He turned into a parking garage, bypassing an empty guard shack and a busted gate. On the far side of the garage, another Tahoe sat backed into a parking space, its running lights glowing in the dimness. It was a few years newer than Stewie's, but no less worn.

Stewie swung the SUV around and backed in next to its twin, but left the engine running.

"Hop out. This'll be quick."

Reed swept the garage as he exited the Tahoe, one hand on the SIG beneath his jacket. There was nobody in sight, and no other cars. Just a light breeze smelling of oil and gasoline fumes.

He turned to the new vehicle, where two men dressed in street clothes fanned out, shooting him quick nods but not approaching. He noted oversized bulges beneath their jackets that didn't match their muscled physiques, and guessed them to be submachine guns.

The door of the second SUV popped open, and a third man stepped out. Short, lean, and also dressed in street clothes. He wore a nondescript black baseball cap, and Reed noted the trace of scarring on his neck, disappearing beneath an open collar.

The scars were a mottled mess of bright white and deep red, permanently frozen on his skin as a graphic art piece. Reed had seen that pattern before—on the lucky ones. The unlucky ones bled to death amid the shrapnel, their ears still ringing with the blast of an IED.

Stewie pulled a sucker from his pocket and ripped the wrapper off with his teeth, jerking a thumb at the new guy.

"Guys, meet Pat. Pat, meet the...what did you guys call yourselves?"

"The Prosecution Force," the new guy finished, extending his hand toward Reed. "Pat Harris, CIA Station Chief, Caracas."

Reed took his hand, enjoying a solid grip. Harris remained relaxed but alert as he passed down the row, shaking hands with Turk and Wolfgang. Reed thought he detected a curious glint in the station chief's eye, but Harris didn't ask any questions as he turned to the hood of his SUV and withdrew an iPad from his coat. In the background Reed was conscious of the two guys in street clothes standing with their backs turned, surveying the garage and the surrounding streets.

"HQ says you guys are here about a boat," Harris said, calling up a map of Venezuela on the iPad and zooming out until Reed could see the bulk of South America's Caribbean coast.

"Something like that," he said. "You found one?"

"The Brits did. Russian, we think. Anchored here, at Puerto Pedernales. About three hundred twenty miles down the coast, give or take."

"That's a long hike," Reed said.

"And a rough one. The roads are bad, and there's a storm coming in. If it were me, I'd wait a day or two..." Harris looked up. "But you don't look like the waiting kind."

Reed grunted. "That's correct. What can you lend us?"

Harris jabbed a thumb toward the back of the garage. "We've got an old Land Cruiser you can use. Four-wheel drive—and you'll need it."

"Reliable?"

"Never failed me yet. Once you get near the port, the Brits have their field agent on standby to guide you in. Some woman named Corbyn. I've never met her."

"Sounds good. What about gear?"

"What do you need?"

"Fresh water. MREs, if you have them. And small arms. Light and fully automatic, 5.56 preferably. Three of them."

Harris hesitated, glancing down the length of mismatched men. His gaze pivoted to Wolfgang's leg, and Wolfgang stiffened, his face turning cold.

Harris returned to Reed. "Look. I'm gonna level with you. We're not really a well-equipped operation down here. Since they pulled the embassy, we've been working unofficially on a shoestring budget. Honestly, I was starting to think Langley had forgotten about us. This morning marks the first unscheduled call I've received in weeks, and it came straight from the top."

Harris switched off the iPad, looking a question at Reed. Reed folded his arms and didn't answer.

"I guess it's pointless to ask who you guys are," Harris said.

"We're the good guys," Reed said simply.

Harris laughed dryly. "Right. Of course you are."

He passed the iPad to Stewie, then tilted his head to the back of his Tahoe. Reed followed him as the hatch rose automatically, exposing a carefully assorted field of small arms.

Four FN MK 16 SCAR rifles with shortened, fourteen-inch barrels lay next to each other, alongside eight fully loaded thirty-round magazines. All black. Beyond them sat a pair of twin backpacks, loaded out with MOLLE web pouches attached to their outsides.

"Sixty rounds per rifle," Harris said. "Flashlights, MREs, fresh water, and medical in the packs. Enough for two days, anyway."

"No sidearms?" Reed questioned.

"Stewie informed me that you already have sidearms."

Reed shot Stewie a surprised look. Stewie rattled the sucker against his teeth, shrugging innocently.

"Why four?" Reed said, turning back to the rifles. He already knew the answer, and he didn't like it.

"Stewie's going with you," Harris said. "He'll serve as your local guide and hopefully get you through any checkpoints you encounter. Outside the city, national military and police presence is extremely sparse and easily bought off, but it helps to have somebody who understands the local landscape."

Reed's gaze hardened. Harris held up a hand, lowering his voice.

"I know he comes off weird, but he's a competent officer. He's spent the last ten years in South America. Trust me. You want him."

Reed turned to Turk. The big man shrugged.

"Fine," Reed said.

Wolfgang and Turk retrieved the gear, and Stewie led the two men to the Land Cruiser, leaving Reed standing next to Harris.

Reed lifted his chin toward the scars disappearing beneath Harris's collar.

"Iraq or Afghanistan?"

Harris's gaze dropped. He pocketed his hands.

"Iraq. And you?"

Reed looked across the parking garage, listening as an engine rumbled to life someplace deep in the shadows. The Land Cruiser, he figured.

"Everywhere," he said.

That glint of curiosity shone in Harris's eyes again, but he didn't comment. He started toward his driver's-side door.

"Good luck. I hope you find what you're looking for."

Reed shot him a two-finger salute and started after the engine noise as Harris's bodyguards returned to the Tahoe.

"Hey, ghost," Harris called after him.

Reed looked over his shoulder. "Yeah?"

"Do me a favor. Don't make a mess." Harris slid on a pair of sunglasses, looking suddenly very tired. "These people have suffered enough."

27

The ride was going to be hell—Reed knew that from the first moment the Land Cruiser's heavy doors slammed shut and the windows rattled.

The vehicle was old. Mid-nineties, probably, with worn and sagging seats and a vague smell of gasoline. Turk stowed their gear in the cargo compartment, and Reed took shotgun, expecting Stewie to drive. Before their CIA contact could reach the driver's-side door, however, Wolfgang cut him off, placing his hand on the door and shooting Stewie a look cold enough to freeze alcohol.

Stewie backed off, holding up both hands with the sucker still pinned between his teeth. Wolfgang got in, ratcheting the seat back and fishing for the accelerator with his prosthetic leg. Reed raised an eyebrow, but Wolfgang ignored him, shifting into first gear.

"Which way, Family Guy?"

Stewie passed forward an iPad preloaded with digital navigation, and then they were off, rumbling through the dusty streets and headed east. They cleared the outskirts half an hour later and found a wide, almost empty highway that ran right along the coast. Wolfgang put the hammer down, dodging most of the potholes on the underused asphalt.

With the windows down, Turk unpacked a trio of MREs. Reed's selection was marked *Menu 23 – Chicken with Pasta in Pesto Sauce*. He mixed water into the heater pouch and waited for the promised pasta to warm, then scooped lukewarm penne out of the pouch with the included plastic spoon.

It tasted like...something other than food. Something manufactured, packaged, stored for a very long time, and probably now expired. But Reed couldn't help relishing the cocktail of mediocrity. The flavor unlocked memories long stored—or maybe suppressed—by mountains of gunfire and bloodshed.

Way back to the very beginning. Back to Parris Island, Basic RECON Course at Camp Pendleton...and then Iraq. A long, chaotic journey, with a lot of MREs consumed along the way.

"Diverse menu." Turk spoke through a mouthful of what may have been roast beef. "Superb flavor. Would recommend for a date night."

Wolfgang sniffed his pouch, then deposited the lot of it onto the console with a grimace. "I'll starve."

"Civilians," Turk snorted. Reed joined in the laugh, and Wolfgang smiled, but Reed saw no humor in his eyes. There was only darkness—deep and angry, like a hurricane bearing down on the coast.

Ready to unleash hell on anything in its path.

The highway dissolved into a series of bumpy, winding two-lanes, some of them previously paved, and some of them never paved. Wolfgang locked the Land Cruiser into four-wheel drive and wrestled through the ruts, his prosthetic foot slipping at times off the accelerator.

Reed offered to take over, but the gesture was flatly ignored. The sun rose high over Venezuela as the passing towns and villages alongside the road dissolved into sparser—and much poorer—settlements.

The huts and shacks they now passed made the barrios of Caracas look like the crown jewel of civilization. Many of them were assembled directly out of scraps—sheet metal, busted shipping pallets, and reclaimed wood. Dirt trails led between the houses, and livestock ran in small herds chased by dogs.

The people were thin and gaunt, but without fail they waved as the

Land Cruiser churned past. Reed had lowered his window, the SIG riding within easy reach on his lap as the afternoon breeze wafted through the cabin. He thought about two years previously, the last time he'd been in Venezuela, with Banks.

They had married on a hilltop inland of Caracas. Turk and Wolfgang were there. Reed was on the run at the time and not paying much attention to the predicaments of those around him.

But he didn't remember Venezuela being so poor. So starved of life and hope. Maybe the country had changed since then—or maybe he had. Thinking about Banks and that happy moment up on those hills made his stomach twist. They had nothing then. Only their lives. And somehow...it had felt like enough. Banks was happy.

Where had he gone wrong?

"Thirty minutes." Wolfgang spoke in a dull growl. Reed checked the iPad and confirmed that they were narrowing in on the preassigned rendezvous with Corbyn—the British agent who claimed to have found the Russian sub. It would be another two-hour drive from there to Puerto Pedernales. Corbyn would guide them in and provide intelligence on local security, then stand back while Reed and Turk conducted an intrusion and full recon—after dark, probably. Take Stewie along in case translation was called for. Leave Wolfgang in the Land Cruiser, ready to exfiltrate quickly should anything go sideways.

It wasn't Reed's idea of a great plan. He didn't like having so many people to worry about, but he wasn't expecting a gunfight either. Just a quick look, a positive identification, then fall back to contact Langley and discuss next steps.

About as easy a job as Trousdale had tasked him with since returning to America.

A heavy bolt closed behind Reed, signaling the chambering of a 5.56 NATO round into the breech of Turk's SCAR. Stewie grunted a sarcastic laugh.

"Don't trust Brits, big guy?"

"I don't trust anybody." Turk spoke around a wad of chewing gum from his MRE. "*Little guy*."

Wolfgang slowed the Cruiser as the blinking icon on the screen guided them around a bend in the dirt road. A light rain had begun to fall an hour previously, killing the dust that had clouded their windshield all day but bringing a new curse in its place—mud. A lot of mud.

The Cruiser fishtailed a bit as they reached the bottom of the hill. Around the next bend was the rendezvous—an abandoned service station, marked on the map by a simple white dot.

"Stop short of the turnoff," Reed said, press-checking his SIG. "And keep it in gear."

Wolfgang tapped the brake as the service station came into view. There was another Land Cruiser parked under a slouched awning; an empty block building squatted next to it with all its windows blown out. The station's pumps were gone, as was its sign. Evergreen undergrowth crowded its backside, pressing in near to the second Cruiser.

But no people. No British secret agent.

"You see her?" Wolfgang leaned toward the windshield.

"Flash your lights," Reed said.

Wolfgang reached for the switch, then the passenger door behind Reed popped open, and Stewie shouted in alarm.

"Holy sh—"

Turk swung his SCAR to bear, and Reed pivoted with the SIG. Before any of them could confront the unidentified threat, a slender arm shoved Stewie in the shoulder, and a grinning face framed by sopping dark hair poked through the door.

"Well, go on, bugger. Shove over!"

Stewie's head slammed against the headrest as Turk thrust the muzzle of his SCAR toward the woman.

"Don't move! Who are you?"

The woman rolled her eyes. "Who do you bloody well think I am? Lady Liberty? MI6, assface. Now let me in before I drown to death."

Turk looked to Reed. Reed cast a quick glance around the Land Cruiser, then nodded. Stewie crammed into the middle seat, and the woman closed the door. She ran both hands through her hair, squeegeeing out rainwater as more of the same ran off the rain slicker she wore. She was small—not more than five-five, but looking lithe and fit.

She was pretty, too. Dark skinned, probably biracial. Big brown eyes and flashing teeth.

"What are you gawking at?" she quipped, catching Reed's gaze.

"Corbyn?" he said.

"That's right. Kirsten. And you are?"

Reed didn't answer. He looked to Turk. The big Tennessean still looked pissed to have been jumped.

"Oh, come on," Corbyn snorted. "This isn't East Berlin. You can give me a name, even if it's fake."

Reed grunted. "I'm Reed. That's Turk."

"Stewie." The CIA officer was next to speak, offering his hand. Corbyn shook it with a friendly nod.

"And what about storm cloud there?"

Wolfgang's face darkened a shade, but he didn't answer. He placed one hand on the shifter and glowered into the rearview mirror.

"Where's the boat?"

28

Gray clouds darkened to black, the rain settling in to a steady shower by the time Corbyn guided Wolfgang off the road and took control of the iPad. She shot careful glances around the vehicle, then used her fingers to zoom in on a digital map of the coastline.

"The port is here, about two miles due north. This is as far as I'd take a vehicle. You're better off on foot moving forward."

"Describe it," Reed said.

Corbyn shrugged, enlarging the satellite imagery. "It's pretty much what it looks like. In a shallow valley, hills on either side. Lots of undergrowth right down to the water, and trees overhanging the edges of the river. You've got a concrete dock here, with fingers shooting out for half a dozen small bays. Three of them are occupied. Russian feeder freighters. The sub is here...in the back, behind a line of chain link fences topped with razor wire."

"Security?"

"Pretty minimal, last I was here. Mostly it's just longshoremen—a hundred or so, working one freighter at a time. Lots of heavy equipment and bright lights, but that's kind of a good thing. We'll be invisible so long as we stay in the shadows."

"We?"

Corbyn swept semi-dry brunette hair behind one ear. "Right. We."

"The station chief indicated you were only guiding us in," Stewie said.

Corbyn snorted, stowing the iPad in her backpack and drawing a SIG P226 not unlike Reed's.

"Your station chief can get his head out of his bum. I don't work for him. Technically, this is my op. You lads are just along for the ride."

Corbyn completed a press check on the SIG, moving with the confident fluidity of a woman familiar with small arms. Turk rolled his shoulders in a "what are you gonna do" gesture, and Reed turned back to the Brit.

"What operation is that, exactly?"

"Mine?"

"Right. You looking into the sub?"

"Negative. I'm here about the cargo ships. They're running unregistered routes out of West Africa, carrying God knows what. MI6 wanted to take a look. I discovered the sub by accident."

"You know what you're doing in the dark?" Reed asked.

Corbyn shot him a wink. "Wouldn't you like to know."

She reached for the door and dropped out of the Cruiser before anyone could object. Reed sighed and turned to Wolfgang.

"All right. You stay here and keep the keys handy. We'll radio if there's trouble."

Turk passed Wolfgang a shortwave handset from one of the CIA packs. Wolfgang's gaze swept over it with open disgust.

"You kidding me? I'm going."

"Like hell you are," Reed said. "You see that jungle? It's hardly a running track, and you're hardly a sprinter."

Wolfgang's face hardened, but Reed wasn't in the mood to sympathize.

"Deal with it, Wolf. I let you come along. Take the job you're suited for."

Reed's feet sank into an inch of mud as he dropped out of the Cruiser. The steady rain quickly saturated his shoulders and dripped down his back. Turk checked the CIA bags for rain gear, but despite his knowledge of the weather forecast, Harris had neglected to pack any.

"You lads coming or what?" Corbyn called from the tree line.

Turk and Reed each shouldered a pack, cradling SCAR rifles. Stewie hung his rifle over his back beneath a heavy jacket, taking a machete from the Cruiser as his primary weapon. Then they were off.

Corbyn moved like a cat, sliding amid the jungle foliage and ducking low-hanging tree limbs with all the grace and ease of a Bengal tiger. Stewie followed directly behind, using the machete sparingly to avoid generating needless noise but clearing a path large enough for the two oversized Americans to plow through.

Reed kept his finger just above the trigger guard of the SCAR, checking in with Wolfgang fifteen minutes after entering the jungle.

"Prosecutor to Wolf, comms check."

"Bug off, Prosecutor."

Reed snorted and returned the radio to his belt.

"He's gone dark," Turk muttered.

"I know," Reed said. "Better keep an eye on that."

Corbyn's promised two-mile hike felt more like five and ate up the better part of an hour. By the time they narrowed in on the port, it was full dark, and Reed and Turk stopped to dig night vision goggles out of the packs. Harris wasn't kidding about being underfunded. The units were no less than ten years old, the straps stretched and worn, and the peripherals of their view a little fuzzy. But they worked, and Reed passed a unit to Stewie. Corbyn was already equipped with a cutting-edge Armasight model, sticking to her head like it belonged there.

She held up a closed fist just behind a dense grove of foliage, and the line came to a halt. The patter of ceaseless rain running off oversized leaves generated endless white noise, but as Reed focused, he heard other sounds also.

Heavy engines. Muted shouts. Occasional clangs of metal on metal.

"Directly ahead," Corbyn whispered. "Quiet, now."

She dropped into a crouch, one hand riding the SIG in her belt as she wove around another tree. Reed and Turk followed, fanning out with the SCARs at the ready. Rainwater dripped from his weapon's muzzle as Reed trailed Corbyn to the crest of a rise, dropping to their stomachs for the final two yards. He was now soaked to the bone, mud coating his legs and chest.

It was a damn good feeling.

Reed's goggles flickered as he parted leaves, then washed bright green as he peered into the valley below.

The space was fully illuminated. He made out bright dots where powerful work lights dumped LED light over the port, and the outdated goggles failed to compensate. Shoving them up and away from his eyes, Reed blinked a couple times to clear his vision.

And then he saw it.

Nestled two hundred yards away, surrounded by rusting chain link fence and crawling with dockside workers, lay Puerto Pedernales. The port consisted of a wide pool of sheltered salt water, with the ocean connecting on the northeast side and a river dumping freshwater from the inland jungles to the south. Three massive container ships with built-in cranes sat at anchor, divided by concrete fingers packed with machinery. The lights Reed's night vision had detected were mounted on high poles like stadium lights, blazing down as bright as day as longshoremen scurried to download dozens of containers from each vessel.

There were maybe two hundred workers present, all wearing little white hard hats and neon vests. But they weren't alone. Reed spotted the first gunman standing at the end of a concrete finger, slouched against a shipping container with the familiar outline of an AK type rifle hung over his chest. A quick sweep of that finger revealed five more, and when Reed turned to the core of the port, the black-suited gunmen were like ants. Fully three dozen of them, maybe more, all standing in the rain as though they were impervious to it.

Reed turned to Corbyn. "I thought you said there was no security?"

Corbyn had flipped up the Armasight, deploying digital binoculars in its place. She breathed a curse.

"They weren't here last night, I swear."

Reed dug a pair of binoculars out of the CIA pack, flicking open lens caps and conducting his own slow sweep of the port. He focused over the nearest gunman, that guy at the end of the concrete finger, and watched as the man lit up a cigarette. He had a hard face, scarred on one side, with extra magazines riding in a bulletproof vest and a sidearm strapped to his hip. The rifle was a modern rendition of the classic Kalashnikov design. An AK-12, probably. The preferred implement of the Russian military but also used by a variety of armed forces and security services around the globe.

The guy was legit security, no doubt. With a paramilitary flavor.

"Well," Reed said. "They're here now, and they aren't gonna make this easy. Where's the sub?"

"To your left," Corbyn said. "Other side of the rail lines, along the river."

Reed swept the binoculars to the left, past a row of containers being loaded onto rail cars. He reached the spot Corbyn pointed out, where the darkened mass of the river glided past an unused section of the port, but he saw nothing save deep shadow.

"I don't see it."

"You're looking right at it."

"Yeah, well, these binos are trash. What am I supposed to be seeing?"

"Here." Corbyn passed him her binoculars. They were equipped with night vision, easily compensating for the blast of the LED lights and allowing Reed a balanced view of the darkness beyond the rail cars.

He saw it now. Cloaked by darkness, surrounded by a heavy-duty fence, and secured by five or six more gunmen. It was definitely a submarine—relatively small, probably a fast-attack boat. Maybe Russian. Reed's naval identification skills were too limited to be sure.

He focused the binoculars on the spot and swept the vessel from the stern forward, searching for any identifying marks or shapes. Overhanging trees blocked part of his view, concealing the sub from spy satellites circling outside the atmosphere.

It was a great place to hide. You'd need to be almost on top of it before you even knew it was there.

"Crap," Turk breathed. Reed instinctually removed his gaze from the binoculars, twisting to Turk.

"What is it?"

Turk lay on the other side of Corbyn, next to Stewie. With another pair of the CIA's binoculars pressed to his eyes, he was fixated not on the submarine but on the rail lines nestled under brilliant white light, right at the heart of the port. Turk pointed with one hand.

"Center line, five containers left from the end. Yellow container, bottom of the stack. What does that label read?"

Reed used Corbyn's binoculars to trace a path to Turk's identified crate. He found it easily enough, scarred by heavy use and slick with a muddy film, at some point painted yellow but now as much rust as anything.

Zooming on the back corner, he found the label. Then his heart skipped.

"Lenkov International," Reed said.

"That's what I thought," Turk said. "Check the orange one, two crates to your left. Then the blue one on top of it."

Reed quickly found both. On each one, metal tags bolted near the rear doors were printed with the same bold letters in deep red: Lenkov Intl.

Reed handed the binoculars to Corbyn, offering her a chance to inspect the scene before he spoke. "What's your interest in these crates?"

Corbyn checked the labels before answering, then shook her head. "We're not sure. MI6 tracked the first ship out of Lagos last week, quickly followed by another. The third sailed out of Luanda. All taking suboptimal shipping lanes with less traffic."

"These ships are owned by Lenkov?" Reed asked.

Corbyn lowered the binoculars, nodding. Then her dark eyes narrowed. "You know the name?"

Reed didn't answer. He knew the name, all right. Lenkov International was the primary energy holding of one Stepan Belsky.

"Coincidence?" Turk said.

"Not a chance," Reed answered.

"All right, boys. What am I missing?"

Reed stowed the CIA's binoculars and double-checked the NV goggles. They were still operable, if barely useful.

"I need a closer look," he said. "I want to know what's in those crates. Corbyn, we'll be back."

Turk placed his hands against the ground to stand. Corbyn's hand shot out like a snake, pressing him back down. In an instant, she was on her feet, landing like a cat.

"You two provide overwatch. I'll go with Reed."

Turk glowered. "Hey, missy. This—"

"Is still my op," Corbyn finished. "And don't call me missy, or I'll missy my foot up your bum."

Turk's glower wrinkled into a confused frown. He turned to Stewie. The CIA officer only shrugged.

Reed momentarily debated taking Turk's side, then decided it wasn't worth it. It would only waste time to argue with Corbyn—and besides, he wanted to quiz her about what else MI6 knew.

"All right," he said. "Turk takes overwatch, then. Keep a lookout, and radio us if something comes up. We'll be back within the hour."

He turned to the trees, Corbyn at his elbow.

"Come on, Brit. Let's see if you sneak as well as you sass."

29

The White House

"Ladies and gentlemen, the president of the United States!"

The crowd roared. Maggie felt the cheers in her gut, like a rumbling blast building into overwhelming nausea. She saw the stage and the rising field of spectators in the blurry distance, out of reach but calling to her. Dragging her out of the safe shadows.

Stratton stood behind the podium, raising his hands to the crowd, his face spread into a toothy grin. He turned toward her and held out a hand, his dark eyes flashing suddenly red, his teeth morphing into bloody fangs.

Maggie's heart thundered. She took a step back, reaching instinctively for O'Dell.

He wasn't there.

"...the president of the United States!" Stratton repeated, louder this time, his arm outstretched.

Except it wasn't his voice any longer. The voice was now deep and growled, like the voice of hell in a horror movie. The sky behind Stratton blackened with rolling clouds, and the roar of the crowd amplified until Maggie's eardrums split.

She could feel the blood draining out of her ears. She clamped her eyes shut and turned away from the podium, breaking into a run.

She hit a wall. The darkness around her thickened, and an iron hand closed around her shoulder. Cold and harsh, dirty fingernails sinking into her skin. She looked up, expecting to see Stratton and his demon eyes.

It wasn't Stratton—it was a faceless man dressed in all black, like an executioner. In one hand he held the largest rifle she'd ever seen, with a massive scope and a muzzle wide enough to swallow her arm.

"Come with me." He spoke in the demon voice, dragging her backward. Toward that podium, like an execution scaffold.

Maggie clawed to remove his hand, writhing and jerking free.

"O'Dell!"

The executioner pulled her into the spotlight. The crowd roared louder —no longer calling for their president. Now clamoring for the spectacle.

The executioner hurled her onto the floor. She struck the podium on the way down, its hard corner driving shooting pain through her body, overwhelming her mind.

"O'Dell! Please!"

The muzzle of the rifle swiveled down. The faceless man's head disappeared behind the scope. A loud snap heralded the disengagement of the safety.

"Go to hell, swamp girl."

"Maggie! You're okay. Wake up!"

Maggie's eyes blinked open as fire exploded from that gaping muzzle. The iron hand on her arm was still there, but the nails didn't bite into her skin. It was a gentler grip, paired with a familiar voice.

"You're okay...you're okay now."

Maggie shook, sweat streaming down her face. The darkness around her was shattered by an ornate lamp resting on her bedside table, casting dull yellow light around her presidential suite. As her heart rate began to calm, the trembling subsided. Her darting gaze searched the room, but she couldn't find the faceless man and his gun.

Then she saw O'Dell. He knelt on the floor next to her bed, one hand cradling her arm, his dark eyes peering earnestly into hers. The fear she felt was mirrored in his face—deep concern. Raptured focus.

Maggie winced, the pain she felt in the dream perpetrated by a deep ache in her stomach. She licked sweat off her lips, then placed one elbow against the bed and pivoted herself into a sitting position. O'Dell assisted, and her feet touched the thick carpeting of an ornate rug. The pain in her gut magnified, sharp enough to draw tears.

Maggie blinked them away, digging her toes into the carpeting and bracing both hands over the bedspread. She sucked in a deep breath and forced back the nightmarish images. They faded quickly, but the sounds remained.

The roaring crowd. The demon voice.

"Are you okay?" O'Dell's soft voice was laced with concern. She brushed damp hair out of her eyes, a flush of embarrassment replacing the adrenaline that had swamped her body.

Did I really call for him?

"I'm...I'm so sorry," she mumbled. "Just a dream. I'm fine."

"Let me get you a drink." He hurried to his feet, turning to a coffee bar and pouring a glass from a water pitcher. She sucked greedily on the cool water while O'Dell stood awkwardly next to her, his hand near her arm but not quite touching her.

Maggie finished the glass, her mind starting to clear but still clouded by waves of fight-or-flight chemicals.

It felt so real, just like it had that day in Chicago. The cold wind. The boom of Stratton's voice calling her onto the stage.

The tens of thousands cheering her in one endless roar.

"I'll...I'll be just outside."

O'Dell turned for the door, and Maggie caught his sleeve before she could stop herself.

"No...stay. Please."

Her voice was hoarse. O'Dell turned back, and her gaze traveled up his broad chest, past his swollen shoulders, and into those deep, dark eyes. He wore his work uniform, minus the jacket. His Secret Service–issued Glock 19 was still strapped to his hip alongside his government ID.

Maggie wore nothing but a nightgown, but she didn't care. She slid her hand down his arm to his fingers, tugging softly. Knowing somehow, deep in her gut, that she was crossing an invisible boundary she might immediately regret.

And just not caring.

"Stay with me," she whispered.

O'Dell's fingers intertwined with hers. She saw uncertainty in his face, and his lip trembled, just a little. He glanced self-consciously toward the door. Maggie tugged a little harder.

"Nobody will know," she whispered.

O'Dell slid slowly onto the bed next to her. It creaked with his muscled bulk, and Maggie felt something hot ignite in her stomach. Something like a dormant volcano—a force of nature that had lain dormant for years.

Yet somehow she always knew it was there.

Maggie traced O'Dell's arm up to the elbow, staring into his eyes. She didn't blink. O'Dell's lips parted, and she noted a trickle of sweat creeping down his neck.

Taking his hand in hers, she guided his fingers to her shoulder and gently nudged the nightgown's strap aside. It fell, carrying her neckline with it, and O'Dell inhaled. The pulse in his wrist quickened as his left hand glided up her thigh.

"Maggie," he whispered.

"James."

And then he kissed her. Pulling her close, his mouth against hers. Aching pain and burning desire colliding in her gut all at once as the two of them fell into a tangled mess on the sheets, all moving hands and pressing lips and falling clothes.

A dormant volcano. Finally erupting.

30

Puerto Pedernales, Venezuela

Wolfgang wasn't used to being sidelined. Actually, he wasn't used to working on a team at all. Save for a small handful of missions with Reed—almost all of which had gone sideways—it had been almost a decade since Wolfgang had regularly operated as a member of a unit.

Even then, he was never parked in the rear, relegated to something as trivial as getaway driver. The humiliation of his predicament was mostly self-inflicted, he knew, but he couldn't help the burning in his gut. The irate irritation at yet again falling short of being useful.

Rotating the radio handset on his fake knee, Wolfgang listened to the chatter of the rain on the Land Cruiser's roof and watched the trails of water washing across the windshield. It was humid with the air conditioning off, but he didn't want to waste gas. He had no idea how long Reed would be, and the fuel gauge had dropped beneath half a tank.

Back in Venezuela.

Wolfgang never thought he'd return to South America. It was only a few hundred miles to the west of here, deep in the Colombian mountains, where Wolfgang had lost his leg—and nearly his life. Reed had come through for him on that mission, establishing a brotherhood loyalty that pulled Wolfgang into the Prosecution Force when the quasi-official black ops team was born. But Wolfgang never imagined it would be this way—sitting in the mud and rain, phantom pain racing up his thigh, feeling worthless.

Maybe he should have stayed in New York.

Tilting the seat back a notch, Wolfgang relaxed his body and momentarily surveyed the MRE spilled across the console. He was still hungry... but not quite hungry enough. He turned back to the windshield and measured a long breath.

In and out. Ignoring the phantom pain. The only way to defeat it.

A clap of thunder rippled overhead, melding with the patter of rain. The Cruiser shook just a little, water droplets dancing on the windshield.

But the thunder didn't fade. It continued, a perpetual thumping beat that grew a little louder by the second.

Wolfgang squinted, sitting upright and tilting his head to look upward through the windshield. He caught the underbelly of the chopper only a millisecond before it rocketed overhead, sending a hurricane blast of rotor wash ripping through the trees around him, its tail marked by a single blinking light.

Then it was gone, shooting eastward over the top of the Cruiser. Toward the port.

Wolfgang lifted the radio and keyed the mic.

"Wolf to Prosecutor, over."

No answer. Wolfgang gave Reed five seconds, figuring he might be dug into the mud, focused on something. Maybe not within easy reach of the radio.

"Wolf to Prosecutor, over."

Another five seconds. Then ten.

A crackling voice finally answered, distorted and broken by distance.

"Wolf...Rocky Top...signal...over."

It was Turk's voice matched with Turk's call sign, but that was about all Wolfgang could discern.

"Wolf to Rocky Top. Be advised, unidentified chopper inbound on your location, flying low. Over."

No answer. Wolfgang gritted his teeth and inspected the handset. It was old, like everything the CIA had given them. He checked the rechargeable battery pack and confirmed the connection.

Everything looked good.

"Wolf to Rocky Top, confirm inbound chopper. Over."

Dead silence. Then the headlights broke around a bend in the road, barely a hundred yards ahead of Wolfgang's position. He shrank instinctively into the seat, his hand dropping to the 10mm resting on his lap as the vehicle topped a hill and descended toward his position.

It was a heavy-duty truck—American built, four-wheel drive, quad cab. Jet black with a brush guard and a winch. The bed was covered over by a camper shell, and mud exploded from the front tires as it hurtled down the road like the driver owned the place.

There was no chance of hiding. Wolfgang had parked the Cruiser on the side of the road behind a patch of low undergrowth, but he hadn't taken it deeper into the trees for fear of getting stuck. The truck's headlights blazed across his windshield as the vehicle raced forward, and Wolfgang held his breath.

Keep driving. Keep driving.

The truck stopped. Ten yards out, high-beam headlights blinding him. Ten seconds passed, and nothing happened. Then the passenger-side doors popped open, and two men dressed in all-black tactical gear and carrying AK-type rifles stepped onto the road.

Great.

Wolfgang slid the Glock beneath the edge of his shirt, keeping his shoulders loose as the two men approached the vehicle, one standing back, the other taking point. An LED flashlight flicked on, sweeping across the Land Cruiser's front license plate before it pivoted to the windshield.

Wolfgang lifted a friendly hand, waving once.

The gunman kept one hand on the grip of his AK as he circled toward the driver's-side door. Wolfgang cranked the window down two inches, noting the second gunman standing directly ahead, his rifle held in low-ready.

Nobody else had exited the truck.

"*Estás perdido?*"

The man spoke in Spanish, but he wasn't Venezuelan. A hard face was matched with piercing blue eyes and light blond hair. He was Eastern European, Wolfgang was sure of it. Slavic of some kind.

"*No hablo español*," Wolfgang said.

The guy squinted, sudden suspicion crossing his face. "English? You are American?"

"I'm waiting for my friend," Wolfgang said, tapping the Cruiser's gauge cluster with one finger. "He went to find gas."

The flashlight pivoted to the gauge cluster.

"You have half tank," the gunman said.

"It's broken. Faulty gauge. You know how it is."

Wolfgang shrugged, offering a disarming smile. The guy wasn't buying it.

"Let me see papers."

"Papers? You mean my ID? Funny story, I lost my wallet last night. Too much rum, I guess."

Another relaxed laugh. The guy exchanged another look with his partner, then he swung the flashlight into the back seat.

"Open the trunk," he said.

Wolfgang conducted a quick mental inventory of what remained in the cargo area. Torn MRE wrappers and water bottles. Reed had taken all the weaponry. Right?

He hesitated. Then the radio lying in the console next to him crackled.

"Rocky Top to Wolf...comms difficulty on our end...confirm...over."

The gunman stiffened, then dropped the flashlight as his left arm moved to cradle the AK. The muzzle began to rise, and Wolfgang's gun hand darted from beneath the steering wheel. He swung his head beneath the dash as he lifted the Glock toward the gunman and opened fire.

31

Turk positioned himself in a shallow depression as Reed and Corbyn set off down the hill. With his SCAR propped up on his left arm, he had a clear field of fire across one entire side of the port, with moving targets ranging in distance from one to two hundred yards.

Easy pickings, with a good optic. The SCAR was equipped with an Trijicon ACOG—an excellent optic, but Turk didn't know how long it had been since that optic was sighted in, so he flipped the quick-release lever and opted for iron sights.

Within seconds, Reed and Corbyn were lost in the shadows, leaving Turk to enjoy the slow seep of rainwater saturating his clothes while muddy loam did the same from beneath him.

Good times.

"You guys do this often?" Stewie asked. He was stretched alongside Turk, eating strips of beef jerky from his pack. Turk liked beef jerky, but this stuff smelled like sour ass.

"Do what?" he asked, gently pivoting the rifle to inspect the untamed land surrounding the pier. On the far east side, total darkness consumed the landscape, with tall trees leaning out over the harbor right down to the water. There was a guard shack on their side of the inlet, with a small patrol boat of some kind tied up at a short pier. That arrangement was replicated on the far side of the bay, protecting the mouth of the port.

The port itself was relatively simple. Docks for four ships—three of them occupied—and a river beyond, spilling out of the jungle and into the ocean.

It would be a tranquil little spot, minus all the needless noise and clutter.

"Covert ops," Stewie said. "I assume you work for SAC."

Turk didn't answer. He kept sweeping the rifle, marking Reed's position behind a stretch of low undergrowth at the base of the hill.

"You a Falcons fan also?" Stewie asked.

"Titans," Turk grunted.

"A Tennessee man! That's cool. Born there? Got a family?"

"What the hell is this, twenty questions?" Turk growled. "Chill, dude."

Stewie shrugged, gnawing on another strip of jerky. "Just trying to pass the time. We don't get a lot of company down here."

"So it seems."

Turk adjusted his position, keeping his finger ready just above the trigger as Reed knelt in the darkness, extending his rifle toward the port.

What the hell.

Reed fired. His muzzle spat flame, but Turk barely heard the shot over the din of the port. A hundred yards away, the propane tank on the back of a forklift ruptured, followed almost immediately by a cascade of white rice exploding from a falling pallet. Security guards stationed around that half of the port turned toward the commotion, and Reed and Corbyn dashed from the shadows.

Turk smirked.

A dull crackle sounded from the radio next to him. He kept his trigger hand wrapped around the SCAR's grip while retrieving the handset from his side. Wolfgang's voice was garbled as it filtered through the tiny speaker. Turk caught only one clear word.

"...Prosecutor..."

Turk keyed his mic. "Wolf, this is Rocky Top. Your signal is FUBAR. Confirm you've got me. Over."

The radio fell silent. Wolfgang didn't reply.

"Our equipment is a little outdated," Stewie said apologetically.

"No joke." Turk hit the mic again. "Rocky Top to Wolf. Comms check. Over."

Long pause. Then Turk felt something in the base of his skull. A distant but persistent throbbing. Like soft thunder. Or...

"—inbound chopper—"

Wolfgang's transmission came through as a mere fragment, but it was all Turk needed to hear. He pivoted instinctually toward the sky just in time for the throb to become a pound, and then a small black helicopter burst out of the clouds. Flying low with its landing gear deployed, it beat back the rain and glided downward, ripping straight for Reed's position along its final approach.

Turk didn't bother reaching for the radio. Reed and Corbyn were already taking cover as the chopper flashed overhead. The bird beat a path onward, streaking for a cluster of office buildings built at the back of the port. The edge of a helipad was visible just beyond it—a detail Turk hadn't noticed before.

"No way," Stewie hissed. He was propped up on his elbows now, binoculars held to his face as he traced the aircraft's progress toward the helipad. "That's Moreno's bird!"

Stewie pried his gaze away from the binoculars, turning disbelieving eyes on Turk.

Turk was no longer concerned about the chopper. Reed and Corbyn were now busy accessing the rusty orange shipping container—Reed covering Corbyn with his SCAR while the Brit snapped pictures with a phone.

But unbeknownst to both of them, two of the black-clad gunmen were marching straight toward their position, circling in from the nearest container ship, only seconds from spotting them both.

"Rocky Top to Prosecutor! Tangos inbound. Repeat, two tangos inbound at five o'clock. How copy?"

No answer. Turk's pulse rose a notch, and he repeated the transmission. The radio didn't so much as chirp.

"What is this crap?" he snarled, slinging the radio toward Stewie before bringing the SCAR into his shoulder. He flicked the selector to semiautomatic, finding the front sight post inside the rear ghost ring and drawing a long breath.

A hundred yards. Maybe a hundred and ten.

Absolute child's play.

"Come on, Reed..."

Corbyn was shutting the crate. Reed was sweeping the perimeter, still ready with his rifle.

But he'd never see the gunmen. Not until it was too late.

Turk laid a finger on the trigger.

32

Corbyn was even better at sneaking than sass, sliding into high gear and leading the way down the hillside with catlike grace. Reed hurried to keep up, running heavy with the pack on his back and the SCAR slung over his chest. They made a crisscross pattern down the vegetation-infested slope, working gradually westward toward a shadowy portion of the port farthest away from the nearest ship.

Corbyn slid on her side into concealment behind a gnarled bush as Reed panted in behind her, crouching and keeping his rifle at the ready. The steady rain continued, fully saturating them both, but at least there was no longer any need for the night vision. The stadium lights that illuminated the port were glaringly bright, but they all pointed inward. From fifty yards away in the thick darkness, Reed had a clear view of the path ahead while remaining completely concealed from the gunmen pacing the perimeter of the port. The nearest ship loomed out of the water, tied off to the dock and groaning as its built-in crane lowered yet another container toward the pier, where a four-legged mechanism on wheels waited to cart it toward the rail lines.

The din of noise was now overwhelming. Grinding motors, clanging metal, and a constant chorus of shouting voices, all in Spanish. Reed could have fired off a gun, and nobody would have heard it.

Corbyn retrieved her binoculars from her belt pack and commenced sweeping the port again.

"What are you doing?" Reed said.

"Video."

Reed used his own binos to survey the containers. Not all were marked by Lenkov plates, but as he inspected the ship itself, he saw Lenkov's logo spray-painted on the near side of the superstructure.

This was a Lenkov show, no doubt. But what was Belsky shipping in such great quantities into Venezuela? And why?

"I want to look inside one of them," Reed said.

"Me too. How about the orange one, there?"

Corbyn pointed to where a stack of containers sat together, waiting to be loaded onto rail cars. The nearest was painted rusty orange, its secured doors drenched in shadow by the shelter of the others. They sat about eighty yards away, on the far side of a ten-foot fence. Not an easy target, but after crossing the clearing and circumventing the fence, plenty of concealment waited for them on the other side.

At least until the rail car crane removed that concealment. The orange crate was maybe sixth in line, and the crane moved methodically. Fifteen minutes?

"There's a gap in the fence, just opposite that light pole." Corbyn pointed again, and Reed marked the spot. A sixty-yard dash through bright stadium lights. They'd need a distraction.

Sweeping his gaze back to the right, Reed searched the pier, looking past a trio of gunmen in all black to an open crate set by itself at the end of a concrete pier. A small forklift ran in and out of the crate, a Venezuelan driver unloading pallets marked in bold, black Spanish.

Dry foods, Reed thought. Supplies for the longshoremen.

"Get ready," he whispered.

Shouldering the SCAR, he flicked the selector to semiautomatic and exhaled slowly. There was an Aimpoint sight affixed to the top of the weapon, but Reed had left it turned off, deploying the flip-up ghost ring sights instead. As disappointing as the rest of their CIA-issued gear had been, he didn't want to rely on an optic that might not have been calibrated in years. Iron sights, even flip-ups, were more reliable.

"What are you doing?" Corbyn hissed.

"'Murican stuff," Reed whispered. Then he pressed the trigger.

The SCAR spat a steel-core bullet with a loud crack, barely audible amid the clamor of the port. The green-tipped round sliced across the open water and collided with the exposed side of the forklift's propane fuel tank, resulting in an immediate rupture. A cloud of propane exploded into the air and the forklift stopped, the driver knocking a control lever as he bailed out. The pallet he'd been moving hit the ground, and white rice exploded across the pier as all three of the black-clad gunmen pivoted toward the commotion.

"Go!" Reed hissed, smacking Corbyn on the shoulder. The two of them jumped the low brush line and hurtled across the gravel lot to the fence. Pivoting to run along it, Reed stretched his long legs to keep up with Corbyn's aggressive sprint, noticing a lopsided jerk to her every stride, coinciding with her left foot striking the ground.

They reached the gap in the fence and ducked through, not bothering to look back as they broke for the container. It was all or nothing now.

Corbyn completed another home-plate slide at the orange crate, biting back a grunt. Then Reed landed beside her on his knees.

"You good?" he asked.

"Brilliant," she muttered, casting a glance over one shoulder. Reed looked back also, but nobody chased after them. A chorus of shouts rang from the pier with the wounded forklift, but all else appeared business as usual.

"What happens when they identify a bullet hole in that propane tank?" Corbyn said.

"I aimed for the weld line. Shouldn't look like a bullet hole."

Corbyn shook her head, pulling herself to her feet. "Bloody Yanks."

The metallic slam of a container landing on a rail car boomed across the port. Reed peered between the stacked containers to see longshoremen unchaining the crane in preparation for another lift.

"Let's go," he hissed.

Corbyn clicked her flashlight on, using her phone to snap pictures of the end of the crate before she consulted the latch. The container wasn't locked, but there was a metal security tie in place with a date tag written in Cyrillic.

"Have to break it," Reed said. "Stand back."

Corbyn slid aside, and Reed pressed the muzzle of the SCAR through the gap in the security tie. The thin wire snapped with only gentle pressure against the rifle. The tie fell away, and Corbyn wrestled the latch open while Reed remained on lookout.

Corbyn shoved the latch upward and moved to tug it free, then froze.

"What's that?" she said.

"What?" Reed checked his six. Nothing there.

"You don't feel it?"

"Feel what?"

A light clicked on behind Corbyn's gaze, and she flattened herself against the container.

"Chopper! Get down."

The vibrations in the concrete registered with Reed's mind just as Corbyn called for him to take cover. He hadn't heard the aircraft. He could barely hear himself think amid the chaos of the port, but only moments after he ducked, the bird roared overhead, barely a hundred feet off the ground, all black and sleek. It was a Eurocopter of some kind—an executive transport, with wheels instead of skids.

Moreno's chopper.

Reed recognized it from earlier that day, but almost before the thought could register, the chopper was gone, racing toward the back of the port beyond the office buildings.

Reed's mind descended into temporary deadlock, thrown off by the unexpected aircraft. Why hadn't Turk radioed him? And more importantly —why was Moreno here?

It didn't matter. Not right now. They were almost out of time.

"Move!" he called.

Corbyn was already back on her feet, tugging the door open. An overwhelming stench of heavy grease wafted out almost as quickly as her flashlight blazed in, spilling light over the container's contents.

Pipe. *Lots* of pipe. Thick walled, black, about eight inches in diameter, stacked inside roughhewn wooden carriages and strapped to the inside walls of the container.

Corbyn frowned, and Reed made a rolling motion with one hand.

"Take pictures! We've got to roll."

Corbyn went to work on the pictures, and Reed lifted his radio.

"Prosecutor to Rocky Top. Wrapping up down here. Advise about aircraft and new arrivals, over."

No answer. Corbyn moved to close the crate, and Reed smacked the radio against the side of the SCAR.

"Prosecutor to Rocky Top, come in. Over."

Still no answer. Reed checked the handset. The digital screen glowed green, displaying the preselected shortwave channel and a battery charge readout, but when he cranked the volume up and pressed the key, no sound signaled the transmission.

Great.

"Comms down," Reed hissed. "Let's—"

"*Ruki vverkh!*" A cold male voice cut Reed off from somewhere to his left. He pivoted in that direction, already raising the SCAR.

Turk got there first.

From a hundred yards up the hillside, a flash of orange marked Turk's position, the gunshot rendered almost inaudible by the clamor of dockside machinery. The oncoming gunman went down, his head exploding like a falling melon. Turk's rifle spat fire again, and the next guy toppled around the corner, spilling an AK and grasping at his neck as blood sprayed like a geyser.

"Go! Go! Go!" Reed pushed Corbyn and flipped his SCAR to full auto.

33

Chaos erupted across the port in mere seconds. Reed pivoted around the line of containers, opening fire into the faces of another two gunmen racing toward the sound of battle. The sixty-yard sprint across open gravel to the gap in the fence now looked like a suicide route, with additional shouts ringing from their right, in the direction of the rail lines.

"This way!" Reed called, turning back toward the containers and ducking into a narrow alley between them. Corbyn pressed in close behind him, her SIG drawn, her body relaxed. No hint of alarm invaded her calm eyes, and that reassured Reed a little. If he was going to be stuck down here getting shot at, at least he was stuck alongside somebody with guts.

Kneeling at the edge of the alley, Reed watched as a dozen more black-suited men with AKs stormed by, running toward the office buildings where the chopper had landed. They ran in tight formation, shoulder to shoulder, rifles held at high-ready.

Not the stance of men expecting to come under fire. Reed counted the shots in his head and figured he'd fired maybe six times—plus Turk's two. A lot of noise, even under the mask of clanging crates and throbbing engines. Clearly, port security knew something was wrong, but save for those unlucky bastards who stumbled upon Reed and Corbyn, nobody knew exactly what.

"Can you swim?" Reed asked.

Corbyn kept her back against a crate as she cast frequent glances behind her. "Well enough. What's your play?"

Reed pointed ahead, behind two of the three container ships to where the river spilled into the harbor. It was maybe thirty yards wide, inky and dark, with a slow current pressing out to sea.

"Make it to the river, get under the dock. Then drift out to sea. Once we're well outside the harbor, we'll circle back to shore and rendezvous with the team."

Corbyn looked over her shoulder again—still thinking about a mad dash up that hill, Reed thought. A quick retreat to her original plan of escape.

She hadn't been doing this very long.

"You'll never make it up that hill," Reed said. "It's an open field of fire, fully illuminated. And they're looking for us now. Best shot—"

A shout cut him off—a shout in Russian, from directly behind them. Corbyn turned, and Reed heard boots hit the ground. Then a gunman appeared in the alley gap, silhouetted by the stadium lights, facing away from them. Corbyn raised her SIG, but Reed clamped a hand over her arm, holding a finger to his lips.

The gunman called to somebody out of sight, his back still facing them. More shouts accompanied more boots. Reed held his breath, not daring to move. Sweat dripped down Corbyn's face, and the muzzle of her weapon trembled. The gunman looked at his feet, kicking at bloody gravel. Following the trail.

Then he looked right at them.

Great.

Corbyn opened fire like a kid on their first turkey shoot. Five rounds of 9mm tore through the guy's exposed neck and face, just above his body armor. He toppled backward in a spray of blood, and Reed yanked her arm.

"So much for stealth. Let's go!"

They broke out of the end of the alley, dashing frantically for cover behind the crane parked next to the rail lines. Rifles cracked and heavy rounds ricocheted off the crane, whistling through the air like death hornets as Reed scrambled for cover behind the rear wheel. He pivoted around the tire and opened fire beneath the crane, spraying hot lead back down the alley. Screams were accompanied by silenced guns, but then Reed heard a shout from someplace high overhead—the bow of the nearest container ship.

He rolled and raised the SCAR, then watched the guy's head explode under another crack shot from the ridgeline.

Nearly two hundred yards—now Turk was just showing off.

"On your feet! To the river!"

He grabbed Corbyn by the arm and yanked her forward. The river was another hundred yards, and between them and the welcome water lay a field of pallets, small crates, and coiled anchor chains. The longshoremen were long gone now, clearing out in a panicked horde as heavily armed security closed in from the office buildings—dozens of them. Twice as many as Reed had initially observed, all wielding AK-12s and dressed in full body armor.

And they weren't just gunmen—they were mercenaries. Reed knew the look. No flags or precise cohesion to their uniforms. No regulation to their personal grooming. Long hair, beards, tattoos...guns for hire.

Rifles cracked and bullets bit concrete as Reed led the way from cover to cover, sliding in behind a pile of heavy anchor chain and rolling onto his stomach to return fire. The SCAR chattered in short, three-round bursts, unleashed more green-tipped hell into the faces of two more mercenaries pushing their luck and not diving for cover. Reed took his time, keeping his breaths measured as he moved from target to target.

Then the SCAR locked back on empty, and for the tenth time that night, Reed cursed Harris. Bad binoculars, broken radios...and only two mags per gun.

Reed dumped the magazine and slammed in his single reload, then crumpled behind the heavy chain as a storm of whistling lead ripped overhead, pinging off the chain and spinning toward the bow of the freighter. Corbyn lay next to him, rolling out from time to time to return fire with her SIG. She was on her second magazine also, and blood ran from a bullet graze on her right arm.

Reed attempted to roll left to get a few shots off, but the oncoming fire was too intense. The mercenaries were shooting without regard for damage of port property, dumping hundreds of rounds per minute on the two intruders dug in behind the heap of chain. There wasn't even time for Reed to lead another dash for the next point of cover—a shipping container, resting halfway between their current position and the river.

And then what? There would never be time to drift out to sea. The belt of mercenaries was closing in.

"That hill's not looking so bad now, is it?" Corbyn snarled.

Reed looked to the ridgeline, hoping to see orange starlight marking Turk's participation in the fight—for what good it would do. But he saw nothing. The ridge was dark, and the thunder of AK-12s was deafening.

They were cornered.

34

From the ridgeline, Turk watched as Reed and Corbyn vanished into the alleyway between stacks of shipping containers. The four mercenaries they left in their wake lay bleeding out on the gravel, rifles strewn around them. An alarm sounded from someplace near the core of the port, where the helicopter had landed. The longshoremen were fleeing like a tide of ants all scurrying for their hill while a new wave of black-clad gunmen jogged toward the piers.

In layman's terms, the whole situation was going to hell in a handbasket.

"Try him again," Turk snapped, tossing the radio to Stewie. The CIA officer lay on his stomach, binoculars pressed to his eyes, surveying the unfolding chaos beneath him with a macabre fascination.

Shouldering the SCAR, Turk surveyed the illuminated space between Reed's alley and the gap in the fence. If Reed sprinted now, he might have a shot at making the fence line, but he'd almost certainly never reach concealment at the base of the hill. A fire team of four more mercenaries was moving up the length of containers from the direction of the nearest ship, cradling rifles and gaining speed as they spotted the bodies of their comrades.

Great.

Turk traced them with his SCAR, conscious of his limited ammunition and exposed position. He was concealed but not covered—too much muzzle flash, and he'd be a sitting duck.

"Come on, Reed..."

Stewie dropped the radio, shaking his head. "It's dead." The CIA officer returned to the binoculars, pivoting left toward the helicopter.

"More security coming in," he hissed. "Twenty...maybe twenty-five men. And wait...somebody is boarding the chopper. They're gonna take off again."

"Moreno?" Turk asked.

"Lord, no. This is some fat sucker. Long beard, huge gut."

Turk looked up from the rifle. "Where?"

Stewie pointed, passing him the binoculars. Turk focused on the spot, still cradling the rifle with his shooting hand.

"I'll be damned," he whispered.

"What? Who is it?"

Turk tossed the binoculars as the chopper spun to life. Pivoting to the port, he laid a finger on the trigger as the lead man stopped at the first body. An instant alarm overtook the small crowd, and Turk saw hands reach for radios.

Not good.

"What now?" Stewie hissed.

"You believe in God?" Turk asked.

"Not really."

"Pray anyway."

The mercenaries fell into a diamond formation, rifles pointed outward as they proceeded down the length of containers. The lead man crossed the mouth of the alley Reed and Corbyn had disappeared behind, and Turk rested his front sight post over the guy's neck.

But he didn't fire. The mercenary was faced away from Reed. Turk waited.

"They're coming in from the left!" Stewie said.

Turk broke focus, just for a moment. He looked left and saw the two dozen men Stewie had identified streaming toward the ships like an oncoming tidal wave, leading with their rifles and moving from cover to cover.

Then he heard gunshots.

Snapping his gaze back to the alleyway, Turk saw the mercenary go down in a spray of red. Then Reed and Corbyn appeared from the opposite end, dashing for cover behind a heap of oversized anchor chain. Gunfire erupted on all sides, orange muzzle flash blinking across the port like crazed Christmas lights. Reed and Corbyn made cover behind the chain and briefly returned fire.

But it was no use. By accident or bad luck, they had run straight into a dead end.

Turk swung his rifle up and picked off a gunman at the bow of the nearest container ship, splitting his skull open and sending his rifle toppling toward the pier. Then he swept his gaze down the length of the port.

Searching.

"We've got to go!" Stewie said. "There's no saving them now. Get back to the Cruiser and contact Langley."

Turk snorted, ignoring him. He'd already worked his way up the port, all the way to the helipad. The helicopter was gone now, as were the longshoremen. But there was no escape that way. Far too many enemy combatants lay dug in behind effective cover, keeping Reed's and Corbyn's backs to the empty ocean.

"Did you hear me?" Stewie snapped. "We've got to split!"

"You know why you've never heard of us?" Turk shouted, sudden anger shattering his disciplined cool. "Because we don't *exist*. Got it? We're expendable! We leave them here now, and we leave them to die."

He twisted right, tracing the port the other way. Beyond the ships. Down the edge of the harbor, to the little guard shack clinging to the hillside.

And that patrol boat.

Jumping to his feet, Turk abandoned his pack, taking only his spare magazine.

"Come on," he snapped.

Stewie stumbled to follow, fumbling with his gear. "Where are we going?"

"Upriver," Turk said. "We're about to get wet."

35

"What now?" Corbyn shouted.

Her arm was coated in a thin sheen of crimson, her body pressed close to Reed. The hail of gunfire had subsided a little, but every few seconds Reed stole a couple shots off the top of the chain pile—just enough to keep the line of mercenaries from advancing.

Until he ran out of ammo, anyway. Which wouldn't be long. He guessed he had maybe ten rounds left, plus whatever good his SIG could do. Then they would be dead or captured. No other option. Turk might have made it back to the Land Cruiser, where he and Wolfgang could strategize a rescue, but Reed wasn't banking on it.

"On my signal, you dash for the river," Reed said, spraying rain from his lips. "I'll run back for the containers and draw their fire."

"Are you looney?"

"Get under the dock and see if you can drift out into the harbor. Stay low to the water and swim hard."

"I'm not splitting on you. On my count, we both go for the river."

Reed bit back a curse. "We'll never make it if—"

Another barrage of gunfire rang off the anchor chain. A stray ricochet bit Reed's forearm, ripping through his sleeve before whistling into the night. Rolling out, he unleashed a three-round burst before ducking for cover again.

The mercenaries were getting close. Barely thirty yards now.

"We'll never make it without drawing fire!" he finished. "I know what I'm doing. Now get your ass off the ground and—"

Corbyn held up a hand, her wide eyes fixated on the river. The second container ship blocked their view of the open harbor, but as a momentary break in fire rendered temporary quiet, Reed heard it too.

A boat engine. A *big* boat engine, howling in from the harbor, racing toward their exposed side. And then he heard another sound—a sound that never ceased to turn his stomach, no matter the context.

Heavy machine gun fire.

"Get down!"

He grabbed Corbyn by the shoulders and pinned her down, flattening himself against the chain and wriggling to put as much cover between himself and the river as possible. It was a useless effort—he knew that even as chain links bit into his back. Heavy slugs raced up the concrete pier, sending clouds of disorienting dust exploding into the air while those bullets zipped ever closer toward their targets, and Reed knew he was screwed. He was screwed, and so was Corbyn. But it was his fault. He should have risked the hillside from the start.

Reed closed his eyes and thought of Banks. Thought of that heart-piercing moment when the only woman he'd ever loved walked out of their little home, his son riding alongside her.

Everything he had in the world, vanishing in an instant. For what? For *this*? For his own meat-headed insistence on dropping into hellholes to be shot at?

What was he *thinking*?

Hot anger boiled in his stomach, and Reed's eyes snapped open. He shouldered the rifle, pointing it toward the river. Ready to take somebody with him. Ready to eat the consequences of his own moronic foolishness.

Then the boat burst around the end of the container ship, spinning in mid-water, the bow-mounted machine gun blazing hellfire across the port.

But not at him.

Reed's heart lurched as he watched tracer rounds rip across the concrete piers, shredding into the ranks of mercenaries as screams tore the air. The boat was some kind of small patrol vessel, built with a heavy outboard motor hanging off the back and the fifty-caliber machine gun mounted on a swivel up front. Stewie stood behind the center console controls, guiding the vessel straight toward the pier.

And Rufus Turkman stood behind the machine gun, dumping five hundred rounds a minute into the dug-in ranks of mercenaries.

"Go! Go!" Reed yanked Corbyn by her bloody arm. They both sprang across the pier, heedless of their exposed sides as they raced for the river. Reed didn't bother to leapfrog from the anchor chain to the shipping container—he broke straight for the boat, knowing Turk's ammo supply wouldn't last much longer at his present rate of fire. Pot shots from the mercenaries whistled by their heads as the boat slammed into the pier and bounced immediately away. Stewie struggled with the controls, beckoning them on while the fifty cal thundered louder than Moreno's chopper.

Reed pushed Corbyn from behind, and they both dove headlong into the boat. The vessel rocked violently as they landed, gliding back from the pier. Stewie screamed, and blood sprayed across Reed's face. He saw the CIA officer go down, clutching his thigh as more blood gathered on the boat's floor. The chugging of the machine gun slowed, breaking into short bursts now as waves of heat from the weapon washed backward over the boat.

"Get us out of here!" Turk shouted.

Reed scrambled to his knees, reaching for the controls. Bullets shattered the meager glass windshield and pinged off the control panel. He found the throttle and snatched it open, yanking the wheel to the right. The boat banked hard and tore through the black water, headed upriver as Turk pivoted on his feet to keep the fifty cal pointed toward the port. Hot wind swept past Reed's face as he yanked the vessel back to the left just in time to avoid an overhanging tree limb. The hulking black mass of the submarine raced by to their left—oh, it was Russian, all right. Surrounded by a heavy fence and more armed guards. Whistling lead perforated the air, and everything stunk of gunpowder and blood.

The machine gun went silent, and Turk dropped into cover beneath the gunwales.

Reed kept driving, plowing straight ahead into the inky blackness as the Venezuelan jungle swallowed them whole.

36

Washington, DC

Stratton left his Tahoe at the curb, accompanied by two black-suited Secret Service agents as he pushed through frosted-glass doors into the restaurant. Built in the seventies as a French bistro and undergoing numerous rebrandings and rebirths over the next four decades, The Capital Social no longer identified as a French restaurant. It didn't even serve French food, but it was easily Stratton's favorite place in DC.

A little pretentious, maybe. An odd sort of dusky decor with a gold-trimmed bar, foggy mirrors, and crimson carpet underlaying a multi-leveled dining room. Some might call it dated, or even a little grungy. But the food was delicious, the atmosphere calm. And best of all, the doors were always open.

At two a.m. after a long, brutal day, in search of a quiet nook to enjoy a good meal and a private conversation, Stratton could think of no better place.

The maître d' greeted Stratton by name—another touch he appreciated—then guided him in person to his favorite table, a booth in a dark corner where he could sit with his back to the wall and remain undisturbed for the duration of his meal. With the Social being an established favorite of so many politicians and lobbyists, the *undisturbed* part was crucial.

"May I take your drink order, Mr. Vice President?"

"The usual, please. And a water."

"Of course, sir."

Stratton's bodyguards took a table fifteen feet away, ordering coffee and remaining relaxed but alert while he scanned the menu. Not that he needed to—he always ordered the same thing. Filet mignon, with one skewer of grilled shrimp, a side of asparagus, and a half slice of chocolate cake. Perfection.

The maître d' returned with his drink—Pappy Van Winkle, twelve year, neat—and Stratton settled into the booth. He was two sips in when his dinner guest arrived. Tall and lean, dressed in a simple black suit with a deep blue tie and no flag pin, the guy stopped to be patted down by Stratton's bodyguards before proceeding to the table.

"Mr. Vice President." He ducked his head.

Stratton gestured for him to be seated, not bothering with a greeting. He'd known Sam Hyler—formerly *Special Agent* Sam Hyler—for nearly twenty years. His personal contact at the PPI. His bloodhound with a nose the size of Texas, capable of sniffing out the truth almost anywhere, given enough time.

Even in DC.

"Good evening, monsieurs." A server appeared with a polite smile, clutching a notepad. Despite the Social's long disassociation with French cuisine, the vernacular remained.

"Would you like to order an appetizer?"

"I'll have the usual," Stratton said, surrendering his menu.

"Just water for me," Hyler said, his voice croaking with the rasp of a heavy smoker, which he was. That was part of the reason he lost his special agent title, all those years ago. Not for the cigarettes so much as the black tar heroin. Hyler had been an addict at one time, and might still indulge in heavier recreations than nicotine, but he had shaken the heroin habit, and he was such a good investigator that Stratton didn't care what he smoked in his free time.

The server departed, and Stratton placed his finger over the top of his water straw, drawing a few drops of filtered water and depositing them into his Pappy, followed by a gentle shake of the glass and a long sip.

The water neutralized the bite beautifully while preserving the flavor. Stratton thought he could drink an entire bottle.

"I reviewed the files," Stratton said.

"You have questions?" Hyler asked, all business as always.

Stratton did have questions. A lot of them, most of which Hyler couldn't possibly hope to answer. But he decided to start someplace simple.

"You didn't include an executive summary with your findings packet," Stratton said. "Why not?"

Hyler indulged in an uncharacteristic smile, short-lived and very dry. "Do I really need to answer that?"

"I didn't hire you simply to dig up the facts," Stratton said. "I value your interpretation."

Hyler looked away. He drummed one finger on the table and shifted uncomfortably.

"It's a delicate issue," he said at last.

"Which part?"

"The entire thing. You asked me to investigate connections between Harold Cunningham and Lenkov International. And Lenkov International is owned by Stepan Belsky, an exiled Russian oligarch who is currently being hunted by the Bureau."

"Is that right?" Stratton played it cool. Hyler grunted.

"With respect, Mr. Vice President. I earn my money. I still have contacts in the Bureau. They keep me fed."

"And what are those contacts telling you now?"

Hyler shrugged. "That they aren't the only ones looking for Belsky. The Agency has an interest. So does Homeland...and the White House."

Hyler finished the sentence by looking Stratton dead in the eye. Stratton didn't blink.

"I don't know why you'd include us on an investigation into the president's attempted assassination," Hyler said. "Seems like the Bureau has you covered. But the connection between Cunningham and Lenkov is outlined in the documents I sent you. I'll leave those facts to your own interpretation."

Stratton sipped bourbon. The server came with a tray of bread and Hyler's water. When she left, Stratton leaned across the table.

"I'm not asking you to point fingers, Hyler. That's my job. I'm asking you if Cunningham is in bed with Lenkov."

Hyler tore into a piece of bread, chewing slowly. "Did you read the documents?"

"What I could understand. It's a lot of legalese and accounting—all Greek to me. Hence why I typically rely on your executive summary."

Hyler swallowed bread. He nodded slowly.

"They're in bed together," he said at last.

"How deep?"

"Deeper than an English teacher and his eleventh-grade student—and just as covert."

"What are they up to?"

Hyler sighed. "I'm still digging into that. It seems to be some manner of highly complex crude oil deal. A lot of refinement and exportation agreements. But the weird part is..."

"What?" Stratton pressed. Hyler shrugged.

"Well. The volumes are huge. Off the charts. Cunningham Enterprises is negotiating the purchase of just over a billion barrels over the next three years. Lenkov doesn't have the oil fields to fill that order—not even close. They couldn't fill half of it."

"You dug into Lenkov's oil holdings?"

"We dug into everything," Hyler said flatly. "Lenkov is peddling goods they don't hold. And Cunningham must know it."

"Is it possible they're negotiating the sale of something else? Using oil as a stand-in for some type of black-market deal?"

Hyler shrugged. "Now you're asking me to speculate. That's not my area of expertise. I'm simply reporting the facts."

Stratton pondered, surveying the handful of late-night patrons gathered to eat. In the back of his skull, a dull pounding heralded the presence of an oncoming headache. Something he probably deserved, skipping this much sleep and drinking this much alcohol. It had been only three months since he won election on Maggie's ticket, but he felt five years older. And looked it, too.

"Why isn't the FBI looking into this?" Hyler said. "If Cunningham is somehow involved with Lenkov in an illicit way—"

"Use your head, Hyler," Stratton cut him off. "My family are longtime buddies with the Cunninghams."

"You're trying to shield them?"

Stratton snorted. "Harold? Please. I wouldn't piss on the man if he were on fire."

The server brought Stratton's plate—the meal neatly arranged over gleaming china. He went for the steak first, slicing through rare meat that oozed a little blood when he sank his fork into it. It was cooked to perfection.

Hyler straightened, finishing his water. "I'll keep digging, Mr. Vice President. Let me know if there's something specific you'd like me to focus on."

He slid out of the booth. Stratton spoke through a bite of filet. "You said a billion barrels?"

"A little more, actually. A million a day, over three years."

Stratton chewed the rich meat, still fixated on his plate. Hyler ducked his head and stepped out, leaving him alone in the quiet booth.

But Stratton's mind wasn't quiet. It spun like a circus ride in high gear, all lights and noise and swirling surroundings.

A billion barrels.

Maybe it was something else—some other expensive commodity Cunningham felt the need to hide behind the shroud of an oil negotiation, but Stratton didn't think so. He thought it was exactly what it looked like—an economy-boosting mega load of black gold.

An earth-shattering fortune in the making. A kingmaking deal.

The kind of thing worth killing a president for.

37

Venezuela

The gunfire faded as the patrol boat roared into the jungle. Black water washed against the bow, and the sheet metal skin of the vessel shook with each turn up the curving waterway. The river was narrow, with low-hanging limbs trailing the water and leaving a pathway only about ten yards wide to navigate through. As Reed eased back on the throttle, he heard a soft scrape of sand and rock against the bottom of the boat and looked back to see muddy water kicked up by the propeller.

The river was growing rapidly shallow. It wouldn't be long before they were forced to ditch the boat altogether and return to the jungle.

"Everybody okay?" Turk appeared from the bow, his shirt clinging to his sweaty chest as he extended a fist toward Reed.

Reed bumped it, then tilted his head toward the back of the boat.

"Stewie's hit. Take over."

Turk accepted the controls, and Reed moved to the stern, kneeling next to the motor where Stewie was stretched out in a shallow pool of blood. He'd taken a round to his left thigh—a steel-core 5.45-millimeter slug, probably, the standard diet of an AK-12. It was a vicious and destructive round, capable of mass damage on impact.

Stewie was lucky—Reed felt an exit wound on the back of his leg as Corbyn wrapped her belt just above the wound and cinched down, her flashlight held in her teeth. Stewie grunted in agony, his face a little pale.

The blood flow subsided, and Corbyn tied off the belt.

"Enough whining," Reed said. "Damn Pats fans. Rough life without Brady, am I right?"

Stewie's eyes bulged. "This wasn't what I signed on for!"

Reed thumped his leg, and he cried out. "The bullet missed both your arteries and your femur. Count your blessings."

The boat shuddered as it scraped bottom again. Muddy water sprayed over the stern, and Turk worked the throttle. The motor surged into reverse, but the boat didn't move.

They were grounded.

"Time to bail," Turk said, looking over his shoulder. Reed traced his line of sight deep into the trees and wondered how far they had traveled. The boat moved at a good clip for much of their journey inland. Ten minutes? Fifteen?

Maybe a couple miles, and he already knew there weren't many roads serving this region.

"Was there another boat?" Reed asked.

"There was," Turk said, cutting the motor and retrieving his SCAR. "Not anymore. I hit it with the fifty on our way in."

"Hoorah," Reed grunted. "Nice job."

Corbyn took the flashlight out of her mouth, dropping the mag on her SIG. Reed noted only four rounds remained as she slammed it back home, tucking the weapon into her belt-less pants.

"You Yanks sure know how to make a mess," she said. "Are we *trying* to kick off a world war?"

Turk was busy sifting through a locker built beneath the boat's steerage controls. He dumped out a tangle of old rope and a rusty machete before coming up with a first aid kit and a single bottle of water.

"Painkillers?" Stewie rasped.

"Sorry, bud," Turk said. "Painkillers thin your blood. Grin and bear it."

He passed Corbyn the bottle. She took only a sip before helping Stewie to swallow most of the rest. Reed finished the final gulp and tossed the bottle into the boat.

"We'll carry him," he said, slinging the SCAR over his shoulder. "Can you take point?"

Corbyn dropped out of the boat with the flashlight in one hand, the water rising up to her thighs. Sloshing through the tangle of tree branches, she led the way to a slick bank infested by tangled undergrowth. Reed and Turk followed, carrying Stewie high enough above the black water to keep his wound clean. Once the four of them were safely back on dry land, they set the wounded CIA officer on his back amid a nest of fallen leaves and took a moment to assess their situation.

Most of their equipment was gone. Between them, Reed and Turk had only thirty-five rounds remaining for the SCARs and a couple dozen 9mm cartridges to share with Corbyn and her SIG. Turk had brought one backpack, and Corbyn drew a handheld GPS from the cargo pocket of her pants. It was waterlogged but still operational, with a full battery.

One point for MI6 in the way of preparation. Reed was going to tear Harris a new one if they ever made it back to Caracas.

"I saw Belsky," Turk said. Reed's gaze snapped up from Corbyn's GPS, but the Brit appeared less impressed.

"Who now?" Corbyn said.

"Where?" Reed said.

"Getting into Moreno's chopper," Turk said. "He was headed for the port when the gunfire started—he got out pretty quick. But it was definitely him. Fat, hairy sucker."

"*Who* is Belsky?" Corbyn pressed.

"He's the man we came here to find," Reed said. "He owns Lenkov International."

"So all those shipping crates?"

"Right." Reed nodded.

"I thought you wanted the sub?"

"Only to find Belsky," Reed said. "We think he was smuggled into the country on board."

Reed wiped sweat from his forehead and looked back toward the river, listening intently. He still heard no sounds of approaching watercraft, but it would only be a matter of time.

"We've got to get back to Wolfgang," Reed said. "The Land Cruiser is still our fastest way back to Caracas. Stewie will need medical care."

"You think he's okay?" Turk said. "Wolf, I mean."

"He should be. He was well outside the action. Best bet, when the comms went down, he decided to wait it out. He may have heard the gunfire and relocated, but he'll wait a little longer for us. How far to the Cruiser?"

Corbyn fiddled with the GPS, inputting coordinates and waiting for it to compute.

"Eight klicks," she said. "Dense jungle, all the way."

Turk glanced down at Stewie. The CIA officer lay trembling on the ground, his eyes clamped closed. His face had washed pale, and a trickle of blood still oozed from his saturated pants leg.

"He won't make it," Turk said. "He's done."

"Should we put him down here?" Corbyn said, a faint smirk playing at the corners of her mouth.

Stewie's eyes snapped open. "*Put him down?* Like a dog? What's wrong with you people?"

Reed held up a hand. "Chill, hotshot. It's called morbid humor. You learn to enjoy it when you're being shot at." He gestured toward the jungle. "If we carry you, can you hang in there?"

"Do I have a choice?" Stewie spoke through gritted teeth.

"Not really."

"Then I'll make it. Stop asking stupid questions."

"That's the spirit," Reed said. "Turk, grab that machete and rope from the boat. We'll put a stretcher together and carry him that way. Corbyn, you'll have to take point."

Turk grunted an acknowledgment and waded back into the river. Corbyn lowered the GPS.

"What's your interest in this Russian?" she asked.

"Classified," Reed said simply.

Corbyn snorted. "Classified my ass. I'm the bloke with the GPS. I've earned a little transparency."

Reed measured her steady stare, noting the calm rise and fall of her chest with each breath. Despite the near-death experience, the gunfire, and the hectic boat ride, she remained perfectly cool.

Corbyn had experienced combat before. A lot of it. Not just an MI6 spook. She had been a soldier.

"Three months ago our president was shot," Reed said.

"Right..."

"Belsky hired the shooter."

Corbyn blinked. "Are you serious?"

"As a heart attack."

"So you're here to..."

"Extract him. By any means necessary."

38

Puerto Pedernales, Venezuela

Even through the thick metal walls of the shipping container, Wolfgang could hear the chaos consuming the port. Shouting voices, pounding feet. The grind of machinery and the perpetual clang of fresh containers landing on steel and concrete.

He could still smell the gunpowder in the air—a metric ton of it. Of course, he couldn't see when he was dragged out of the pickup truck and thrown in this box like a dead animal. The Russians had blindfolded him. But the stench of combat was as plain as a familiar signature—Reed Montgomery had been here. Things had gone sideways.

And they had not ended in the Russians' favor.

Just the thought of it brought a dull smirk to Wolfgang's aching face. His lips were swollen, and each breath sent slicing pain up and down his rib cage. The mercenaries had done a number on him after extracting him from the Land Cruiser. He shot one of them, crouching behind the dash as the second guy opened fire with his AK, blowing out the windshield in short order.

Wolfgang slid out of the open door and recovered the dead man's rifle.

The gunfire ceased, and he wormed his way to the front bumper, ready to engage.

And then he felt the sharp bite of an angled muzzle brake driving into his neck.

Apparently, three Russians had left the truck, not two. One of them had circled wide and come in from behind. A smart move. A move Wolfgang should have been ready for, but he was too hyped up on adrenaline and bloodthirst to care.

He *enjoyed* shooting that guy. He hadn't shot anyone in over a year—not since well before Collins had died. All the gathered rage boiled over into a double-tap to the face, literally blowing the mercenary's brains out as heavy 10mm cartridges tore through.

Even after they disarmed him, stripped his prosthetic leg away and spent ten minutes beating him with it, the anger remained like some kind of unholy fire burning deep in his gut. Wolfgang relished the pain. He *deserved* the pain. And the millisecond he was given an opportunity, he was going to return the favor—with interest.

Metal hinges groaned, and bright white light flooded the container as the door swung open. Wolfgang spat blood and looked away. He lay on his side, his hands hogtied to his single ankle, helpless to shield himself from whatever came next.

He didn't care.

Six legs appeared in front of him. Two pairs were black-clad, black-booted, with traces of blood gleaming on black leather. His blood, probably. The third pair of legs were stubby and thick, with loose black dress slacks and casual shoes bulging under the pressure of fat ankles.

They all three stank.

One guy spoke in Russian, toeing Wolfgang in the chin and rocking his head back. Wolfgang gritted his teeth and grinned into the blaze of a flashlight, his lips coated in blood.

The Russians held a short conference, then the light changed hands, and the guy in the slacks huffed forward. He squatted in front of Wolfgang, a bulging stomach riding atop thick thighs. Wolfgang smelled sweat and stale breath.

"*Who* are you?" the guy growled in accented English.

Wolfgang licked his teeth. "Wouldn't you like to know?"

His voice rasped, barely sounding human over a dry tongue. The fat guy shifted the light, pointing it against the wall to remove the glare. Wolfgang blinked his way back into focus. The fat guy morphed from an indistinguishable blur into a hairy brown blur, with a thick beard and a wide face.

Wolfgang laughed. "Well, look who it is. You know, we've been looking for you."

Belsky gritted his teeth, grabbing Wolfgang by the jaw and sinking his fingernails into unprotected skin. Wolfgang barely felt it.

"*Who* are you?" Belsky repeated.

"I'm really not supposed to say," Wolfgang hissed.

Belsky drove the flashlight hand across Wolfgang's face, smashing into his nose and driving his head against the metal floor. Wolfgang blinked, suddenly dazed. Gasping for breath, he managed a weak nod.

"Okay, okay. I'll talk."

Belsky wrenched his jaw around again. "What is your name?"

Wolfgang licked his lips. "Promise you won't tell?"

Belsky shook him, blasting his face with enraged spit. "Name!"

"The name is...Bond. J-James B-Bond."

Wolfgang could barely finish the sentence as he broke into a laugh. Belsky hurled him down, driving a sloppy kick into his exposed stomach. It hurt, but nothing like the heavy prosthetic leg had. Wolfgang kept laughing, tears streaming down his face as he curled into a fetal position.

Belsky turned to his men, snapping orders in Russian. One of them ran off while the other grabbed Wolfgang by the shoulders and hauled him up with a powerful heave.

Wolfgang's head rolled, blood and snot running down his face. He spat, still laughing like a demented drug addict.

"You know, if I were you," Wolfgang rasped, "I'd be hauling ass right now."

Belsky shoved the flashlight beneath Wolfgang's throat, closing his mouth and forcing his chin up.

"You laugh now, American. You will beg for death before we are finished with you."

Wolfgang blew saliva from his lip, managing another weak smile. "Promise?"

Belsky swore in Russian and drove his fist into Wolfgang's face. The world spun as Wolfgang's head snapped back, his body going limp. He was vaguely aware of the mercenary dragging him by one arm out of the container and across rough concrete. Another set of meaty hands grabbed his ankle and hoisted him off the ground, and then a bag was pulled over his head, thick and black.

It was difficult to breathe. Wolfgang felt his mind leaving him as the whine of a jet engine was joined by the blast of rotor wash.

He hit the ground again—carpet this time, pressed against his bound hands. The helicopter roared, and doors closed.

Wolfgang struggled for another breath, and then he simply gave up, embracing the thick darkness instead.

39

The Kremlin
Moscow, Russia

Early morning in Moscow was miserable, much as it always was in February. A thick snowfall from the night before had piled atop now frozen mounds of previous precipitation, leaving the entire city locked in a prison of white, gray, and bitter cold.

Nikitin had lived here so long, he barely noticed anymore, or cared. Despite his dacha on the Black Sea and the photoshoots he commissioned of himself carrying a surfboard out of the waves, Nikitin didn't really care for the outdoors.

He'd done his time in the bitter cold, lugging a heavy rifle across snow-bound mountains. The world could now be conquered from behind a polished wood desk, safe inside the warmth of his presidential suite. Nikitin preferred it that way.

Pouring himself another measure of bitter Russian tea, Nikitin sat alone in his executive office behind a tablet computer and used his finger to scan through the email. There were photographs—a lot of them, snapped mostly with cell phones by the detachment of mercenaries he had deployed to Venezuela. Those photographs told the story better than the summary report next to them ever could.

Twelve men dead. A field of expended brass. One captured, unidentified American.

And at least four more, on the loose.

Nikitin flung the tablet across the room, grinding his teeth as it shattered against the stone fireplace. Shoving his tea aside, he snatched up his desk phone and hit zero for his secretary.

"Mr. President?"

"Get him on the line," Nikitin growled.

"Yes, sir."

Nikitin hit the speaker button, then leaned back in his chair, clenching the headset against his leg. He wanted to bash it against the desk.

Better yet, he wanted to bash it against Belsky's thick, brainless skull.

Fool.

The phone rang, reaching Belsky's secure mobile number. Nikitin's knuckles turned white around the handset, shaking against his leg. He waited. Belsky didn't answer.

The call routed to his secure message box instead. Nikitin leaned toward the phone, speaking through his teeth.

"*Find the Americans*," he snarled. "Or this is the end of you."

40

George Bush Center for Intelligence
Langley, Virginia

"Mr. Director, I've got Station Chief Harris on the line for you."

O'Brien had barely made it into his office before the call came in. He punched the speaker button as his secretary spoke from the next room. It was six a.m., but she always beat him to the office. She had for his entire eight-year tenure as head of the CIA.

"Put him through," O'Brien mumbled, still blinking himself awake. Despite a few decades of practice dragging himself out of bed before the sun came up, O'Brien wasn't a morning person. Were it up to him, he'd run this office ten to ten every day, but the intelligence world operated on the clocks of all the places where that intelligence was being mined, not the place where it was interpreted.

That put him on a perpetually changing schedule—Moscow one day, Beijing and Pyongyang the next, Tehran and the Middle East the day after that.

Who needed sleep, anyway?

"Mr. Director, this is Station Chief Harris, Station Caracas. Good morning, sir."

"I know who you are," O'Brien said. "Why are you calling?"

O'Brien already knew why. It was rare for him to speak directly with most station chiefs, let alone the SC of a station as unimportant as Caracas. Harris was calling because O'Brien had given him explicit orders to do so if anything went wrong with the Prosecution Force.

It was that reality, coupled with two hours of sleep, that made O'Brien want to punish Harris for following orders.

"I'm afraid there's been a development, sir. With the PF."

O'Brien unlocked his computer and waited while it loaded. He ran a hand over his face and slurped coffee from his desk mug. It was cold, but the caffeine jolt helped.

"What happened?"

"I sent one of my local assets along with them, as you requested. He went offline four hours ago, and we haven't been able to reestablish contact."

O'Brien wrinkled his nose in disgust. "What do you mean, *offline*?"

"We sent him with a GPS messaging device and locator beacon. We lost signal with both around two a.m. Haven't received contact since."

"He's probably sleeping," O'Brien snorted. "Do you actually have something, or are you just wasting my time?"

Long pause.

"I just thought you'd want to know, sir."

"Yeah, well, I don't. Call me when you have something important."

O'Brien hung up, twisting his cold fingers around the handle of the mug. His computer loaded, displaying the bank of files he'd been reviewing the night before.

The top file? DOD records for one Reed David Montgomery, ex-Marine and longtime criminal fugitive, now officially pardoned by POTUS. A strange, sordid story featuring a lot of big gaps and unanswered questions.

Questions like, how had Trousdale met Montgomery in the first place? What was the nature of their off-the-books relationship, and why was Trousdale so willing to let Montgomery off the leash at the first opportunity?

O'Brien had been around a long time. He knew what dirt smelled like, even when he couldn't put his finger on it. There was something here. Something Trousdale didn't want the world to know about.

And he was going to find it.

41

Venezuela

Progress through the Venezuelan jungle was brutally slow. Corbyn led the way, using the rusty machete from the patrol boat and doing her best to cut a trail. But she was a lot smaller than Reed or Turk, and the path she left between the tangle of jungle undergrowth was seldom large enough to allow passage for both big men and their makeshift stretcher. Reed frequently had to bull his way straight through tangled vines and waist-high bushes, doing his best to keep from dumping Stewie right into the mud.

For his part, Stewie gritted his teeth and bore the pain without complaint, not so much as cursing when Turk slipped and slammed his injured leg into a rubber tree. Stewie grunted and sweated a lot, but Corbyn's emergency tourniquet was doing its job. So long as they reached the waiting SUV and implemented more permanent medical care soon, he should survive.

"That peg-legged bastard better be waiting," Turk grunted.

Reed didn't say anything, but he had his own concerns about whether they would find Wolfgang where they had left him. The position of the Land Cruiser was sufficiently removed from the port so as to shelter it from any likely observation by the mercenary security team, but Reed hadn't expected that security team at all, and if Wolfgang heard the gunfire, he may have proactively relocated to remain hidden, relying on Reed to radio him for extraction.

It was a lot of ifs and maybes, but the Land Cruiser still represented the best means of transportation back to Caracas, where they could find medical care for Stewie.

"One klick to go," Corbyn said, pausing to catch her breath for the first time since leaving the river. Reed rested his end of the stretcher in the crook of a tree and fished a water bottle out of his CIA pack. He half expected the bottle to have a hole in it, given the reliability of Harris's gear to date, but the water was cool and clean. He sucked down half while Turk shared a bottle with Stewie, then passed his off to Corbyn.

The British agent leaned against a tree, the machete stuck in the mud next to her, a subdued grimace creasing her face as she guzzled water. Reed had observed her favoring one leg as she cut the trail, seeming to limp over perfectly level ground, almost as if her right leg were a little shorter than her left. It was a sharp contrast to the catlike grace he observed when they first infiltrated the port, but he knew the limp wasn't the result of a fresh injury. What he saw now carried all the characteristics of an old war wound, inflamed by intense physical activity.

"You ex-military?" he asked, accepting the empty bottle back.

Corbyn grunted, wiping her mouth with the back of one hand.

"RAF," she said. "Chinook pilot."

Reed watched as she squatted, wincing a little as her bodyweight descended over her hips.

"What happened?" he asked.

Corbyn sighed, resting her back against a tree. Her eyes closed, and for a moment he wondered if she had heard him. Then she grunted.

"RPG. Iraq. Went down pretty hard."

"I'm sorry," he said. "Your guys make it out okay?"

Corbyn blinked, and her eyes rimmed red. She looked away and didn't answer.

Reed tucked the bottle into the pack and slung it over his shoulders. He extended a hand to Corbyn.

"Come on, Brit. You ain't done yet."

Reed knew something was wrong before the Land Cruiser was even in sight. As they neared the crook in the road where they had left Wolfgang, something about the air felt a little too still. No rain forest life buzzed in the trees or crept along the loamy jungle floor, and as Reed held up a fist and the four of them froze a hundred yards from the tree line, a faint odor tinged the heavy jungle air.

Gunpowder.

Turk smelled it too, and they quickly deposited Stewie on the ground, Reed taking point with his SCAR held in low-ready. He selected each step with care, navigating behind the largest trees he could find to stay under cover as long as possible.

The Land Cruiser waited right where they'd left it, resting on the outside edge of the ditch beneath the low-hanging canopy of a moriche palm. Reed approached from the rear and caught the soft gleam of a reflective taillight under the bright glow of the moon.

And then he noted that moonlight gleaming off something else—on the left side of the vehicle, sprinkled across the ground.

Shattered glass.

"Going left," Reed whispered. "Cover me."

Turk fell into a kneeling position behind a tree and signaled with two fingers for Reed to proceed. Rotting leaves padded Reed's footsteps as he circled toward the Cruiser's driver's side.

The driver's window was shattered. He saw that before reaching the tree line, also noting brass rifle casings littering the ground, along with bullet holes in the windshield. Dried blood stained the dirt and was smeared across the driver's door—where a body had fallen against it, Reed figured.

But there were no bodies here now, and no Wolfgang. The dirt road was completely silent, the Land Cruiser cold and still.

Reed slipped out of the trees and jogged into cover alongside the Land Cruiser, conscious of Turk's position of cover fire thirty yards back amid the trees. Pressing his back against the vehicle, Reed moved swiftly to the shattered driver's window and peered inside.

There was no blood on the seat, and no body. Fragments of windshield coated the dash, and bullet holes tore through the upper half of the driver's seat. The back seat was empty, as was the cargo area. The keys still hung from the ignition.

But on the floorboard, small brass objects gleamed under the glow of his rifle-mounted light—too small to be rifle casings, but much larger than your average handgun brass. They were spent 10mm cartridges. Five of them, all scattered around the floor where they'd fallen after being spat from Wolfgang's Glock.

Reed's stomach fell, and he cast a quick look up the roadbed and into the jungle beyond. Then he looked over his shoulder and whistled once.

Turk appeared like an apparition, his rifle held at the ready as he approached the vehicle. He met Reed at the front bumper, where half a dozen rifle casings littered the mud—Russian 5.45 brass.

"Shoulda shot more of those suckers," Turk muttered.

"I've got an ugly feeling you'll have another chance," Reed said, crouching to scoop a casing out of the mud. It wasn't actually brass; it was steel. A common thing in Russia.

"You think he's alive?"

Reed looked back into the jungle, his heart rate rising into an angry thump. He wasn't angry at Wolfgang. The mercenaries had taken them all by surprise, and that wasn't anyone's fault. He was angry at himself for ever allowing Wolfgang to come along in the first place.

"There's no blood in vehicle," Reed said.

"There's blood on the outside."

"I think Wolfgang shot somebody. There's ten-millimeter brass on the floorboard. I'm guessing he got out through the back, or maybe the side. Then they got a gun on him, and he had to surrender."

"So he's still alive."

Reed stood, not answering. Returning to the driver's-side door, he stuck a hand through the shattered window and twisted the key. The dashboard lit up, and the engine coughed. Reed released the key and started for the trees.

"Come on. We'll load Stewie in the back and get him to medical care."

"And then?" Turk pressed. Reed could hear the angry tension in his voice. The undertone that spoke the challenge that Turk wouldn't dare to say out loud.

You're not gonna leave him.

Reed stopped, facing his old battle buddy over one shoulder.

"And then we're gonna find Wolfgang and waste whoever took him."

42

The White House

For the first time since joining the Trousdale administration nearly eighteen months earlier, Stratton was forced to go through Maggie's schedulers to arrange a last-minute meeting with the president.

He didn't really want this meeting on the records. He would have preferred to not have consulted anyone at all, simply ducking into the Oval for a brief conversation prior to the daily political grind reaching its midmorning fury.

But then, if he and Maggie were still on such casual terms, there might not be cause for this meeting at all.

Stratton waited in a plush lobby chair outside the closed door of the Oval, two envelopes riding his lap. The first was legal sized and packed thick with documentation. All the most critical documents from PPI, paired with his own boiled-down summary of their contents.

The second was letter sized and slim. It was unsealed, contained only one sheet of paper, and on the face he'd addressed it with only two words: *Madam President*.

Sitting outside the Oval like the freshman congressman from a district whose largest city nobody had ever heard of, Stratton couldn't help but feel the blood rush to his face. With every White House aide and West Wing busybody who passed, he felt a little more inclined to toss both envelopes in the shredder and return to the Naval Observatory. Cut his duties back to those strictly assigned to the VP and hang Maggie out to dry.

He didn't deserve to be treated this way. He'd worked too hard, proven himself too many times, sacrificed too much. He'd given everything to play second fiddle to the Trousdale White House, not just because he craved political power in his very marrow, but because he actually believed in Maggie.

Stratton closed his eyes and drew a deep breath. He knew he wouldn't shred those documents. He knew he wouldn't get up and leave. Not until he was kicked out, anyway. Until that day, he would rise early and go to bed late, giving everything he had to this administration. Because that was his job.

His country deserved it.

"Mr. Vice President?"

Stratton opened his eyes. An aide had just stepped out of the Oval Office, holding the door open. She offered him a polite smile.

"The president will see you now."

Stratton walked in alone. The Oval Office was fresh with morning fragrance, the carpet newly vacuumed, a gas fire burning amid artificial logs in the fireplace.

Maggie sat behind the desk, a copy of the *Washington Post* spread out in front of her amid a continental breakfast and a coffee tray. She didn't look up as he approached, sipping coffee and slowly turning a page of the paper. Stratton stopped in front of the desk, the envelopes cradled under one arm, and stood awkwardly while Maggie proceeded to read.

She looked good. He couldn't help but notice it, but he wasn't sure what had changed. Her face was still tinged with yellow, and the coffee trembled a little as she took a sip. She still sat hunched over, and he could see the pain in her eyes as she set the cup down.

But something…something was different. A slight shade in her cheeks. Something about her aura.

"Good morning," she said at last. Her voice was all business, and she didn't invite him to sit. In months past, Stratton wouldn't have asked.

Somehow, he now felt pressure to stand.

The door opened behind him, and O'Dell stepped in. Stratton watched the big bodyguard out of the corner of his eye as O'Dell crossed the room, standing tall and walking with a soft spring in his step.

Maggie looked up, and a faint smile touched her lips. That vague shade of red Stratton first noted in Maggie's cheeks brightened just a little, and her back straightened.

"Good morning, James."

O'Dell didn't answer, ducking his head awkwardly and suppressing a smile as he helped himself to the coffee tray. Maggie didn't take her eyes off him while he mixed cream and sugar, then helped himself to one of the two seats across from her.

I'll be damned, Stratton thought.

He should have seen it coming. He knew Maggie had a special affinity for her bodyguard, and during her darkest days of recovery from the sniper wound, O'Dell had seldom left her side. Stratton had been so busy holding the country together, he hadn't really stopped to consider where that situation was headed.

Good for her. He couldn't help but think it. Everybody needed somebody.

"What do you need, Jordan?"

Maggie addressed him while smearing cream cheese over a bagel. Stratton shifted hesitantly, suddenly very aware of O'Dell sitting next to him. O'Dell seemed just as uneasy, but he didn't get up to leave.

"Madam President, I'd prefer to speak in private."

"I trust James with my life, Jordan. Don't you?"

She faced him for the first time, both eyebrows raised. Stratton pursed his lips and didn't answer. He simply nodded.

Lifting the envelopes from beneath his arm, he deposited them both on the desktop without comment. Maggie scanned them but didn't reach out to retrieve either one.

"What's this?"

"The first contains the identities of your enemies, ma'am. The second contains my letter of resignation."

The room went dead quiet. Maggie's bright eyes fixated on the twin envelopes before she slowly lowered the bagel to her plate. She looked to O'Dell, and for a moment Stratton thought the bodyguard might be dismissed after all.

Instead, she turned back to Stratton.

"Explain."

"Not long after you were shot, while Montgomery was still hunting Belsky, one of his people came to see me. Some guy I'd never met before. He confronted me about my involvement in your attempted assassination. Montgomery had uncovered a link between Belsky's oil company and an American energy firm called Cunningham Enterprises, based in Chicago."

Maggie's eyes narrowed, but she didn't interrupt. Stratton drew a deep breath and continued.

"Cunningham Enterprises is managed by Harold Cunningham, the patriarch of the Cunningham family...and longtime friend of mine. After Montgomery discovered the link between Belsky and Cunningham, his next step was to confront me. The most obvious beneficiary of your death."

The room had turned icy still. Stratton's collar felt tight, and he wanted to tug on it with one finger, but he didn't. He knew he was laying it on hard, dumping fuel on the fire of any suspicions Maggie may already hold, but he didn't have a choice. If she was to believe anything he was about to say, she needed to know he wasn't holding anything back.

Not even his own neck.

"Why didn't you tell me this before?" Maggie said. Her voice was as cold as the room but remained calm.

"I never intended to keep it from you," Stratton said. "But first I needed you to heal. And more importantly, I needed to know if Montgomery was right."

Maggie broke eye contact, her gaze flicking to O'Dell. For his part, the bodyguard had rested his cup on his knee and was facing Stratton, his eyes narrow with suspicion, like a dog fixated on a potential intruder.

"I hired a private investigatory firm to dig into Cunningham," Stratton continued. "Not just the company, but Harold also. His family. Everything. They've spent most of the last three months poking through anything they could get their hands on, public records or otherwise. What you see in the first envelope is the result of their investigation."

Maggie glanced at the envelope. She still didn't pick it up.

"And?" she prompted.

"Cunningham Enterprises is in bed with Lenkov International. Deep. They've signed a multiyear purchasing agreement for crude oil—a bigger order than Lenkov can hope to fulfill with current resources. I can't prove that Cunningham had anything to do with your attempted assassination, but I can speculate."

Stratton stopped, as though waiting for permission. Maggie's gaze was glued to his. She nodded once.

"I don't know where the oil is coming from, but I'm going to hazard a guess it's some sort of illicit arrangement. Since taking office, you've championed American energy independence, emphasizing domestic production and renewables. Things that directly threaten deals like these. When it became obvious you had a shot at reelection, I think Belsky made arrangements to have you killed, figuring that either we'd lose the election, or I would take your place."

"A friend of Cunningham's," Maggie said, her voice still cold.

Stratton nodded. "Yes, ma'am."

A long period of frigid stillness encapsulated the three of them, Maggie's gaze pivoting again to the envelope, but still she didn't pick it up. Laying both hands in her lap, she turned back to Stratton.

"Since you're telling me this, I suppose I'm expected to assume your innocence."

Stratton held his chin up, allowing himself to tap into his own indignation for the first time. Fueling the frustration and personal outrage he'd felt from the first moment Maggie had turned cold on him.

He understood why. But knowing why did nothing to assuage the sting.

"No," Stratton said.

"No?" Maggie raised both eyebrows.

"No, Madam President. What I'm telling you shouldn't be the reason you assume my innocence."

Maggie sat forward, wincing in pain and flushing a little. Her lips parted, but Stratton cut her off.

"You should assume my innocence because, since the first *day* you phoned me about the vice presidency, I have dedicated my life to the service of this administration. From Capitol Hill to the West Wing to the campaign trail. Even while you lay unconscious, fighting for your life, *I* have fought for *you*. I have defended you, protected you, advocated for you, and shielded you from things you'll never know about, because that's my job. It's my job to roll out of bed every morning and lie down on the tracks to derail whatever freight trains are headed your way, so that you can do your job—lead this country."

Stratton felt a tremor in his voice, and his eyes stung. He swallowed hard, but he didn't stop.

"I have sacrificed family, political affiliation, and my own better judgment to be a part of this administration. Because I believe in it. Because I believe in *you*. And the more they come out swinging, trying to take you down, the more I believe in you. The more I believe that this fight is only just beginning, and you need me by your side. Just like you need him."

Stratton faced O'Dell. The bodyguard's eyes were still narrowed into suspicious slits, but there was a hint of openness now. Just a trace.

When Stratton turned back to Maggie, he saw none of the same. Maggie was as flat as a granite wall.

"I can be a tremendous asset, Madam President. I can be an absolute savage. I can hunt your enemies and drag them screaming and bleeding into this office by their hair. And I want to. But I can't serve the presidency if the president doesn't trust me."

Stratton relaxed his shoulders. Embraced the punch line. "That's why you hold my resignation. Inside those envelopes you'll find everything you need to have me out of this office permanently. Probably enough to land me in prison, if you wanted. I leave that up to you. I serve the president."

Stratton finished his spiel with a slight duck of his head, and then he simply stood, hands behind his back, body relaxed. Like a man waiting to see if a firing squad would cut him down.

And ready to embrace death if it did.

Maggie said nothing, one finger tapping her desktop slowly. The envelopes still untouched on her desk. The moment dragging into a minute. Then five.

The phone rang, shattering the stillness like a gunshot. O'Dell jumped, but Maggie calmly hit the speaker button.

"Yes?"

"Madam President, Director O'Brien is requesting a conference call. He says he has an update for you."

"Very well. I'll take it in the Situation Room."

"Yes, ma'am."

Maggie hung up, then stood slowly, looking frail again. But not weak.

"You say Cunningham struck an oil deal with Lenkov?"

"Yes, ma'am." Stratton gestured to the envelopes. "It's all there. I just don't know where the oil is coming from."

Maggie looked to O'Dell. Then she turned to the door.

"Maybe I do. Come with me."

43

Maggie's heart pounded as she led the way out of the Oval, blood rushing to her face and her head swimming. She wasn't sure if it was anger or surprise that overwhelmed her the most. Maybe a little of both, not only at the gritty truth Stratton had just dumped on her, but at how bluntly he'd been willing to dispense it.

There was no self-preservation in his words. No defensiveness in his posture. Just more of the raw honesty and undercurrent of confidence that first attracted her to him as a potential partner.

And now left her questioning him.

Taking the elevator into the West Wing basement, Maggie remained silent as they descended toward the Situation Room, O'Dell standing close to her side. His hand brushed her arm, and she knew it wasn't by accident. It brought a momentary smile to her face, numbing some of the burning pain in her stomach.

She walked slowly to her seat at the head of the long table, motioning for Stratton to sit next to her. Easing into the plush leather, she grimaced and steadied herself against the table edge. The room was empty save for the three of them, a large screen at the end of the table already illuminated with the White House logo, ready to receive O'Brien's secure transmission from Langley.

O'Dell poured her a glass of water, and Maggie hit the intercom on her phone.

"Put him through."

The screen blinked, and then O'Brien's bald head appeared in a flash, his owl eyes blinking behind those trademark round glasses. He looked more tired than usual, and a little pissed off.

It wasn't a good sign.

"Mr. Director, what do you have for me?"

O'Brien wasted no time with formalities, cutting straight to the chase.

"We just received an update from the Prosecution Force, ma'am. They think they've found Belsky."

Maggie's heart skipped. She listened intently as O'Brien recapped the last two days of operations, beginning with a tip from MI6 about a Russian submarine and concluding with a gunfight someplace east of Caracas. When he reached the part about Belsky, he dumped the facts with no mention of his prior insistence that Belsky was dead.

No mention, and no apology. Maggie barely noticed, focusing on the relevant details of the report and glancing sideways at Stratton when O'Brien described containers loaded with industrial paraphernalia. Specifically, according to the CIA's subject matter experts...oil-drilling paraphernalia.

Stratton met her gaze, and she knew they were both thinking the same thing.

One large oil contract...and a wealth of untapped Venezuelan oil.

"Where are they now?" Maggie asked. "The team."

"They're holed up in a CIA safe house in Maturín. It's a midsized city halfway between Caracas and the port. One of our assets was escorting them and got shot in the leg. He'll need medical."

"Can they make it back to the city?" Maggie questioned.

"We'd prefer not, ma'am. They've made quite a mess at the port. Montgomery claims multiple kills of these...'mercenaries.'"

O'Brien made air quotes as he used the word, and that angry undertone returned to his voice. It irritated Maggie for some reason, but she brushed it aside.

"Take care of your asset, and keep Montgomery on standby. Can you meet again at eleven?"

"Of course, Madam President."

"I'll see you then," Maggie said. The screen went black, and she looked at Stratton, rubbing the edge of the table and thinking. Deciding.

Deciding whether she could afford to trust him. What it would cost her if she made the wrong call. Stratton had been right about one thing—she needed him right now. More than ever. And he'd been right about a second thing, also. Outside of his link to her potential assassins, he had never given her a reason to mistrust him.

And yet...

"Call Secretary Gorman and General Yellin," she said, addressing Stratton. "We'll meet here at eleven. If they can't arrive in person, get them on video."

Stratton ducked his head in acknowledgment. Maggie sighed and leaned back in her chair, facing the blank screen.

"I think we found your oil."

44

Venezuela

After grinding out of the jungle and back onto the pothole-infested streets of rural Venezuela, it was Stewie who gave Reed his next destination—a CIA safe house on the outskirts of the city of Maturín. Someplace where the team could lay low, Stewie could seek emergency medical care, and next steps could be planned.

The "safe house" was really more of a "safe shack," owned and occupied by an indigenous auto mechanic who believed he was being paid by a Canadian minerals company to make his home available on short notice for their employees. Reed thought the guy probably knew better, but he also probably speculated that the arrangement was a front for a South American drug cartel, not the Central Intelligence Agency.

Regardless, the man opened his doors without hesitation or question, giving not so much as a second glance to the shot-up Land Cruiser. He directed them to lay Stewie on his battered kitchen table, and ten minutes later, a doctor was at the door, ready to stitch up the gunshot wound and administer painkillers.

The doctor didn't ask questions, finishing his work in half an hour and leaving the house without further comment. Meanwhile, Corbyn borrowed the mechanic's phone and made a series of relay calls to her people in Caracas, who in turn contacted Langley, eventually bringing Reed on the line with an unidentified speaker using a computer-distorted voice.

It was an unsecured line—Reed couldn't blame the CIA for being cautious. But he didn't have time to beat around the bush, either. In short order, he outlined the situation at the port, focusing on the highlights—Belsky, the mercenaries, the containers, and most importantly, Wolfgang.

The computerized voice directed him to send photographs to an obscure email address, then the call ended abruptly. Reed tossed the phone down in irritation, storming back into the little living room, where Stewie lay stretched out across the couch. He was jacked up on hydrocodone now, probably high out of his mind but at least no longer in pain. Turk stood by the door, pacing irritably, his rifle riding his back like a book bag.

The mechanic had seen the weapons and seemed completely unconcerned. The guy must be well paid.

"What's the update?" Turk asked.

"They asked me to email pictures," Reed said. He hit send on his phone, waiting for the slow international cellular service to transmit half a dozen photographs. It would take ten or fifteen minutes for them to find their way into the CIA inbox, and probably twenty or thirty more for them to filter through however many firewalls and filters stood in place to ensure nobody who intercepted the unencrypted email could know what its final destination was.

And in the meantime…they were just sitting on their hands.

"I'm waiting to hear back from my superiors," Corbyn said. "They'll be keen to learn more about those mercenaries, I'm sure. They might want more pictures."

"They're on their own," Reed said. "I didn't come down here on a photoshoot. I came to nab Belsky, and now we've got to find Wolfgang."

"Belsky may have fled the coop by now," Turk said.

Reed shook his head. "Not a chance. You saw all those shipping containers—all those mercenaries. Belsky's cooking up something big down here. Something he won't abandon, and the fact that he's using Moreno's chopper indicates that Moreno is involved. I'm betting Belsky flew back to Caracas."

Reed ran a hand through sweaty hair, tensing as footsteps tapped on the wooden porch outside. He reached instinctively for his SIG as Turk swung his rifle around and Corbyn checked the window.

The Brit waved a hand. "It's just the mechanic. Let him in."

Turk opened the door, and the mechanic stumbled in with a big smile, his arms laden with an aluminum dish. Reed's nostrils twitched as the rich smell of seasoned rice and meat flooded the room. The mechanic rattled off something in Spanish, setting the dish down on the recent operating table and gesturing to it invitingly.

"*Muchas gracias*," Reed said, offering a nod.

The mechanic smiled again and left the way he came, leaving Turk to bolt the door. The three of them settled around the table, uncovering fresh tortillas and a blend of brown rice and braised pork. It smelled delicious and reminded Reed how hungry he was.

This certainly beat MREs.

Reed filled a tortilla and chowed down, his mind spinning as he focused on the problem at hand. Not Belsky.

Wolfgang.

The farther they chased Belsky, the hotter things would become in Venezuela. Presumably, whenever they finally captured him, they would need to vacate the country immediately. Which meant they had to find Wolfgang first. But before they could do that, they would need to refit. Find clean clothes, a lot more ammo, and electronic gear that actually worked.

Filling another tortilla, Reed wrapped it tight and walked to Stewie's couch. The CIA officer lay with his head on a cushion, his eyes closed, but Reed could tell he wasn't sleeping.

"How do you feel?"

Stewie cracked a dry smile. "Like I just blew a twenty-eight-to-three lead."

Reed rolled his eyes. "Who told you I was a Falcons fan? I literally never said that." He offered the tortilla. "Here. It's good."

Stewie grimaced as he sat up, accepting the makeshift burrito and taking a tentative bite. He nodded in surprised satisfaction as Reed squatted next to him.

"Listen," Reed said. "I need your help."

Stewie chewed slowly, studying the food and becoming suddenly pensive.

"Why do I feel like you're about to ask me to break the rules?" he asked.

"I don't know. Why do you?"

Stewie looked over the top of the burrito, still chewing slowly. Then he set it down.

"Look. I'm not supposed to say anything. But..."

"But what?"

"Harris wasn't the one who assigned me to accompany you."

"What do you mean?"

"That order came from up the chain. Way up the chain. They wanted me to...monitor you."

Reed wiped a thin layer of sweat from his forehead. Somehow, what Stewie said didn't surprise him, and he didn't have to think long about who would have given that order.

O'Brien.

"You guys are off the books, aren't you?" Stewie asked.

"We don't exist," Reed said.

"And somebody near the top doesn't trust you."

"So it seems."

Stewie thumped his chest with one fist and belched. He finished the burrito and wiped his hands.

"What do you need?" Stewie asked.

"Firepower—a lot of it. And some tech that actually works. We'll get you someplace safe, then we're going after Wolfgang."

Stewie didn't answer immediately. He sat propped up on the couch, wincing as he lifted a finger to pry pork out of his teeth. After a moment, he faced Reed.

"There's an armory in the city, hidden in a basement underneath the embassy. They never cleared it out when they pulled the ambassador. I'm not sure what's in there. The Marines would have used it for their embassy guards."

"So it's good stuff," Reed said. "That'll do. How do we get to it?"

"You'll need Harris. He's got the passcode."

"Will he squeal?"

"I don't know. Harris is a good guy, but he's a rule follower. It all depends on Langley. Surely, they want Wolfgang back as bad as you do."

Reed's pocket buzzed, and he dug the phone out. There was a new email from that bizarre address—no salutation and no signature. Just one simple line.

Stand down, remain in place. Await further.

Reed rotated the phone for Stewie to read.

"Does that answer your question?"

Clicking the phone off, Reed pocketed it and walked back to the table, where Turk was chowing down on his fifth burrito.

"Pack it up. We're moving out."

Corbyn appeared from the house's little bathroom, limping just a little on her right leg. She'd scrubbed her face and pulled her hair back into a ponytail. She looked tough as nails.

"What's new?" she said.

"The CIA ordered us to stand down."

"And?" She raised both eyebrows, a mischievous twinkle in her eye. Reed liked it.

"And they can make passionate love to themselves," he said. "We're going to get Wolfgang."

45

Caracas, Venezuela

Rivas hoped for a crowd of two hundred, but long before he reached the balcony on the north end of the square, nearly twice that many angry Venezuelans had packed their way across the park and between the narrow streets, cardboard signs at the ready. Rivas could feel the tension in the air like pulsing sound waves, growing ever louder as the prospect of a National Guard confrontation drew ever nearer.

Moreno didn't tolerate riots. Over the years, Rivas and his followers had learned how to ride the line between protest and riot, amping up the tension in a hope to instigate international support while stopping short of direct conflict with a military force. The National Guard would use tear gas and rubber bullets in abundance, often sending people to the hospital, where pro-Moreno doctors would ignore them for hours or even days until sympathetic nurses stepped in, or else the victims simply licked their wounds and limped their way home.

People had died, yes. Dozens had died since Moreno took power, and those were only the bodies of the protesters. That said nothing of the hundreds more who had disappeared, swallowed into El Helicoide, never to be heard from again.

It was those stories Rivas needed. The secret fuel to ignite a revolution. But for now, he would have to make do with Juan Blanco. He would have to hit Moreno before Moreno could hit him.

"Amigos!" Rivas called, speaking into a bullhorn from the balcony. The restless crowd calmed at the sound of his voice, all eyes and ears turned his way as he advanced to the railing. Rivas was fully exposed here. A prime target for one of Moreno's snipers.

But even Moreno wouldn't dare to press that trigger. Not in front of these people—so long angry. So long hungry. So long suppressed and forgotten.

Rivas dared him.

"It is another sad day for Venezuela," Rivas began. "Another long night without power. Another breakfast without food. Another workday without work. Another pocket full of worthless bolívars!"

Rivas clawed colorful paper from his pocket, wadding it up and hurling it into the faces of his impoverished audience. They didn't so much as blink as the bolívars rained down at their feet. There wasn't enough value there to buy a stick of gum.

"But today, amigos, is sad for another reason. While we suffer and starve at the hands of an economy that Moreno has destroyed, it grieves me to tell you that worse tragedies are at hand. Long have we suspected that our own brothers, our own fathers and mothers and sisters have vanished into the belly of El Helicoide, tortured and abused for speaking their minds. Long have we known of the evil that boils in that place like poison, seeping through the veins of our beloved Venezuela and sucking our lives away!"

A low groan emanated from the back of the crowd, growing steadily louder as it neared the balcony. Fists shook. Gaunt, haunted faces turned dark with rage.

Rivas held up a hand.

"What does Señor Presidente say? He says we should not believe our own eyes! He says our missing loved ones are victims of the cartels—runaways and defectors to the American empire. Do we believe this?"

A rumble like thunder echoed from the crowd. "No!"

"We know the truth! But today—" Rivas broke off, raising a finger.

Holding the crowd in suspense. Drawing them to the edge of the knife. "Today is different, amigos. Today the lies and gaslighting have no power over Venezuela, because *today*, we have a witness. She came to me bloody and beaten, barely able to speak, she was in so much fear. This brave woman could have remained hidden. She should have protected her own life. But Gloria Blanco knows the *truth*, and she will not rest until you know it as well. The truth that President Moreno's secret police broke into her home and kidnapped her husband right before her very eyes. They dragged him away, kicking and screaming, straight to El Helicoide."

A gasp rang through the crowd. Genuine shock and outrage. Exactly the response Rivas needed.

"The charges, you ask? High treason. And the proof?" He let the question hang. Drew it out another long moment before letting the bullet fly. "*None at all!*"

Rivas raised his fist into the air, and the crowd thundered. Fresh faces packed in from the peripherals, crowding toward the balcony. Nearly a thousand people and growing by the minute. The anger that rippled from their voices was electric. Rivas could feel it in the air, making the hair on his arms stand up on edge.

Pent-up rage, ready to break like water out of a dam.

Rivas stepped back, holding his arm toward the open door behind him. "Amigos! I give you a Venezuelan hero...Gloria Blanco!"

Gloria stepped onto the balcony like a vision from the battlefield, her face still swollen, one eye still black. Her clothes stained with blood and one sleeve torn off. She'd long since changed, of course. But it was Gloria's own idea to change back into the tattered clothes before this speech.

The people needed to see.

Gloria took the mic and told her story. Crying between sentences. Mumbling through others. But the thousand plus spectators had fallen deathly quiet now, hanging on her every word. Completely raptured by her story.

As she reached the climax and Juan's arrest, the rage returned. Not like a breaking dam, now. More like a tsunami. Nobody was listening anymore. Signs rose over the crowd, condemning Moreno and demanding freedom.

Somebody lit a torch, and quickly the flames spread like little dots over the heads of an army.

Rivas took the bullhorn back and screamed into the mob. “Señor Presidente! This is the voice of the people. We demand for Juan Blanco to be released. We demand for his charges to be dropped, and for those responsible for his unjust imprisonment to be punished. We demand justice!”

The chant resounded through the crowd, echoing back at Rivas like a boomerang.

Louder now. And louder still.

Then the first voice in the crowd shouted what everyone else was already thinking.

“On to Miraflores! *Viva Venezuela!*”

A torch-wielding protester led the way out of the courtyard, and Rivas looked toward the palace.

Choke on this, Moreno.

46

The Situation Room
The White House

The small knot of people assembled around the table in the Situation Room represented only a fragment of Maggie's complete cabinet, but if twenty months in the White House had taught her anything, it was that the eighty-twenty principle was alive and well in Washington—eighty percent of the power and usefulness of her cabinet was concentrated in twenty percent of its members.

For Maggie, those members were Secretary of State Lisa Gorman, Chairman of the Joint Chiefs General John David Yellin, Attorney General Greg Thomas, White House Chief of Staff Jill Easterling, and Director of the Central Intelligence Agency Victor O'Brien.

What problems couldn't be solved by that nucleus of power players might well lie beyond the reach of democracy altogether, but Maggie had yet to collide with that wall. These five people, plus herself, Stratton, and O'Dell, were an imperfect union, and many of them actively mistrusted and disliked each other—not without cause. But Maggie was astounded by how much they could accomplish in a short period of time.

Especially when she authorized them to bend the rules.

Gorman and Thomas sat across from her at the long table, while Easterling sat at her right elbow, and she placed Stratton to her left. O'Dell lurked in one corner, carving an apple with a steak knife and creeping everybody out. It was a talent he had—something about being around, but not being directly involved in anything, that put people on edge.

Maggie found it absurdly attractive.

The phone in front of Maggie's chair blinked, and she hit the speaker button.

"General Yellin and Director O'Brien are ready, ma'am."

"Put them on, please."

This time two separate screens blinked, and O'Brien's owl face was joined by General Yellin's bulldog one. The general was out of town, touring new facilities at Fort Bragg, but was impeccably dressed in Class A's, as always.

"Good morning, ma'am."

Maggie offered a nod, a sudden flash of abdominal pain racing up her spine and temporarily freezing her voice. She winced and caught Easterling's eye.

Easterling filled the gap with practiced grace, Maggie's petite chief of staff speaking with a mousy voice that somehow still carried the power of a woman not to be trifled with.

"The president called this emergency meeting to address a developing situation in Venezuela. It goes without saying that everything we're about to discuss is strictly confidential, and under no circumstances are any of you authorized to divulge anything to anyone without express permission from the president."

Easterling paused a moment to let her instructions sink in, catching Thomas's and Gorman's eyes before she dove straight into the gritty details.

The hunt for Belsky. The contracts between Cunningham and Lenkov. The shipping containers on the Venezuelan coast.

Gorman took copious notes, scratching on an iPad with a stylus and only pausing twice to stare in disbelief at Easterling—first with the mention of Cunningham and Lenkov, and then with the photographs of the drilling equipment on the coast.

Thomas, O'Brien, and Yellin said nothing, simply listening, their faces blank.

Easterling reached the conclusion of her spiel as the pain in Maggie's gut began to subside. She shifted uncomfortably in the leather chair, searching in vain for a position that would minimize pressure on her healing torso.

She expected Gorman to speak first, bursting in with an outraged monologue on the fragility of international relations, but instead it was Attorney General Thomas who took the floor.

"Let me be sure I understand." His gravelly smoker's voice rasped as he leaned across the table, addressing Easterling, not Maggie. "We hold evidence that a US energy company is conspiring with a Russian oligarch's oil empire to drill in *Venezuela*?"

"We have indicators," Stratton said. "I wouldn't call it absolute proof."

Thomas looked to Gorman, disbelief playing across his face. This time, the Secretary of State took her cue.

"Madam President...there are..." Gorman hesitated, seemingly at a loss for words. "A *plethora* of reasons why this simply can't be what it looks like."

"Such as?" Easterling's voice squeaked, signaling irritation.

"Sanctions, for one," Gorman said. "Venezuela's oil economy didn't just disappear—the Brandt administration sanctioned Moreno into the Stone Age for human rights abuses. We've effectively cut them off from the global market, leaving them to self-destruct. In other words, it's not just a matter of expertise and equipment. Venezuela could drill a billion barrels of crude and it could never leave port. It would be illegal for any American company to purchase it."

"Which must be why they wanted me dead," Maggie said.

Nobody moved. A frigid wave ran around the room, leaving everyone avoiding the president's gaze and waiting for somebody else to speak. It was the reaction Maggie expected, but it still pissed her off.

She was the one who took the bullet. She was the one still fighting for her life, rolling out of bed every day with a hot knife slicing through her stomach. Unstable on her own feet, the ghost of a president past, the mockery of mass media quickly losing all affinity for her.

She took that bullet. Her cabinet could be bothered to find their balls and hunt America's enemies.

"We're looking at an international conspiracy to undermine the integrity and sovereignty of the United States," Maggie said bluntly. "A conspiracy that has, apparently, penetrated right to our heartland. It's dirty money and corrupt power, all balled up into one nasty wad, and I'm going to rip it out by the roots."

"Madam President, this is...over the top." AG Thomas shook his head in disbelief. "What you're suggesting—"

"I'm not *suggesting* anything, Greg. The facts speak for themselves. I want Cunningham buried. What do you need to make that happen?"

Maggie's voice cracked as she spoke, turning suddenly dry. She stopped for breath, and O'Dell appeared at her elbow in a flash, a glass of water in one hand. Maggie guzzled, and Thomas sat up.

"I need *proof*. The conspiracy you're suggesting breaches well beyond circumvention of US trade law. We're talking about high treason here."

"I can get proof," Stratton said. He hadn't moved since taking a seat next to Maggie, sitting straight-backed and stoic. Maggie shot him a sideways glance, and he nodded once.

Gorman held up a hand. "With respect, we're way off target. If half of what we're looking at is true, Cunningham barely matters. Who are these mercenaries the CIA discovered on site at the port? That's a lot of heavy firepower for a drilling operation. If there's even a chance that a foreign military is involved on Venezuelan shores—"

"The personnel at the port are security contractors from Europe," O'Brien said. "Similar to the paramilitary contractors we deployed into Iraq. It's not at all unusual to see large oil companies hire heavy security."

Maggie's gaze snapped toward the screen. Separated by cameras and encrypted internet feeds, she couldn't be sure if O'Brien was facing her or not, but she hoped he saw the steel in her eyes.

There was still a piece of this puzzle that Gorman, Thomas, and even Easterling knew nothing about. The Moscow connection. Maggie had deliberately withheld that information for the time being, both because it was unproven and because she didn't want to muddy the waters.

But if it was true...

"We're going to pursue this investigation as if our national security depends on it," Maggie said. "Director O'Brien, I want you to direct assets on the ground in Venezuela to recover Belsky by any means necessary. Mr. Attorney General, you will partner with the vice president to build a case against Cunningham Enterprises and Harold Cunningham. You will not tip your hand. I want the ax on his neck before he even knows it's coming. Am I clear?"

Thomas hesitated, mouth half-open. Stratton filled the gap.

"We'll get it done, ma'am."

Thomas closed his mouth and nodded once.

"Madam President, if I may."

General Yellin's rumbling bulldog growl rattled the desktop speakers. Maggie pivoted toward his screen.

"Yes, General?"

"You know me, ma'am. I'm a facts guy. I don't often lean on intuition."

"But?"

"I'm just not sure I buy this theory that your attempted assassination was a simple matter of dollars and cents. Cunningham and Belsky may be thick as thieves, but my gut tells me there's more to this story."

The general trailed off, his old face wrinkled into a concentrated frown. Maggie knew his comment was calculated to remind her of the possible Moscow connection, but she still wasn't ready to share that theory with the class. For the moment, it was just a theory. An unproven one so long as Belsky ran loose.

"Mr. Director, I need Belsky—"

"Ma'am, I'm sorry. You need to see this."

Keys rattled on the far side of the screen, then O'Brien's face vanished and was replaced by a screen share. Small white letters streamed across the bottom of a blurry image, rapidly clarifying and zooming into a satellite feed of a sprawling city sandwiched between mountain ridges.

O'Brien smacked two more keys and the image zoomed, that string of letters still running, a military clock in the top right-hand corner reflecting current time in Washington.

"This is a live feed," O'Brien said.

Another two revolutions of the zoom, and the buildings became visible but still looked hazy, as though they were trapped on the other side of a fog. Maggie squinted.

The picture closed to almost street level, focused on the heart of downtown.

And then Maggie saw it. Smoke. Hordes of people. A burnt building and the irregular jerk of a lagging video feed as a truck ran off the street and plowed into a building, then exploded.

It was Caracas—and the city was in chaos.

47

Caracas, Venezuela

It was almost noon by the time Reed drove the Land Cruiser to the top of a winding mountain road and looked down into Venezuela's capital city. Stewie lay in the back, rolling around on a makeshift bed, biting back pain-filled grunts while Turk looked after him and Corbyn rode shotgun. With the shattered windshield kicked away, cool mountain air raked through the vehicle and brought with it a faint but distinct smell—smoke.

Reed hit the brakes and pulled to the side of the road, looking out over the wheel and down into the valley. The city was still ten miles distant, but from this altitude it looked like something constructed of LEGOs, all clustered together between mountain ridges. Midday sun beat down amid low-hanging clouds, and right from the heart of downtown, a black column of smoke drifted toward the sky.

"Turk, hand me the binos." Reed reached his hand back and retrieved a pair of the CIA's crappy binoculars, aiming at downtown and adjusting the focus.

What had initially appeared as a single column of smoke Reed now recognized as a conglomeration of drifting columns, all wound together and carrying in a black cloud toward the sky. Multiple buildings near the core of the city seemed to be on fire, but any other detail was obscured by smog and distance.

"Is this normal?" Reed asked.

"I've never seen anything like it." Corbyn sat next to him, using her superior MI6-issued binoculars to map out the city. "The fires are too far apart to have spread from a single location."

"More electrical problems?" Reed asked.

"Maybe." Corbyn didn't sound convinced.

Reed looked back to find Turk administering morphine through a syringe into Stewie's arm.

"Keep him awake," Reed said. "He's still got work to do."

Dropping off the brake, Reed started into the valley. After driving through Caracas previously, he wasn't too concerned about the battered Land Cruiser drawing attention. They had sprayed the blood off with a water hose at the safe house, and the bullet holes and missing windshield looked like par for the course among the ramshackle vehicles they passed on the Venezuelan highway. But if the smoke rising from downtown Caracas meant what it usually meant in a place this destitute, remaining covert would be the least of their worries.

"Stewie, I need directions," Reed called to the injured CIA officer as they approached the city outskirts. The faint smell of smoke had strengthened as they left the mountains and rolled into the ramshackle barrio suburbs of Caracas's southern district, but what struck Reed most was the complete stillness of the homes.

They were empty. Nobody was around. It had been strange when they first drove in from the airport, but it had also been early morning. Now, at nearly midday, he expected to see some people.

There was no one.

Turk wrestled Stewie into a seated position behind Reed where he could get a look at the buildings they were passing. Stewie leaned back in the seat, looking a little flushed and sweaty. Reed caught a glimpse of him in the rearview mirror and immediately noticed the red cheeks and watery eyes.

He looked to Turk, and Turk shook his head. So much for whatever antibiotics the doctor at the safe house had administered. Stewie's leg was swollen to almost twice its healthy size, and what skin Reed could see had turned a dark cherry red.

"You crapping out on me?" Reed called over the roar of the motor.

Stewie wiped his face with the back of one hand, shaking his head weakly. "Hell no."

"Good. Pay attention. I feel like we're on the wrong side of the tracks."

Stewie peered out the window, studying the passing streets and looking vaguely confused.

"Should be a four-lane coming up," he said. "Make a left."

"Left?"

"Right."

"Right or left?"

"Left, dammit!"

Reed swerved around a metal trash can rolling empty through the streets. They were a mile or two inside a neighborhood, and Reed still hadn't seen more than a dozen people—all women and children. The four-lane Stewie described was really just a wider two-lane, with a passing lane down the middle and a motorcycle lane along one side. It wound out of the mountains, leaving the barrio and leading into a slightly more developed shopping district. Reed saw people now—middle-class people, in semi-decent cars. There seemed to be an electric tension in the air, with everyone crowded around radios and TVs behind foggy glass storefronts. He saw neither cops nor military as the Land Cruiser bumped across a small bridge and he took a right toward the heart of the city.

"Our field office is just east of town," Stewie rasped. "In an old satellite building. Stay off the main highways...there could be police."

Reed didn't need to be told twice. He stuck to surface streets, avoiding the major thoroughfares as the distant smell of smoke grew ever stronger. In the distance, Reed heard a horn blare, and as he blazed through an intersection, Corbyn shouted and pointed toward his window. Reed looked left just in time to see a wall of people marching down a parallel street two blocks down, standing shoulder to shoulder. Cardboard signs and penlights of orange mixed with the swarm, and then they were gone. Tall apartment towers and office buildings drowned them out as the Land Cruiser hurtled down another narrow one-way.

"Take the next right," Stewie said. "We're almost there."

Reed kept one hand on the wheel, the second cradling the SIG in his lap as they broke from between the buildings and he pulled a hard right, then immediately slammed on the brakes.

Barely fifty yards ahead, a wall of soldiers marched straight toward them, riot shields linked together in a Roman wall, a bullhorn blaring for them to get out of the vehicle.

Reed ratcheted the Cruiser into reverse and slammed on the gas. Tires spun and they shot backward, but it was already too late to reverse the way they came. A dull pop resounded from ahead of the SUV, and a can of tear gas came arcing through the air, bouncing off the hood. Reed caught a trace of the gas filtering through the open windshield, instantly stinging his eyes and throat.

"Brake! Brake! Brake!" Turk shouted.

Reed slammed on the brakes again, bracing himself against the wheel and wrenching his head around. The Cruiser slid to a screaming halt, barely twenty yards ahead of the wall of people Reed had seen not five minutes prior. They had come out of nowhere, spilling out of side streets, waving signs and torches, their voices a collective roar as they marched headlong toward the soldiers.

Shit.

Reed yanked the shifter back into first gear and dumped the clutch, but instead of lunging forward, the Cruiser simply lunged, then stopped cold, the engine choking off.

"What the bloody hell are you doing?" Corbyn shouted.

Reed reached for the key, looking down to the dash. The fuel gauge still read a quarter tank. He hit the key, and the engine coughed. Directly ahead the soldiers approached, and another pop heralded the arrival of more tear gas—this time bouncing off the street ten yards ahead. Behind them the marching horde closed in, engulfing the Land Cruiser without any care for its occupants or the tear gas raining from the sky. Reed pulled the neckline of his shirt over his face and tried the key again. The motor struggled as bodies surged around them like a river.

The engine wouldn't start. It turned over and choked off, and Reed thumped the dash. The fuel gauge dropped from a quarter tank to bone dry.

"Bail!" he called, coughing through the shirt. "We'll finish on foot."

Corbyn was the first to drop out of the vehicle, leading with her SIG and pivoting to the back door. Turk followed her, half dragging Stewie behind him as Reed shoved his door open and forced his way into the crowd. He dragged the SCAR behind him, keeping the weapon muzzle-down and behind his back.

It was a useless attempt at remaining covert. One of the Venezuelans crushing in next to him saw the rifle and screamed, her soft brown face washing pale as she stumbled back and pointed.

"*Soldado! Soldado!*"

Three or four of the bigger guys wielding torches turned on him like starved dogs, eyes blazing hatred above handkerchiefs tied around their faces.

Reed didn't wait for a conversation. He bolted into the Land Cruiser, fighting his way over the center console and rolling out of the passenger door. Turk supported Stewie at the edge of the street, beckoning Reed into an adjoining alley as a storm of pops signaled a barrage of tear gas.

"Come on!"

Reed charged through the crowd and into the alley. Corbyn was already ten yards down it, jogging with the pistol at her side, searching for the next turn. Reed stumbled over heaps of trash and shallow gutters running with mucky water as he helped Turk to support Stewie. The CIA officer looked ready to pass out, his head rolling as his mouth fell open.

Reed grabbed him by the chin and smacked his cheeks a couple times.

"Stewie! Wake up, jackass! Which way?"

Stewie blinked, breathing in ragged bursts. He looked down the alley and shook his head.

"Straight!" Reed called. Behind him, boots landed on the roof of the Land Cruiser with heavy thuds, followed by rising shouts. They reached the end of the alley and looked down an empty street, running parallel to the street they had just abandoned.

"Left?" Reed jostled Stewie. "Is it left?"

Stewie blinked, his eyes passing slowly down the street. Then he simply slumped.

"He's done," Turk said.

"Freaking wimp," Reed growled. "Corbyn! He's down."

Corbyn crouched behind a set of concrete steps, ten yards away. Reed made eye contact, and the Brit tilted her head down the street.

"Come on! I may have an idea where to go."

She left cover and started down the street, leading with the SIG. Reed hesitated only a moment, then helped Turk to shoulder Stewie. The two of them jogged to keep up, turning their backs to the riots while Reed hoped like hell Corbyn wasn't leading them straight off a cliff.

48

The Situation Room
The White House

"What the hell am I looking at?"

Maggie knew it was a riot. It didn't take a rocket scientist to know that. But her initial instinct—that Reed had somehow touched off a stick of dynamite in Caracas—was quickly extinguished by a more rational reality.

Reed wasn't even in Caracas. He was hours away, and besides. There were thousands of people storming those streets. The CIA's spy satellite captured masses of what appeared to be civilians gathering near the core of the city, around a park that O'Brien informed her was called Bolívar Square. Smoke rose from several small bonfires built of trash and rubber nearby, and marching lines of Venezuelan national police moved in to subdue the crowds.

"It's a protest of some sort," Gorman said. "Probably political. They aren't uncommon, ma'am."

"This violent?" Maggie asked.

"Sometimes. Political tension is at an all-time high in Venezuela."

Maggie studied the screen while Gorman rattled through a summary of Venezuelan politics. Hugo Chávez, Cesar Moreno, and Luis Rivas, the

American-recognized opposition leader. She already knew some of it. She cared about none of it.

Only one thought rang through her mind as she studied the chaos unfolding through the streets of Caracas—how did Belsky fit into this? Because, logic and circumstance be damned, she was convinced he did.

"Greg, thank you for your time," Maggie said, still not looking away from the screen. "Jill, would you show the attorney general out, please?"

An edgy nervousness crept over the room. Maggie could feel Easterling's eyes piercing into her with surprise and probably irritation, but she didn't argue, and neither did Thomas. The two of them got up, collected their things, and left the Situation Room in short order.

Maggie turned directly to Gorman.

"What's happening here?"

Gorman tapped a pen against her lip, watching the monitor. O'Brien's face now appeared on an adjacent screen, his glasses reflecting blue light again.

"Rivas has been staging escalating protests for months," Gorman said. "His usual justification is that Moreno has been illegally imprisoning Rivas's supporters."

"Is that true?"

"The CIA would know better than I, ma'am. But I would guess so. Moreno has a long history of imprisoning political opponents. He may carry the title of president, but for all intents and purposes, he's a dictator. If you give my department a day or two, I'm sure we could develop a more comprehensive understanding of the situation."

"Rivas claims a man named Juan Blanco was arrested and imprisoned at the national intelligence headquarters," O'Brien said. "Rivas delivered a speech two hours ago to instigate the riot. Blanco's wife was there."

Maggie pivoted toward O'Brien. The director didn't look up from his computer screen.

"Like the secretary said," O'Brien continued. "The CIA would know."

"What's our diplomatic position with Rivas?" Maggie addressed Gorman again.

"What do you mean?"

"We recognize him as president?"

"Well...yes. Loosely. It's a delicate situation. Moreno still controls the country."

"But if Moreno were displaced, Rivas would be our recognized leader?"

Gorman didn't answer. Sudden concern flashed across her face. Maggie sat back in her chair, feeling flushed and very tired. But her mind was alive. It spun with all the information she had accumulated over the past week, arranging and rearranging all the possible directions and outcomes, searching for the best possible cocktail.

"I'm not sure what you're suggesting," Gorman said slowly.

Maggie looked to Stratton, measuring her VP's calm posture and steady gaze. Her strained mind reevaluated once again whether she could trust him. Whether the exception was an exception, or whether it was a glimpse into his true character. And whether she could afford to waste time wondering.

Stratton nodded once. A commitment. A vote for himself.

For whatever it was worth.

Maggie turned back to the table.

"All right, Lisa. There's something you should know."

Gorman's face paled just a little. The slight pallor of a woman suddenly confronted with information she might not want to hear. Maggie dove headfirst anyway, leading right with the heart of it.

Wolfgang. His nameless Russian contact. The Moscow connection. Belsky's escape to Venezuela via a Russian submarine.

And now the drilling equipment. Three massive shiploads of it.

By the time Maggie had finished, Gorman looked ready to choke. She sat with her pen frozen over her notepad, not moving and not speaking. Her lips parted just a little.

"So you see, Madam Secretary," Maggie said. "We don't have a couple days. Whatever is happening in Venezuela, it's directly linked to my attempted assassination. We're playing some kind of shadow game with somebody behind a curtain, and that somebody just might be President Nikitin."

Gorman's mouth closed. She looked to Stratton, then the general, as if to ask them if they already knew. Neither man so much as blinked.

"I don't even know what to say. This is...way beyond the purview of what we've been discussing."

"It's what we've been discussing all along," Maggie said. "You just didn't know it. Director O'Brien has a team in place in Venezuela as we speak with the object of bringing Belsky home. But there's something bigger at play here. Somebody sponsored Belsky not only to kill me, but also to go into Venezuela and reestablish their oil industry, after which that oil would be sold directly to the United States. Whoever is behind that—whether it's Nikitin or somebody else entirely—they clearly think they can undermine US foreign diplomacy and sidestep our sanctions. It's a direct threat to our sovereignty."

"We..." Gorman hesitated. "We need more information, then. We need to know what we're dealing with. *Who* we're dealing with."

"We don't have time for that," Maggie said. "It's been three months since I was shot, and save for a battle-scarred Russian blown to hell on a yacht, we've made zero progress on tracking down whoever is responsible. They're *playing* with us. Tossing around an oil scheme right under our noses, using our own people. Circumventing our sanctions. We need to stomp this like the cockroach infestation it is. I want to hit back—hard."

The alarm in Gorman's face grew. She'd been here before—they both had, with Maggie pushing for bold and direct action and Gorman pleading for diplomacy.

"Madam President, with respect. The situation in Venezuela is extremely volatile. Their people are starving, their infrastructure in tatters. The government is corrupt in its very DNA, siphoning off what little wealth exists long before it reaches the people. They import everything. Their entire economy depends on a trickle of oil production. It's an ugly situation, and—"

"Would Rivas change that?" Maggie demanded.

"Ma'am, no. I can't have this conversation. I won't engage in regime change."

Gorman's voice grew increasingly frantic, but before she could continue, it was General Yellin who broke in.

"I agree with the secretary. Any attempt by the United States to instigate or support regime change would carry dramatic consequences for our national security. The Moreno regime is militarily allied with China and may also be linked to Moscow. We cannot—"

"I hear you, General!" Maggie held up a hand. "I'm not suggesting a regime change. All I'm asking is whether Rivas would be an improvement for Venezuela? That's a simple question."

Gorman froze, mouth half-open. She looked at her notes, as if they might lead her out of the fire. Then she simply shook her head.

"I don't know, ma'am. Moreno is a despot, but he's the devil we know. Rivas could wind up being worse."

"But if he were in power, he would be indebted to us?" Maggie pressed. "We could lift the sanctions. Put Venezuela back to work."

"Ma'am, again. What you're talking about is beyond illegal, it may not even be moral."

"You don't know *what* I'm talking about, Madam Secretary, because you won't let me finish my damn thought!"

Maggie's voice rasped, and her heart thumped. She felt suddenly lightheaded and braced herself against the table's edge. O'Dell closed in next to her, but she pushed him back.

"Mr. Director, does this Rivas guy have a plan, or is he just setting things on fire?"

O'Brien looked as didactic and calm as ever, but exhaustion tinged his voice. "I really couldn't say. We've not had direct contact with him. I would assume he has a strategy, but sometimes these resistance leaders get comfortable just...resisting. Regardless, I concur with the general and Secretary Gorman. Instability in Venezuela is not our friend."

Maggie's hand snapped toward the screen. "Does *this* look like stability to you?"

Nobody answered.

"Look. Lisa. I'm not suggesting regime change. But we can't allow a Russian energy foothold of any sort in the western hemisphere—especially one with an underground oil deal feeding directly into America. If Rivas could be leveraged to sabotage that arrangement, wouldn't that be worth discussing?"

Gorman didn't blink. Her narrow white fingers twisted around a pen, bending it until Maggie thought it would crack. She looked toward the general.

Yellin remained quiet and pensive.

"Things never improve when you dislocate power," Gorman said. "Look at Iraq. Afghanistan. Africa—"

"Give me a break, Madam Secretary. Dislocating power is what America does. Look at the British Empire. The slave trade. You can cherry-pick the times things went wrong all you want, but if—"

"I'm not cherry-picking a damn thing! What you're suggesting is reckless, illegal, and I won't have a part in it." Gorman stood bolt upright, the pen snapping in her hand. Her face flushed bright red, and nobody moved.

Maggie didn't blink. She sat with her chin up, eyes blazing. Defying Gorman to say one more word.

Gorman stood with the broken pen in one hand, her lip trembling. Then she ducked her head and turned for the door.

"My apologies, Madam President. You'll have my resignation within the hour."

"Madam Secretary, you are not excused!"

Gorman marched straight for the door, not even flinching. Maggie's back stiffened, and hot fire streamed into her blood. She made as if to stand.

Stratton beat her to the punch, rising out of his chair like a rocket, his voice booming in the enclosed space.

"*Madam Secretary!* You will *not* abandon your president!"

Gorman stopped, frozen at the door. Maggie felt a chill rush down her spine as Stratton snapped his fingers and gestured to O'Dell.

"Mr. O'Dell, if you please."

O'Dell sprang into action like a dog let off a leash. Fast-walking to the door, he cut Gorman off and folded his arms, blocking her path.

Gorman looked back. The crimson in her face darkened, and Maggie couldn't tell if she was more outraged or embarrassed.

Stratton gestured to her chair.

Gorman's bottom lip twitched. She seemed frozen in place. Then she simply melted, turning on her heel and retreating to her chair without a word. O'Dell remained at the door, and Stratton faced the screens.

"Now, then. The president has made her instructions clear. Mr. Rivas is our diplomatic ally, and he's clearly in distress. Mr. Director, you will contact your assets in Caracas and have them reach out to Rivas directly. Find out what assistance he requires. General Yellin, the White House requires a brief of the military's readiness to confront unfolding instability in the region. Please make that happen. And Madam Secretary, you're right. This is an incredibly complex issue. Please have the State Department prepare a full analysis of what options the White House may leverage to bring stability back to the region."

Stratton looked to Maggie. She sat huddled in her chair, suddenly very hot, her blood churning. The anger she felt only moments prior remained, but she was back in control now.

Maggie nodded, and Stratton pushed his chair beneath the table. "All right. Let's get to it."

49

Caracas, Venezuela

Reed had encountered riots and social unrest in third-world nations before—many times. Running down the street, supporting Stewie with one arm and wielding the SIG with the other, he could feel the tempo of rising angst pumping through the city like a heartbeat, and it didn't take a genius to know that it was getting worse.

The crowd had collided with the police—or soldiers, or whatever they were. Reed could hear the commotion on the far side of the block as the pop of tear gas cannons was overwhelmed by outraged screams and repeated chants. More than just a protest, the rage of the mob was boiling into something far worse than what a line of guys in riot gear could manage.

Reed didn't want to be around when things boiled over.

Jogging while Stewie's feet dragged along the pothole-infested asphalt, Reed followed Corbyn, trusting that she had some clue where she was going. The British spy led the way with that lopsided lope, still favoring one leg. When she collided with an unexpected pothole, Reed saw the agony ripple across her face.

But she didn't stop.

"Two more blocks!" she called.

Reed grabbed Stewie's belt and lifted the little CIA officer off the ground, breaking into a run as Turk followed suit on the other side. Somewhere behind them, a gasoline explosion detonated with a chest-thumping roll of thunder and a familiar rush of heat. A tire came hurtling down the street next to them, bouncing off the curb and nearly knocking Reed off his feet.

"That one!" Corbyn pointed toward a three-story brick building with bars over its windows, built into a lineup of similar buildings with a pair of Chevrolet Tahoes parked out front, battered and dusty. Reed recognized one of them as Stewie's daily driver and escalated his run to a sprint, shoving Corbyn from behind. They cleared the last intersection amid a scream of rubber on asphalt as an incoming car swerved to avoid them.

Then they were on the doorstep, and Reed's quick eyes swept a solid steel door, painted to look aged but completely rust-free. Surrounded by a steel frame, with a covert camera in one corner and a tooth-shaped logo printed above a short string of Spanish.

Reed dropped Stewie and pounded on the door with one fist.

"Open up!"

He looked back down the street to see a burning car sitting at the top of the hill a hundred yards away. It was surrounded by locals with water hoses and buckets, all fighting to extinguish the blaze before it consumed their meager homes.

A losing battle.

Reed pounded again. "Open the hell up!"

An electronic bolt rumbled on the back side of the door, then it swung open, and Harris spilled out. He surveyed the small crowd in momentary confusion, then jerked his head inside. Turk pulled Stewie's unconscious body through the door, and Corbyn slid in ahead of Reed. Then the door slammed shut, and the electronic bolts slid into place.

Reed slumped against the nearest wall, panting and wiping sweat from his face. His heart thundered, and his head felt light. He hadn't run that hard in too long.

"What happened?" Harris demanded. "Is he dead?"

Reed scanned the room. It was a dark foyer, with high walls covered in peeling wallpaper, and battered wooden floors. Probably a house, at least originally. Certainly not a dentist's office. Joining Harris was a woman in jeans and a T-shirt, already on her knees next to Stewie alongside an open first aid kit. A third man appeared at the end of the hall, dressed in a rock band T-shirt and smudged plastic glasses, with shoulder-length blond hair tangled and dirty, a half-eaten sandwich in one hand as he surveyed the chaos openmouthed.

"He took a round to his leg," Turk panted. "Didn't Langley call you? He's got an infection. And he doesn't handle combat well."

Turk wiped his face and proceeded to the end of the hall, swiping the blond guy's sandwich and consuming half of it in one greedy bite. "Thanks."

"We haven't heard a thing from Langley," Harris snarled. "I thought you guys were still on the coast." He knelt next to Stewie, checking his pulse before palming his forehead.

"My God, he's burning up. Jackie, let's get him on the couch."

Harris and the woman hefted Stewie's slender frame down the hall, through a small kitchen, and into a living room arranged with two couches and a small TV. They stretched Stewie across the couch, then Jackie went to the kitchen for ice water. Harris turned immediately to Reed.

"Did you start this?" He pointed toward the street.

Reed ran through a bullet-point summary of the events at Puerto Pedernales, followed by their retreat to Caracas. Harris listened in irritated silence, breathing a curse now and then but not interrupting.

"So you have no idea where your man is?"

"We were hoping you might," Reed said. "Any idea where the Venezuelans would take him?"

"Only if he was taken by Venezuelans. Did you say Russians?"

"They sounded like it. I honestly wasn't hanging around to confirm. We'll need to get in touch with Langley, and then I need to refit. Stewie indicated you might have an armory hidden beneath the embassy."

Harris said nothing, measuring Reed's gaze for a long moment before turning for the kitchen. Reed followed, scanning a room cluttered by all the indicators of multiple people hacking survival with little or no support from the outside. Boxes of canned goods and dry food heaped against one wall. Dirty laundry and personal items scattered over every flat surface.

It all looked very slipshod, and Reed found it easy to understand why Harris felt abandoned.

"This is all they give you?" Reed asked.

Harris dug two bottles of water from a cabinet and tossed one to Reed. Corbyn and Turk were busy making more sandwiches while the blond guy made nervous chitchat.

"This was a satellite field office," Harris said. "A place to stage covert missions, back in the day. After Moreno ordered our embassy to close, of course we couldn't house the station there anymore, but they still want assets in Caracas. So here we are...like a French resistance club, pretending to be a dentist's office."

A distant boom brought Reed's attention back to the window. He could still smell burning rubber, but overall, the commotion of the riot sounded softer than it had five minutes prior. Whatever the nature of the instability outside, it was moving away from them. For now.

"What about that armory?" he pressed. "Your last loadout left something to be desired—particularly in the electronics department. I need fresh comms and more ammo. A lot more."

Harris shook his head. "Sorry, chief. Not happening. I've got enough of a mess as it is. We're trying to remain covert down here. Hard enough to manage with riots popping off three times a month. Worse with a man down."

"They have my man," Reed growled.

"Yeah, well. They're probably gonna keep him, too. Hate to break it to you, cowboy. It's kind of a zoo around here."

Harris dropped his empty bottle in a trash can and moved back to the couch where Jackie was leaned over Stewie's chest with a stethoscope.

Reed stepped to the table where Turk was chowing down on his third sandwich. The blond guy was gone, and Corbyn had stepped into the bathroom. Turk ate in greedy bites, tearing off ham and cheese with the SCAR still cradled in one arm.

"You catch that?" Reed said.

Turk grunted. "He'll sing a different tune with a SIG down his throat."

Reed shook his head. "Take a breath. It does us no good to get forceful if we don't even know where Wolfgang is. We need intelligence first."

"Gonna be hard to get," Turk muttered. "Like he said. It's a zoo down here. Should we start with Langley?"

Reed hesitated. It was a logical option, but he didn't like their odds with O'Brien. The director had already demonstrated his mistrust—and perhaps disgust—with Reed and his team. He might well tell them to take a long walk off a short pier or, worse yet, simply ghost them. Leave them to rot.

All you're good for is being shot at.

Reed remembered O'Brien's barb and wanted to throat punch him. He turned back to Turk, but before he could speak, a door groaned open someplace beyond the living room, and the blond guy stuck his messy head into the hall. He was wearing headphones now, with a microphone pulled away from his lips.

"Hey, boss!" he called. "I've got Langley on the line. They say it's urgent."

Turk frowned. "Do they know we're here?"

Reed shook his head. "Not unless rock-band over there told them."

Harris stood from the couch, dusting his knees off. "Come on, cowboy. If you've made a mess, you're gonna take the fall for it."

50

The room Reed followed Harris into was exactly what he expected it to be—lined with soundproof foam, crowded with multiple desks, and absolutely crammed with computers. The nerve center of a makeshift intelligence station.

The blond guy sat in a rolling desk chair, situated behind a bank of screens as big as an aircraft carrier, his smudged plastic glasses sliding down his nose as he worked a mouse and keyboard like a drum set, banging and clacking away.

As the three of them stepped in, the blond guy motioned for Turk to close the door, then he smacked a key, and a speaker on the table in the middle of the room glowed green. Harris pulled up a chair.

"Station Chief Harris online. Go ahead, Langley."

"Chief, this is Director O'Brien. Thank you for taking my call."

Harris twitched, visibly surprised and maybe a touch alarmed. He shot an accusatory glance at the blond guy, who merely shrugged.

"Of course, Mr. Director. What can I do for you?"

A long pause. Reed stepped closer to the table, Turk at his elbow. A large part of him wanted to castigate O'Brien right there on the spot, but he held his tongue. For all he knew, O'Brien still thought they were in Maturín. May as well keep it that way.

"I understand you've had a bit of a disturbance down there," O'Brien said.

"You could say that, sir. We haven't had a chance to put out any feelers yet. But it looks like another one of Rivas's uproars. Maybe a little worse than usual. There have been a few fires."

"Any specific intel on how far Rivas plans to take this?"

"No, sir. We're working on it."

Another long pause. A pregnant pause. The kind of pause Reed was used to hearing from O'Brien before he said something that he really didn't want to say.

"The president has directed me to ask you for a favor," O'Brien said at last.

Another surprised twitch from Harris. Maybe worse than the first.

"Yes, sir?"

"She'd like for you to make direct contact with Rivas and...find out what he's up to. Find out if he needs...assistance."

Harris frowned, confusion and maybe frustration washing over his face in a torrent. "She'd like us to...what, sir?"

"You heard me," O'Brien snapped. "Make contact with Rivas and find out what the hell is going on."

"Sir...with respect. We don't have the assets for that. I'm a man down right now. I'd have to go myself, and that could blow my cover."

"So blow your cover. We'll extract you later, if necessary. These are the president's instructions."

"Maybe the president would like to give us time to clean up her last favor before she asks for a new one," Reed snapped, pushing in behind the table.

Momentary soft static filled the line—the calm before the storm. Then the outburst came. "Montgomery? Is that you?"

"You're damn right it's me. We just limped in from the coast, dragging one of your officers with us. He's sweating out an infection on the couch as we speak, but that's your problem. My problem is Wolfgang. We're getting him back, and you're helping. Now I need to know—"

"*Shut up!*" O'Brien's voice snapped through the speaker, just sudden enough for Reed to pause. "What you're going to do is *stand down*. All of you. You've made one hell of a mess, Montgomery. Just like I knew you would. It's chaos down there, and I've got to clean it up."

"You can't seriously blame this circus on me." Reed snorted in disbelief.

"I'll blame anybody I want. Perks of the job. Now get the hell off this call."

Reed folded his arms, making no move to exit. Harris looked up, his eyes a little pleading. He motioned to the door.

"Come on." Reed jerked his head, and Turk followed him out. As he closed the door, he heard O'Brien tearing into Harris.

"We should pour the heat on," Turk muttered. "Make O'Brien squirm."

"Why bother? He doesn't know where Wolfgang is, and he's not going to help find him. O'Brien would be happier to leave us rotting in the jungle."

Corbyn appeared in the living room, her face freshly washed, her hair dripping water. She looked surprisingly spry considering the morning's action, but she still favored her injured leg.

"Hello, boys," she said. "What gives?"

"Not the CIA," Turk growled.

"You heard from your people?" Reed asked.

"Jackie back there says I can have a go on the computer as soon as her boss is finished. I'll touch base with London and see what's kicking, but I doubt they've heard anything about your man."

Corbyn shrugged apologetically. Reed only grunted. Leaning against the wall, he chewed the inside of his cheek and stared at the opposing wallpaper. It was faded and curled at the edges, depicting a repeating floral pattern from hardwood to ceiling.

Like politics, he thought. All polished and pretty, but really just the same crazed circus printed over and over again.

"Don't you think it's strange that Trousdale isn't asking about Belsky?" Turk drawled.

"What do you mean?"

"She was hell-bent on finding him. Now that we have, she seems to have moved on to whatever Rivas is up to."

"You're assuming O'Brien passed on our message," Reed said.

"You think he's holding out on her?"

"He's got a hard-on for us, that's for sure."

Turk shook his head in disgust. "I could be picking out baby paint right now."

Reed looked up, and Turk looked away.

"Say what?" Reed said.

"Nothing," Turk mumbled.

"*Baby* paint? Is Sinju pregnant?"

Turk only grunted. "I told you she was acting strange."

"You made it sound like she's just being moody. You never said a thing about a baby."

"Yeah...well. Protection ain't perfect, apparently."

His voice was heavy with disgust, but a grin crept across his face as he said it. Reed matched the smile and held out a hand.

"Congrats, brother. You're gonna make a terrible father."

Turk accepted the shake and the accompanying one-arm hug while Corbyn stood back, a soft smile on her face, not intruding. As Reed released him, the door swung open, and Harris appeared. Momentary confusion crossed his face as he caught the tail end of the embrace, but he quickly dismissed it.

"You guys get in here."

Corbyn joined them, and Harris shut the soundproof door. He ran a hand through his hair.

"Okay, look. Here's the deal. I've got to go out and make contact with Rivas. Find out what the hell is going on."

"I didn't realize station chiefs were in the habit of conducting field work," Reed said.

"We're not. Stewie is my street guy, but obviously he's out. Hunter is worthless behind anything but a keyboard, and Jackie is our resident medic. She'll need to look after Stewie. So that leaves me."

"You know where to find him?" Reed asked.

"Usually. He's got a few headquarters and places he sleeps, but it's not all that secretive. Rivas's revolution is more of a cold war. There are plenty of little sparks—protests and occasional riots—but generally Rivas knows he's outgunned, and Moreno knows he can't get away with simply murdering Rivas."

Reed tilted his head toward the street. "This feels like more than a spark."

Harris nodded. "I'm afraid you're right. Probably why Washington wants a double-check. I'll be gone a few hours. You guys stay put. We'll solve your problems when I get back."

Harris reached for a folded shoulder holster resting on a nearby table. Reed cocked his head.

"Rivas is an established leader? He has a network?"

Harris shrugged. "You could say that. He doesn't have an army, if that's what you're asking."

"I don't need an army. I need locals with their ears to the ground."

Harris thought about that, buckling the holster in place. Then he nodded.

"Yeah. He's got people."

"Then we'll come with you."

Reed started for the door. Harris held up a hand. "Hold up. Director O'Brien—"

"To hell with O'Brien. He's not the one getting shot at. If Rivas has contacts, those contacts might know where Wolfgang is. They might even know where Belsky is. And the sooner we find those two, the sooner the big guy is picking baby paint. Okay?"

Harris looked up at Turk. He let out a tired sigh and offered a smile. "Boy or girl?"

Turk shrugged. "I don't care."

"You see?" Reed said. "He doesn't care. And neither do you. Let's roll."

51

Venezuela

Wolfgang had no idea where he was. After a two-hour ride in the helicopter, he was confident his captors hadn't yet removed him from the country, but beyond that it was anyone's guess. They'd kept him hooded and tied the entire time, his leg still missing, lying on the floor of the chopper with occasional boots driving into his stomach during the flight.

Then had come a gentle landing, followed by a decidedly not-gentle transfer onto the ground, where two smelly guys hoisted him up and hauled him across grass and gravel, inside a building with what sounded like a concrete floor, and then down multiple flights of steps.

Wolfgang knew they were steps, because he felt every single one, dragged along like a piece of secondhand furniture all the way to the bottom. Then came more concrete. Another door that groaned on its hinges. A cold room that echoed with every footstep.

They threw him on the ground and slammed the door behind them, leaving Wolfgang and his single leg, still hogtied on the floor.

He was numb enough then to tune the pain out and simply endure the discomfort, rolling from time to time in an effort to ease his cramped muscles, but there really wasn't much to be done about his predicament.

Wolfgang was screwed—imprisoned someplace in a hostile country, maybe by locals and maybe by mercenaries, bereft of his team and almost certainly on his own.

He wouldn't blame Reed for leaving him here. Reed had his own problems to deal with, and he'd warned Wolfgang not to come. Wolfgang only hoped he had a chance to take a couple of these suckers with him. He'd rip a throat out with his bare teeth, if he had to, and laugh while his victim choked.

The final note in a long, sad orchestra.

He didn't have long to think about it. Barely an hour after depositing him in this makeshift cell, the door opened again, and twice as many people entered as before. Wolfgang identified them by the different sounds of their shoes on the cold concrete—at least two pairs of military-style boots, one pair of something that shuffled and slid, and then the thick and heavy smack of the fat guy's slab feet.

Wolfgang didn't need to identify the sound to know that Belsky had returned. He could smell him.

"*En la silla*," a smooth voice said.

That prompted heavy hands to grab him by his arms. A knife sliced away the rope connecting his bound hands to his feet, and relief washed across his body. The hands hauled him up, slamming his ass into a metal chair. Duct tape stretched and peeled free of its roll as his leg and chest were restrained to the chair, his hands still bound behind him.

And then the hood was yanked off.

Wolfgang coughed and blinked, his eyes adjusting slowly to a flood of light from directly overhead. Hair and sweat further impeded his vision as he spat blood on the floor and gasped for clean air.

Clean air wasn't to be had. Belsky was too close at hand.

"*Agua*," the smooth voice said.

One of the soldiers who had tied him to the chair appeared with a bottle and thrust the mouth between Wolfgang's lips. He guzzled cool water, capturing as much as he could while much more ran down his face and into his lap. The bottle was yanked away far too soon, but it served to clear his dry throat.

Wolfgang offered a weak grin. "Much obliged, assholes."

He lifted his head, still squinting into the light. He knew where Belsky was. He could smell him on his right side.

The smooth-voiced man sounded like he stood directly ahead, just beyond the halo of light.

"Who's in charge here?" Wolfgang rasped. "There's a cockroach in my bed, and the water's cold."

"*Shut up!*" That was Belsky. The stinking Russian appeared at the right-hand edge of the halo, growling down at him with breath strong enough to kill a small animal.

Wolfgang winced. "Sheesh. Don't they have mouthwash in Russia?"

He didn't even try to dodge the fist. Belsky's meaty hand caught him in the jaw and snapped his head back, lights and stars spinning. Blood ran into his throat from a busted lip, and Wolfgang fought to spit it out. One of the soldiers grabbed him by the hair and yanked his head up.

"Enough!" the smooth voice snapped, in English this time.

Wolfgang spit blood into his own lap. The light moved, shining against the wall instead of his face and allowing Wolfgang a clear view of the room. The man who stood in front of him was tall and lean, dressed in an immaculate white suit with a white tie. He wore a Venezuelan flag pin on one lapel and sported a clean beard with slicked-back salt-and-pepper hair.

Wolfgang knew he was a politician without needing to ask, and after blinking his eyes back into focus, he thought he recognized him.

Moreno?

"Welcome to Venezuela, Mr....?"

Wolfgang spat more blood and grinned. "My friends just call me Bond."

"Bond...hmm. You are a funny man."

"Not all of us can be the prom king."

Moreno smirked, but Wolfgang didn't think he got the joke. Taking a slow step forward, the Venezuelan president leaned into the light and spoke more softly than ever.

"*Who* are you?"

Wolfgang didn't answer. Moreno's eyes narrowed.

"American, yes? You look like an American. You *act* like an American. Traipsing around, poking your nose where it does not belong. Always the way with Americans."

The disgust that crept into Moreno's voice was barely disguised. Wolfgang merely shrugged.

"Who are your friends?" Moreno pressed.

"Friends?"

"The people at the port." Moreno enunciated each word into a snarl.

"What port?"

Moreno straightened slowly, adjusting his jacket. He stepped back and nodded once.

Wolfgang closed his jaw, expecting another blow. Instead, two cold metal prongs rammed into the base of his spine, and a millisecond later, a bolt of electricity raced through his back. Wolfgang went rigid, his head ratcheting back as he shook uncontrollably. He couldn't close his eyes. He couldn't even scream. It was enough voltage to shut his entire body down, and waves of pain came like an endless tide.

When the shock finally ceased, he still shook, pressed against the chair and gasping for air. His muscles spasmed in and out of cramps, adding continued agony to go along with the burns on his back. Wolfgang's face dropped, and he fought for air. Moreno knelt in front of him again, grabbing his chin and wrenching his face up.

"Who are your friends?" All the elegant calm was gone from the president's voice. Saliva sprayed Wolfgang in the face, and Moreno's fingers sank into his jaw like claws.

"Who are they?" Moreno roared.

Wolfgang gritted his teeth, not bothering with a quippy retort. Instead, he gulped up all the blood, saliva, and snot pooling in his throat and blasted it into Moreno's face.

Moreno stumbled back, clawing at his eyes and shouting. A fist flew out of the darkness and smashed into Wolfgang's face. He rocked backward and hit the chair, the world around him spinning.

Moreno screamed something at one of the soldiers on his way to the door.

Then the pain returned. Worse than before. And longer.

Wolfgang went rigid, the edges of his vision turning black and tunneling out, but his mind wouldn't quite shut off.

The pain just kept coming.

52

Moreno scrubbed his face until it felt raw, hurling rag after rag into the stairwell as he marched out of the basement and back into the polished hallways of Miraflores. Finding the first of a myriad of bathrooms in the mansion, he plunged his face into a sink and used soap to wash away the muck of American blood and snot.

His hands shook. Not just with anger but with maddened frustration. A frustration born out of nearly a decade of stepping out of bed every morning only to run straight into one wall after another.

Ripping off a paper towel, Moreno swabbed his face and stared into a mirror, still shaking. His shirt and jacket were both wet and stained. His face haggard, his eyes bloodshot with rage. He looked like some kind of rabid animal, backed into a corner, desperate and vicious.

Not like a president.

Moreno put both hands on the sink and closed his eyes, pushing the visions of horror away and imagining, just for a moment, that things looked as they should. He wasn't interrogating American scum in the basement of his own house alongside a stinking Russian pig. He wasn't making deals with the devil, under the table, desperate to resurrect an economy already on its deathbed.

He wasn't waging an endless war with half of his own nation, fighting for the respect and loyalty that he *deserved*.

He should have been like Chávez. No, better than Chávez. Twice as wealthy. Even more powerful. Influential across the western hemisphere and into the East. Pumping black gold in an endless river that rivaled the Amazon. Walking the streets of Caracas without need for bodyguards, his adoring people gathered to cheer him the way they cheered the *Comandante*.

Moreno had earned it. He'd given his *life* for Venezuela, sacrificing his youth and happiness to build the Bolivarian Revolution. To build a brighter future for all Venezuelans.

Moreno had been there when Chávez tried and failed to launch that revolution in '92. He'd been there when the *Comandante* finally rose to power in '99, and the true work began. Moreno was on the inside, serving in any capacity demanded of him, climbing over the bodies and earning the number two position in all of Venezuela, Chávez's obvious replacement upon the beloved leader's eventual death.

Moreno had seen how the revolution was built. Not the elegant, romantic picture painted for the media, but the true story behind the curtains. All the brutal and corrupt things the Chávez regime had done to bring peace and prosperity to Venezuela. Necessary things.

Sacrifices for the *people*.

Moreno had partaken in those sacrifices. And yes, he'd spilt blood. Gallons of it. Whatever the *Comandante* required.

And now this. Where had he gone wrong? Why did the people still refuse to *believe*?

Moreno opened his eyes, arms shaking against the sink. He ripped a hand towel free and raked it across his face, then slammed his fist into the mirror. Glass shattered, raining across the floor, and a trickle of blood ran from the back of his hand. Moreno wrapped the towel around it and stumbled back, staring at his shattered reflection.

It looked no worse.

The door swung open, and familiar smacking steps rang on the marble. Moreno didn't need to look up. He could already smell Belsky.

"Are you all right, Señor Presidente?"

Belsky spoke in a slow, condescending drawl, like a man half drunk. Moreno saw disgust in the Russian's eyes. Disgust for *him*. As if that swine could look down on anyone.

"Our benefactor is calling," Belsky said. "He requires an update."

The benefactor.

Renewed outrage boiled beneath Moreno's skin. He wanted to grab a shard of the shattered mirror and cut Belsky's throat with it.

How *dare* the benefactor call, demanding updates? It was Moreno who was enabling this partnership. It was Venezuela and her vast fields of untapped oil that provided an opportunity. The benefactor should learn his place. He should get in line.

He should take updates when Moreno gave them, and not a moment before.

But even as the thoughts coursed through Moreno's pounding head, he knew they were a fantasy. He could pretend to be on top all he wanted, but if the situation was really that good, he wouldn't have needed the benefactor in the first place. He never would have made this shitty deal.

The benefactor had him in a corner, and everyone knew it.

Moreno wiped his hand with the towel. He adjusted his tie and smoothed his hair. Even in the broken mirror, he looked like a mess. But the ritual of looking his best, even when nobody was looking, gave him a little confidence.

Moreno followed Belsky outside, and they took the marble stairs to the second level, down another hall into his executive office. From the wide picture windows that overlooked Caracas, Moreno saw smoke in the air. More of Rivas's protests, spilling out of control. The National Guard had been occupied since dawn corralling this one, dispensing tear gas and brute force at Moreno's orders.

It wasn't working. Rivas was making the rounds with his bullhorn, demanding the release of Juan Blanco from El Helicoide. Of course, Blanco wasn't in El Helicoide. He was still imprisoned alongside the American, beaten to a pulp and probably unconscious.

Rivas's desperate stunt to bring public attention on Blanco only served to confirm what Moreno already suspected—Blanco was indeed a traitor and somehow very valuable to the resistance. But knowing that didn't bring

Moreno any closer to breaking Blanco, and now even if he did, he couldn't publicly use that information to attack Rivas.

The resistance leader had beaten him to the punch, bringing public ire against the arrest instead of the crime. Anything Moreno accused Blanco of now would look like an excuse.

Damn him. Damn that American-sponsored dog.

Moreno settled behind his chair, drawing a confident breath before he punched the call-waiting button on his phone. Belsky motioned for the speaker button, and Moreno reluctantly pressed it.

The benefactor didn't keep them waiting. His voice was computerized as ever, yet strangely familiar.

"Are you running a country, El Presidente, or a war zone?"

The voice was heavy with venom, but Moreno didn't recoil. He remained straight-backed and proud.

This was *his* country.

"Leave internal matters to Venezuela," he said. "I know what I'm doing."

"I'm not sure you do. My men report a dozen fatalities at the port. There are Americans on the loose. Do you know what that means?"

Moreno could hear the growing anger, despite the distortion. He leaned toward the phone.

"It is the American puppet—Rivas. I will deal with him."

"See that you do, or this will be the end of our arrangement. Trust me when I tell you, you do not want to disappoint me."

The benefactor hung up. Moreno's blood boiled. He punched the end call button anyway, just in case Belsky could be fooled, and left the chair, facing the window.

The sky was hazy with black tire smoke. Most of it was concentrated near Bolívar Square, and in one place he could see red lights flashing where fire engines fought a blaze near an apartment building.

Most of the fires were harmless, he knew. Mere piles of trash and rubber that Rivas's followers deliberately ignited in order to instill chaos and fuel the perception of revolution. It was all a tug-of-war between him and Rivas—and they were both fighting over the same thing.

The middle people. Those who were undecided or disengaged with politics, too lost in their own struggles to care. Rivas needed those people to rise up for any revolution to succeed.

Moreno needed them to remain right where they were, cogs in a broken economy, until he could fix that economy. Once the storied wealth of the *Comandante* was a mere morsel compared to the feast Moreno was prepared to serve, there would be no doubt about who Venezuela's true leader was.

He would be more than a hero. He would be more than Chávez.

Moreno would be a god...if only he could break the hold of the American empire once and for all.

"What are you going to do?" Belsky taunted. His voice was thick with condescension.

Moreno turned from the window. "You want to see who is president?"

Belsky grinned.

Moreno snatched his phone up, mashing the button for his secretary.

"*Sí*, Señor Presidente?"

"Get me General Vargas. We have a national emergency."

53

Caracas, Venezuela

They left Stewie on the couch, still sweating but already looking better under an IV drip of antibiotics. Reed and Turk reloaded their SCARs from a safe in the soundproof room, and Corbyn topped off her SIG.

The Brit had made contact with MI6 via a secure messaging system and received an immediate reply advising her to assist the CIA and gather intel.

"Bullocks," she laughed, shutting the computer off. "Somebody's gonna get canned for that one. They never write blank checks, but hell. I'll take it."

She joined the Americans in the Tahoe, and Harris launched into the chaos-gripped city. The burning vehicle down the street had been extinguished, and the tide of rioters had moved on. Reed could still hear their angry voices somewhere across the city as the sun arced behind the smoke toward the western mountains.

"Does this happen often?" he asked.

Harris sighed, wrestling the Tahoe around a wide rut in the middle of the street.

"Rivas stirs the pot as often as he can. It's the only way to keep his supporters active."

"You really think things would be different if he were in power?"

Harris actually laughed. "Night and day. But not because of Rivas."

"What does that mean?"

Harris blazed through a stop sign, not even slowing, keeping one nervous eye on his rearview mirror.

"Look around you. This place used to be a Mecca of South American culture. Second-best economy in the western hemisphere, by a long shot. Everybody who wasn't trying to get into America was trying to get into Venezuela."

"Oil money?"

"Right. And Chávez. A complete crook, by most accounts, but a cunning politician. Everything you see today, all the poverty and worthless money, came after that oil empire collapsed. Chávez spent money like a madman when oil prices were high and got caught with his pants down when prices fell. But that's not why the oil industry never recovered."

"Why, then?"

Harris jabbed a thumb at Reed. "Because of us."

"Come again?"

"America. Washington. The Brandt administration, and a couple presidents before him. We've sanctioned Venezuela almost as hard as North Korea, and maybe Moreno deserves it, but there are side effects. Collateral damage."

"That wouldn't be the case with Rivas?"

Harris shrugged. "I'm not a politician. I just know that Rivas is our guy, and once you have a guy, you can't switch teams without losing face. So here we are. If Rivas ever took power, I'd bet my pension those sanctions evaporate overnight and American oil companies roll ashore within the month. Next thing you know, we're Venezuela's new best friend."

Reed looked out the window toward a distant column of smoke. He didn't want to admit it, but he knew it was true. He'd seen it in Iraq. Sometimes it was about politics, sure. And he certainly hoped human rights played a role.

But more often than not, it was simple dollars and cents.

"Can Rivas be trusted?" Reed said.

"What do you mean?"

"I mean is he going to sell us down the river at the first opportunity?"

"He's a pragmatist, but he doesn't deal with Moreno. So long as we're all shooting in the same direction, we'll be fine."

Very reassuring.

Harris flicked his headlights on and navigated down a narrow, winding street. The city was quieter here, farther removed from the fighting only a couple miles away, but the tension was still there. Reed could see it in the nervous gazes of the people they passed, all shrinking inside their homes and regarding the decidedly government-looking vehicle with suspicion.

Wherever they were, it wasn't a stronghold of the Moreno regime. These people mistrusted both authority and outsiders.

At last Harris stopped the Tahoe next to a busted sidewalk, leaving the engine running while he surveyed the darkening street.

"Which one?" Reed asked.

Harris lifted his chin toward a three-story brick townhome, battered by age and so thick with dirt the mortar looked black. The windows were blacked out from the inside, and nobody stood at the door. By all appearances, the place was completely vacant.

"Are you sure?"

"If he's home."

Reed reached down to double-check the SCAR, and Harris shook his head.

"Rifles stay here."

"You're kidding, right?"

Harris snorted. "He's the number one target of a corrupt regime, and he doesn't know you from Adam. All the guns stay here. Stay with them, if you like."

Reed shot Turk a look. The big guy was chewing gum in the back seat, looking irritable. But he shrugged and rested his SCAR in the back seat, drawing his pistol and tucking it like a baby next to the rifle.

Reed reluctantly followed suit, noting that Harris kept his gun housed beneath his jacket.

"They know me," Harris said. Then he cut the engine and bailed out of the Tahoe.

As Reed approached the townhome, he thought he saw a glimmer of light behind one of the windows. It appeared, then vanished in a flash, just long enough to confirm that somebody was waiting inside. And they were watching.

Harris led the way up the steps, keeping his hands in the open as he neared the door. He never had the chance to knock. The heavy wooden door swung open as they reached the porch, revealing a black hall behind and a short Venezuelan man wielding an AK-47.

Reed stiffened, instantly regretting his decision to leave the rifle, but the Venezuelan didn't brandish the AK. He kept it pointed muzzle-down, riding in the crook of his arm as he beckoned them in.

Harris gestured Reed, Turk, and Corbyn ahead, then took up the rear. The door closed behind them, encasing them in darkness, then overhead lights flashed on and two more men wearing sidearms appeared. Reed and Turk were pushed against the wall and quickly patted down while Corbyn was searched in front of them. The process was quick and thorough, leaving no room for anything larger than a penknife to remain hidden.

Reed was impressed. He kept his hands up and his body relaxed until the search was complete, listening as Harris spoke calming Spanish to the guy with the AK.

"Rivas is here," Harris said at last. "But only one of you can come."

Reed and Corbyn both stepped forward at the same moment. He faced her off with a raised eyebrow, then pushed ahead.

"Sorry, hotshot. I'm the one missing somebody."

Corbyn leaned against the wall, arms crossed, looking pissed. Reed left Turk with her and followed Harris up a narrow wooden stairway. The guy with the AK fell in behind, walking easily and still looking relaxed, but Reed noticed he kept his eyes moving and the AK's trigger within easy reach.

Nobody's fool.

At the top of the stairs, another heavy door blocked their path. The guy with the AK directed Harris to knock, and Reed noted a camera mounted to the ceiling above the doorframe. A long second passed, then the bolt slid, and the door swung open.

The space beyond was nothing like he expected. There were no walls of small arms, no windows covered in bulletproof steel, and no more bodyguards.

Instead, the room was small—some type of converted living area, with a fireplace and a large dining room table piled high with documents and maps. Only four men stood inside, and two women. They were all gathered around the table, wearing worn street clothes and looking exhausted as the newcomers entered.

Reed picked out Rivas immediately. He was of average height and less than average build. Jet-black hair and eyes that matched. Skinny to the point of looking malnourished.

But when Reed and Harris stepped into the room, Rivas was the first to look up. He stood with a confident squaring of his shoulders and a tight but genuine smile, circling the table without fear and extending a hand.

"Señor Harris, it is good of you to come."

Harris shook the hand, then introduced Montgomery as his "associate." Rivas didn't blink at the obvious innuendo, offering Reed a strong grip.

"I am sorry that our paths cross on such a difficult day for my country. Although perhaps that is why you are here."

"In part," Harris said. "My bosses in Washington are understandably concerned about the instability. I was asked to extend our condolences for the turbulence, and—"

"We're looking for a man," Reed said, cutting him off.

Enough bullshit.

"A man?" Rivas raised both eyebrows.

"An American man. White, about six foot two, slender. He has a fake leg."

Rivas looked back to Harris. Harris shrugged apologetically.

"I take it this man..." Rivas hesitated, returning to his table and sitting on the edge. "He was lost here in Caracas?"

"In the countryside," Reed said. "And he wasn't lost. He was taken."

"By Moreno?"

"Possibly. Or by some of his associates."

"Ah. Associates. Men like you."

Nobody said anything. Rivas folded his arms.

"I am sorry, señor. You find me at a very difficult time. I am missing people of my own."

Rivas looked out the darkening window, his gaze growing distant. Reed couldn't tell if it was an act or not, but if it was, it was a good one. Rivas looked the part of a war-weary leader, starving the way his people were starving.

"Washington asked me," Harris said slowly, glaring at Reed, "to inquire about the nature of today's...disturbance."

Rivas laughed, but he didn't smile. "Disturbance? Is this what my allies call our distress?" He shook his head. "Moreno has taken a man hostage. His name is Juan Blanco. We are protesting his unjust arrest."

"We're aware of that," Harris said carefully. "We heard your speeches. What I'm asking now is how far you're going to take this?"

"As far as we must," Rivas said. "Was it not your own Martin Luther King who once said that injustice anywhere is a threat to justice everywhere?"

Rivas held his chin up. Reed narrowed his eyes.

"What does Blanco know?" Reed said.

Rivas's gaze snapped toward him a little too quickly. "Excuse me?"

"Moreno wouldn't have taken him and you wouldn't be burning the city down unless he knew something."

Rivas looked to Harris. Harris repeated the apologetic shrug.

"You are a shrewd associate, Mr. Montgomery."

"I do what I can."

Rivas walked to the window and stood a long while watching the last light of day fade. It seemed to take his strength with it.

"Blanco worked as an aide inside Miraflores. He managed to obtain, but had yet to deliver, a certain computer drive."

"What was on it?" Harris pressed.

Rivas looked over one shoulder. "Videotapes. Torture porn. Depictions of Venezuelan political prisoners being beaten, raped, and interrogated inside El Helicoide. Or so Blanco claimed."

Rivas left the window, and the man with the AK moved in to close the curtain.

"It is no secret that Moreno has done this for years. The FAES hunts opposition for sport. Men and women are arrested, never to be seen again. El Helicoide's doors swing only one way, as they say. But...we could not prove it."

"So you want the tapes," Reed finished. "Why is that important?"

Rivas shook his head, snorting derisively. "This is not obvious?"

Reed didn't answer.

"Venezuela is at war, Mr. Montgomery. With herself. And both sides are losing. I cannot overturn this regime with rhetoric alone. The people are tired and broken. But many of them see no reason to change. It is, as you say, *the devil you know*."

"You need something to push them over the edge," Reed said.

"I need something to prove who the monster really is. I need a nail for the coffin."

"So what's with the riots?"

Rivas shook his head, holding up a finger. "Protests, Mr. Montgomery. We call them protests."

"Okay. Protests. Why?"

Rivas settled into a chair at the end of the table. The small circle of men and women around him hadn't spoken since the Americans had arrived. They seemed defeated—and maybe a little suspicious. Reed couldn't blame them.

"We launched the protests in order to disarm Moreno...just in case Blanco talked. It is a war of words, yes? Nobody can blame us for espionage if we blame them for kidnapping first."

"How's that going?" Reed asked.

Rivas drew breath to reply, but just then a phone rang at the end of the table, and the woman seated there snatched it up. She withdrew into the corner and spoke quietly.

Rivas shook his head. "Not well."

The woman finished the call and turned around, her face blanching white. She set the phone down and spoke quickly in Spanish to the table. Reed caught only two words, but they were enough: *Moreno* and *army*.

Rivas cursed and reached for the phone. "This has gone on long enough!"

He began to dial. Reed stepped past Harris and put a hand on Rivas's arm.

"How did you know Moreno took Blanco hostage?"

Rivas looked up. "What?"

"You didn't say he was missing. You said Moreno took him hostage. How do you know?"

"His wife was a witness," Rivas said.

Reed shook his head. "No. It's more than that. You said yourself that the others have gone missing and nobody knows where, but with Blanco, you were certain. How?"

Rivas hesitated a long second, seeming to weigh his options.

"We have a man," he said slowly. "On the inside."

"El Helicoide?"

"No. Miraflores."

Reed motioned for him to put the phone down. The others around the table were already busy working their phones, making calls. Making arrangements.

Ordering the end of the riots, probably. Reed couldn't blame them. It was bad enough to fight riot shields and tear gas. They would be no match for bullets.

"We're also looking for a Russian," Reed said. "A fat guy, with a long gray beard. He's been using Moreno's chopper, so he might well be with him. They might have taken my friend to Miraflores also. Keep everybody in one place, out of sight."

"What are you saying?" Rivas said.

"I'm offering you a deal. Call your inside man. If you can find my friend, and find the Russian, I'll get Blanco back for you."

Harris pushed forward. Reed stiff-armed him without looking, still holding Rivas's gaze.

"You will...help us?" Rivas asked slowly.

"Isn't that what allies are for?" Reed nodded to the phone. "Contact your man, and find mine. I'll take it from there."

54

The Presidential Residence
The White House

The breath slowly vacated Maggie's lungs as she slipped into the water. It was hot—as hot as she could stand it, designed to thin her blood and relax the spasming muscles all up and down her back. She descended into the tub until the water reached her chin, her entire body tingling with racing fire.

But she didn't get out. She pressed her back against the porcelain and breathed evenly. Relaxing. Embracing the heat. Releasing the stress of the day and turning her mind once again to her own survival.

Maggie had never been a very spiritual person. Growing up in Louisiana, she identified as Roman Catholic—because of course she did. There was a lot she liked about the Church. The way it drew the community together, unifying everyone around a shared set of values and priorities for themselves, their children, and their future.

Even so, thoughts of God and a greater meaning were distant at best as the turmoil of the presidency descended upon her with all the wrath of the other place. When the White House physician inquired about her spiritual health, Maggie was surprised. Even a little offended. It seemed a deeply personal, intrusive question. What did her spiritual health have to do with anything? What did that term even mean?

"Life itself is nothing more than the union of the soul with the body," the physician said. "For your body to heal, that connection must be strong."

It sounded like a load of hogwash at the time, but as the brutal days of physical therapy, the stacks of medicine bottles, and all the sleepless nights began to wear at her mind, Maggie gave in. She found the rosary beads her mother gifted her when she was elected governor, and she prayed nightly. Then twice a day.

Now she found herself praying for strength and wisdom almost all day long, and doubting whether she deserved either. Amid all the chaotic moments that had consumed her presidency, there hadn't been a lot of time for navel gazing. Not a lot of time to question whether she was the woman for the job.

But now, alone in the bath...she wondered. She doubted.

What am I doing here?

Maggie slipped a little lower in the water, dropping until it washed over her skull, and she heard her heart thumping in her ears. She closed her eyes, and the nightmares returned almost instantly. Stratton on that stage with his demon voice. The executioner standing by, wielding his oversized rifle.

The black sky opening like a grave, ready to consume her.

But this time she didn't shake. She didn't scream or fight back the visions. She ran toward them, hobbling when the pain almost drove her to the ground but not stopping. She threw herself at that executioner, heedless of his gun. Barely noticing the hot agony that ripped through her gut as he opened fire.

He'd shot her once. Let him try again.

Maggie broke the surface, gasping for air, water streaming down her face. A stiff knock rattled the door, followed by the semi-alarmed voice of her personal steward.

"Ma'am? Are you okay?"

"I'm fine, Angie." Maggie gasped, still seeing the horrorscape in her mind but not caring anymore. She was sick of being afraid.

"There's a call for you, ma'am. Secretary Gorman. Would you like me to have her hold?"

Maggie rubbed water out of her eyes, peering around the oversized White House bathroom. It wasn't opulent, just comfortable.

"No, Angie. Put her through."

Maggie leaned out of the tub and scooped a phone off the floor. It slipped in her damp hands, but she got it to her ear.

"Lisa?"

"Madam President...I'm sorry. Is this a bad time?"

"Not at all. I'm glad you called."

Long pause. Maggie knew what she needed to say, but she also knew Gorman needed to make the first move. There was a delicate balance of power at play here. A tug-of-war between grace and authority.

"I wanted to apologize for my behavior this afternoon," Gorman said. "It was unacceptable to walk out that way, especially in front of other members of the cabinet. You'll have my resignation in the morning."

Maggie winced. She had hoped Gorman would back down on that tact. Maybe grace was needed more than power.

"I accept your apology, Lisa, but I cannot accept the resignation. I need you. Now more than ever before."

"Do you, Madam President? With respect, this isn't the first time we've crossed wires over foreign policy. I realize my approach is conservative, but to be honest with you, I've seldom felt that my viewpoints were valued."

Maggie held in a sigh, leaning into the tub. She closed her eyes and thought quickly. Gorman was right—they'd crossed wires a number of times. And yes, Maggie seldom agreed with Gorman's diplomacy-heavy approach.

But she still needed Gorman. If for no other reason than to stabilize the State Department and manage America's allies while Maggie hunted down her enemies.

"Doesn't disagreement make us stronger?" Maggie asked. "Iron sharpening iron, and all that."

"Only if we let it, ma'am. The State Department is a cornerstone of our democracy, but lately I've felt that your approach to foreign policy is incompatible with my own. You didn't choose me as secretary. I won't make this difficult on you. I'm happy to step aside."

"Lisa, wait." Maggie sat up. "It's true, we see things differently. But that's part of what makes any administration strong. If I've done a poor job of appreciating the wisdom you bring to the table, that's on me. But you can't abandon the administration in the middle of a crisis."

"It's been one crisis after another for two years, ma'am."

"I know, right?" Maggie laughed softly, but Gorman didn't join.

"Look," Maggie said. "Promise me you'll stay until we resolve this issue in Venezuela. Hang in there that long. Then we'll talk. Okay?"

"I can't condone or support regime change. It's too dangerous."

"I'm not asking you to. I'm only asking you to stand by our allies. We're obligated to lend a hand, are we not?"

Long pause.

"I suppose that depends on what you mean by *lending a hand*."

Maggie tried not to grit her teeth. "It means we stand up for freedom, Lisa. That's all it has ever meant."

Another protracted pause.

"Can I count on you to see us through this crisis?" Maggie pressed.

"Of course, Madam President. I serve the nation."

Maggie breathed a silent sigh. "Thank you, Lisa."

She slid the phone back into its cradle and pushed stringy wet hair out of her eyes. Her back ached. Her head throbbed.

But it was her mind that felt run over by a dump truck. No amount of hot water could ease the tension.

Gorman was right. It had been one crisis after another, and something told Maggie that the events in Venezuela were only a gateway to more of the same.

55

Caracas, Venezuela

From the roof of Rivas's headquarters, Reed had a clear view of downtown Caracas. The protests had moved northward under Rivas's direction, concentrating around the core of the city, where Moreno was least likely to deploy lethal force.

There were too many witnesses. Too many of his own supporters. Rivas might be a ruthless pragmatist, but he wasn't stupid.

Reed bummed half a pack of cigarettes off the guy with the AK and stood chain-smoking them by himself near the edge of the roof, the SCAR leaned against the wall next to him. The tobacco was good, if a little rawer than he was used to. More like the flavor of a cigar than a cigarette, but that was probably a good thing. Fewer chemicals.

Reed dragged on his smoke and listened to the distant sound of sirens mixed with the ever-present roar of a few thousand voices, all chanting the same thing. This far away, they sounded like soft thunder. He couldn't tell what they said and knew it didn't matter.

Nobody was listening to them. Not Moreno. Not even Rivas. Caught in the middle of a power struggle, used as pawns in a chess game of politics, these people were soldiers on a battlefield they could never own.

Reed knew, because he'd once been a soldier. He knew what it felt like to be shot at on behalf of people who didn't care whether you lived or died. Fat men behind sprawling desks, dealing the lives of young Marines like poker chips.

Rivas didn't feel like one of them. But how could you really tell? Given enough time, enough power...what would he become?

The roof hatch groaned behind him, but Reed didn't need to look. He recognized Turk's heavy footsteps as the big Tennessean joined him, accepting a cigarette without needing to ask for it. He lit up and sucked down, and Reed found himself very glad to not be alone. The rooftop was cold, and looking out over the city, he suddenly felt very far from home. Thoughts of Banks storming out returned to his mind, and he wondered where she was. Who she was with.

If she'd ever listened to his voicemails.

Reed didn't worry about her. If there was ever a woman who could look after herself, it was Banks. He didn't worry about Davy, either. Banks looked after their son like a mama bear after a cub. She was a great mother.

But he did worry. He worried about himself, even though he knew it was selfish. He worried about what he was becoming, and what he was doing with his life.

He'd spent years fighting for freedom. Dreaming of peace. Longing for a little home and a loving family and football to watch on the weekends. He'd bled for that. Banks had bled for that.

And he'd let her walk right out the door...for what? For *this*? More gunfire? Another man's war?

He'd been a damn fool. He should have fought for her. Pulled her in and never let go. Given her whatever she wanted. A big city, a small apartment, a music career—who cared? He could live in the city. He could live in another country. He could live *anywhere* she was safe and happy. So long as he had his family.

So long as Davy had his father.

"This is the last one," Reed said.

Turk cocked his head.

"The last op," Reed clarified. "I'm going home. I'm done."

Turk grunted. Sucked in a deep lungful and breathed out slowly.

"Me too."

The haze gathered around Reed's head, and he embraced the sudden calm, blocking out the distant roar of voices. Tuning out the hell of Venezuelan heartbreak. And simply focusing on his family.

Banks's smile. Davy's laugh.

It could be a good life, if only he would stop sabotaging it.

"You gonna buy that house?" Turk asked suddenly.

Reed drew on the cigarette. Held his breath and enjoyed the burn. Then he shook his head. "No. I don't think I am."

"Something more rural?"

"Actually, I was thinking of going the other way. Maybe a bigger city."

"No kidding?"

"Banks never had her shot with music. She deserves that. I don't want her to look back and regret."

"No more musical place than Music City. Sinju really likes it."

"And you?"

Turk shrugged. "I…hate it. Too much concrete. But you know."

Reed laughed and finished his smoke. He reached into the pack for another and found it empty, so he crushed it under his foot instead and pocketed his hands.

"What are we gonna do, Turk?"

"I was thinking about starting a gym. Like, one of those ugly block buildings with crude equipment. These West Coasters will pay good money to be screamed at while they do pushups. You wanna join?"

Reed laughed. "Sure. I'm good at screaming."

"Great. We can call it Jarhead Fitness…gotta good ring to it!"

Reed bumped his fist, but his mind was far from thoughts of building leases and exercise equipment. None of that would matter until they found Wolfgang.

Wolfgang…and Belsky.

As if on cue, the roof hatch blew open again, and the guy with the AK stuck his head out, calling in Spanish and beckoning. Reed jogged across the roof and followed him down a ladder into the house. The room they had left Rivas in only two hours prior was now abuzz with action, all of Rivas's associates huddling around the table and shuffling sheets of paper back and forth as they chattered in agitated Spanish.

As Reed reached the table, the buzz died almost completely, dejected and angry faces overtaking the excitement of only moments before. Many of Rivas's aides turned from the table in disgust, leaving only Rivas to greet Reed and Turk.

"What happened?" Reed demanded. "Did you find them?"

Corbyn pressed in next to the small crowd as Rivas ran a hand over his face and settled into a chair. He looked ready to drop.

"The American is missing a leg, yes?"

"He has a fake leg."

"Well, not anymore." Rivas pushed a tablet across the table, and Reed scooped it up. He wasn't sure what he expected to see—photographs of Wolfgang tied to a chair, now missing both legs, maybe. Instead, he saw a satellite map of Caracas, drawn straight from Google. A yellow pin marked a place near the core of the city.

"Miraflores?" Reed said.

Rivas nodded. "Your friend is held prisoner in the basement. My contact says the Russian is there also. Big man, long beard. Never showers."

"That's Belsky," Reed muttered, zooming in the screen. "Tell me about this building."

He tapped the presidential palace. Rivas shrugged.

"What is there to tell? It's like your White House. Much security. Our best hope is for Moreno to transfer your friend to El Helicoide. We could perhaps rescue him on the way."

Reed ignored Rivas, zooming in on the palace and inspecting the layout. The building consisted of a large, square mansion with an open courtyard right in the middle. Built around that mansion was a high wall, not quite a rectangle, but close. The complex as a whole looked a little like a box within a box, with the interior box shifted toward the top of the exterior one, leaving a larger section of greenspace near the bottom.

Reed zoomed in on that greenspace and found what he was looking for —a round pad, maybe built of concrete, with a white *H* painted on it. Zooming back out, he selected a tool to measure distance and dropped a pin directly on top of the *H*, then drew a straight line northward, out to sea.

Seven miles to the coast. Then another twelve to reach international waters. Maybe...eight minutes.

"Corbyn. Get over here."

The Brit pressed close alongside the table. Reed pointed to the yellow line between Miraflores and the Gulf of Mexico.

"You were a helicopter pilot?"

Corbyn frowned. "What are you talking about?"

"You can fly a chopper?"

"I flew one in the RAF...years ago. What's up?"

Reed ignored her, looking instead to Turk. He didn't have to voice the plan evolving in his head. Turk was tracking right alongside him, and nodded once.

"Rivas, you said your man is held prisoner inside Miraflores? This Blanco guy?"

Rivas nodded slowly. "*Sí*...in the basement, probably."

"And you have a man on the inside?"

"Yes..." Rivas looked suddenly uncomfortable. "What are you thinking?"

"We'll get them all," Reed said. "Hit the palace directly. Infiltrate to the basement, then exfiltrate off the lawn."

"Are you crazy?" Rivas and Corbyn both spoke at once. Reed simply zoomed out on the tablet and gestured to the greater cityscape.

"We'll need a distraction to pull military forces away from the palace. Something big enough for Moreno to worry about. More than a protest. Where is this Helicoide you've been talking about?"

Rivas stood, circling the table and reaching for the tablet. "Have you lost your mind? I'm not trying to start a civil war! Moreno is deploying troops into the city. I must pull my people back."

"And then what?" Reed pressed. "Business as usual, next week. Do you know why that Russian is here, Rivas? He's here to pillage your country. To suck your single greatest natural resource right out from under your feet and sell it offshore. Nowhere in that equation does anything change for your people. Moreno just gets richer and more secure by the barrel."

"This is not the way," Rivas said, shaking his head. "This plan of yours will get people killed!"

"Of course it's gonna get people killed! But it might just save a few hundred thousand more from starvation over the next decade."

Reed glowered in disbelief, then tossed the tablet down. "Look. I didn't come here to rescue Venezuela. I came here to arrest Belsky, and now I have to get my friend back. You can do whatever you want, but if Wolfgang and Belsky are inside Miraflores, that's where we're going, with or without you."

Rivas turned irritably to his circle of aides. A whispered conference was held in Spanish, snapping with passion as arguments and counterarguments were made. Corbyn moved down the table, her voice low as she spoke out of the side of her mouth.

"Are you out of your mind?"

"Usually," Reed said. "But not this time."

"I don't have authorization to participate in direct action!"

"You won't be. You'll just be hauling our asses out of there once we're done."

"I don't have a helicopter. I haven't flown in years!"

"Moreno has a helicopter. You'll be fine."

Corbyn flushed, drawing breath to protest. Then Rivas returned. His circle of aides had grown quiet, but Reed could still feel the tension amid them. Glares mixed with wide-eyed looks of hopeful desperation.

The face of a brewing revolution.

"I don't have an army," Rivas said. "I can't attack anything."

"You won't need to," Reed said. "All you need to do is draw out his armed forces."

"I won't risk my people," Rivas pressed. "How am I supposed to engage the military without loss of life?"

Reed scooped up the tablet again and zoomed in on another large building, well south of Miraflores, on the far side of a wide highway.

El Helicoide.

As he focused on the spot, the dim yellow light built into the ceiling overhead flickered suddenly and went out. Everybody looked automatically to the bulb, waiting for the blackout to pass and the light to return.

The bulb buzzed, then flashed on again. Reed looked to Rivas.

"I think I have an idea."

56

The White House

Stratton hadn't left the West Wing all day. Bent over a half-eaten chicken Caesar salad from the Navy Mess, he huddled inside his cramped vice presidential office across from Attorney General Thomas, a slew of documents from PPI scattered across the desk.

Thomas sat with a pen in one hand, shuffling through the mess and rattling off questions like a machine gun while Stratton ate. They were good questions—the who, what, when, where, and how of a prosecutor warming up to an investigation—but the disbelief in the attorney general's voice was palpable.

Clicking his pen shut, Thomas leaned back in his chair and shook his head. "Jordan...what you're suggesting..."

Stratton gestured to the documents with his fork. "I'm not suggesting anything, Greg. I'm proving it."

"This isn't admissible!" Thomas said. "Half this stuff was illegally obtained. I can't run an investigation on this shit."

"So call Bill," Stratton said, referring to FBI Director William Purcell. "Get his people on it."

Thomas pointed to the documents. "You're not hearing me. *If* this is true, you don't want an investigation linked to the White House. Don't you see the conflict of interest here? The president does not want to launch a witch hunt against America's business elite. You've got a tiger by the tail. I don't—"

The phone on Stratton's desk rang. He scooped it up without checking the ID.

"Stratton."

"The president requests for you to return to the Situation Room, sir. Alone."

It was O'Dell. His voice carried the same dry detachment Stratton had become used to, but there was exhaustion in the undertone.

"Of course," Stratton said. "Be right there."

He hung up and stood. Thomas nearly spilled the stack of papers heaped in his lap.

"Where are you going? You can't just leave me in the middle of this."

Stratton slapped the AG on the shoulder, heading for the door. "You'll be fine, Greg. Call Bill and put something together. The only way out is through, all right?"

Thomas spluttered. Stratton ignored him. Back in the hallway, he guided himself down a level to the Situation Room, where Secret Service agents stood guard just outside the room and O'Dell waited for him.

O'Dell moved for the door, but Stratton put a hand on his shoulder.

"Just a moment."

O'Dell turned on him, his dark Cajun eyes strained and focused. He started to speak. Then he simply stopped.

Stratton measured the gaze, retracing his memories of the last two hours in the Situation Room. The way O'Dell hovered near the president, never leaving her elbow. Tense and alert, like a watchdog ready to sink his teeth into anyone who threatened her.

A watchdog...and something more.

"The president asked you to watch me?" Stratton asked.

O'Dell said nothing.

Stratton grunted. "I thought so."

Again O'Dell reached for the door. Stratton caught his arm.

"James...listen to me."

O'Dell stiffened, pulling his arm but failing to yank it away. Stratton kept his voice calm.

"You're on the inside of a very dangerous game now. What happens in this room...the things the president tells you at night...that knowledge could destroy her. Do you understand me?"

O'Dell's chin lifted. Stratton released his arm, adjusting his own coat.

"What I'm trying to tell you, James, is you've never given me a reason not to trust you. But if you think for a moment that you've got some kind of special access...tread carefully. The millisecond you become a threat to this administration, I will rip your throat out and leave you to bleed on a White House sofa."

Stratton finished the monologue with a long, cold stare. He saw surprise, and then maybe confusion swirling behind O'Dell's dark gaze.

Then the president's bodyguard smiled, just a little.

"So noted, Mr. Vice President."

Stratton held his hand toward the door, and O'Dell opened it. The two of them stepped into the Situation Room to find Maggie huddled over the table, Director O'Brien and General Yellin visible on screens.

"Where have you been?" Maggie snapped, looking up from the table.

"It's my fault, ma'am," O'Dell said. "My apologies."

Maggie's gaze narrowed, but she simply waved a hand at the door. "Sit down. We've got Montgomery on the line."

Stratton took his seat, surveying the room and noting the conspicuous absence of Secretary Gorman. He put two and two together and knew what Montgomery was about to say even before he spoke. Maggie punched a key on the phone.

"Go ahead, Reed."

The now familiar voice of the Prosecution Force's leader crackled through the phone, distorted by distance. Inside of sixty seconds he outlined a scheme bold enough to make Hollywood blush, but nobody around the table interrupted him. When Montgomery finished, Maggie hit mute on the phone and pivoted to the screen on the wall.

"General Yellin. Can you make this work?"

The general didn't hesitate. "We have an asset in the Gulf that we could reroute. Flight time may be a little longer than eight minutes, but unless the Venezuelans deploy air forces, that shouldn't be a problem."

"Director?" Maggie pivoted to O'Brien. Unlike Yellin, O'Brien looked anything but stoic. His owl face was set in a series of hard lines, his cheeks a little flushed.

"Madam President, I cannot endorse this course of action based on existing intel—"

"Dammit, Victor. I'm not asking for your endorsement. I'm asking whether the CIA still holds an arsenal inside the embassy?"

A long pause. O'Brien pushed his glasses up his nose, then nodded. "I believe so, ma'am."

"Terrific." Maggie faced Stratton, both eyebrows raised, a clear question in her face.

Not asking for his opinion. Not even asking for his judgment.

Asking for his trust.

Stratton suddenly understood why he had been asked to return to the Situation Room, even while Gorman hadn't. Maggie was giving him a chance here. A chance to be on the inside of the inside.

Stratton looked sideways at O'Dell and saw the challenge in the big man's face. Then he returned his attention to Maggie.

"It's a no-lose situation, ma'am. We recover our people, recover Belsky, and deal a potentially fatal blow to the Moreno regime. Whatever the Russians are up to in Venezuela, it's reasonable to conclude that they need Moreno. If Rivas were to take power, you could revoke the sanctions and send our own people to drill. Win-win."

"That's the general idea," Maggie said slowly.

"I completely disagree." O'Brien's voice broke from the speakers on the wall. "This is an ill-advised and potentially disastrous scheme. You're putting all your chips in on shaky intelligence, at best. If this Blanco guy isn't found inside Miraflores, or if he doesn't hold the tapes he claims—"

"Then we're all SOL," Maggie snapped. "Tell me something I don't know. Jordan?"

Stratton sat next to her, staring at the phone. Weighing the odds. The unspoken question hanging over them all like a cloud was whether they could trust the man on the other end of that phone. If Montgomery could deliver—if he could pull this thing off without leaving American fingerprints—the payoff would be earth-shattering. But if even one domino fell out of line, the consequences would be hellacious. Possibly overwhelming, not to mention politically lethal.

And yet...

And yet Maggie wasn't the only one on the warpath. Stratton felt the outrage deep in his gut when he surveyed those PPI reports. His own people had turned against him, conspiring in the dark to displace his boss and clearly expecting him to serve their best interests after the fact.

Well. To hell with that.

"I say we do it," Stratton said. "Kick 'em in the teeth, Madam President."

A dry smile crept across Maggie's face. She nodded slowly, and Stratton saw the hint of respect in her bloodshot eyes. It was a look he hadn't seen in weeks—it felt good.

Maggie hit the mute button.

"You still there, Reed?"

"Just enjoying the hold music," Montgomery muttered.

"The arsenal is there. Have your local contact get you inside."

"What about my LZ?"

"I'll take care of your LZ, son," Yellin said, his deep voice booming over the wall-mounted speakers. "You just get there safely with the package in hand."

"Reed," Maggie said, leaning toward the speaker. "We're putting a lot of chips on this bet. Okay? I need it to pay out."

Montgomery snorted. "Don't worry, Madam President. I'm fully prepared to be disowned and blacklisted if things go sideways."

"That wasn't what I—"

"Sure it was. That's why you pay me the big bucks. Director O'Brien?"

Long pause. O'Brien drew a belabored breath. "Yes?"

"Place a call to Caracas and tell Harris to play ball. He's getting squeamish."

Montgomery hung up, and the room went still. Maggie remained bent over the table, focused on the phone. She looked spent, and Stratton felt the sudden urge to place a gentle hand on her shoulder.

O'Dell beat him to it, closing in beside her and taking her hand. Maggie wiped sweaty hair from her forehead.

"You've all got work to do," she said. "Let's get to it."

Yellin and O'Brien dropped off the screen, and Stratton stood, buttoning his jacket.

"I'll be with Thomas," he said. "We're putting something together."

Maggie nodded.

"You should get some rest, ma'am," Stratton said gently. "We can't do this without you."

Maggie laughed. "You could probably do it better without me, but I won't give you the chance. Keep me posted on things with Thomas."

"Yes, ma'am."

Stratton headed for the door, then stopped just short of the exit. He turned back.

"Ma'am, if I may."

"Yes?"

"I understand why you excluded Secretary Gorman from this meeting, but regardless of what happens tonight, you're going to need her."

"I know," Maggie said.

"I've known Lisa since she was in the Senate," Stratton continued. "A word of advice? She's easier to win over ahead of time."

"I'll call her," Maggie said.

Stratton reached for the door. "Chin up, Madam President. We're about to nail your enemies to the wall."

57

USS Boxer
528 nautical miles east of Panama Canal
Caribbean Sea

The eight-hundred-forty-three-foot warship looked like a miniature aircraft carrier from a distance. Flat-topped, riding high over stormy whitecaps north of the South American continent, *Boxer* was the sixth US-flagged warship to bear the name since the capture of *HMS Boxer* from the British during the War of 1812.

Naval warfare technology had evolved considerably since then, and even though *Wasp*-class amphibious ships were already becoming outdated and phased out by the new *America*-class ships, *Boxer* still represented more than your average can of whoop-ass, ready and eager to be deployed anywhere in the world where whoop-ass was called upon.

Equipped with a standard air wing of a dozen or more helicopters and between six and ten F-35B Lightning II fighters, *Boxer*'s real secret weapon was launched via a well deck built into the vessel's broad stern—a flotilla of fast-attack vessels, loaded with as many as seventeen hundred US Marines.

She was the ultimate answer to the age-old problem of how to secure beachheads with maximum efficiency, and as far as Captain Kurt Anderson was concerned, *Boxer* was nothing short of a work of art. He'd held the title of her commander for barely three months, and already *Boxer* had been transferred from Norfolk to San Diego, necessitating yet another cross-country move for his road-weary family. While the Navy paid for moving containers to ship their battered furniture, Anderson himself steamed the warship at a stately twenty-two knots all the way down the East Coast and now into the Caribbean Sea, headed for the Panama Canal.

He wouldn't admit it to his irritated wife or disgusted children, but Kurt Anderson was having the time of his life. His first major command, a long and beautiful cruise, and the prospect of lengthier tours into the Pacific lying ahead. All at just forty-two years old.

It was good to be in the Navy.

"Captain's on the bridge!"

The officer of the deck chimed out as Anderson ducked through a narrow sea door and into *Boxer*'s control center. As the sun faded and left the Caribbean Sea awash in darkness, there was little to see through the bank of windows facing the bow. Dull lights marked the flight deck while illuminated control panels reflected on the black glass. For many sailors, it was the most boring time of the day—the end of a long watch, or the start of an even longer one, leading through the night.

But for Anderson, there was something about the gentle peace of the night, matched with the perpetual hum of the vessel's machinery, that relaxed him. No, it was more than relaxing. It spoke to his very soul.

He nodded to a few of the officers scattered around the cramped space as he navigated to a window, cupping hot coffee in both his hands. Outside, a warm breeze whispered over the deck and pulled at the secured rotor blades of a Super Stallion helicopter lashed to the deck.

It was warm down here—a lot warmer than Norfolk, and San Diego would be warm too. The kids should be happy. Sure, it was a new school, and new friends, and yet another new house. And yes, their tour through SoCal would probably last only so long as it took the Pentagon to station them farther west, maybe in Japan.

But wasn't that part of the fun? Never knowing where you'd end up next? Always on the move.

A light flashed on a nearby control panel, and the watch officer stationed there responded by lifting a phone handset. He spoke mechanically into the mouthpiece, then looked over one shoulder.

"TAO requesting to speak with you, sir."

Anderson took the handset, sipping coffee from his free hand. "Anderson, go ahead TAO."

"Incoming transmission from Washington. Request for you to join me at CIC."

"Roger that, Mike. Be right down."

Anderson hung up and exited the bridge, swinging down a series of one-way stairwells and narrow halls as heavy waves sent tremors through the heavy ship, nearly spilling his coffee. Anderson negotiated the swells with practiced ease, ducking into *Boxer*'s Combat Information Center, or CIC.

The room was dark, as always, illuminated by the green and red of flashing radar screens and navigation displays built around the perimeter and filling the room's core. A boring place to be for ninety-nine percent of any cruise, but as the very nerve center of combat readiness the moment action erupted, it was a place Anderson was familiar with from his own tenure as Tactical Action Officer, or TAO.

Those memories were good ones, stationed on a range of military ships around the world. He felt comfortable in the CIC.

"What've you got, Mike?"

Anderson stopped next to his TAO's desk, holding an overhead brace as *Boxer* tilted into another oversized swell. The TAO looked up from his desk and handed Anderson a torn sheet of printer paper without comment.

Anderson scanned the heading as he sipped coffee, enjoying the warmth in his throat.

And then nearly choking on it.

"They want us to do *what*?"

58

Caracas, Venezuela

The US embassy in Caracas lay dark and desolate in the southeast corner of the city, its flagpole bare, the tangle of razor wire arranged around the top of the perimeter walls gleaming under the glow of a soft moon. The gates were closed and barred, the guardhouse empty, and the best Reed could see from across the street in the passenger seat of Harris's Tahoe, the entire complex was completely vacant.

It was a haunting image, and it struck home a lot harder than he expected. Just knowing that the flagpole nestled in the courtyard beyond the gate once proudly displayed the Stars and Stripes, and now stood naked in the hot Venezuelan breeze, sent a strange chill down his spine.

It kind of pissed him off.

"There's a secondary entrance around the back," Harris said, his foot on the brake but the Tahoe still in gear. "We can access the basement from there."

"This place under surveillance?" Reed asked.

"I doubt it. After Moreno expelled the ambassador in 2019, they kept their people on our backs for months. Just harassing us, mostly. Making stops and threatening arrests as we came and went. That's why we relocated the CIA station across town—to the dentist's office. It's been more than a year now. I doubt they've got anyone here."

Reed scanned the streets of Venezuela's embassy district, marveling at how dark it was. He'd visited embassies before, including taking a tour of Washington, DC's embassy district, where nations from around the world planted their flags amid the proudest architecture of their culture.

It was usually a bright, thriving place. A lot of people with diplomatic immunity, cruising the streets and touring the local attractions.

Venezuela's embassy district couldn't be more different. It felt somehow dead, as if the life had been sucked from the air of this place. Nobody wanted to be friends with Venezuela, it seemed.

Or maybe Moreno didn't want to be friends with anybody.

"Clear?" Reed asked.

Turk grunted from the back seat alongside Corbyn. "Looks good to me."

Reed waved two fingers at Harris, and the CIA station chief navigated away from the curb, circling the street as he gnawed absently on a toothpick.

"I really can't believe we're doing this," he muttered.

"Believe it," Reed said. "They're illegally holding an American citizen without due process. This is what happens."

Harris snorted. "No. This most definitely is *not* what happens."

"Yeah, well. It is tonight." Reed reached for the door handle as Harris pulled to a stop. As he stepped out of the Tahoe, he could smell distant smoke on the air. Burning rubber and debris. But no noise. Rivas had called his people back in accordance with the plan, rallying them someplace south of downtown, leaving just enough protesters behind to occupy Moreno's forces as the Venezuelan army took control of the city. As they had navigated the long way from the dental office toward the old embassy, Reed had noted military-style trucks rolling into downtown, loaded with men in dark green uniforms, all wielding assault weapons.

Ready to grind their boots into the throats of their own people. A lot of lousy cowards, in his mind. He wouldn't hesitate to gun them down if faced with the necessity.

Harris cut the engine and followed them to a narrow gate built into the embassy wall, now overhung by an unmanaged shrub and nearly blocked.

Using the keyboard to enter a code, he wrestled the gate open and led the way down a darkened sidewalk.

Reed walked with one hand resting on his SIG, Corbyn at his side. Upon learning of his scheme to extract Belsky and Wolfgang out of the presidential palace, Corbyn at first appeared completely unwilling to play ball.

But then Turk called her a chicken, and Reed again raised the necessity for the helicopter. He saw a strange light in her eyes at the mention of the aircraft—a light that grew only brighter the more he focused on that element of the scheme.

Corbyn was like any pilot in Reed's experience. Completely obsessed with flying and, by no fault of her own, long robbed of the opportunity. She was won over on the second attempt and thus far hadn't lost her nerve. Reed had no doubt that she was operating well outside the mandate of her MI6 deployment, but so long as she didn't leave them hanging on the extraction, he really didn't care.

Harris stopped at an exterior metal door framed by stone with two security cameras facing them. Both cameras were black and lifeless, and the door was held closed by a heavy chain and a padlock. Harris went to work on the lock, the toothpick still sliding around between his teeth as he talked quietly.

"The embassy is now considered Venezuelan property," he said. "But there's kind of a diplomatic etiquette to these things. It would be aggressive for Moreno to seize control. And he knows there's nothing here. So..."

The chain rattled free, and Harris looked over his shoulder. Then he clicked a flashlight on and shone a light over the path ahead.

The hallway was ghostly. It reminded Reed of abandoned hospitals after natural disasters. Loose scraps of paper lay strewn across the tile floor, doors hanging open and abandoned furniture scattered from room to room. Harris led the way with the flashlight blazing a trail, his free hand resting on his CIA-issued Glock 19.

At the end of the hall, Harris bypassed a turn to head into the heart of the embassy and accessed another secure door instead. It was built of solid steel, marked with black paint, the official label once mounted alongside it now torn away. Harris worked the mechanical keypad and the lock clicked open, then they proceeded into a stairwell, marching down two levels of metal steps.

"I have the strangest feeling," Corbyn said. "That this is going to land me in prison."

Reed snorted. "Cheer up, Brit. You hang around long enough, we'll show you all kinds of good times."

At the bottom of the stairs, they faced another hallway, this one paved in blank concrete and framed by solid block walls. Reed noted dormitories on either side as they proceeded to the end and paused momentarily as Harris's light flashed across an abandoned pair of brown leather boots.

USMC issued, with the anchor, globe, and eagle stamped into them. Reed had seen a few thousand of those boots and worn more than a few pairs himself.

"The security garrison evacuated to Colombia," Harris said. "They were some good people."

"Best in the Corps," Reed said. "Everybody wants embassy guard duty. Cushy job."

"Beats Iraq, anyway," Turk laughed.

The final door at the end of the hallway was built entirely of steel, vault-like in appearance, with a giant circular handle and a combination dial. Harris held the flashlight in his mouth while he worked the combination, turning the bolt handle to a deep metallic *thunk*.

"All right, hotshots. Keep your hands out of your pants."

He hauled the door open, spilling bright light into the secured compartment beyond. Corbyn breathed out a soft whistle, and Turk broke into a grin.

"Now we're talking."

Reed accepted the flashlight from Harris and scanned the walls.

Row after row of USMC-issued small arms filled racks, all bolted to the wall. M16 select-fire rifles, M4 carbines, fifty or more Beretta M9 sidearms, a rack full of twelve-gauge Mossberg shotguns, three crates of grenades, boxes full of pepper spray and tasers, tear gas and flash bangs.

Every conceivable tool for the defense of a US embassy.

Reed circled the table stretching down the middle of the small room, laden with ammunition, and found what he was looking for beneath a shelf in the back. Only a small box of it—enough to blast away a blocked gate or a collapsed wall.

C-4 plastic explosives.

"Got it," he said, toeing the box out.

Harris scooped the package up, then turned for the door. Turk laughed and held up a hand.

"Hold up there, buddy. We're ain't done."

"Are you kidding me?" Harris sounded irritated. "We've got to go."

Reed found an empty USMC duffel bag shoved beneath one of the shelves, and together he and Turk packed it full of a pair of M4s from the rack, thirty magazines of steel-core ammunition, flash bangs, fragmentation grenades, and canisters of tear gas.

"Enjoy the moment, Harris," Reed said. "It's not every day you get to raid Santa's workshop."

Turk shouldered the bag, and Harris beckoned impatiently. He bolted the vault behind them before jogging back down the vacant halls to the Tahoe. Crashing into the back seat, Turk went to work stripping down and inspecting both rifles before ramming loaded magazines into their mag wells. Harris started the engine and drove quickly away from the embassy, his phone buzzing from the console. He answered in Spanish and listened for a moment, then hung up.

"That was Rivas. His people are good to go."

"And the targets?"

Harris opened the message app on his phone. A link waited that transferred automatically to the built-in navigation app, marking a blue line out of the city, up the mountainside, to a rural spot in the middle of nowhere. Twenty plus miles outside the city.

"There," Harris said.

"Is he sure?"

"He's betting his presidency on it."

Reed accepted the M4 Turk passed forward. "All right, then. Let's blow this sucker and get the hell out of dodge."

59

Caracas, Venezuela

Rivas stood at the edge of a square surrounded by barrios as his protesters returned. They were tired, battered, and many of them red-faced from indirect contact with tear gas. Many more had sustained rubber bullet strikes and held their sides as they staggered up the street, casting nervous glances over their shoulders in the direction of Moreno's National Guard.

Only it wasn't just the National Guard pouring into the city to subdue the protests. The Venezuelan army was there also. Three or four hundred armed soldiers, dressed in full combat gear, accompanied by armored vehicles and even a tank.

It was the tank that pushed Rivas over the edge. Moreno had ground his heel into the face of the opposition ever since stealing the election of 2018, but he'd never gone this far. He'd never deployed heavy weaponry before, ready to blow his own people into bloody chunks.

Images of Tiananmen Square flashed across Rivas's mind at the sight of the Russian-built T-72 rolling down Avenida Bolívar, and he knew the time had come. The Venezuelan military had yet to open fire on their own people, but that was only a matter of time. For better or worse, Rivas had to push his chips in.

Moreno would go down *tonight*, or Rivas would fall in front of that tank.

"Luis!" One of Rivas's unofficial cabinet members appeared at his elbow, fear straining his exhausted features. "Over half have gone home. We don't have enough people."

Rivas surveyed the crowd packing in among the barrio. Maybe two hundred people, with a few dozen more trickling in. A fraction of what he had hoped for. A fraction of the thousand or more angry protesters who had taken to the streets earlier that same day, ready to make their voices heard.

For what the American had planned, Rivas needed hundreds more. A couple thousand would be ideal. Enough to overwhelm the National Guard and drive the military into panic mode.

"It is enough," Rivas said, projecting confidence he didn't feel. His lieutenant paled, pushing in front of him as Rivas moved toward the crowd.

"Luis! You can't do this. Did you not see the tank?"

"Didn't you?" Rivas challenged.

The man stopped, his mouth open. Then his arm fell away from Rivas's sleeve. Rivas put a gentle hand on his shoulder, speaking softly enough to isolate the conversation.

"This is our moment, amigo. If we do not stop this tyrant tonight, our children will slave under his heel for generations to come. They will bleed and die because we were too afraid to bleed and die for them. Do you not feel it in the air? Venezuela is calling our names."

Sudden quiet fell around them, and Rivas looked up to see the battered crowd pressing in. The barrio became still as the breathless protesters waited, too tired to move any further. Too defeated to even lift their heads.

Something hot ignited in Rivas's gut at the scene. Something angry. He pressed through the crowd to a nearby shack and snapped his fingers at the young man standing there. The Venezuelan sported a black eye, dried blood running in streams across his mouth. He looked ready to drop.

"Help me up," Rivas said, motioning to the roof.

The young man bent and interlaced his fingers. Rivas grabbed a windowsill and scrambled upward, crawling over an awning and rolling onto the flat roof. Sheet metal popped and bent under his weight, but Rivas ignored it. He pulled himself to his feet and turned to the darkened crowd.

"Amigos! Do you hear that sound?"

He gestured toward downtown, four or five kilometers away. Too far to hear anything, but that wasn't the point. The small crowd turned their faces toward the invisible approach of Moreno's army, and he knew they felt the pressure. They felt it like a knife on their throats.

"That is the sound of tyranny coming for you! But not just you. For your children, and for their children. For all Venezuelans—from Colombia to the mountains and into the jungle. The despot in Miraflores has deployed an army to hunt you down. *Your* army, that swore an oath to protect Venezuela with their lives, will instead turn their guns on their own people."

A murmur of anger mixed with agitated fear. In the back of the crowd, Rivas noted half a dozen battered protesters turn for the streets, ready to slip away quietly. He yanked a flashlight from the hand of the bodyguard standing next to him on the rooftop and shone it toward the deserters.

"No, amigos! You cannot leave now. Your country needs you!"

Some of the protesters turned back. The rest kept walking. Rivas felt fear building in his gut—a reality of doom, pressing home. He had to say something. Something powerful enough to bring them back, even as that tank bore down like an invisible fist.

"I will be the first to die!"

He shouted over the barrio, and the stillness returned. The protesters closest to the edge turned back, looking over their shoulders, swollen and bloody faces twisted into defeat.

But not leaving. Not yet.

"My amigos, you elected me as your president. While the despot in Miraflores has refused to concede the government, this has not changed my obligation to my country. My obligation to sacrifice my life for Venezuela! If you turn from me now and leave me alone on this street, I will still stand for you. I will stand in the way of this tyrant and be the first to be crushed by his abuses."

Rivas felt tears in his eyes as he spoke. His throat closed, and he swallowed hard, stepping to the edge of the roof. His bodyguard reached out, grabbing his hand. Rivas pulled away. The barrio was dead quiet now, all eyes pointed at Rivas.

"I will die for Venezuela, amigos. There is no greater honor for your president to have than to surrender his life for yours. But..."

He pointed the flashlight to the sheet metal, allowing the light to bounce back over his body, making him appear taller than he was. Giving him a little more confidence.

"If you will *fight with me*, we do not have to lay down our lives to this tyrant. While the world watches, we can say *enough* to his corruption. Enough watching our children starve, our friends disappear. Enough watching Venezuela's wealth evaporate amid a sea of worthless bolívars! We can take *back* what is ours."

"Moreno has deployed the army!" somebody shouted. "They have a *tank*!"

"Yes, amigo! Yes, he has. And have you asked yourself why? Never before has he done this. Why now? It is because he smells change in the air. He knows Venezuela has had enough. We are ready to *fight*. Not just for ourselves, but for our children. For all of Venezuela, tonight is the night. Will you stand with me? Will you drag this tyrant into the grave he deserves?"

Dead silence. Rivas looked into the crowd, pleading. Desperate.

All his chips on the table.

"*Viva Venezuela.*"

The voice was soft and faltering, coming from someplace directly beneath him. Rivas looked down to see his shaken lieutenant standing near the base of the house, still terrified.

But no longer silent.

"*Viva Venezuela!*" he said again, stronger this time. "*Viva Venezuela!*"

The call was repeated from somewhere in the back. Rivas's bodyguard approached the edge of the roof and thrust his AK into the air.

"*Viva Venezuela! Poder para el pueblo!*"

The cry was repeated across the barrio, and the bodyguard hit the trigger, squeezing off a short burst of automatic fire. The sound seemed to galvanize the crowd, shooting lightning energy between the shanty homes and electrifying the crowd.

"*Viva Venezuela!* Down with the tyrant!"

Rivas felt the thunder in his chest, building ever louder, anger replacing the defeat of only moments before as Mateo continued to lead the chant.

Dropping off the roof, Rivas found his lieutenants in a knot near the door, screaming at the sky with fists raised. Infuriated enough. Pushed to the brink, and then pushed over the edge.

Channeling the rage of an entire nation.

"Find flashlights!" Rivas said. "As many as you can. And make the bombs! When the American gives the signal, we march on El Helicoide."

60

Palacio de Miraflores
Caracas, Venezuela

Moreno couldn't hear the chants from the distant hillside barrios where the traitor Rivas and his rioting rabble had fled, but his soldiers reported them. They had run the protesters out of downtown, pushing them into the hills at the nose of armored vehicles and a couple of Soviet cast-off T-72 tanks.

Moreno had given orders for the military to hold their fire—the tanks weren't even loaded. But Rivas and his people didn't know that, and the show of force was paying off. Order was returning to Caracas, and Moreno was beginning to feel control again. And yet he couldn't shake a feeling in the back of his mind that the second shoe was about to drop.

"Señor Presidente! I have General Vargas on the line."

Moreno turned from the picture window and lifted the phone from his desk.

"Yes, General?"

"We have driven the resistance into the outskirts, Señor Presidente. With your permission, we will press ahead and make arrests."

Moreno looked over his shoulder, into the invisible darkness where Rivas and his scum lay hiding. For nearly four years he'd tolerated the

American puppet—indulging his existence even while Rivas worked night and day to undermine the Moreno administration, pumping a steady stream of lies into the poverty-stricken barrios. Leveraging their hardship into rage at the wrong target.

Blaming Moreno when they should have blamed the American empire and their storm of back-breaking sanctions.

Rivas was a thorn in Moreno's side and would continue to be so for years to come. Moreno had planned to wait until his partnership with Belsky turned the economy around before he dragged Rivas into Bolívar Square and strung him up by his ears.

But Moreno was tired of waiting. He'd tolerated this traitorous chaos long enough.

"Bring me Rivas," he said. "Alive. If anyone gets in your way...do what you have to do."

"*Sí*, Señor Presidente. It will be done."

Moreno hung up and stood with his hand resting on his phone. He could hear the heavy footsteps in the hallway—the smacking rhythm of leather on marble.

Belsky.

The doors swung open, and the stinking Russian rumbled in like one of Moreno's tanks, marching for the desk with his gut jiggling over stubby legs.

The pig.

"The benefactor wishes to speak with you," Belsky snarled. "You have made a real mess, Señor Presidente."

As if on cue, the phone rang again. Moreno's eyes blazed at the Russian as he motioned for his people to close the doors. He lifted the phone.

"Yes?"

"An American warship has just rerouted for your coast." The computerized voice sounded angry. Maybe it always sounded angry. Moreno was a little angry himself.

"What do you mean?" he demanded.

"Exactly what I say. You have foxes in the henhouse, Señor Presidente. The Americans are making a play."

Moreno sneered, suddenly very tired of the innuendo. Very tired of being told how to run his own country.

"Let them try. By morning there will only be one president in Venezuela."

"You had better hope so, señor. Our arrangement is dependent on your ability to deliver. Am I understood?"

Moreno hung up and glared at Belsky. The fat Russian smiled in return, his flushed face half hidden by shadow.

Moreno dialed zero for his operator, requesting General Vargas again. His chief military official answered in record time.

"*Sí*, Señor Presidente?"

"Double your men," Moreno growled. "Load the tanks. Take the barrios by storm. *Bring me Rivas*."

61

Miranda, Venezuela
Outside Caracas

The mountainside south of the city was steep, a gravel road leading to the row of four-legged transmission towers mounted at the top. A heavy electrical buzzing rattled through the power lines a hundred feet overhead as Harris cut the Tahoe's engine and Reed, Turk, and Corbyn bailed out.

Reed led the way through waist-high grass, cradling his newly acquired M4 while the plastic explosives rode in his pack. A hot breeze swept the mountain top, and far below the city spread out before him in a twinkling pattern of a million tiny lights, with obvious black patches where the poorest barrios were served by the most unreliable electricity.

Stopping under the sprawling legs of the transmission tower, Reed tilted his head back to scan the lines. There were nine of them, clustered in groups of three, draping down from the tower and across a shallow valley to the next hilltop before plunging toward the city. Half a million volts surged through those lines, feeding a full third of the city from a hydro plant somewhere to the south, deeper in the mountains. As he placed a hand on one of the four legs supporting the tower, flaky rust broke away, and he felt a tremor of wind shooting down the superstructure.

The tower was old. Decades old, probably. Ripe for an accident.

"This one," Reed hissed. He slid to his knees and removed the pack, working in tandem with Turk while Corbyn stood watch and Harris remained in the Tahoe. A quick application of C-4, shaped to match the inside cavity of the angled steel leg, held in place by duct tape, and wired with a remote detonator. The process required only thirty seconds per leg, with wires draped between to ensure all four charges detonated in unison.

Complete chaos, unleashed USMC style.

"When I heard the 'Murica jokes, I kinda thought they were just jokes," Corbyn muttered.

Reed wiped sweat from his forehead and double-checked his work. The charges were secure, the detonators packed tightly into the moldable explosive. Ready to blast.

"We never joke about 'Murica," Reed said, leading the way back to the Tahoe. He held Corbyn's door. "Especially when explosives are involved."

He grinned, and she shook her head.

"This is gonna be one hell of an after-action report."

Reed took shotgun and directed Harris down the gravel service road to the next tower. They had just enough C-4 left to rig two more legs, which should be enough to bring both towers crashing down, ensuring a complete loss in power. Reed set the charges while Turk held a flashlight, and then they were back in the Tahoe, retreating out of the mountains.

Back into Caracas.

Harris dropped them at the dental office before returning to the mountains—back within radio detonator range to await Reed's signal.

"Don't fall asleep," Reed warned him. Harris merely shook his head as he stepped on the gas. In the distance, Reed heard the grind of heavy engines pounding their way out of downtown, moving toward the barrios. As of yet, there was no gunfire.

But that would change. And soon.

Reed found Jackie waiting just inside, a Glock 19 held at her side as she let them in. He saw uncertainty in her face, but not fear. Harris had already advised her of the evolving situation. She probably thought it was as crazy as Harris did.

Stewie still lay on the couch, bandaged up with his leg lying on a pillow. He looked comfortable, all things considered. The swelling had gone down quickly, and he was no longer flushed. Jackie's IV was working its magic.

Reed knelt next to him, patting his shoulder.

"We're outta here, little buddy. Gonna need your Tahoe."

"Reckon we'll meet again?"

"Honestly? I kinda hope not."

Stewie laughed. "Keys are in the kitchen. Give 'em hell."

Turk found the keys, and the three of them headed for the door.

"Hey, Montgomery!" Stewie called after him.

"What?"

"Nobody does it like Brady, am I right?"

"Pound sand, Masshole."

Stewie's Tahoe was as smelly as Reed remembered as he took shotgun, leaving Turk to drive. Corbyn was busy in the back seat, reviewing her gear and stretching her right leg. She grimaced a little each time she fully extended it, and Reed thought her hip looked a little swollen, but he wasn't about to comment on that.

Turk drove aggressively, leading them away from the incoming sounds of mechanized military and deeper into the darkest sections of the barrios. Dull streetlights illuminated their path, and occasional flashes of yellow marked a lifting curtain as a frightened Venezuelan stole a glimpse of the passing Tahoe.

But nobody blocked their path. It was as though the entire city were inoculated with fear, now holding their breath in the shadows, waiting to see what would happen next.

As they approached Rivas's headquarters, that tension escalated. Reed could feel it in the air long before the two armed men stepped out of the shadows, demanding that they roll down their windows and identify themselves before allowing passage. The shacks and shanties gathered around the narrow streets were fully dark, their windows blocked, most of the occupants invisible, but Reed knew they were there.

He could sense the presence of hundreds of tense people, all waiting in the darkness, bracing themselves for action. It was an odd instinct—something he picked up in Iraq. An ability to detect the calm before a storm.

After parking in front of Rivas's three-story presidential headquarters, Reed led the way into the building, this time being allowed to retain his weapons. He found Rivas right where he'd last met with him, bent over that dining room war table, drawing on a map with a black marker. Outlining a strategic plan of attack.

Rivas looked up when Reed entered, his eyes asking a question his lips didn't voice.

"We're good," Reed said. "Ready on your signal."

Rivas wrapped up his meeting with the cluster of nervous lieutenants gathered around the table. They dispersed on his command, leaving Rivas and his bodyguard alone with Reed and his little band. Rivas wiped his forehead and stepped around the table.

"I hope you understand, American. I am risking everything tonight."

"I understand," Reed said simply. "So are we."

Rivas said something in Spanish over his shoulder. The bodyguard with the AK appeared, and for the first time, Reed noted that the man wore full combat gear. Boots, a bullet-proof plate carrier, extra magazines, and a headband wrapped around his skull like freaking Rambo.

"This is Mateo," Rivas said. "He is my personal bodyguard. He will accompany you tonight."

Reed laughed softly. Rivas didn't blink, and neither did Mateo.

"Um, no," Reed said. "No, he won't. Keep him with you. I've got everything I need."

"Mateo is a good fighter," Rivas said. "He spent many years in the Venezuelan army, fighting the Colombian FARC on the border. You will be well served to have him."

"I don't doubt his skill set," Reed said. "I simply don't need another man to look after, especially one I've never fought with before."

"You are taking the Brit," Rivas challenged.

"The Brit flies helicopters. Does Mateo fly helicopters?"

Rivas glared, and Mateo asked a confused question in Spanish. Rivas held up a hand, closing on Reed.

"This is not an option for you, my friend. Mateo is more than just assistance for you. He is a guardian for Venezuela."

"To make sure I don't seize power?" Reed snorted.

"To make sure you don't kill Moreno," Rivas retorted. "This plan of yours is very dangerous. Very bold. But if it goes too far, much more harm will come to my people."

"I'm not killing Moreno," Reed said. "I wouldn't waste a bullet. All I want is my friend, and the Russian. Then I'm out of here—permanently."

Reed had barely finished the sentence before a thunderclap shook through the air, followed a short second later by a second clapping bang. The building shook, and a pane of glass across the room cracked but didn't shatter. Turk jogged to the window, peeling the curtain back to look in the direction of the blast, but he didn't need to. Reed already knew what it was from the moment his ears first registered the noise.

"Tank shell!" Turk called. "Incendiary round. Time to go!"

Reed turned for the door. Rivas grabbed his arm, sinking his fingers in. "Mateo goes, American. These are my terms."

Reed looked over his shoulder, half-tempted to deck Rivas and leave him bleeding out on the floor. Half-tempted to tell him he wasn't in a position to be making demands.

And then he decided he simply didn't care. Another thirty seconds of squabbling, and that Russian tank might lob a round right into this living room.

"You speak English?" Reed demanded.

Mateo looked blank.

"*Estás listo?*" Corbyn broke in.

Mateo responded by racking the heavy bolt of his AK and saluting Rivas on his way to the door.

Reed pulled his arm free of Rivas's hand and led his team toward the street, Rivas calling out from behind.

"God be with you, Montgomery!"

Outside, the air was thick with the sulphury smell of tank fire, and a hundred yards down the street, a barrio shack burned.

Moreno's men were coming, and just like Mateo, they were ready to kill.

62

Palacio de Miraflores
Caracas, Venezuela

Rivas's inside man could hear the distant thunder of tank fire as he descended the stairs into the basement of the presidential palace. It was a sound he recalled all too well from his years in the armored division of the Venezuelan army. Cast-off T-72B1s, purchased a decade ago from the Russian Federation.

Now turned on the people of Venezuela.

It had been years since Jorge Garcia had transitioned from the military to Moreno's private palace guard, and the experience had only reinforced what he had suspected his entire life—the glory days of Chávez's revolution were long, long gone. If they ever existed in the first place. Corruption poisoned the very core of Venezuela's government, saturating a presidential regime that was so far removed from the true problems of the people it claimed to represent, that the daily events inside Miraflores felt like happenings on another planet.

Moreno had no earthly clue how bad his people were suffering, but Garcia did. He'd been touched more personally than most—had lost more than most. He sat alongside his young wife's hospital bed as the cancer devoured her. Maria died slowly, and in a lot of pain, but despite Garcia's most desperate pleadings, the Venezuelan doctors refused to administer chemotherapy, or even morphine.

They claimed Maria was too far gone. Medical care would be a waste of limited state resources, even for the wife of a presidential guard. They were better off saving that medicine for patients with more hopeful prognoses.

Garcia almost bought it. But the evening Maria died, as they wheeled her body out of the hospital, he caught sight of the man being treated with chemotherapy in a private room. The door opened for only a moment, but the face was clear—a face Garcia had seen a dozen times before.

It was Moreno's uncle, a dear friend of the president, and a man known to be dying of terminal cancer.

He received treatment anyway, even while Maria's body grew cold, and Garcia's soul grew colder. From that night onward, Garcia dedicated himself to the service of Venezuela, connecting with the resistance, feeding them whatever limited information he could mine from inside Miraflores. He worked alongside Blanco to recover the tapes, and when Blanco was captured, Garcia remained vigilant to feed Rivas any update he could.

Garcia was only too thrilled when Rivas called with details of the coming mission. Even more thrilled by Rivas's special request—a request the resistance leader trusted Garcia alone to execute.

And Garcia would be only too happy.

He found his way past the security operations center in the basement, acknowledging some of his fellow guards and remaining calm as he poured a cup of coffee, then wandered casually into the mechanical room.

Beyond the boilers, computer cages, and HVAC equipment, a bank of generators lined the far wall. They were purposed for backup use only, ready to kick in and feed the greedy needs of the Miraflores complex in the event of a full power outage.

That sort of thing happened a few times each year, usually only for an hour or two at a time. But tonight, Rivas warned, the blackout would last much longer. And it was critical for Venezuela that the generators would not be operational.

It took Garcia the better part of fifteen minutes to fully disable all four units. He wasn't an electrician and knew little about mechanical things beyond tanks, so he cut multiple wires and pulled several plugs just to ensure that the job was effective, pausing now and then to crouch in the shadows as doors opened and his fellow guards passed through.

Nobody wandered to the darkened rear of the room, where the generators lay. There was no need too. Garcia slashed enough wires to lay all four units low, then stowed his tools in a darkened corner before proceeding out of the mechanical room, down another dank hallway, and into the unofficial prison of the Moreno regime.

Juan Blanco lay in the back, chained to a wall, clinging to life by a thread. He was joined by an American with only one leg.

It was the American Garcia needed to see.

Acknowledging the sleepy guard reading an American porno mag next to the steel gate, Garcia sipped his coffee and made as if he were simply stretching his legs halfway through a long shift. Nobody suspected him. Garcia supervised nighttime security operations a few times a week. He wasn't an officer, more of a senior enlisted man. Somebody the other guards trusted.

The guy let him pass without so much as a second glance.

Inside the row of narrow prison cells, Garcia slurped coffee and walked slowly. The American lay all the way at the end, stretched out on a battered and stained mattress, his breath whistling through a busted and swollen face.

Moreno and his FAES goons had done a number on the guy, working him over for hours on end. Garcia had been helpless to intervene, but he didn't think the American had talked. The guy must be made of iron.

Garcia stopped in front of the door and glanced over his shoulder. Nobody had joined him in the dank prison block. It wasn't a place most of the guards relished visiting.

"Gringo, can you hear me?" Garcia whispered.

The American stirred on the mattress, lifting his head a few inches. His eyes were swollen almost shut, his lips busted, dry blood encrusting his face.

"I have a message for you," Garcia whispered, facing the door now, speaking out of the side of his mouth.

"Who..." The American struggled to get a word out. Garcia cut him off.

"Don't talk, just listen. My message is from a man called Prosecutor. He says...be ready."

The American struggled to sit up, gasping for air. "Wait. He said—"

"Be ready," Garcia hissed. Then he hurried back down the hall and out of the prison block, his heart beginning to thump as he switched his mind to the next phase of his mission. The part he was so eager to sink his teeth into.

The special request of Luis Rivas.

63

Caracas, Venezuela

The distant crash of Moreno's tanks grew louder as Turk piloted the Tahoe out of the barrios and back toward downtown. Reed heard the rattling growl of at least two tracked vehicles, plus an unknown number of armored troop carriers and foot soldiers.

All around them amid the inky shadows between flickering streetlights, Reed observed Rivas's supporters fleeing their homes in organized order, many carrying darkened flashlights, others cradling armloads of glass bottles loaded with gasoline.

Molotov cocktails. A pitiful weapon against the brute force of a Russian tank, but those tanks would become mired in the narrow streets of empty barrios long before they received word of Rivas's real target.

And by then, Reed would be in position to strike his own.

Turk swung wide into the outskirts, blowing through traffic lights and quickly losing a Venezuelan police car who gave temporary chase. In the back seat, Corbyn navigated using an iPad while Mateo sat dead quiet, his face graven into cold stone, his AK-47 riding his lap.

"Mateo. You want some paint?" Reed reached into his pack and withdrew a tube of black grease paint. He, Turk, and Corbyn had already applied it, muting their skin from the glare of overhead lights. Not that those lights would be a problem much longer.

Mateo looked confused. Corbyn translated in Spanish, and he ducked his head and accepted the tube, quickly smearing it across his cheeks and under his eyes.

"What's his deal?" Reed said.

"What do you mean?" Corbyn asked.

"I mean I need to know this jackass isn't going to shoot me in the back of the head."

Corbyn spoke a few words in Spanish, and Mateo paused with the face paint. A grin crept across his wide mouth, and he muttered a reply.

"He says he would need a full magazine for you," Corbyn said.

"Sounds like he's given it some thought," Turk said.

Reed rotated in the seat. Mateo spoke again, his grin fading.

"Moreno arrested his brother," Corbyn said. "Mateo thinks he was murdered. That's why he deserted the Venezuelan army and joined Rivas."

Mateo met Reed's gaze, his face now blackened by paint, his eyes cold and dark. He muttered a few more words.

"There is a price on his head," Corbyn said. "For treason."

"How much?" Reed asked. "I could use the payday."

Corbyn translated, and Mateo grinned again. Reed faced the windshield again as Corbyn called a turn onto a darkened street. They were someplace near the outskirts of downtown, pulling into an empty parking garage outside a tall office tower. The city around them felt suddenly very quiet and dark. Reed felt a chill up his spine, and not for the first time that night he thought of Banks and Davy.

Safe and sound, a world away. Waiting for him.

He hoped.

Turk stopped the Tahoe next to a curb, leaving it in gear as he ducked his head beneath the visor to survey the streets. They were now just half a mile from Miraflores, nestled in a quiet part of downtown that Reed marked as a business district by the high towers and logos plastered across ground-level glass doors.

In the distance, he heard the pound of the military vehicles moving up the mountainside, matched with the repeated blare of bullhorns ordering all citizens to return to their homes. Dim streetlights running the length of the boulevard illuminated their path to a checkpoint three hundred yards away. The roadblock was constructed of simple sawhorse street blockades, staffed by Venezuelan soldiers in full combat gear.

Reed swept them with a pair of the CIA's binoculars, searching for and failing to find one key component of what should have been standard-issue gear.

"Night vision?" Turk asked.

"Negative. We're golden."

Reed stowed the binoculars and dug through a pack of additional CIA gear, all taken from the locker at the dental office. Night vision headsets were pretested and charged with fresh batteries, and Reed adjusted the harness of his before sliding it on. The fit was good. Corbyn and Turk donned theirs also, but Mateo waved his set away.

"He says he has fox eyes," Corbyn said.

"Yeah, okay." Reed shook his head. "I think we'll keep Spanish Rambo in front. I'm not trying to get shot in the back."

Corbyn drew her SIG and fit a CIA-issued suppressor to the muzzle, twisting until snug, then chambering a round.

"Still gonna wind up on my ass for this," she said.

Reed grunted. "Stop acting like you aren't loving every minute."

He dug another CIA-issued radio from the pack and dialed in to the correct channel. Keying the switch, he was rewarded with a digital chirp.

"Prosecutor to Tooth Fairy, sitrep. Over."

Turk grinned from the driver's seat. Harris's call sign had been his idea, and the CIA station chief was none too thrilled with it.

"In position," Harris answered. "Viewing multiple fires on the hillside from barrio district. Light small arms fire. Recommend executing when ready."

Reed surveyed the small team, feeling an unease creep into his stomach. It wasn't the mission ahead. All things considered, he felt pretty good about that. The interior layout of the palace was a relative unknown, but breaching unknown buildings was part of the job, and Rivas's inside man would be his secret weapon.

What bothered Reed now were the two teammates he had limited to no direct experience with. He didn't mind having Mateo along—an additional gun was always a good thing—but he couldn't afford to be slowed down if Mateo couldn't keep up.

And he absolutely *needed* Corbyn to deliver.

"You good for real?" Reed shot the Brit a piercing stare, reinforcing his point. She checked the fit of the suppressor before tucking the weapon into her jacket and nodding.

"Brilliant. Let's kick some ass."

Reed held the gaze a beat longer, then looked to Mateo. The Venezuelan sat with his rifle held close, looking past Reed to the blockade down the street. Pure murder in his eyes.

Reed keyed the mic. "Prosecutor to Tooth Fairy. Execute when ready."

"Copy that, Prosecutor. Execute in five...four...three..."

Reed looked over his shoulder through the back glass. Toward the rolling foothills leading into the mountains, marked by a few thousand streetlights. A little like a Christmas tree.

And then he heard it. A distant crescendo of concentrated explosions, followed an instant later by a wave of black, passing down the hill and ripping through the city. Lights vanished, and the city was drenched in instant, inky darkness.

A full blackout.

"Go," Reed snapped.

Turk's foot dropped off the brake, and the Tahoe surged forward.

64

Palacio de Miraflores
Caracas, Venezuela

Moreno had the windows open, listening to the irregular pound of tank cannons and small arms fire echoing across the city. From his executive office on the top floor of the presidential palace, the noises sounded like distant fireworks, without any of the brilliant lights. He could smell the smoke, though. Whenever the wind turned toward Miraflores, he imagined he could hear the screams.

Behind him, Belsky sat at the breakfast table in the corner, chowing down on a full Venezuelan spread, smacking and slurping like a dog. The sounds agitated Moreno, like nails on a chalkboard, working on his already strained nerves. Making him want to drive Belsky's head through a block wall.

Moreno paced, his hands working in and out of fists, a trickle of sweat running down his back. He felt the sudden urge for very strong Venezuelan rum and turned for the liquor cabinet.

Then the lights snapped out. All at once, the entire office suite was saturated in darkness. Belsky stopped chewing, and his silverware hit the table.

Moreno froze, then turned quickly toward the window. The thunder of tanks in the distance pounded even louder now as two cannons fired in unison, but he couldn't see anything. The entire city was black. Every window and streetlamp dark in an instant.

The door burst open, and a flashlight swept across the room. "Señor Presidente! Are you here?"

"What the hell is going on?" It was Belsky who spoke, spewing angrily toward the security guard.

"We've lost all power," the man answered in Spanish, fumbling with his radio. The device chirped, and a short exchange prompted a curse.

"The generators aren't responding, señor. We're working on it."

"Get the lights back on!" Moreno shouted. "And get me a radio. I want General Vargas on the line!"

The guard dropped his head back to the radio, rattling off orders as Belsky exploded out of his chair.

"What are you doing?" the Russian demanded.

"This is getting out of control," Moreno answered, gesturing blindly toward the windows. "The whole city is black! I'm calling back the army."

"Find your balls, fool," Belsky snarled. "Take control!"

"I can't control anything without electricity!" Moreno screamed.

His guard appeared, thrusting a radio into his outstretched hand. Moreno found the call switch and barked into the mic.

"General? Are you with me?"

"*Sí*, Señor Presidente! We are in the barrios, but we've lost all light."

"Are the rioters counter-attacking?" Moreno pressed.

"No, señor. We've encountered almost no resistance. We're using the tanks to launch tear gas, but..."

The general trailed off. Moreno thought he heard more radio chatter in the background before the audio cut. Temporary panic edged into his system, and he reached for the call key again. Then Vargas's heavy voice boomed across the handset.

"Señor Presidente! I have just received word. The rioters are mounting an attack at El Helicoide. Five hundred, maybe more. Lights and firebombs. They are marching on the building!"

The panic that Moreno felt only moments before quickly converged into absolute fear.

El Helicoide.

How could he not see this coming? It was so perfectly obvious. Rivas had campaigned for months against Moreno's use of the Venezuelan intelligence center, claiming that the building was a prison where Moreno's political enemies were held, interrogated, and tortured.

They were bold and dangerous claims, but the one thing Rivas lacked was proof. El Helicoide was under the full control of Moreno's regime, staffed and manned by loyal supporters and a bureaucracy of military and intelligence officials drunk off their own power. The truth about what happened in the multi-leveled, top security building was a strict secret, and Moreno denied Rivas's claims across the board.

But if Rivas gained access to El Helicoide...if his supporters obtained evidence of what happened there...

"General!" Moreno growled. "Move all your troops to protect El Helicoide. Surround the building and cut them off. Use whatever force necessary. Under no circumstances is anyone allowed to enter that building."

"Understood, Señor Presidente. I will keep you updated."

Moreno threw the radio down, turning back to the darkened windows. He ran both hands through his hair and felt the sweat coating his scalp. Without the HVAC units, it was already growing warm in the building.

"Where are those generators?" he roared.

Footsteps pounded in the hallway, but nobody answered. Moreno leaned out the third-floor window and looked south—toward El Helicoide. He could see an orange glow reflecting from the horizon. In the street beneath him, a platoon of infantry soldiers fast-marched in that direction, rifles slung over their chests, boots thundering on the pavement.

"You seem terribly distressed, Señor Presidente," Belsky taunted, his voice thick with the hints of inebriation. He'd been drinking all evening and did not seem the least concerned by the night's developments.

Moreno whirled on him but didn't answer. Belsky flashed a grin.

"Do you have skeletons in your closet?"

Moreno marched past him, throwing the door open and calling to his guard. It was still pitch black in the palace, save for the irregular sweep of flashlights darting down the halls as security and staff worked to bring the lights back on.

"Yes, señor?" The guard appeared at his elbow.

"Go to the basement!" Moreno snapped. "Bring me the American. And bring me a gun."

65

Turk piloted the Tahoe down the street and took a hard right just short of the barricade. The soldiers looked temporarily confused by the sudden approach of the vehicle, but as soon as the headlights snapped past the turn, they were again awash in darkness.

Directly ahead, Reed saw the looming outer walls of Miraflores, spilling over with dripping vines that reached for sidewalks planted with towering oak trees. Turk cut the headlights, and Reed snapped his night vision down, illuminating the path ahead in flickering green.

"Side gate," he said, pointing ahead. "Park on the curb."

They rocketed through a main intersection, and Reed glanced left to see a small knot of soldiers gathered at Miraflores's main gate. Even in the brief glimpse, he could clearly see the chaos consuming their ranks under the pressure of the sudden blackout. Flashlight beams flicked across the street, but nobody moved to accost the speeding black SUV.

"There!" Reed marked the side gate built into the palace's exterior wall —a flat black metal door built into the stone, just wide enough to allow two men to walk shoulder to shoulder. It was unguarded, rising eight feet up the twenty-foot wall and surrounded by shadow.

Turk hit the brakes and stopped the Tahoe just outside the gate. Reed piled out, leading with his M4 and quickly taking position near the front bumper to cover the others while they bailed out. Mateo moved with practiced ease, swinging out and automatically covering Reed's back with his AK while Turk ran for the gate.

It was time to see if Rivas's inside man was worth a damn.

Turk reached the door and pressed his back against the wall next to it, rifle at the ready. Then he reached out and rapped on the metal with gloved knuckles.

A moment passed. Then two. Reed kept his rifle zeroed on the door.

Then the door swung open, and a single man in a dark presidential guard uniform stepped out. He saw Turk, and his face paled. Turk's lips moved, speaking the preassigned password.

The guard answered. Turk shot a two-finger wave toward the Tahoe, and Reed, Corbyn, and Mateo charged to the wall.

"Inside," the guard said. "Quickly."

The five of them slipped into a narrow hallway, pitch dark save for the soft light of the moon glowing some twenty feet ahead. The guard shut the door and bolted it, then swept off his hat and mopped sweat off his forehead.

"I am Garcia," he said. "You are the American?"

He didn't address Turk; he addressed Reed. Whether by instinct or some prior information Rivas had given him, he seemed to know who was in charge.

"That's right," Reed said.

"Your friend is in the basement," Garcia said, driving straight to the point. "I will show you. The Russian is with President Moreno. We will go for him afterward."

"What about the helicopter?" Corbyn pressed.

"The helicopter is on the pad, behind the palace. After we reach the courtyard, I will direct you, but you must go on your own."

"Are there guards?"

"*Sí.* Two, maybe three men..." Garcia hesitated. Then he shrugged. "This is your problem."

Reed shot Corbyn a look. She bit her lower lip, then nodded. "I'll manage."

"We must hurry now," Garcia said. "Follow me."

He led the way down a concrete tunnel and into a decorative garden just inside the walls. Tall trees and manicured bushes surrounded a winding man-made creek, ending in a pool and a fountain. The fountain was silent and the park empty. Garcia directed Corbyn to split immediately to the right, pointing toward the helicopter. The Brit shot a two-finger salute at the rest of the team before moving quickly through the shadows with the SIG at her side, working her way to the back of the complex.

Reed swept the rifle across the building rising in front of them—a three-story structure built of white block with a Spanish-style adobe roof. Venezuela's national colors flapped from a flagpole someplace high overhead, but he didn't see any security.

No people at all.

"This way," Garcia said, motioning toward the building. "Quietly, now."

Reed caught a thumbs-up gesture from Turk before he turned to Mateo. The Venezuelan cradled his AK like an old friend, the stock pressed against his cheek, his finger stiff just above the trigger guard. He met Reed's gaze and nodded once.

Reed fell into position just behind Garcia, leading with his M4, and then the four of them rushed for the main building.

66

Moreno heard the commotion echoing down the marble hallways long before it reached his executive office. The lights were still off, but one of his guards had brought a propane lantern to cast hissing light around the room.

Belsky stood from the table, his hand dropping toward the 9mm Beretta strapped to his hip as both doors burst open, and three guards appeared. They were all big men, but they struggled to carry the convulsing American, two men holding his arms while a third carried his single leg.

The American coughed and kicked, managing a glancing blow to one man's groin before all three dumped him onto the hard marble. One of the guards pressed a handgun into the base of the American's skull while another saluted Moreno and handed him a Beretta.

Moreno circled the flailing leg and approached the man's head, crouching next to his face as the American continued to thrash. He racked the Beretta, chambering a fresh 9mm round before he pressed the muzzle into the American's cheek.

The prisoner became suddenly still, and Moreno jammed the muzzle deeper into his already bruised flesh.

"No more games, gringo. What do you know about this?"

Moreno gestured toward the empty blackness outside the palace. The

American's jaw ratcheted open under the pressure of the Beretta, but he didn't answer. He just grinned—crazed and depraved, like he had when tortured, his eyes gleaming with absolute fearlessness.

"What do you know?" Moreno shouted, drawing back the Beretta and pistol-whipping the man in the side of his face. The American's head cracked against the marble, and he grunted.

Then Moreno heard another sound. Not so far away, muted by walls and windows, but most definitely coming from *inside* the Miraflores compound.

Automatic gunfire.

"I know...," the American rasped, still grinning, "...that you better *run*."

67

Garcia led the way through the park, circumventing the creek and moving toward a darkened corner of the main building. Through his night vision goggles, Reed detected two guards jogging toward the main entrance, carrying AKs, apparently agitated. He didn't think they had been detected, however. Whatever was drawing the attention of the two guards, it was still outside the main wall.

Rivas's riots were making an impact.

Garcia held up a fist at the edge of the park, bringing the four of them to a halt behind a row of bushes. Peering out into the darkness, Garcia made a quick sweep of the perimeter, his gaze fixating on a point high on the external wall. Reed followed his line of sight and noted two guards standing at the top of a narrow tower, their gazes fixed on the main gate. From that perspective they looked directly across the park, their peripheral vision almost certain to be alerted by any further progress toward the main building.

Reed shifted his M4 into his shoulder, but Garcia shook his head, holding up a hand. Reaching for his belt, the Venezuelan retrieved a radio and keyed the mic, speaking softly but with command.

Reed adjusted his night vision and saw one of the guards drop his hand to an identical radio. Then both men moved quickly to the wall, leaning out to look down into the street. Turning their backs to Miraflores.

"Go!" Garcia hissed.

He returned to his feet, leading the way across the park. Reed felt Mateo fall in behind, and looked over his shoulder to see Rivas's bodyguard jogging backward, covering them with the mouth of his AK like an absolute veteran.

Maybe it wasn't so bad to have him along after all.

They reached the block face of the main building, and Garcia turned eastward, running down a smooth concrete sidewalk toward the main driveway. Ahead Reed saw an armored limousine resting under a portico, its jet-black windows glowing green through his goggles. Beyond it a metal gate opened into a tunnel, and Reed knew there to be a courtyard beyond.

Garcia didn't make for the portico. Instead, he turned abruptly around a bulge in the wall, and held up his fist just outside another secured metal door.

Reed and Turk slid in behind him, their rifles riding in low-ready while Mateo pressed his back against theirs, still covering their six. Garcia produced a key card from his belt, glancing nervously over his shoulder as he scanned it. A red light turned green, and the door lock clicked.

"*Alto! Quién va allí?*"

The voice shouted from the portico, and Reed snapped in that direction to see another guard appear from the tunnel, wielding a flashlight in one hand with an FN P90 slung across his chest. For a split second they all froze, hoping his attention was arrested by a disturbance other than the four intruders.

No such luck. Reed saw his face twist into an alarmed grimace, and the flashlight dropped as the P90 swung upward.

Then Mateo fired. The rolling *chunk-chunk-chunk* of fully automatic AK-47 fire split the stillness like thunder, and the guard went down in a spray of blood. Garcia yanked the door open, and Mateo pressed from behind, shouting almost directly in Reed's ear.

"*Vete! Vete!*"

68

Corbyn followed Garcia's directions toward the back of the complex. Using her MI6-issued night vision, she was able to make out a narrow security path running just inside the main wall, circling the outside edge of the park she'd left Reed and his team in before crossing a secondary gate on the east side and heading behind the primary building.

The bulk of the Miraflores complex rose in elegant grace and style as a multi-floor mansion, directly to her left. White block looked soft green through the goggles, with a slate roof lined by dead security cameras.

At least, she hoped they were dead. The power was cut, and the generators disabled. MI6 would have further layers of energy redundancy in place to fuel their most critical systems, but it didn't take a genius to know that the Venezuelan government was no MI6.

She just hoped the chopper was in working order and ready to fly. Garcia seemed confident about it, but they'd all be screwed if he was wrong.

As she approached the secondary gate and looked beyond a small guardhouse toward the back of the property, she caught her first sight of the aircraft. Only a tail rotor was visible, fully encased in a shroud with a rudder protruding from the top. The rest of the chopper was invisible, lost around the corner of the mansion, but she could tell by the tail alone that it was some manner of Eurocopter.

Corbyn knelt in the shadows next to the wall and spent the next sixty seconds surveying the rooftops and windows, searching out anyone who might spot her during her sprint across the drive, behind a parked limousine, and into the back of the compound. Her reconstructed right hip throbbed with pain, and she knew that running would send further blasts of discomfort shooting all the way up her spine and into her skull.

But better to be uncomfortable than dead.

"Alto! Quién va allí?"

Corbyn's heart lurched. She pressed her back against the wall, her head pivoting automatically toward the voice. It came from someplace to her left, back toward the mansion. A glimpse of light brightened her goggles—maybe a flashlight, reflecting against the block wall.

Then a blast of automatic gunfire ripped through the night. The figure went down, and Corbyn sprang into action, bolting full-speed across the drive and circling the back corner of the mansion. Her SIG cleared her jacket as she pivoted toward the helicopter, running almost face first into a sprinting guard.

The SIG popped three times, spitting suppressed slugs into his chest and neck, stopping him in his tracks. Corbyn's heart thundered as she peered left, searching for more guards. She made out the back entrance of the mansion, cloaked in darkness, with two more guards rushing toward her. Both brandished P90 submachine guns, but she could already tell they couldn't see her.

Corbyn shrank back into the shadows behind the body and raised the SIG.

69

Garcia pushed the door open, and the four of them shoved inside. Turk fell automatically into point, following Garcia's directions to turn left down a wide hallway. Reed noted polished marble and automatically rolled onto the balls of his feet to mute the slap of his heavy boots. A high ceiling was lined by darkened light fixtures, gaps in the wall to his right opening out over a darkened courtyard decorated by tall green plants and more water features.

Nobody moved to block their path down the long hallway ahead, but Reed heard the voices. Shouts in Spanish, boots thundering along a walkway someplace overhead, with occasional flashlight beams spilling over the courtyard.

Moreno's guards, launched into overdrive by the voice of Mateo's AK. Terrific.

"Right turn!" Garcia signaled with his free hand, the other still wrapped around a Glock 17. Turk had barely made it around the corner before he opened fire, blasting a hail of steel-core ammunition down the next hallway amid shouts and screams from invisible combatants.

Reed slung himself against the wall, pulling his M4 into his shoulder as the rolling *thunk* of Mateo's AK thundered to his left. The Venezuelan had dropped into a kneel and was firing back down the hallway the way they had come.

"Turk! What've you got?" Reed shouted over the gunfire as Turk leaned around the corner and dumped the rest of his thirty-round mag.

"Four or more! P90s." Turk pulled back from the corner. "Changing!"

He dumped his mag, and Reed ripped a fragmentation grenade from his chest rig and yanked the pin.

"Frag out!"

He slung the grenade around the corner, and all four of them instinctively braced for the blast. Glass shattered and the marble hallway thundered, then Reed felt hot lead whistling past his face from invisible shooters somewhere behind.

"Move! Move!" He threw his elbow into Garcia's back, and Turk stormed around the corner, ready with a fresh mag.

There was no need. The combatants around the corner had fallen prey to the grenade, now bleeding out in crumpled masses of shredded flesh. Turk splashed through the blood and opened fire again at a target somewhere down the hall. Reed traced his line of sight to a uniformed guard dug in behind a stone planter, firing blindly toward the oncoming Americans. Turk couldn't get a bead on him from the left side of the hall, but he was a wide-open target for Reed's M4. The handgun went silent, and Reed turned to Garcia.

"Where next?"

Garcia looked confused, temporarily disoriented by the gunfire. He blinked rapidly and shook his head. Reed grabbed him by the arm and shook him.

"Hey! Snap out of it. Where is the American?"

"Downstairs," Garcia choked. "Basement!"

Turk moved automatically into the lead again, Reed falling in behind Garcia. They made it barely five yards before Mateo shouted from behind —a long string of angry Spanish.

Reed looked back to see the Venezuelan pointing through one of the gaps in the stone wall, out across the courtyard to another hallway running along the second level of the mansion. Reed followed his line of sight just in time to see a small crowd of men rushing across a similar gap in the wall —a tall man in a perfectly white suit followed by a short, fat guy with a thick beard. Then three guards, carrying a man dressed in all black between them.

A man with only one leg.

"They're making for the chopper!" Turk shouted.

The words barely left his lips before the high-pitched snarl of a P90 submachine gun ripped through the night, and a spray of fine concrete dust exploded from the wall over Turk's head. Reed hit the ground and pivoted toward the gunfire. A starburst of muzzle flash lit a window on the third level over the courtyard, cutting across the open space and showering their position with fully automatic fire. Before he could bring his M4 to bear on the spot, similar bursts erupted from down the hall the way they had come. Bullets skipped off the marble next to Reed's feet, and Mateo slumped against the wall.

"Smoke! Smoke!"

Reed tore another grenade off his chest rig and flung it through the open window into the courtyard. A moment later, a soft pop and hiss signaled the arrival of thick white smoke, but the P90 continued, now joined by two or three of its twins.

"We've got to move!" Turk shouted.

Reed felt through the darkness to his left, touching Mateo's arm. The sleeve was slick with blood, and Mateo jerked back.

"*Déjame!*"

"I'm not leaving you anywhere," Reed growled. "Where are you hit?"

He felt through the Venezuelan's jacket and found the source of the wound beneath the rib cage. A gunshot, probably from a P90. It felt like a small entry wound.

Then he felt two more.

"Montgomery!" Turk shouted. "Move, *now*."

"Mateo is hit!"

"Leave him! They're gonna reach that chopper."

Mateo shoved Reed with an angry hand, his dark eyes blazing upward.

"*Vete!*" he snarled. "Go now."

The message was clear. Reed saw unbridled rage in his eyes. That dark, venomous look he'd seen before in the eyes of the suppressed and abused. A fire only blood could quench.

He released Mateo and nodded slowly. Pulling two more fragmentation grenades from his chest, he passed them to the Venezuelan and squeezed his shoulder.

"Good luck."

Mateo lifted his AK, propped against the inside wall of the hallway, and turned back toward the voice of a handgun popping from down the hall. Reed smacked Turk on the arm, giving him the go-ahead. Turk bolted toward the next turn, Garcia just behind, Reed covering their rear.

As they pivoted around the corner, a fresh storm of gunfire opened behind them, and Reed looked back to see three or four guards armed with P90s entering the hall. Turk led the way around the bend onto the north side of the courtyard as Moreno's guards broke into a run after them.

Then a floor-shaking blast ripped through the air, and clouds of dust exploded from the courtyard windows directly over Mateo's position.

Reed met Turk's gaze for a split second in the mayhem, and Turk nodded once. Then the three of them sprinted toward the back of the complex.

Toward the chopper.

"There!" Garcia shouted.

Reed looked ahead to see a door blast open, and a Venezuelan soldier dressed in full combat uniform stormed out of a stairwell beyond. He shouted and held up a hand behind him.

He never finished the sentence. A burst from Reed's rifle drove his body against the wall and cut him down as they reached the door. Reed slid right and directed his rifle through the gap just in time to catch the next guy in the throat. The M4 blew half his neck away, and he fell like a tree. Garcia pressed in and opened fire with his Glock, sending more bodies to the floor as a chorus of panicked shouts erupted from the stairwell.

Another handgun popped, and Garcia staggered back, clutching his arm. Turk hurled him aside and shouted over the chaos.

"Belsky!"

Turk's M4 barked, and somebody screamed. Then he and Reed barged through the door, climbing over the bodies of three fallen guards to find three more men in a tangled mass on the steps beyond.

Stepan Belsky, Cesar Moreno, and Wolfgang Pierce.

70

Wolfgang lay at the bottom, his head driven into the marble edge of the steps, blood running from a busted lip. Moreno stood with one leg pinned under the body of his fallen guard, clawing at the stairway railing and holding a pitiful outstretched hand against the mouth of Turk's M4.

And Stepan Belsky, obese oligarch and would-be murderer of the president of the United States, turned tail and clawed his way up the steps, one hand pouring blood from a gunshot wound to the palm.

Reed didn't hesitate. He opened fire on the steps, showering Belsky's face with fragments of marble and slate and sending the fat Russian crumbling amid screams of pain. Turk reached down to grab Wolfgang's arm, and Moreno crawled backward against the wall, tears streaming down his face.

"Please! Don't hurt me. I am the president! You cannot kill a president!"

"Tell that to this asshole," Reed snarled, driving his shin into Belsky's crotch. The Russian collapsed against the steps, and Turk shoved his rifle muzzle against the back of Belsky's skull while Reed secured his arms with a wire tie.

"What the hell are you doing here?" Turk said, shooting Wolfgang a derisive grin.

Wolfgang struggled to sit up, but his hands were bound behind his back, and the effort brought searing pain to his face. Reed left Belsky to Turk and helped Wolfgang up, slicing his bonds with a quick flick of his knife.

"You good?" Reed said. "Where's your leg?"

Wolfgang slumped against the wall, gasping a little. He shook his head. "Russians...took it."

"Okay. Hang in there. We're gonna get you out."

Reed smacked him on the back as Turk hauled Belsky onto his feet and shoved him with the muzzle of his rifle. "Move, jackass!"

Belsky stumbled out of the stairwell as another burst of handgun fire erupted from someplace down the hall. Metal bit the wall, and Belsky screamed in panic.

"Pull me back in!"

Turk ignored him, resting his M4 over Belsky's shoulder and spraying bullets across the courtyard.

"Tangos inbound," Turk called. "We gotta move!"

Reed turned back to Moreno, Garcia standing over him with his Glock pressed to the president's throat. Reed knelt and retrieved a fallen radio handset from one of the dead guards, pressing it into Moreno's shaking hand.

"Call off your men."

Moreno almost dropped the radio. Garcia fell into a squat and drove a right hook into Moreno's jaw, hard enough to snap his head against the wall.

"*Llámalos!*"

More gunfire pounded. Reed felt a bullet skim his shoulder blades, and he grunted, pressing closer to the wall.

"Reed!" Turk shouted. "We gotta go *now*!"

Reed snapped his knife open and grabbed Moreno by the hair, hauling his head up. The president's face turned deathly pale, but he stopped fighting.

"Do what he says!" Reed shouted.

Moreno took the radio and screamed panicked orders into the mic. Garcia stayed on him, coaching him through a series of commands. The gunfire from the courtyard subsided, and Reed passed Garcia a pair of wire ties to secure Moreno.

"He's all yours," Reed said.

Garcia tossed the ties on the floor, still pointing the Glock.

"You should leave now," he said.

Reed stopped, his gaze dropping to Garcia's finger. It was curled around the trigger, the weapon still pointed at Moreno's skull. Dark fire burned in Garcia's eyes—the same merciless hatred Reed had seen in Mateo.

"No!" Reed stepped forward, reaching for Garcia's hand.

He was milliseconds too late. Garcia fired. Once, twice, three times. Moreno's skull exploded like a melon, blood and gore spraying across the marble steps as Reed slid to a stop, heart thundering.

Garcia sobbed, mumbling in Spanish as he crumbled into a kneeling position, the Glock still clasped in his hands. Reed recognized a single word, repeated over and over.

"*Maria...Maria....Maria...*"

"Montgomery!" Turk's shout shattered Reed's stupor, galvanizing him back into focus. He grabbed Garcia's shoulder, shaking him.

"Come on! You've got to move."

Garcia looked up, eyes flooded. He shook his head.

"Go, amigo. God be with you."

"*Montgomery!* Now or never!"

Reed released him, staggering back. Garcia looked back to the shattered body of the president, then gently lifted the Glock and pressed the muzzle beneath his chin.

Reed turned for the door, waving two fingers ahead. Turk drove his knee into Belsky's lower back, shoving him into the hall and pivoting immediately right—toward the chopper. Reed held his rifle with one hand, propping up Wolfgang with the other.

They made it halfway to the exterior door before Garcia's handgun cracked thunder behind them. One last time.

Turk rammed the door open, cuffing Belsky across the ear as he stumbled. Outside the back door, a trio of Venezuelan presidential guards lay dead on the concrete, shot through the head with a small-caliber weapon. The air thundered with the beat of the jet-black Eurocopter vibrating on the helipad fifty yards away, Corbyn seated in the cockpit, beckoning them on.

Behind him, Reed heard automatic gunfire and the rapid pop of a pistol. Men screamed, and an alarm sounded as lights flashed on.

The generators were back online.

Reed leaned into Wolfgang and dragged him along, making for the open side door of the chopper. The aircraft hopped on the helipad as Corbyn adjusted the cyclic, but it didn't leave the ground.

A stray bullet from the open door behind them whistled over Reed's shoulder and pinged against the chopper, followed by the rattling snarl of another P90. Turk stumbled, grabbing his hip and slamming into Belsky. The Russian half turned, almost as though he were going to run toward the sound of the guns. Turk grabbed him by the hair and jerked him forward instead, falling into the chopper as it skipped sideways on the helipad.

Reed pushed Wolfgang through the door and spun on his heel, clamping down on the M4's trigger and spraying lead indiscriminately toward the mansion. Concrete dust erupted into the air, and Reed felt a hand on his arm.

"We're good! Get on!"

He fell backward, finding the edge of the helicopter's floor with his ass and kicking off the ground just as the chopper lurched upward. Starbursts of P90 muzzle flash blazed from a window, and tiny 5.7-millimeter bullets ricocheted off the chopper's side and bit Reed in the shin. He almost dropped the M4 as Corbyn swung hard left, banking directly over the top of Miraflores and gaining altitude rapidly.

Reed grabbed the base of a leather seat and held himself inside as the blackened city grew small beneath him. The chopper passed through a thin cloud of smoke, and Reed tasted rubber. Then he saw a flash of bright orange someplace to the south, glowing near the base of the mountains. Too large to be streetlights alone, too orange to be anything less than an inferno.

An armored truck was engulfed in flames, casting flickering light over a tide of Venezuelan soldiers, beating a retreat under the face of a surging mob.

Rivas's revolution was under way.

Reed hauled his legs inside, pressing one hand over the bullet wound in his shin. He couldn't even feel it. Masses of adrenaline coursed through his system, blocking out the pain and unleashing unholy euphoria in his skull. The thrill of survival.

Peering over his shoulder, Reed found Turk seated in one of the leather chairs, the muzzle of his M4 pressed into Belsky's back. The obese Russian glared fury at Reed, blood and snot running down his face and into his tangled beard, but he didn't try to fight. His hands were still bound behind his back, and complete defeat hung over him like a cloud.

"Cheer up, asshole," Reed shouted, hauling himself into the nearest chair. "I hear Gitmo is delightful this time of year."

Corbyn leveled the chopper off several thousand feet over the city, then turned north. Hot wind ripped through the open doors and tousled her hair, but Reed could still see the grin she wore—full mouthed, like a kid on Christmas.

He turned to find Wolfgang riding the floor just inside the right-hand door, his leg hanging off into the emptiness beyond, his swollen and battered face turned into the wind. As Corbyn completed her turn, Caracas spread out beneath them, almost totally black, with a cluster of fiery red near the core of the revolution.

A city on fire, in more ways than one.

Wolfgang ran a hand over his bruised face, then turned toward the cabin and gestured to the gold-plated ice chest mounted just behind the cockpit. The lid was open, and it was stocked with two bottles of unchilled Dom Pérignon.

"Hand me that," Wolfgang rasped.

Reed raised an eyebrow but retrieved the nearest bottle. Wolfgang fought with the foil-encased cork, then gave up and smacked the neck against the doorframe of the chopper. Glass shattered, and a volcano of champagne erupted over Wolfgang's lap.

He turned the bottle up and guzzled, straight from the broken neck, most of the costly drink washing over his face and down his shirt. As the bottle emptied, Wolfgang twisted and flung it into the rushing darkness, a crazed grin stretching across his battered face.

"*Viva Venezuela*, suckers!"

71

The Situation Room
The White House

Nobody spoke as the satellite images played across the bank of screens on the wall. First, total blackness. And now, specks of blazing red and orange.

Maggie couldn't see the rioters. She couldn't see the hundreds of soldiers marching down the streets, rushing to defend a place called El Helicoide. But Director O'Brien assured her they were there, as proven by infrared imaging delivered from a spy drone launched off the amphibious assault ship *Boxer*.

To her, it only looked like darkness. So much darkness.

General Yellin hung up a phone at the end of the table, clearing his gravelly throat. "I just received confirmation from *Boxer*, ma'am. The Prosecution Force landed safely. Belsky is in custody. I gave orders for them to push the helicopter overboard."

Maggie nodded slowly, still fixated on that orange dot in the middle of the screen. A burning tank, O'Brien had said. Or maybe a truck.

"See that they do," Maggie said, pivoting toward Yellin. "We were never there, General. We had nothing to do with this."

He ducked his head in understanding and reached for the phone.

Across the table, Maggie could feel Gorman's piercing eyes on her. Ice cold. Maybe angry.

Maggie ignored her, addressing the screen where O'Brien's face was displayed instead.

"Terminate the feed, Victor. Contact your people in Caracas, and make sure they scrub away any fingerprints."

O'Brien didn't answer. He simply cut the satellite visual, and a moment later, he disappeared from the screen also. She could sense tension in his face. Unspoken thoughts, much like she sensed from Gorman.

Problems for later.

"Congratulations," Stratton said, lifting a coffee mug next to her. "Mission accomplished."

Maggie said nothing, still staring at the blackened screen. Then she moved to stand.

"It's been a long night. Let's all get some sleep, and we'll debrief in the morning."

Stratton and Yellin stood. Gorman reached for her purse, then her face darkened as her cell phone flashed. She took the call, and her cheeks washed pale. Lowering the phone, she faced Maggie.

"Ma'am...we're receiving a call from Moscow."

Maggie stopped behind her chair. She looked quickly to Stratton and saw the concern in her gut reflected in his face. Then she resumed her seat and nodded.

"Put it through."

Gorman spoke into her cell, and a moment later the phone in front of Maggie rang softly. She almost reached for the speaker button, but she opted for the handset instead.

"Madam President, I have President Nikitin on the line for you."

"Go ahead," Maggie said.

The phone clicked, long-distance static and distortion smoothing out as the signal was adjusted. When Makar Nikitin spoke, she recognized the voice. Clear English, with a subtle accent. Products of a Western education. She'd spoken to him before. It hadn't been a friendly conversation then, and she didn't expect one now.

"Congratulations, Madam President. You've got yourself your own little revolution."

Gorman leaned across the table, motioning to the phone. Pleading for Maggie to place it on speaker.

Maggie ignored her.

"You must be confused. I have no idea what you're talking about."

A dry, tight laugh without an ounce of humor. "Play your games, you American bitch. The world will know the truth. You just made a very costly mistake."

Maggie leaned out of the chair, her voice growing very cold. "You know, Makar. There are things you can know, and there are things you can prove. I guess we're both lucky they aren't one and the same."

She slammed the phone down over the receiver. The room rang with the snap of plastic on plastic, and nobody moved. Gorman looked ready to cry, clutching the edge of the table with white knuckles. Stratton and Yellin stood by the door.

Maggie drew a long breath, forcing her mind back into calm. Regaining control.

Being the president.

"Thank you, gentlemen. That will be all."

Stratton ducked his head, and he and the general left the room, leaving Maggie and Gorman alone for the first time.

"Don't say it, Lisa," Maggie said. "Just don't say it."

72

USS *Boxer*
Caribbean Sea

The Navy corpsmen were good at their jobs, if a little lacking in bedside manner. Reed and Turk were quickly swept off to *Boxer*'s infirmary, where they were placed in immediate triage and prepped for surgery. Reed's bullet strike was the result of a ricochet, with minimal real damage to his leg despite a lot of bleeding.

Turk was hit in the left buttock by a 5.7-millimeter round, and the bullet had lodged in deep. By the time the slug was removed and they were both patched up and placed in adjacent beds of the sick bay, Reed figured that *Boxer* had churned well outside the reach of Venezuelan air forces.

Even if he was wrong, he felt safe behind the shelter of *Boxer*'s fighter pilots. The best in the world.

Relaxing on the pillow, Reed closed his eyes and inhaled recycled and filtered air, just enjoying being still for a moment. He didn't think about Belsky, or Wolfgang. He didn't even think about the men he'd killed or the chaos they had left behind. Those were bridges too far—battles he couldn't hope to win.

He just thought about Banks, and Davy. And he prayed they were still waiting for him someplace back home.

"Too bad about Moreno," Turk drawled. He was conscious but heavily doped up.

Reed opened his eyes. "What about him?"

"Gonna make things a lot worse, him being dead," Turk said. "For Rivas, I mean."

Reed shook his head. "Rivas wanted him dead from the start. If I had my guess, he ordered Garcia to murder him."

"How you figure? He told us he wanted Mateo to keep Moreno alive."

"Exactly," Reed said. "So that after the fact, we wouldn't suspect him. Think about it, Turk. There's only one president now. No question who's in charge."

Turk grunted, and the two of them fell quiet for another long stretch.

Then Reed laughed. A dry chuckle at first, growing rapidly louder until it filled the sick bay, and one of the corpsmen stuck his head through the door to check on the disturbance.

"What the hell is wrong with you?" Turk said, grinning himself. "Are you doped up?"

"Probably," Reed said, tears rolling down his cheeks. "I was just thinking...I can't believe you got shot in the ass."

Turk's face darkened as Reed continued to laugh. He looked away, pretending to be disgusted.

But then the grin returned. And shortly after, so did the laugh. They both laughed, holding their sides with tears rolling down dirty faces until the corpsman banged on the door and shouted for them to keep it down.

Reed relaxed into the pillow and thought about everything that lay behind—and everything that lay ahead.

He wasn't finished fighting. But he was damn ready to fight for something else.

"Call it a day, Turk. Let's go home."

73

One Week Later
Chicago, Illinois

It had been decades since Harold Cunningham felt fear overtake him, but it was overtaking him now, clouding his mind and driving out his better judgment. On the fortieth floor of his lakeside executive office building, he shoveled a laptop and a sheaf of documents into a briefcase, snapping at his secretary as he barreled toward the door.

"Send everyone home! Don't talk to anybody. I'll call you from the plane."

He reached the golden face of a bank of elevators and smashed the button with the back of his fist, his heart thumping. His mind obsessed with that stack of documents housed in his briefcase.

Subpoenas. Dozens of them. Flowing directly from the US Department of Justice, delivered by order of US Attorney General Greg Thomas.

They hit him like a curve ball, streaking in from a blind side he didn't know he had and smacking him right in the face. There had been no warning from his plants inside the FBI. No warning from his contacts in the DOJ. Not the first sniff or hint of an investigation of any sort.

It simply exploded on his desk, all at once. His phone ringing off the hook with calls not just from his army of lawyers and business associates but also from the press.

How the *hell* did the press know about this?

Somebody was targeting him. It was a complete torpedo job—he could smell it. Had Belsky sold him out?

Had Nikitin?

The elevator dinged at the ground floor, and he burst through the lobby, shoving past the doorman and erupting into the brutal Chicago cold. His limousine waited at the curb, ready to cart him to the private airfield where his personal Gulfstream G550 waited to fly him directly out of the country.

The Bahamas, first. Then someplace more remote. Maybe South America. Somewhere he could lay low until the overwhelming force of fifty billion dollars printed him a get-out-of-jail-free card.

It wasn't a question of if, simply when. And while that process swung into motion, Cunningham would be occupied with another project—finding the son of a bitch who sold him out.

At the bottom of the frozen steps, Cunningham's driver waited by the door, ducking his head and pulling it open. Cunningham ignored him, slinging the briefcase in ahead of him before settling into the welcome warmth. His face was already so cold he didn't smell a thing at first. The driver shut the door and circled toward the limousine's front as Cunningham grimaced and coughed.

The limousine was full of smoke. Billowing from someplace near the front of the vehicle, thick and heavy, obscuring his view.

Cunningham reached for the window switch, but it wouldn't work. He flipped the lights on instead, illuminating the elongated compartment and revealing the source of the pollution.

Seated at the front end of the vehicle, leaning back on the Italian leather with one suit leg crossed over the other, a Churchill cigar clamped between his teeth, was Vice President Jordan Stratton.

"Howdy, Harold."

Cunningham's eyes bulged, and he erupted out of the seat, smacking his head on the low ceiling.

"Jordan! What the hell—"

"Watch your head, there. Would be a shame to lose it."

Cunningham collapsed back into the seat, rubbing his bald skull. His hand shook, and he reached for the built-in intercom phone. It wasn't there.

"What is this?" Cunningham snarled.

Stratton drew on the cigar, a grin creeping across his face as he exhaled through his teeth. "I was going to ask you the same. Don't you know it's illegal to flee a federal investigation?"

Cunningham blinked, then his face flushed red. The frustrated rage he'd felt all morning boiled out of his gut like a volcano.

"*You*. This is you?" His fist shook as he slammed it over the briefcase. Stratton laughed.

"I really wish I could take credit, Harold. Fact is, I've never liked you. Had a thing for your daughter, once. I really dodged a bullet there, didn't I?"

"You snotty little shit! You have no *idea* who you're screwing with."

"A corrupt American energy conglomerate, tangled in the sheets with an even more corrupt Russian oligarch, both linked to the attempted assassination of the president of the United States. Actually, Harold. I have a pretty good idea."

Cunningham's breath whistled through clenched teeth. He lifted a finger toward Stratton, jabbing it at him as though it were a knife.

"You can't prove anything."

Stratton tapped his cigar with one index finger, dumping a long column of ash across rich black carpet. He laughed. "If that's what you think, I'm guessing you haven't spoken to Belsky recently."

Cunningham's palms went cold. He didn't move.

Stratton drew on the cigar, blasting more wretched smoke into the cabin and shaking his head. "I shouldn't be surprised. I guess you don't get a call when you check in to Gitmo. You know, they tell me he's got one hell of a singing voice...and all *kinds* of stories to tell."

Cunningham shook. It was all he could do not to hurl himself across the floor of the limousine and grab Stratton by the throat right there in the middle of downtown Chicago.

"I'll have you out on the street for this," he snarled. "Your family will starve to death like the scum you are. You'll never be able to show your face in public. I'll rip down every—"

A hard knock rang against the glass of Cunningham's door. He stiffened, his head snapping toward the sound.

A black glove pinned an open ID wallet against the glass, displaying an FBI shield and a matching plastic ID card.

"Harold Cunningham! I'm Special Agent Fields with the FBI. Step out of the car, please."

Cunningham's gaze returned to Stratton. The vice president sat with the cigar in his teeth, a wolfish grin spread across his face.

"Shame about the Bahamas."

The door opened, and the gloved hand closed around Cunningham's arm. He stumbled out amid a storm of bright flashes and camera clicks. A knot of reporters packed in around him, joining the half a dozen FBI agents who spun him against the limousine like a captured drunk, handcuffs clicking around his wrists.

"Don't drop the soap, Harold!" Stratton called from the limousine. "I'll send you a cigar."

Cunningham ignored the hail of questions erupting from the reporters as the agents hauled him toward a waiting Suburban. The bitter Chicago cold saturated his face, and the fear he'd felt all morning completely consumed him.

74

The Oval Office
The White House

It rained for almost ten days straight, leaving the Rose Garden a soggy mess and the sky a roiled mass of dark clouds. Washington was fully consumed by the death throes of winter, and as Maggie stood by the window that overlooked the South Lawn, she longed for the days when the mucky snow was gone for good and green grass would poke through.

She needed the warmth in her soul. Not just because Washington was a hostile change in climate for a born-and-bred Louisianan, but because she craved the hope that every spring promised. She needed to believe she wasn't staring down the barrel of the end...for everyone.

Maggie cupped hot coffee and looked over her shoulder to the couch beyond her desk. O'Dell sat with one leg crossed over the other, picking apart a fresh copy of the *New York Times* with all the zeal of a freshman congressman.

Since the development of their romantic relationship, they had both agreed that a post as her personal bodyguard was not the most ideal arrangement, and O'Dell had reluctantly hung up his badge and gun for the position of special advisor to the president.

It was a sufficiently vague title as to allow him to always be close, without initiating too many prying questions from the media—at least for now. But O'Dell took the title seriously, committing himself to a thorough understanding of the nation's concerns, ready to brief Maggie at a moment's notice about anything from developments on Wall Street to droughts in the breadbasket.

It made her smile, watching him squinting at the newspaper, a notepad resting on the couch next to him. There was a lot she could say about what attracted her to James O'Dell, but the absolute loyalty, the relentless dedication...it was as rare and precious as gold.

The office door swung open, and an aide poked her head inside. "I have Secretary Gorman ready to see you, ma'am."

"Show her in, please."

The door closed, and O'Dell stood.

"Meet me for lunch?" Maggie asked.

O'Dell smiled, retrieving his notebook. "Wouldn't miss it."

He left the room, and she watched him go, her gaze dropping impulsively to the tight cut of the seat of his pants.

The tailor had done a hell of a job.

Gorman stepped inside, her shoulders squared, her chin up. She wore a conservative blue skirt with matching blazer, her black-and-gray hair swept back from a face lined and strained. Maggie couldn't help but think she looked a lot older than she had when they first met, barely two years prior. The office had taken a toll on them both.

"Good morning, Lisa. Will you close the door?"

Gorman pushed the door closed, her free hand clutching an unmarked envelope. Maggie already knew what it contained, but she wasn't going to indulge that inevitability. Not yet.

"This won't take long, ma'am," Gorman said.

Maggie motioned her to take a seat, sitting on the couch across from her and sipping warm coffee. The rush of caffeine felt like heaven itself in her exhausted body.

"Can I get you some coffee?"

"No, thank you, ma'am." Gorman settled into the couch but didn't lean back. She remained upright on the furniture's edge, that envelope resting on her lap.

Maggie decided to wait for Gorman to make the first move. To break the glass and reach for that inevitable switch.

"You know why I'm here, ma'am," Gorman said. She laid the envelope on the table and pushed it toward Maggie. "You'll find my resignation enclosed."

"And you know I won't accept it," Maggie said.

"You can't keep me from quitting."

True enough.

Maggie looked into the coffee and measured her next words. She wasn't very sure where to begin, but she knew what she wanted to say. Gorman might think she was quitting on principle, but in Maggie's view, she was quitting out of frustration. Maggie had done a poor job managing this corner of her cabinet since taking office. She accepted blame for that, but she couldn't accept the consequences of it. With the turmoil boiling across the pond, she needed a reliable State Department now more than ever.

"Why are you quitting, Lisa?"

"I think you know, ma'am."

"Maybe I'd like to hear it from the horse's mouth. In summary."

Gorman smoothed her skirt. Straightened her back.

"Okay. In that case, I'm quitting because I no longer believe I can serve this administration."

"That's a very diplomatic answer."

"I'm a diplomat, ma'am."

"Were you always?"

Gorman didn't answer.

"You're from Arizona, right? Tucson."

"Yes, ma'am."

"I hear it's nice there. I've only been once, when we were campaigning. I didn't really have time to look around."

Gorman remained stiff and unmoved. Maggie sighed.

"Lisa, I'm not a politician. I'm just a swamp girl. Where I come from, people are very blunt. They say it like it is, even when it's ugly. That's the only way I know how to operate. Do you understand?"

Gorman remained stone-faced.

"I know you want to quit," Maggie said. "But if you'll indulge me, I'd really like to know the truth. Blunt and ugly. The way we say it down in the swamps."

Gorman's lip twitched. Maggie could tell she wanted to burst and was battling with herself. She interlaced her hands.

"Okay, Madam President. If that's what you want."

"It is."

"I'm quitting because this administration has become a dumpster fire of bad policy and reckless decision-making. From the moment you took office, the chaos of this White House has spilled around the globe and left disaster in its wake. Despite my years of expertise and best efforts to save you from yourself, my counsel is universally disregarded in favor of dangerous military action, much of which is probably illegal. I'm quitting because you don't have a damn clue what you're doing, and I won't stand by and watch this administration burn the world down out of sheer stupidity."

Maggie lifted the cup, sipping coffee and allowing herself a moment to digest the lambast. None of it surprised her, and most of it was reasonable, if maybe a little self-righteous. She knew she would need to endure this fire if she had any hope of talking Gorman off the ledge.

Hazards of the job.

"Well, that was blunt," Maggie said with a smile. "I appreciate it."

"If you're trying to talk me out of it, you can't," Gorman said. "I can't be a part of this any longer."

"A part of what, exactly?"

"All of this. The blatant disregard for foreign policy. The illegal use of paramilitary forces to manipulate global events—"

"The Prosecution Force officially disbanded earlier this week," Maggie said. "I fired them."

Gorman hesitated, caught off guard. Maggie sat back on the couch. Strictly speaking, she was stretching the truth about Reed and his team. She hadn't fired them, they had quit, and she still wasn't entirely sure why. But maybe it was for the best.

"You were right about them," Maggie said. "They got the job done, but at a price. We now find ourselves in the most precarious international situation since the Cold War. Russia is on the offensive, Venezuela is in chaos, and the American people are scared. Maybe because they don't understand what's happening. Maybe because they've already lost faith in this administration. Frankly, it's a diplomatic nightmare, and you were right about something else, also. I don't have a clue what I'm doing."

Gorman's lips parted, then closed. She adjusted her seat and looked at the carpet. It was the first time Maggie had ever seen her secretary of state caught off guard—a rare moment of vulnerability.

Maggie needed to pounce on it.

"I can't make you stay, Lisa. No more than I can make these problems evaporate. But I don't have the luxury of simply walking away. For better or worse, the American people have entrusted me to lead them through the fire, and that fire is now burning hotter than ever. We know Russia had a hand in my attempted assassination, but unless and until Belsky turns on Nikitin, our evidence is strictly circumstantial. Even then, short of declaring war, what options do I really have?"

Maggie let the question hang, knowing it would trigger Gorman's natural diplomatic instincts against military action. Knowing that it would lead her mind to the same inevitable conclusion Maggie herself had been forced to face.

Russia had won this round, even if Maggie had survived a bullet to the gut. Nikitin had left her with no direct option of retaliation short of World War Three, and that was a possibility she couldn't possibly consider.

"What I'm trying to say, Lisa, is that these problems aren't going away. We're stuck in the long game now. Chess, not checkers. Keeping the peace while placing a foot on Russia's neck is going to require a lot of finesse, a lot of strategy, and a *lot* of expertise. A lot of the right people."

Gorman's mouth closed. She lifted her chin. "Madam President, I can't—"

"I'm not asking you to stay, Lisa. I'm asking you to consider the kind of legacy you want to leave behind. My daddy never finished high school, but he taught me to never leave a place until it was better than how I found it. You may not have made this mess, but this mess was made on your watch, and if you leave now, you will be abandoning your country in her greatest hour of need. I know that's not the kind of woman you are."

Gorman's eyes turned cold. Maggie held up a hand.

"I know what you're thinking. You won't be strung along. And that's fair. So what if you and I engage in a little diplomacy? What if we make a deal?"

No answer. Maggie folded her hands. "I will commit to moving more slowly. To listening to your advice and leveraging your expertise, and I won't micromanage the State Department. I will commit to no further illegal, covert military action, and to include you in any further operations from the outset. You will be an integral part of this administration, like you should have been from day one."

Gorman took her time responding, still sitting stiff. Still playing hard to get.

But Maggie knew she wasn't going anywhere.

"And in exchange?" Gorman asked.

"In exchange, you will do what you swore an oath to do—you will serve this country. You will not abandon this administration in the heat of the fire. You will keep the confidence of this White House and be prepared to roll up your sleeves when it's time to get dirty. You will embrace the reality of the shit storm we find ourselves in, and you will help me lead this country out of it. You will *be* the chief diplomat of the Free World...come hell or high water."

Gorman drew a long breath. She looked down at her hands and gently twisted the class ring on her right ring finger. Maggie had never noticed it before, but she recognized the emblem of Dartmouth.

An esteemed college. A lifelong politician, accustomed to the old ways. But the Trousdale administration was the new guard, and times were changing.

She would either jump ship or face the storm.

Gorman rose slowly, and Maggie rose with her. The secretary of state lifted her head and offered her hand.

"It would be my honor, Madam President."

75

Caracas, Venezuela

The week following the riots at El Helicoide was the worst of Rivas's life. Like never before, Venezuela descended into pure chaos.

Homes burned. Businesses were vandalized. The worst of society capitalized on the collapse of law and order to pillage Caracas, sacking grocery stores and marketplaces while police, the National Guard, and the Venezuelan army threw down their weapons and simply watched.

Moreno was dead. He was found in Miraflores, lying amid nearly two thousand empty rifle and pistol cartridges and two dozen dead presidential guards. He was shot through the head with a Glock 17, and his murderer, Jorge Garcia, lay next to him with a self-inflicted gunshot wound blasting a hole through his brain.

A dead hero, although Rivas would never admit it. He could never admit to any of the events that preceded the murder of Cesar Moreno, or his suspicions about what part the nameless Americans had played. The world had questions—and so did the shattered body of Moreno's government. Questions about what had triggered the riots, who had attacked Miraflores, and what had become of Moreno's helicopter.

But Rivas wasn't answering. He didn't have to—he was on the offensive himself. Shortly after Moreno's death, Juan Blanco had been recovered from the secret prison beneath the presidential palace, and just as he promised, Blanco delivered the El Helicoide tapes.

Rivas publicized them immediately. While Moreno's vice president scrambled to seize power, video clips of illegal interrogations and torture spilled across the globe, painting an undeniable picture of the cruelty and corruption of the Moreno regime and quickly eroding what remained of Moreno's support.

Rivas would be president—everyone knew that. As the recognized leader of the Venezuelan state, he had already invited the Americans to reopen their embassy and had requested foreign aid for his starving people. Without Moreno's military to stand in their way, the Americans were quick to respond, deploying not only mass shipments of food and medical supplies but also a State Department delegation sent to advise the Rivas administration on the reconstruction of the Venezuelan economy.

They had a particular interest in the millions of barrels of untapped crude, ripe to be drilled. President Trousdale was willing to lift all former sanctions on the Venezuelan state.

America was ready to buy oil—billions of dollars of it.

Standing on a mountainside overlooking Caracas, Rivas was only vaguely aware of the people gathered around the trucks and armored vehicles behind him. After Moreno's death, a large portion of the military had defected and declared their loyalty to Rivas, providing him with an instant boost in both legitimacy and power. He'd put them to work, converting their assault vehicles into tools of restoration, distributing the food and medication the Americans brought in by the shipload.

Bringing hope to a broken people and cementing in everyone's mind that he, Luis Rivas, would be more than a leader. He would be their savior. A knight in shining armor.

A leader Hugo Chávez never dreamed of becoming.

Rivas relished the moment, tasting the warm South American breeze and smiling.

Viva Venezuela.

The power felt amazing.

76

Tyler, Texas

Reed stopped the rental car halfway down the long driveway and looked past a field of towering pecan trees to the antebellum home built in a clearing, a hundred yards away. Two Range Rovers and a Porsche SUV sat next to a red Volkswagen at the foot of the sprawling front porch, catching winter sunshine while leaves drifted across the gravel.

The home was beautiful. Very old, but well maintained and tastefully upgraded. The columns were polished and gleamed with fresh paint. The yard was manicured and dressed with evergreen bushes and dormant drift roses.

Everything about the place smacked of wealth and privilege. Not the hard-won success of a life dedicated to industrious entrepreneurship or the reckless misapplication of windfall millions from a sports contract.

No. This was old money. East Texas oil money, probably. A wealth that rolled like a snowball across multiple generations, growing through careful husbandry and a relentless dedication to *the family* above all else. And in that respect, it was the last place Reed expected to find Banks. It took him a full week to think of it—and a little help from one of Wolfgang's old contacts. But now that he was here, it all fit like a glove in his mind. Bereft of the family stability she craved, where else would Banks turn?

Reed knew that Banks hated her mother, so it said something for her to be here. It was a statement. A thumb in Reed's eye.

Maybe he deserved it.

Letting his foot off the brake, Reed rolled up to the house and parked next to the Volkswagen. It was thick with Texas dust, the little stick figure family pasted to the back glass barely visible under a few hundred miles of road grime. He piled out of the rental, enjoying the sun on his face as he shut the door. His body ached from the long drive out of Dallas—the nearest major airport, still over two hours away with traffic.

But something deep inside of him ached worse. A cold reality that he'd been a fool, and it might have cost him.

At the top of the steps, Reed mashed the doorbell and waited for footsteps to tap over original hardwood on the other side. The woman who answered was exactly as Reed expected. Tall and stately, dressed in a needlessly fancy pair of slacks and a loose southwestern style blouse. Gray hair pulled back behind a severe face.

Very tired eyes. They reminded him of Banks, a little.

"Ms. Morccelli?" Reed asked.

"Ms. O'Hara," the woman corrected, her voice smothered under a blueblood Texas accent. "And you are?"

"I'm Reed," he said, pocketing his hands. "I'm here for my wife."

The coldness in the woman's eyes turned a little colder, and she folded her arms behind the screen door. Like some kind of guardian.

"I know she's here," Reed said simply. "I'd rather not kick the door down."

"I understand you do a lot of that," the woman said. "You're a..."

"Marine. I was a Marine. But now I'm just a guy...and I really want to see my family."

O'Hara's eyes softened, just a little. Her shoulders dropped.

"She's around back. But you should really—"

Reed ignored her, dropping off the porch and circling the house. Texas wind brought the smell of a barbecue grill to his nostrils, and as he reached the back corner of the house, a child's laughter joined the smell. A happy, familiar sound.

Reed found Banks under a pecan tree, pushing Davy in a little yellow swing. With every push, their son chuckled happily, his mouth glimmering with baby teeth, his bright eyes fixed on his mother.

Banks wore jeans and a University of Texas T-shirt, laughing with Davy at each push. She didn't see Reed until his foot landed on a fallen pecan, crushing it in the afternoon stillness.

Banks looked up, allowing Davy's feet to collide with her stomach as he continued to laugh. For a long moment she just stared, her hair swept by the wind, wide blue eyes fixed on him.

He saw a lot in those eyes. Pain and confusion. A lot of anger.

All things he deserved.

"How did you find me?" she demanded.

"I...called some people."

Davy's swing began to slow, and the child held out both chubby hands, crying for more. Banks scooped him out and placed him on her hip, standing straight-backed. Reed didn't turn to look, but out of the corner of his eye, he saw her mother had stepped onto the back porch.

Probably glaring at him with that hawkish scolding. It was easy to see why Banks didn't like her.

"Why are you here?" Banks said, her voice still cold. "I made my position clear. I'm done with the government work. Done with Trousdale. Done with—"

"I quit," Reed said. "I quit last week. So did Turk."

Banks didn't move. Her bottom lip trembled, and she clenched her jaw to stop it. Reed saw her eyes rim red, but she held her head up.

Proud. Independent. Standing her ground.

"Look," Reed said, taking a cautious step forward. "All I want is you. All I want is my family. I know I've taken so much from you...I've taken your life. I want to give that back. We can move to Nashville. We can get an apartment, and you can sing. We'll find you a record deal. I'll become a cop...or a banker. Hell, I don't know. I'll figure it out. Just please...don't walk away again. You're all I have."

Banks's eyes watered. She looked at the ground and sniffed, holding

Davy closer. Reed took a step forward, and she shook her head. He reached out and touched her cheek, gently lifting her chin. Tears dripped down her face.

Despite the sadness in her eyes, he thought she'd never looked more beautiful.

"I never wanted you to change," she whispered. "I never cared about music, or Nashville. I just can't share you anymore. I need you to be mine."

Reed wrapped his arms around the two of them and pulled them in close, burying his head in her shoulder and feeling his own eyes sting. He held them very close and smelled their hair, Davy cooing and slobbering on his shoulder. His little family fit in his arms like a treasure.

His treasure. And he was never letting them walk away again.

"You've got me," he whispered. "I'm all yours."

77

Toronto, Ontario
Canada

From a bench in Coronation Park, Wolfgang had a partial south-facing view of Lake Ontario—sheltered on one side by the mass of the Toronto Islands and Billy Bishop Airport. Directly ahead of the park, the mouth of a sailboat marina was dotted by small cutters riding at anchor, most of them with their sails wrapped tight, their decks vacant of any visible occupants.

Even in early March, it was still cold in Canada. Still bitter. And so was Wolfgang.

The brand-new prosthetic latched to his right leg was the best money could buy. Wolfgang had spared no expense on its purchase, having it custom crafted out of carbon fiber and titanium, with a little compartment built into the fake calf large enough to store a Glock 29 and a fake passport.

Not a bad upgrade, all things considered. Wolfgang no longer felt robbed when he looked at his shoe and felt no flesh or bone beneath the sock. It was all spilt milk. Another thing lost that he would never forget but could no longer afford to be chained down by.

It was time to move on.

Wolfgang checked his watch and noted that it was eight minutes past the agreed-on meeting time. He glanced up the length of the park, searching for cops or security. Oversized families with too many adults, or people sitting on park benches pretending to read iPads behind sunglasses. Things that may have spooked the man he came here to meet.

There was nothing. A few children played in the grass fifty or sixty yards away. A young couple walked one of those new poodle-hybrid dogs along the waterfront. Wolfgang didn't see anything that should spook his contact.

Another five minutes, he thought. Then he would split.

The bulky Russian appeared in three, slipping out of the park and taking the waterfront pathway to meet Wolfgang on the bench. He wore blue jeans and tennis shoes, American style. But no jacket. Only a long shirt that barely concealed the handgun Wolfgang knew he carried.

Ivan settled onto the bench next to him without so much as a greeting, then tipped back a water bottle and guzzled something clear that was most definitely not water. He sighed with satisfaction, belched, and reached for the cap.

"Aren't you going to offer me a drink?" Wolfgang asked.

Ivan stopped, the cap hanging over the bottle. He raised both eyebrows, then offered Wolfgang the bottle. Wolfgang tipped it back and took a long pull of harsh vodka, burning all the way to his stomach, where the liquor pooled and built a fire.

It tasted good. Wolfgang liked it.

"*Nu ee nu*," Ivan muttered. "And I thought you didn't drink."

"Things change, Ivan," Wolfgang said, returning the bottle. "The world spins on."

Ivan nodded thoughtfully. "*Da*. So it does. At least until we stop it."

He capped the bottle, then set it on the bench next to him, relaxing in the sun. He looked warm. Even comfortable.

Wolfgang was cold—a coldness he felt in his very bones. But it no longer bothered him. He was ready to embrace it.

"Where did you go?" Wolfgang said.

Ivan sucked his teeth. Rocked his head. "Someplace...where I could work."

"You couldn't work in America?"

Ivan snorted. "Many years ago, you once told me, *just because we understand each other does not mean I trust your country*. This ax cuts both ways, Amerikos."

"Fair enough. Your intel was good, for what it's worth. It seems Belsky was in deep with some guy named Cunningham, in Chicago. There are links back to Moscow, but...I don't know what became of that."

"They cut you out?" Ivan asked.

"Something like that. The rest of the team quit. I was always the third wheel...the man on the outside. I think the CIA is trying to distance themselves from us."

Another derisive snort from Ivan. "This is always the way with people who work behind a desk. They use you until you are spent, then you either get your own desk...or you go away."

"I don't think they believe it," Wolfgang said. "The Moscow connection. Or maybe they do and don't know what to do about it. Regardless, I'm out now. I'm a free agent. And I want work."

Ivan tilted his head, raising an eyebrow. "You want *work*?"

"You know what I mean, Ivan. Don't make me say it."

"If you mean what I think you mean, you shouldn't be afraid to say it."

"Okay. Fine. I want back in the game. There's still work to be done. Like you said yourself, Nikitin is a madman, and he won't stop. You're going to keep fighting that. I want to help."

Ivan took a long pause, twisting the cap off the bottle with his teeth and sipping slowly. Then sighing.

"You do not know what you ask for," he said slowly. "This is big problem. Bigger than either of us. When two large dogs are locked in small space, they can only circle each other for so long. Eventually they fight. This is situation with my country and yours."

"Except it's not that kind of fight. It's not an open challenge. Nikitin is throwing rocks and hiding his hand. Trying to chip away at the Free World."

Ivan laughed. "The *Free World*. Always such an obnoxious thing to say. As if tyranny is only found in places where it is most obvious."

"I'm not here to argue ideology with you, Ivan. I'm here because two months ago I lost the last thing I had left to live for, and if I don't find a way to replace it, I'm checking out. Do you understand me? I need work. I need a reason to get out of bed. Do you want to help or not?"

A long pause. A deep inhale. Then Ivan stood up.

"I will call you. We will see. But...it is better for you to work with the people you know."

"They quit," Wolfgang said again. Ivan smiled sadly.

"Men like this—men like *us*—they never quit. They only pretend. Give them time."

Ivan extended his hand, and Wolfgang stood. Their fingers clasped, and Wolfgang gave as good as he got. The old Russian smiled, blasting Wolfgang with vodka breath, then leaned in close.

"There is...other option."

"What?" Wolfgang raised both eyebrows.

"You could...get a dog."

"Go to hell, Ivan."

Ivan laughed and smacked him on the arm. Then his face turned serious, and he nodded slowly.

"I will call."

He turned back down the waterfront and left Wolfgang standing in a fresh blast of lake wind, cutting him right to the bone. Chilling him to his core.

But not shaking him. Not anymore.

Because one way or the other, he knew the fight wasn't over.

The world was still spinning.

And he wasn't checking out.

FIRESTORM
THE PROSECUTION FORCE THRILLERS Book 5

When tragedy strikes Reed Montgomery, revenge is the only way forward.

Former Force Recon Marine and covert operator, Reed Montgomery, has finally hung up the rifle. The White House has disowned him. His team has disbanded. He's now embracing the quiet life while his wife pursues a life-long dream of becoming a music star.

Life is good. But it's far too quiet, and for an assassin like Reed, quiet never lasts.

The blasts detonate only yards from the stage, sending red hot shrapnel ripping through the crowd and across the band. As Reed watches in horror, the love of his life topples to the ground in a field of blood—and the carnage has barely begun.

Across America, TV screens are dominated by a smooth-talking man with an Arabic accent. He claims responsibility for the attacks, identifying himself as the head of a brand-new terrorist network who will hold America accountable for her sins.

With the promise of further attacks hanging over the nation, Reed prepares to abandon retirement and hunt his enemies, no matter the cost. But with the White House unwilling to reestablish the Prosecution Force, Reed is pushed to act alone.

He assembles his own team. Loads his own weapons. And will carry this fight to the ends of the earth.

ABOUT THE AUTHOR

Logan Ryles was born in small town USA and knew from an early age he wanted to be a writer. After working as a pizza delivery driver, sawmill operator, and banker, he finally embraced the dream and has been writing ever since. With a passion for action-packed and mystery-laced stories, Logan's work has ranged from global-scale political thrillers to small town vigilante hero fiction.

Beyond writing, Logan enjoys saltwater fishing, road trips, sports, and fast cars. He lives with his wife and three fun-loving dogs in Alabama.

Sign up for Logan Ryles's reader list at
severnriverbooks.com/authors/logan-ryles

Printed in the United States
by Baker & Taylor Publisher Services